Praise for Bianca D'Arc's
Keeper of the Flame

"I have missed this world, filled with fantasy and passion, and I welcome Ms. D'Arc's Dragon Knights back for more adventures. I look forward to more stories in this world, but be warned; this one is as hot as a dragon's flaming breath at times."
~ *Long and Short Reviews*

"*Keeper of the Flame* is fantastic! The storyline is fast paced, filled with action and hotter than the flames that Hugh and Lera use as part of their magic. [...] I hope author Bianca D'Arc has many more such books up her sleeve, because I am ready and raring to read the next one."
~ *Fresh Fiction*

"There's a lot that D'Arc infuses into this series that takes dragons onto a whole other level. The worldbuilding is unique and executed well and the writing is always stellar."
~ *Under the Covers Book Blog*

Look for these titles by
Bianca D'Arc

Now Available:

Brotherhood of Blood
One & Only
Rare Vintage
Phantom Desires
Sweeter Than Wine
Forever Valentine
Wolf Hills
Wolf Quest

Tales of the Were
Lords of the Were
Inferno

Dragon Knights
Maiden Flight
Border Lair
The Ice Dragon
Prince of Spies
Wings of Change
FireDrake
Dragon Storm
Keeper of the Flame
The Dragon Healer
Master at Arms

Resonance Mates
Hara's Legacy
Davin's Quest
Jaci's Experiment
Grady's Awakening

Gift of the Ancients
Warrior's Heart

String of Fate
Cat's Cradle

StarLords
Hidden Talent

Print Anthologies
Caught by Cupid
I Dream of Dragons Vol. 1
Brotherhood of Blood

Keeper of the Flame

Bianca D'Arc

SAMHAIN
PUBLISHING

Samhain Publishing, Ltd.
11821 Mason Montgomery Road, 4B
Cincinnati, OH 45249
www.samhainpublishing.com

Keeper of the Flame
Copyright © 2014 by Bianca D'Arc
Print ISBN: 978-1-61921-695-2
Digital ISBN: 978-1-61921-367-8

Editing by Amy Sherwood
Cover by Angela Waters

This book is a work of fiction. The names, characters, places, and incidents are products of the writer's imagination or have been used fictitiously and are not to be construed as real. Any resemblance to persons, living or dead, actual events, locale or organizations is entirely coincidental.

All Rights Are Reserved. No part of this book may be used or reproduced in any manner whatsoever without written permission, except in the case of brief quotations embodied in critical articles and reviews.

First Samhain Publishing, Ltd. electronic publication: February 2013
First Samhain Publishing, Ltd. print publication: March 2014

Dedication

First and always, my work is dedicated to my Mom, who I miss every single day. And to Dad, who I've gotten to know so much better in these past three years since losing the center of our mutual universe. It's been tough finding my way, but I think (hope) I'm on the right track now.

And to the readers who make this all possible. I've gotten to know many of you through the various conferences and events I go to and you are the real reason I keep going and keep trying to tell my stories as best I can. You are my motivation and my dear, good friends. Thank you from the bottom of my heart.

Prologue

"You are no child of mine!" Her sire's voice made her cringe toward the opening of the cave.

"Papa," she pleaded, but he would not listen. He never listened. Not to her.

He only listened to his warriors and those with whom he plotted the downfall of some woman she didn't know. She was too young to really understand, but she learned more each day, hiding her deformed body in the background.

"I should have put you down when I first saw your ugly face. Get out! Die in the snow for all I care. You should never have been born!"

He swiped at her, and in her fear, she scrambled too close to the cave's edge. Tumbling downward in the cold night air, she cried out in terror, but no help came. She had a long way to fall.

She twisted, hoping to find something to grab onto. She tried everything she knew or had seen—unfurling wings that were too weak to support her. But they did slow her down.

The ground rushed up to meet her and she landed on four paws. Safe.

And scared. In a place she'd never seen. Walking on the ground.

She'd never been outside the cave before and everything down here was different. Dark, scary and cold... So cold.

She curled up in a corner out of the rain and cried herself to sleep.

Chapter One

What the hell was he doing here? Hugh had done a lot of crazy things in his life, in service to his family, country and kind, but this had to be one of the craziest. Creeping around in a land not his own was nothing new to him, but he'd never been spying in a land where he stood out so badly from the rest of the population.

A land where he couldn't even shift to his dragon form if things got tough. Not even to stretch his wings. The thrice-damned gryphons saw to that. Everywhere he looked over the city of Alagarithia in the Doge of Helios's domain, gryphons flew. In formation or in pairs, singly or in groups, they were everywhere.

He hadn't been able to fly in over a month now, as he got the lay of this foreign land where gryphons dominated the sky. His brother had sent him here undercover as a result of a prophetic vision. The seer, Shanya, had had a vision and his brothers had sent him winging off to places dragon folk had never visited before. At least none of the dragons of Draconia.

To Nico's credit, the Prince of Spies had checked with Drake and his Jinn network before sending Hugh on this mission. The famous musician known as Drake of the Five Lands had counted Helios as one of *his* lands when he'd been a travelling bard.

Jinn traded in Helios too. Not the few dragon shifters of the Black Dragon Clan, but other, extended clansmen. If Hugh ran into trouble, he'd look for help among the Jinn. Being a black dragon meant something among those people.

Among the natives, it could only mean trouble. At least until Hugh figured out if the gryphon army that ruled the skies

Keeper of the Flame

was there to fend off dragons. One lone dragon against so many gryphons was terrible odds, and Hugh preferred not to try his luck with all those hawk-headed flying lions on patrol. So he remained firmly on two feet for the foreseeable future while in this strange land.

He would have preferred the straightforward approach, but Nico had convinced their older brother, Roland, the King of Draconia, to approach the Doge of Helios with caution. Nico had married into that den of spies, the Jinn Brotherhood, and become their de facto king, since his wife was their hereditary queen. Nico and Arikia—Riki for short—were more a ceremonial couple than actual rulers, but they held the respect of the elusive, canny and altogether too crafty Jinn.

Hugh had always felt like he was the odd man out. There was a long line of male heirs to the throne of Draconia, and Hugh was neither heir nor spare. He was just one of many. Third in line should the worst happen to Roland and Nico.

He'd never coveted his brother's throne. Roland had risen to power early, after the brutal murder of their parents. Barely able to cope after the loss, Roland had been forced into leadership of both humans and dragons alike in their homeland of Draconia. Hugh knew it hadn't been easy for him, but Roland had proven himself a good king, willing to put aside his own desires time and again for the benefit of his subjects, be they two-footed or winged.

Draconia prospered, even while her enemies plotted against the peace and stability of the land. Draconia had wealth in both people and resources. Few went hungry in such a rich land, and the freedom both people and dragons enjoyed was anathema to some of her neighbors. Neighbors who kept probing for weak spots along the borders and seeking ways to destroy her most fearsome protectors, the dragons and knights who defended the land.

Which was part of the reason Roland had sent Hugh here, to Helios, in secret. Shanya's vision only provided the excuse. For too long, conflicting rumors had come to the royal court

11

about Helios. Some claimed they were colluding in the plots against Draconia. But Drake himself had brought news from the Doge about possible threats against the royal family. Drake vouched for the Doge, but he wasn't so sure about the advisors or those in other positions of power.

King Roland and his advisors didn't know what to think. Helios had always seemed a very far-off place with which they had little contact except through diplomatic channels. Such contacts were always of the most benign variety—assurances of neutrality and overall peaceful intentions. But had such words hidden a snake in the grass? Was Helios secretly involved in the plots to destroy Draconia?

And most importantly, had the Doge of Helios orchestrated the deaths of the former king and queen of Draconia and aided in the kidnapping of the daughters of the House of Kent, only newly returned? If so, such treachery could not be ignored. It might well mean war.

At the very least, Hugh needed to discover if Helios was truly a friend or the worst of foes.

Winter rains in Alagarithia were truly awful. Hugh had been told they didn't last long, but they persisted while the wind blew from the north, bringing bone-chilling rain and snow off the water. Lucia had remembered a great deal about the city in which she'd been born, even though she hadn't lived there long. Hugh had spent an enjoyable dinner back in the Castle Lair in Draconia with Lucia and her husbands, the knights Kaden and Marcus and their dragon partners, Reynor and Linea. Lucia had told him all she knew about Alagarithia, though she'd been smuggled out of the city as a young girl when her family was slaughtered.

She remembered the rains, though. Hugh now understood why. Even gryphons stayed in their nests during the winter rains and the city hunkered down to endure the cold. Hugh wasn't so lucky. He would have loved to build up the fire in his rented room and hide for the duration, but he had work to do. Shanya's vision had been of cold rain from the north, so whatever was going to happen, it would be while the north wind blew and the weather of this normally temperate city was at its worst.

Hugh was as wet and miserable about it as anyone in Alagarithia, though he wasn't quite as cold. Even in his human form, Hugh was a dragon. He carried that fire within, no matter what he looked like on the outside. It was something to be grateful for as he watched people huddling under doorways in tattered oilskins in the poorer parts of the city. He wore an oilskin coat as well, though his was in slightly better repair. His guise was that of a traveler and Hugh tried to look as plain as possible, neither prosperous nor poor. He adopted the guise of someone who was not an easy or fat mark for those who populated the less scrupulous parts of the city.

Drake, the famous bard and newly made knight, had given him pointers on blending in, though little could be done about Hugh's larger-than-normal stature. Of all his brothers, Hugh was the tallest and broadest across the shoulders. In dragon form, he was the largest as well, though only by a foot or two when measured from tail to snout and wingtip to wingtip.

Hugh tried to slouch, but it was hard for someone as tall as he was to appear a more normal height. Still, he did his best, adopting the loose gait Drake had taught him and casting his shoulders downward. He did his best to look unremarkable, though truth to tell, most of the inhabitants of this lower-class part of Alagarithia were too caught up in their own semi-frozen misery to be looking at another fellow sufferer too closely.

Few walked on the slushy streets and even fewer in the back alleys that bordered the cliff face. Similar to Castleton—the city that had grown up around the base of the castle in which Hugh had been born—this city was built with a rock face on one side, the sea on the other. The cliff and the sea met, leaving only one front on which a potential enemy could mount a land-based attack.

The waterfront was well protected by Alagarithia's famous fleet of ships and the gryphons took care of the cliffs. For it was in the caves that pockmarked the cliff face that most of the gryphons had built their nests. They flew from their lofty perches almost constantly. A trail of workers who cleaned their few belongings and did tasks their talons were not suited to walked up and down the small paths and stairs cut into the rock during daylight hours.

This wasn't the safest place for Hugh to be hiding, but it was the most unexpected. The taverns in this part of the city catered to the working class and shady deals of all kinds were transacted in the back alleys every day. If there was information to be had, this was the place to learn it. Or so the Jinn had claimed.

The biting wind and icy rain pelted everything in almost horizontal slices, making most sensible folk stay indoors. It was the perfect opportunity for Hugh to scope out the Jinn trader Nico had arranged as an emergency contact. Hugh would not speak to the man this day, but he would learn the various approaches to his trading post and commit them to memory should it become necessary to seek his aid.

That task firmly in mind, Hugh used his slouched gait to cross the area around the Jinn trader's colorful wagon a few times. He never got close enough to be seen by the occupant of the red and yellow conveyance that doubled as his shop wherever he put down stakes. Nobody stirred in the rain as it worsened and turned to true ice.

Sleet lashed him, but Hugh wasn't cold. Not really. He wasn't even really wet, except for the places the wind had whipped his coat away from his body from time to time.

He was about to head back to the inn, having learned all the pathways to and from the trader's wagon when he became aware of eyes trained on him. Hugh didn't flinch. He didn't stop or deviate from his path. The eyes followed. The sensation of being watched increased as he walked along a darkened alley—the closest one to the cliff face he had yet traversed.

Hugh let his senses expand, opening his mouth slightly to taste the wind, but the eyes stayed cautiously upwind of him. He got the fleeting impression of an inhuman growl and then he heard the telltale pad of four feet. Not two.

Little feet. Taking little steps.

Someone's pet? Hugh didn't think so, though the size sounded about right—the intelligence behind the pattern of the little paws stalking him was unmistakable. Curiosity flavored its movements. Hugh's dragon senses told him all this just from the sound of its paws hitting slushy ground.

A dainty sneeze sounded from around the corner just ahead of Hugh. The creature was running parallel to his path, watching him from the side alleys between the clustered buildings in this part of town.

Hugh made a decision and slowed his steps. Sure enough, a small furry head peeked around the corner to look at him. It drew back sharply when it saw him and he got the impression of wet fur and a forlorn look on a small cat's face. At least, it looked like a cat from what he could see of it.

It had mottled gray fur and sad gray eyes. It looked like a cat, but the quick glimpse he'd gotten had not looked like any housecat he had ever seen. Hugh was familiar with domestic cats since every Lair had a few that hunted mice and kept the places free of vermin. It wasn't uncommon for dragonettes to have a pet if they had no peers their own age to play with. Cats never seemed to be afraid or antagonistic to dragons. The same could not be said for most canines, unfortunately.

Hugh stopped in his tracks and waited. The little creature seemed to be in distress, but still curious enough to watch him. Something was off about the animal. For one thing, its eyes held even more intelligence than an ordinary cat. For another, it wasn't hiding from the rain, even though it was obvious the little thing was miserable. Hugh wanted to know more.

A moment later his patience was rewarded when the small creature poked its head around the corner again, a little at a time. At first, Hugh could only see half its face. When Hugh kept still, the little one moved closer, exposing its head fully, watching Hugh with those big, sad, gray eyes.

It blinked once and Hugh sighed. He needed to know more, but his first instinct was to help this poor bedraggled kitten. For he could see now, it wasn't fully grown, even though it was larger in size than a fully grown house cat.

Perhaps it was the young of one of the big cat varieties that were said to roam this land. Hugh didn't know, but he wanted to find out. He wanted to learn this little one's story and help protect it.

Backing against the wall of the nearest building, Hugh crouched down, putting himself nearer eye level with the creature, hoping to put it more at ease. He remained there, unmoving, willing the cat to come to him.

Slowly, paw by paw, it moved out from around the corner and that's when Hugh realized what he was dealing with.

The cat had wings.

Which meant it wasn't a *cat* at all. It was a gryphon.

Not a normal gryphon. Not the ones he was used to seeing around here. Those had the back end of a cat and the head and wings of a predatory bird. This little one had the body and head of the cat plus long feathered wings that dragged behind the poor creature. Was this some new kind of gryphon? Or a different species entirely?

Hugh had no idea, but he knew a creature in distress when he saw one. He could not leave this little one alone in the freezing rain. In all likelihood, it would be dead by morning if he left it on its own. Hugh would not have that on his conscience.

Hugh sat, his back against the wall. He didn't feel the cold, though he certainly noticed the way the wet ground soaked his pants. They would dry. So would he. What was important now was that he get the little gryphlet to come to him so he could help it.

There was no doubt in his mind that this odd kitten was a youngster. Probably just a baby. He would never be able to live with himself if he left the young one to suffer and probably die in this awful weather.

The kitten stopped, eyeing him warily as Hugh sat in the mud. He opened his hands, showing the wary kitten that he held no weapon, or anything else, for that matter. Hugh kept his motions slow and steady, his posture as unthreatening as possible.

He was rewarded as the baby gryphon came closer to him, inch by inch, moment by moment.

"Hello." Hugh spoke softly, coaxingly, as the kitten stopped a few feet from him. He'd seen gryphons talk aloud in his brother's court. He knew they could, but he had no idea at what age they mastered the skill.

"Hi," the youngster answered, its head cocking adorably to the side. The gryphlet watched Hugh suspiciously, but didn't run away.

"My name is Hugh. What's yours?" Again, he was careful to keep his tone friendly and soft-edged.

"Hoo." She tried his name but didn't get it quite right. Hugh was charmed. "Am Misborn. What dey call me."

"They?" Hugh's tone invited confidence, though inside he was appalled and angered that anyone should call an innocent child by such a name.

"Mama an' Papa." The gryphlet moved closer and sat in the mud on Hugh's right.

"Can I call you Miss? You're a girl, aren't you?" Hugh hadn't gotten a good look at the creature's hindquarters, but he suspected he was talking to a female. He still didn't like the name, but perhaps she didn't know what it meant. Shortening it to something more respectable was his best option at this point.

"Tink ssso." The youngster's head drooped with fatigue and

17

she seemed to lower her guard a bit more. "Why Hoo magic?"

Hugh wasn't exactly certain what the gryphlet meant by her question. It was possible she sensed the magic that lived inside him, deep in the place where the dragon shared his soul. It made sense. Gryphons were also creatures of magic. Perhaps that was what had drawn this little one's interest.

It put Hugh in a bad position, but his conscience wouldn't let him leave this little girl behind. No matter what it cost him personally. Princes of Draconia protected the helpless and innocent no matter what land they were in.

"Do you need magic, Miss? Is that why you were following me?"

"Tink sso," she repeated. "Can I sstay?" Like the few gryphons he'd met in Draconia, she had trouble with the letter S, but less so than the gryphons with beaks. Her soft mouth formed words better, though she was only a baby and had limited vocabulary and the typical problems with pronunciation that most young creatures seemed to have.

"Stay with me? Yes, little one." Her uncertain tone nearly broke his heart. She sounded as if she'd truly expected him to reject her. Poor baby. "Are you cold? I will share my coat with you if you like." He lifted his arm and untied the flap that held his oversized oilskin closed on that side.

The coat was more like a cape that tied at various points, allowing water to sluice downward. It wasn't the easiest thing to get in and out of, but it had the advantage of excess fabric that helped ward off the rain. This kind of coat was common enough as to be unremarkable and he could carry much beneath it should he want to smuggle anything on his person.

He lifted the excess fabric and the kitten scrambled under it faster than he would have believed. She was shivering and miserable, her small body skinnier than he'd expected.

"Hoo warm," she observed as she settled next to him. She'd tucked her body around him, her wings under his arm, her front paws resting alongside his leg, her head turned to look up at him.

Wrapping the folds of his coat over her back and legs, only her head stayed uncovered as she watched him. Hugh let out a tiny tendril of his magic to warm her rapidly, gratified when her little body ceased shivering and her eyes closed momentarily in delight. He felt the way her magic touched his and accepted the energy he fed to her in a gentle trickle so as not to overwhelm her senses.

"Are you hungry?"

Her eyes popped open. "Yess!" Her verbal pounce reinforced the idea and Hugh had to struggle not to laugh. She really was the cutest little thing, bedraggled as she was.

"I have a meat pie in my pocket. You can have it."

He pulled the waxed paper out of his inside pocket and unwrapped the treat within, holding it for her. Surprisingly dexterous paws took the pastry-wrapped meat from him and brought it to her mouth. It was gone in three bites and she looked to him for more even as she licked her paws clean. He noticed she favored one, but she was quick to hide it and he didn't get a good look.

"More?" she asked, distracting him from his train of thought.

"Not with me. But I can get more. I have a room nearby where we can both get out of the rain. Would you like that?"

"Hoo take me wif?" She seemed so hopeful. There was no guile in this brave youngster.

"Yes, little one. I cannot leave you out here in the cold. Will you come with me?"

"Yess. Go wif." She leapt to her feet under his coat and looked at him eagerly. No doubt she was hungrier than her dainty manners had led him to believe.

"All right." Hugh stood and kept his arm raised so that at least some of the freezing rain was blocked over her little body. "Come with me and we'll both get dry, warm and fed."

19

She trotted at his side energetically at first, but soon began to slow her pace. Hugh finally stopped and bent down to her, meeting her eyes so he could gauge her reaction.

"Is it all right if I pick you up and carry you? You can stay warm under my coat that way and we can get there faster."

Her answer was to raise her front paws to rest on his thigh. It was clear she wanted up.

Hugh took a moment to untie the flaps on his coat completely, then make an opening in front where she could look out if she liked. She was an intelligent creature who needed to trust him. Keeping her in the dark—literally—would do nothing to further that trust.

Once there was room under the hanging flaps of the coat, Hugh reached down and lifted her easily into his arms. The rain had turned to sleet and snow. No one saw him lift the large winged cat into his arms and walk on as if she weighed nothing at all.

Hugh had the strength of a dragon even when he was in human form. The little gryphlet was no burden at all for him as he held her shivering body close to his chest. She'd gotten cold again during their short walk no matter how much he'd tried to shield her from the rain.

Hugh was thoroughly wet now. Wet, muddy and a total mess, but he was warm. The kitten seemed to soak up his warmth and her shivering stopped again in short order.

They walked through the alleys, heading away from the cliffs, toward the safer working-class part of the city where he'd taken a room. Opting not to be murdered in his bed, Hugh had chosen one of the better inns to sleep in. He'd rented a room for the next week and paid half in advance to keep the innkeeper friendly.

Arriving at the door with a giant kitten under his coat, her head peeking out from between the folds near his chest, Hugh realized there was no way to hide her. The noise level from within the inn was higher than normal, probably because so many had chosen to seek shelter from the storm in the taproom.

There was a back entrance and Hugh made for it, but it was also the area where the innkeeper kept his spare barrels, and he was out there on the covered porch, wrestling with an empty when Hugh approached. He could have waited until the innkeeper went back inside, but Hugh needed to feed the kitten and for that, he'd need an ally in the kitchen. Who better than the owner of the establishment? If Hugh couldn't talk the man around, they could always find another inn.

But the man had seemed kind. Hugh had observed him taking less than the standard amount for lunch from a nearly blind old woman the day before and giving extra portions to her as well. The man seemed to have a big heart and Hugh was counting on that inner kindness to help him help the gryphlet as well.

"Sir." Hugh spoke in a quiet, unhurried voice, hoping to put the man at ease. "May I have a word with you?"

The innkeeper looked out into the sleet and spotted Hugh standing by the steps to the covered porch. Hugh had dared not go closer until he'd warned the innkeeper of his presence. It wouldn't do to startle the man.

"Certainly. What is it you have there?" The man squinted, looking through the gray precipitation, staring hard at the gryphlet's head poking out from the coat.

"That is what I wanted to talk to you about." Hugh stepped closer, moving under the end of the covered porch and shrugging his coat open wider so the innkeeper could see more of the baby gryphon in his arms. "I found her in the street. She is very young and in need of food and warmth. I will understand if you wish me to go elsewhere." He kept his tone calm and quiet. To his relief, the man stepped closer.

"Fell out of your nest, eh, little one?" The innkeeper addressed the gryphlet directly, his gaze rising from her eyes to Hugh's with grim understanding. "Aye, you can both bide here.

It was good of you to bring her. I have seen this before."

"Often?" Hugh couldn't help but ask as he stepped forward, farther under the covered porch, heading toward the door. The innkeeper opened the door so he could pass through and their eyes met.

"No." The innkeeper shook his head, a grim cast to his features. "Not often. Thank the Lady."

Hugh wasn't sure whether the man thanked a female deity or perhaps the Lady Doge who ruled this land. It didn't much matter. What mattered now was getting this poor, bedraggled kitten warm and dry. And fed. The little cub had to be starving—Hugh could feel the bones of her ribs sticking out beneath her skin.

The innkeeper led the way down the dim hall toward the bedchamber Hugh had been given. It was worth noting that the older man apparently didn't want the gryphlet in the busy common room, even though the fire was roaring in there, where many people had gathered on this gloomy, sub-zero day.

"I'll send the boy up with coals for the fire and food for the youngling," the innkeeper said as he bustled ahead of Hugh and his burden. "Blankets and nesting material too, though you'll have to promise to keep her safely back from the fire. This lass is too young to know the danger."

"No fire," Miss piped up, holding up one paw that Hugh now saw was singed. "Hoo warm."

Hugh shared a grim expression with the landlord who had opened his door with the master key. "Perhaps some salve for her paw? If you have any."

"I'll see what the missus has from the stillroom." He blocked Hugh's path when he would have entered, holding his gaze with a hard look. "You seem to know your way around gryphons." It was more question than statement.

"Not gryphons, exactly." Hugh shrugged. "In my travels I have become familiar with many different creatures. They seem to like me as much as I like them."

"They are often better judges of character than most men, I reckon." The innkeeper nodded once and moved aside. "All right then. If you would see to her for the night, we'll see what must be done in the morning. If anything."

"I would be most obliged if you could send dinner to my room. I will pay..." Hugh tried to look reluctant, knowing the rough traveler he posed as would balk at spending extra coin—or at least make a show of objecting.

"No need. The boy will be along soon with food and supplies for the nestling. Just tell him if there's anything else."

"Thank you," Hugh said politely as the innkeeper closed the door, leaving him inside with his precious burden.

The room wasn't warm yet. No fire had been lit in the grate. The innkeeper's son would bring a coal to get the blaze going. Hugh didn't need that, of course, but it would raise suspicion if he lit his own fire, and he'd have to expose his ability to the gryphlet. She was just a baby, really, and couldn't know how important it was for him to keep his dragon half secret from the people of this land.

Hugh still didn't know if Helios was friend or deadly foe to dragon folk. Until he figured that out, he would have to keep a low profile. Taking in a rejected gryphon nestling wasn't exactly the way he had planned to do that, but his honor wouldn't let him do anything else.

Half dragon, Hugh was a strong believer in fate. Some things were just meant to be. Perhaps finding this baby gryphon in need was part of the grand plan fate had in store for him. Or perhaps not. Hugh would likely never know either way.

Hugh settled on the lone chair in the small room, preferring not to transfer the wet mud from his clothes to the room's single bed. Miss stayed happily in his arms, cuddling close to his chest for warmth. She jumped a little when the innkeeper's son knocked once before entering at Hugh's word.

He held a small wooden bucket and a metal scoop that held a hot coal with which to light the wood and tinder already in the grate. Miss watched the young human with wary interest. She jumped when the fire caught in the fireplace, but Hugh soothed her, holding her close in his arms and stroking her drying fur.

"I'll be back in a tic with towels and hot water so's you can clean up, sir," the boy said as he headed for the door. "Da said heat first, then cleaning stuff, then food." He ticked off his tasks on his fingers as he headed out the door. "Ma's burn ointment is in the bucket, sir."

Hugh thanked the boy as he left and spent a few minutes coaxing Miss off his lap. She was truly afraid of the fire, which was a healthy instinct when not taken to an extreme. Hugh hooked the handle of the bucket with his foot and dragged it over, having been not entirely successful in dislodging the kitten. He found a small earthenware pot with a square of gingham fabric tied over the top, which proved to be a fragrant burnjelly salve he'd seen before. Humans who lived among dragons often had need of such things, unfortunately, so it was a staple of many Lair homes.

"Can I see your paw?" he asked the gryphlet politely. "This salve will make it feel better and in a few days it will be good as new if we keep it clean and apply more salve morning and night. I promise."

She looked at him suspiciously, keeping her paw hidden. Perhaps she wasn't ready to open herself up for more possible pain at the moment. He still had work to do in gaining her trust.

"How did your paw get singed, little one? Did you stray too close to a fire?"

"Wuz warm," she said finally. "Wanted warm, but hurt."

"Fire can hurt, but it is also a good thing. See that fire in the grate?" Hugh pointed to the source of heat. Miss's gaze followed reluctantly. "It can keep you warm. It can help dry your wet fur. It is also a source of light so we can see each other clearly. Although I suppose you have excellent night vision, don't you?" His question was rhetorical since the youngster probably didn't even realize she could see better at night than most humans. "People also use fire to heat their food. Cooking certain foods makes it safe for them to eat, though I think you probably prefer your meat raw, don't you?"

"Hungry," she mewled and Hugh's heart broke again for the bedraggled little waif.

"We'll take care of that soon. The innkeeper is sending food for us both. We just have to be patient a little longer. In the meantime, we should get clean and dry." He shrugged off his coat and let it drape back, over the chair. He was wet through and through, but a controlled blast of his own internal heat dried his clothing from the inside out.

He stroked warm hands over Miss's fur, drying it and sweeping bits of twigs, mud and other debris from her coat. Where most of the gryphons he'd seen were brown, gold or even red in color, Miss had a gray and white striped pattern to her coat. Her baby fur dried fluffy and full, giving her a fuzzy look that was utterly adorable.

She purred a bit as she warmed up and began to dry out. Her wings were still wet and Hugh encouraged her to spread them out so he could see to them as well. She'd dragged the tips on the ground behind her and some of the shafts were caked with mud. It would crack off cleanly when dry, he hoped.

She unfolded one wing at a time as he worked, relaxing more and more as Hugh and the fire warmed the room. She was dozing lightly when the boy returned. He placed a loaded tray on the room's single table and began unpacking the heap of stuff on top.

"Towels and spare blankets," he said as he put the neatly folded stack near Hugh, who put them to good use almost immediately. "A bowl of tidbits for the little miss." The boy seemed in awe of the gryphon, not sure how to approach. Hugh held out one hand for the bowl and the boy gave it to him.

Hugh carefully checked the meat scraps inside the bowl, selecting one to give Miss. It wouldn't do for her to gorge herself

25

and become ill. He would watch over her eating until she was sated and more secure. She perked up when she scented the meat and lifted her head. He held half a chicken breast—top quality meat, he was pleased to note—in his hand, allowing her to take it from him with her paws. He watched her injured paw with particular interest, plotting how to treat it once she was done eating.

"If you want to help her, you can give her the rest of the chicken, one piece at a time. It's best she doesn't eat too much too fast just now after not having eaten for a while." Hugh gave the bowl back to the boy. He seemed enchanted by the gryphlet and thrilled at the prospect of helping her.

With a tentative expression, the boy held out the next piece of chicken. He smiled with joy when Miss snatched the meat out of his hands and began chewing it daintily. While she ate, Hugh used the towel to work on her fur a bit more. She was almost completely dry, except for her large wings, and much cleaner than she had been just an hour ago.

The boy watched, enthralled, when Hugh spread one of her wings to its full length with Miss's absent-minded cooperation. She was busy eating and didn't seem to be paying attention to what he was doing.

"She is going to grow up on the big side, eh?" the boy asked, seeing the largeness of her wing.

"I believe so, yes," Hugh confirmed. "She has a very large wingspan for her body size right now, but I have little doubt she will grow into these very impressive feathers."

Hugh was proud for no reason he could think of. The gryphlet was not his. She was merely a stray he had picked up out of the kindness of his heart. He would have no influence on her future as an adult. There was no reason he should feel so proud of what she would no doubt become. Still, he did feel pride in her and for her. She was going to be a beautiful creature with uncommon talents and if her reactions so far were anything to go by, a beautiful soul.

If nobody managed to crush her spirit before then.

Hugh didn't like that idea at all. Not one bit. But what could he do?

It was simple, really. He would do what he could for her while he was here. Beyond that, he had no idea. Maybe the Jinn could take her in when he had to leave. He had to come up with some solution that would protect this precious creature. He just didn't know what that solution would be at the moment. Perhaps fate would step in once more to provide it.

"Will that mud come off her primaries?" The boy's voice broke into Hugh's dark thoughts. "Da said to bring you a kettle you can keep over the fire so you have warm water for washing. I'll also bring a pot of cold water for drinking, miss, so you won't go thirsty." The boy addressed the gryphlet directly.

"How know name?"

The boy's gaze went from her to Hugh in confusion. "I've been calling her Miss as a short form of what her parents called her," Hugh explained with a grimace only the boy could see.

Understanding dawned over the boy's features, along with an unexpected compassion as he turned back to the gryphlet.

"Da taught me the polite way to address young females is to call them miss. Like Miss Jenny who teaches me letters and Miss Sara who helps Ma in the stillroom. Married ladies are called Missus. Since you're a young female, it's only polite to call you miss, miss."

The kitten scrunched up her little nose and made a mewling sound that probably was laughter. At least the boy seemed to interpret it as such. He laughed with her and tentatively reached out to touch her uninjured paw.

"I burned my arm once," the boy said in a slow, careful way. Hugh had seen the youngster eyeing Miss's injured paw. "Ma's salve works wonders, miss. See?" He held up his forearm and pulled back his sleeve to reveal a white scar. That burn had been bad when it had been made.

"Hurt?" she asked, stopping eating for a moment to look at

his arm.

"Yeah, it hurt when it happened, but the salve takes the sting out and makes it heal. You should try it at the very least. I bet your paw hurts something awful, don't it?"

"Hurtss," she agreed, holding up her little paw. It was angry and red, puckered in places where the burns were worst.

"Touch this." The boy held the uncovered earthen pot up to the gryphlet, offering it to her. She sniffed it first and then dared to dip her paw into the wide mouth of the container. It was big enough that she could do so without further injury and Hugh wondered why he hadn't thought of the boy's unique approach.

"Skwissh," she said, cocking her head to the side as she encountered the slippery salve for the first time. "No hurt." Her eyes blinked rapidly in surprise as she pulled her paw out of the jar. It had only a small amount of salve on the tip of the paw, where the burns were worst. If that was all she'd allow, it was at least in the right place.

The boy moved closer and held up one hand, palm outward as he moved it closer. "It takes the sting out, don't it?" His tone was encouraging. He dipped his fingers into the jar and took a dollop of the salve out. "Can I put more on for you?"

This time the gryphlet held out her paw more eagerly. She understood now, Hugh thought, that the salve would stop the constant pain. The boy was a genius. And gentle with his approach to frightened young things. Hugh's opinion of the innkeeper and his family rose with each interaction. When he left, he'd leave them extra coin and good word for their business with the Jinn.

Miss let the boy put more salve on her paw, her fatigue beginning to catch up with her as the pain decreased and she became warm, dry and sated. Hugh motioned to the boy to spread the towels and blankets he'd brought next to the low-slung bed. Hugh would sleep only a foot or so above the gryphlet—if she would accept the fabric nest. If not, he'd figure a way to make them both comfortable for the night. Somehow. Even if he was the one who ended up sleeping on the floor.

Hugh stood, lifting Miss in his arms and placing her in the curl of thick blankets the boy had arranged. He still needed to do a little work on her wings, but the young gryphon was dozing and would probably sleep for a while. Hugh could work the mud out of her feathers as easily while she was asleep as when she was awake, and the boy seemed eager to help.

"Does your father need you in the common room?" Hugh asked.

"Not for a while yet." The boy smiled, speaking quietly. "He said I was to help you and the young miss."

Hugh could see the boy's excitement at the idea. He liked being around the young gryphon with all the open honesty of the young.

"What is your name?"

"Tomlin, sir. You can call me Tom."

"Well, young Tom, you are very good with her. Would you be willing to help me with her wings? She has a few pounds of mud in her feathers that needs to come out. And we might need some kind of oil to help restore her shafts. I haven't dealt with gryphons much. Do you know of anything we could use that you might have in the inn?"

The boy nodded. "I know just the thing, sir. Ma keeps it for the stillroom. I'll come back with the water and the special oil. Just be a tic." The boy was already out the door, away on his errand. Hugh looked at the sleeping gryphon and then at the tray that held his meal. With a shrug, he moved the chair to the table and dug in. He'd need his strength for the hours to come grooming feathered wings.

Dragon scale was so much easier, by comparison. Feathers were too delicate. But the little thing couldn't help the fact that she'd been born gryphon instead of dragon. Hugh would help her as much as he could.

Over the next hour and a half, Hugh and Tomlin cleaned

Miss's feathers and then worked small amounts of soothing oil into the abused shafts. The little gryphon slept through the whole procedure and Hugh thought maybe this was the first time in a long time that she felt safe, warm and well fed. He vowed it wouldn't be the last, no matter what he had to do to give her a secure future.

If he had to, he'd smuggle her out of Helios and bring her back to his land, where he knew she would be welcome. But first he had to get her through the next few days. Hugh thought he'd found allies in the innkeeper and his young son. Time would tell if his instincts were correct.

When they were finished with Miss's wings, Tomlin took the empty trays and left. Hugh settled down in the bed after rearranging Miss's wings comfortably folded along her back. She didn't stir and he expected she'd sleep for several hours.

He fell asleep with one arm dangling off the bed, resting over the gryphlet's back. She probably didn't realize it, but he fed her a steady trickle of magic through the light touch, rebuilding her strength little by little. She'd been down to the dregs of her inner energy—starved magically, physically and most likely emotionally as well. Poor little mite.

In the bustling taproom, Tomlin reported to his father as instructed.

"The little miss is asleep. The sir's name is Hugh and he fixed her up. He even let me help put oil on the shafts of her feathers after we got all the mud off." Tomlin was proud of that. He'd always admired the gryphons that flew overhead, but had never been close enough to touch one. Not that they would let just anyone touch them. Tonight had been an honor he would always cherish.

"That was well done. The Lady will no doubt reward you for your service, my lad." Tomlin could hear the pride in his father's voice. "We have to get word to the palace, but this weather isn't fit for man nor beast." The innkeeper grimaced.

"All sane folk are indoors and we're busy enough. I need you here for now. I suppose the little miss can bide here a while. At least until the weather improves and I can spare you to run a message to the castle."

Tomlin couldn't believe his luck. The gryphlet would be staying and he might even get to help her again. He knew he was grinning, but his father was in an indulgent mood. A pat on the head and his father moved off to pour more ale for those weathering the storm in the common room of their humble inn.

It was two days before the weather cleared enough that Tomlin was able to run up to the palace to deliver his father's message. Only hours later, a strange lady arrived at the inn.

Chapter Two

In the two days since Hugh had become the caretaker of a misborn baby gryphon, she had become the centerpiece of the common room. She was too energetic after she woke that first day to stay in a small bedroom. With the innkeeper's indulgence and Tomlin's eager help, Hugh had escorted Miss into the common room before the morning meal, when few people were around.

She was shy of everyone at first and hid behind Hugh's legs, rubbing up against him like the cat she was and tucking her wings close against her body and her tail down between her legs. He'd even felt her shivering in fright against him at first, but with Tomlin on one side and Hugh on the other, she'd finally settled into a nest Tomlin had prepared for her near the fire.

She had the best seat in the house, for during such foul weather, the seats near the giant fireplace were at a premium. Tomlin had to leave after a bit to fetch breakfast for them and to do his chores, but Miss had settled down at Hugh's side. He'd foregone a chair at first, in favor of a spot on the floor where he could keep contact with the scared gryphlet.

He'd taught her the right way to approach a fire so as not to get singed and he covertly gave a bit of his natural healing energy to finish the repair to her injured paw. When Tomlin bounded over with breakfast, he sought Hugh's permission to place the bowl of prime meat tidbits in front of Miss. Hugh checked the contents of the bowl before nodding. It wouldn't do to let her gorge. The amount was about right to give her a good feed without causing more problems. Lady knew, the little miss—as Tomlin had taken to calling her—had already been through enough.

Miss dozed after eating. Warm and well fed, comfortable in front of the fire, she put her feline head down on her paws and fell almost instantly asleep.

Hugh rose from his spot on the floor and took a seat at the table only a foot away to eat his own breakfast. The innkeeper came over to chat with him and run his eye over the gryphlet.

"Tom says she looks better this morning. I'd have to agree." The innkeeper nodded at the sleeping baby. "You've done a noble thing here, lad. And it's clear you have a way with gryphons. Are there many where you come from?"

Now that was a fishing expedition if Hugh had ever heard one, but he was clearly an outlander here. It was only curiosity that led the man to ask such questions when Hugh had rescued a magical creature that few people knew how—or were permitted—to deal with.

"I have met only a few gryphons in my time, and those were not of this land. There is a pair now nesting in Draconia, where I hail from." Hugh decided to stick with the truth. Draconia and Helios were supposed to be political allies. What better way to find out if that was true than by posing as a commoner from his own land. If the common folk of Helios had a problem with another commoner, it would be more likely to come out than if he appeared as a royal prince of the House of Draneth the Wise.

Statesmen would lie to a prince. It was unlikely a middle class barman would lie to someone he considered a social equal or, perhaps, inferior.

Hugh watched to see how the man would react. There was nothing in his outward demeanor to raise Hugh's suspicions. The man merely nodded and moved on with his conversation.

"We have heard tales of strange gryphons appearing in Draconia. It was big news among our flocks for some time and the cause of much conjecture."

Hugh wondered if they'd figured out that the wizard Gryffid was still alive and well on the island south of Draconia where he and his people had hidden from the ravages of time. That's where some of the gryphons now in Draconia had come from. As well as the seer whose vision had sent him on this quest.

Shanya was one of Gryffid's people, one of the thriving colony of Fair Folk who inhabited his island. She'd chosen to come to Draconia with a young emigrating gryphon pair and make her home there. She claimed a vision had led to the move and her gift had already proven valuable to the royal family of Draconia.

"They are amazing creatures," Hugh answered noncommittally, glancing fondly at the sleeping gryphlet at his side.

"You've done well on her wings. Have you trained with gryphon caretakers in your land?"

"No. One of my father's friends trained hunting falcons. I learned a bit of feather care from him when I was young." At least that much was true. One of the knights in his training Lair had once been a falconer. Hugh had helped him a time or two. "It seems I remembered more than I thought, but if there's ought I should be doing for her, please let me know. She seems happy enough now, though still very shy."

"She's probably been through a lot, but she is young. She will recover her spirit in time." The barman rubbed his cloth over the table, wiping off an errant crumb. "My name is Hobson. My friends call me Hob."

"I'm Hugh." He held out his hand and Hob took it, exchanging a firm shake. "You said last night that you'd seen this before." Hugh glanced back at the gryphlet, who shifted her head into a more comfortable position and appeared to still be dozing.

"Once. Rejected by the parents. Left out in the cold to die. It was a very sad thing indeed." Hob's expression was grim. "But not for such delicate ears as the little miss." Hob nodded toward the gryphlet, who had awoken and was looking at Hob with fear in her eyes. "Hello, little miss."

Miss pressed her head against Hugh's thigh, her wings quivering the tiniest bit. Hugh reached down and stroked her back, sending a little tendril of his magic out to her, giving her that lifeline to which to cling as she learned her way in this unfamiliar world.

"Master Hobson is Tomlin's sire," Hugh explained. "He owns this place."

Miss's eyes widened as she looked up at the man across the table. "Hi," she finally said, in a whisper.

That was the first greeting of many offered by the gryphlet under Hugh's supervision. As the common room of the inn began to fill up for the midday meal, quite a few of the patrons came over to pay their respects and coo over Miss. Hugh was indulgent because he sensed no ill will from the people and he felt the leap in Miss's confidence each time someone was kind to her.

He had no doubt she'd seen little kindness in her life to this point. Tomlin delivered lunch and stayed to play with Miss afterward. It was clear to Hugh that Miss was feeling more at ease with each passing minute and she truly liked the boy. It was obvious Tomlin was enthralled by the gryphlet as well.

The crowd thinned after the meal and Hob motioned for his son to stay where he was. Miss was getting more active and even ventured a few feet away from Hugh's side when Tomlin produced a ball the two youngsters rolled back and forth.

Rolling turned to tossing before long as the two children worked off some of their seemingly boundless energy. At one point as they were tussling good-naturedly over the ball, Miss's claws came out and nicked Tomlin's arm, drawing blood. Both youngsters froze as Tomlin gasped in pain.

"Come here, Tom," Hugh ordered quietly. "Let me look at that."

Hugh pulsed a bit of his magic over the shallow wound before wiping away the blood with the sleeve of his black shirt. The wound was healed and would not fester. Miss was so young, Hugh hadn't thought through the fact that she probably didn't know much about her claws and the damage they could inflict on soft human skin. He called out to her and she came to his side.

"Will you give me your paw, sweetheart?" Hugh was as gentle as he could be with this timid little soul.

She held up her front paw, trustingly touching Hugh's outstretched hand. He pressed gently on the soft pads of her toes, revealing the wickedly sharp instruments concealed there. He didn't know how much she understood, so he decided to start out with the basics.

"These are your claws. See how sharp they are?" She nodded, taking his lesson very seriously if her expression was any indication. "They will grow longer and stronger as you grow older. They are your most basic tools and weapons." He gave her the lesson that was given to baby dragons, altering it slightly to fit her form.

"Weaponsss?" she asked curiously.

"Yes." His expression was as grave as hers. "Do you know the difference between good and bad? Right and wrong?" She nodded slowly and he decided to let that philosophical problem go for now. She seemed to have a basic grasp of the concepts after what she'd been through. "You are a good person," he said firmly. He took every opportunity to reinforce her self-image. "Some aren't so good. And sometimes they do bad things. That's when good people step in and stop them. When you grow up, perhaps you'll do that." Hugh didn't know exactly what kind of role the misborn gryphlet would have in this world, but he hoped for the best.

"I sstop bad tingss?" Her head tilted to the side as if considering the idea.

"Yes, dear one. When you are older and bigger. For now, you need to learn the use of the weapons that are part of your body. Tom here doesn't have such weapons. See?" Hugh motioned for Tomlin to hold his hands out so Miss could inspect them. "Humans have fingernails and they can scratch, but they're nothing like your claws. See the difference?"

"I ssee," she agreed. He was gratified by her curiosity.

"And see how thin human skin is? A fingernail will make a scratch on the surface. Show her, Tom, if you would." Hugh gestured to the boy and Tom scratched his own arm, showing her the red mark left behind. She looked closely, studying the mark on the boy's arm. "If you used your claw on Tom's arm, it would draw blood very easily. So you must be very careful to keep your claws in when you play with Tom or any other human, do you understand?"

"Yess. I careful." She turned to look at Tomlin. "I ssowy, Tom."

"It's all right, Miss. It only hurt a bit and it's better now. Don't worry about it. Do you want to play some more?"

Hugh marveled at the resilience of youth. The two scampered off across the room with the ball and began playing again almost immediately. There were no repeats of the claw incident and Hugh noted with a bit of pride that Miss was much more careful of how she touched the boy.

By dinnertime, the common room was again full and Miss was doing better with the folk who came to greet her. She wasn't as shy as she'd been that morning. Playing with Tom had worn off some of her energy and by the time she'd finished eating there was only time to give her fur a quick tongue bath before she curled up in a ball and fell asleep in front of the fire.

Hugh didn't count the day wasted. Instead of going out to gather information, the local people came to him. Some were exactly the sort of people he'd had to find some excuse to talk to in the days prior. The gryphlet was enough of a conversation starter that it didn't seem odd when he turned the conversation to local politics and rumors.

Hugh gathered more information in that single day spent sipping beer in the common room than he had in the week since his arrival. He sat in the common room until well after dinner, waiting only for Miss to stir a little before taking her back to the small room they would sleep in together for a second night.

She was able to walk out of the common room, but she was so sleepy, her steps wove almost drunkenly. As soon as they were out of sight of the other patrons, Hugh picked her up in his arms and carried her. It wouldn't do to show off his unnatural strength in a room full of curious onlookers.

Someone had been in to clean his room, make the bed and freshen the little nest of blankets for Miss. The fire was already lit as well, and the room was toasty warm while the gale whistled outside past the shuttered windows.

Hugh placed Miss in her nest and she wiggled only slightly to find a more comfortable position before falling asleep once more. Hugh did as before, finding his place in the bed and reaching down to touch Miss's back so he could feed her more magic as she slept.

She was almost up to where she should be as far as her energy levels went. By morning, her magic would be replenished and he could work more on her self-esteem and food intake. She was still scrawny. It would take more than one day of eating properly to put weight back on her skinny body.

The next day, Tom was gone in the morning, running some sort of errand for his father. He was back by lunch, which he shared with Hugh and Miss, as he had the day before. Afterward, the two youngsters played farther away from Hugh than the day before, scampering around the common room to the amusement of the few people who lingered over their midday meal.

Their game had brought them back around the room toward Hugh when the door opened to admit a highborn lady, if Hugh didn't misjudge the quality of her cloak. She paused to gaze at Miss with a measuring look Hugh didn't care for, then sought out Hobson for a lengthy chat.

Hugh felt uneasy and was glad when the children resumed

Keeper of the Flame

their place near the fire at his side. They'd tired themselves out and were rolling the ball quietly back and forth as they both sat on the floor at opposite ends of the hearth. Miss was on the side closer to Hugh's chair, for which he was grateful. Should he need to protect her for any reason, she would be close at hand.

Hugh's gaze strayed often to the quiet corner of the bar where the lady spoke in hushed tones with Hobson. The innkeeper seemed to defer to her quite a bit, which only confirmed Hugh's guess that she was someone of a higher social class.

When their conversation finally ended, the woman turned and walked toward the fireplace where Miss and Tomlin were still playing quietly. Hugh watched her. Her gaze was focused on the gryphlet, sparing him only a furtive glance as she'd turned.

He didn't know what to make of that glance. Was it shyness that caused her to stop short of meeting his gaze? Or was it arrogance? He had no notion of her motivation at the moment, but if she came any closer, he would. He'd make a point of it before she got too near the little one.

He thought Miss understood the use of her claws a little better now, but he still doubted she'd know when and how to use them effectively. For now, Hugh had to be her defender no matter what. His honor demanded no less. He'd taken her in. Placed her under his protection. He would defend her against all comers.

Even pretty ones with flowing hair and luminous eyes that refused to meet his.

The woman walked closer and Hugh could see her eyes were a lovely shade of light hazel brown. He noted something else as well. Something that set his teeth on edge. As she reached out one hand toward the gryphlet, she was gathering her power. Magical power. And she intended to direct it toward Miss. Her actions could brook no other interpretation.

"What is your name, little one?" she asked even as her

hand rose and her power released.

Hugh stood abruptly, placing himself between the woman's outstretched hand and the baby gryphon. He took in the strange flavor of her magic and absorbed it. His dragon strength allowed not one smidgen of the questioning magic to return to its owner.

For that's what it had been, he realized now. A magical summons. A question. A request for compliance.

No way was he going to let this strange woman—fine lady or not—use such a thing on Miss. She was only a baby and didn't understand much about magic. She'd most likely give the woman anything she wanted, including her obedience.

Hugh believed such a thing should be earned. Not coerced by magical means. Or any other means, come to that.

"She does not have a proper name yet, milady." Hugh's tone was polite but firm. "We simply call her Miss."

The shy gryphlet rubbed against his leg, her head peeping around his thigh so she could gaze up at the woman. Miss was trembling again, probably picking up on Hugh's tension. He reached downward with one hand and stroked her neck, trying to ease her nerves. She was very highly strung after the ordeal she'd been through, though she was bouncing back bit by bit with the ease of the very young. Hugh would be damned if he'd let this woman scare the gryphlet back into the state she'd been in when he'd found her.

"What did you just do?" The woman's unguarded words betrayed her shock as her wide hazel eyes sought his gaze.

"I will allow no harm to come to this child. She is under my protection." His words were pitched low so that only the woman could hear him.

"I intend her no harm." She drew herself up with indignation, though she was still a head shorter than him.

"Then you will not touch her with your magic. I do not know its origins or intent and I will not allow it to influence her one way or the other." His words challenged her authority and he could see by the fire in her gaze that she didn't like it. Highborn as she was, she probably wasn't used to it.

"And what of you? Are you not influencing her? You are an outlander here. What right have you to one of our citizens?"

"Outlander I may be, but I recognize an outcast when I see one. Your people did not help her when they should have. You do not deserve her."

Something in her deflated at his words. For a split second he almost regretted the harsh truth he'd just spoken. Then Miss's intensified trembling got through to him and he bent to lift her into his arms. Let them see how easily he could carry her. Let them realize he could protect her from all comers.

It was an irrational thought but one that would not be denied. His brother Nico could send another spy to Helios to complete Hugh's mission. One better suited to stealth than a lone dragon in a land dominated by feathered wings instead of scaled ones. Miss's fate was more important at the moment.

"Don't fight," Miss said as her clear eyes gazed up at him with fear in their depths.

"I'm sorry, sweetheart." He crooned to the child, rocking her slightly. "Sometimes grownups have differences of opinion, but it's nothing for you to worry about. You're safe, little Miss."

She nuzzled her furry head under his chin and settled down in his lap as he reclaimed his seat near the fire. The woman—stronger of will than he had expected—sat opposite them at the scarred wooden table. Her cunning gaze took in everything about the way Miss relaxed and sought shelter in his arms. Tomlin stood at his side, fear on his young face.

"Tom, would you fetch refreshments? There's a good lad." He sent the boy off with a reassuring wink though Tomlin looked back over his shoulder several times as he made his way across the common room toward his father and the kitchen entrance.

Hugh continued to stroke Miss's neck and back, trying to reassure her. It was clear she did not like the tension in the air and Hugh regretted scaring her. She was a very sensitive youngster.

The woman watched, saying nothing for several moments. That surprised him. He would've expected any other woman to launch into a barrage of questions or criticisms. Instead, this foreign beauty simply watched him with a measuring gleam in her fascinating hazel eyes.

Tomlin arrived with a tray that held finer crockery than Hugh had seen in the inn before. No doubt Mrs. Hobson was pulling out all the stops for the high born lady visiting her humble establishment. Tea and cakes on a dainty plate were placed in front of her by Tomlin's shaking hands. Something about this lady had even the boy on edge. When Tom had finished setting out the teapot and cups, he took his leave faster than Hugh had ever seen him move. He headed back to his father on the double and stayed there, watching their table with wide eyes.

Miss's head rose and she eyed the goodies on the table. Hugh didn't know if gryphons ate sweets, but he figured a little sugary treat wouldn't hurt her. He picked out a fruit pastry and held it for her. She sniffed at it curiously before her little tongue licked out and took a swipe of the fruit spread on the surface.

Her eyes lit with pleasure a moment before she practically pounced on the rest of the pastry, taking it between her paws as she sat curled on Hugh's lap. Hugh was very aware of the lady sipping her tea and watching them with a deliberate, measuring gaze. He was also careful to monitor the level of magic in the air around her, but so far she hadn't made another aggressive move. She seemed more into watching him than making another move toward Miss. Which was fine with Hugh. He wanted to know more about her.

Not for any personal reason, he assured himself. True, she was gorgeous in a foreign sort of way and there was a sparking intelligence behind her dreamy gaze. There was no doubt she was a beauty of the first water. Not that it mattered to Hugh. If she posed a threat to Miss, he'd take her down just like he'd

Keeper of the Flame

take down anyone or anything that threatened the youngster.

"Mr. Hobson tells me you claim never to have dealt with a gryphon before. Yet you are very good with her." The woman's soft voice sent a shiver down his spine, shocking him. Since when did nothing more than a sexy female voice have the power to make his cock twitch with interest?

"Is that merely an observation or a question?" He sat back in his chair, keeping careful hold on Miss even as he moved instinctively away.

"Mr. Hobson says you are from Draconia." She changed her tactics as she took a dainty bite out of a pastry. "What brings you to Helios?"

"With due respect, milady, that is my business."

Her eyes narrowed but she held whatever her first instinctual words would have been. For a moment she focused on the food before meeting his gaze once more. A challenging light was in her eyes.

"What is the source of your magic?"

A direct question. Hugh had to admire her nerve.

"I was born this way," he countered, stroking Miss's flank with a subtle, deliberate slowness. He noticed her gaze following his hand and liked the way her mouth opened. He could do things to that mouth. Oh, yeah. Very naughty—very pleasurable—things.

"How did you absorb my magical probe?" Her head tilted to the side and he liked the way her gaze measured him. Something odd was happening here. He'd been set to dislike this woman but instead was finding himself strangely attracted to her.

Why? He'd been around courtiers all his life. Many graceful women had visited his bed. Why did he find himself so attracted to this one? Especially when she was so determined to find fault with him and could possibly pose a danger to Miss?

"It is one of my talents." He smiled, unwilling to tell her more.

43

Most dragons were able to absorb or deflect some magic. Hugh had a little extra dose of that kind of skill. Of all his brothers, he was the most skilled at absorbing magical energy and redirecting it. If he'd wanted to, he could have done that to her. He could've turned her magic back on her. But he didn't know who she really was or what she wanted with the baby gryphon. He wouldn't hurt her—or betray the level of his magical skill—unless it became necessary.

"Did you come here looking for a gryphon for some reason?" The suspicion in her voice didn't change its effect on his libido. The more he talked to her, the more he wanted to hear that sexy voice screaming his name as he drove her to ecstasy.

"No, milady." He had to chuckle as he stroked Miss's fur. "She found me. It was the magic, wasn't it, little Miss?" He included the child in the conversation, unwilling to discuss her as if she wasn't there.

"Hoo iss magic," she confirmed with a little nod.

"Who?" The lady repeated the sound, clearly puzzled.

Hugh wanted to kiss away the tiny frown between her eyebrows. Damn. Why in the world was he attracted to *her*? Antagonistic, suspicious and possibly a danger to the baby. She wasn't the sort he should be attracted to. Not now. Not when Miss's very existence could be at stake.

"My name is Hugh," he explained. He didn't have to go into detail about how the child couldn't quite grasp the nuance of how to pronounce his name. A small lift of the lady's full, kissable lips made it clear she was amused by his words.

"So you followed his magic? Is that why you went with this man, little one?" The lady spoke to the gryphlet in calm tones but Hugh sensed no magical attempt to influence.

"Wass cold. Hoo warm. And magic," Miss clarified, as if that was all the reason she needed to follow a complete stranger through the back alleys of the city. "Hoo nice. Ssafe," she added after a moment's pause. She licked her paws, having devoured the pastry in little bites, before lowering her head and resting more fully in Hugh's lap.

The lady studied him. A lesser man would have been intimidated, but Hugh was a dragon prince. One of the biggest, baddest, most dangerous and magical men in any land. It would take more than a hard look from a pretty bit of fluff to intimidate him.

Especially when almost all he could think about was how she would look naked and stretched out on his bed, tied hand and foot, awaiting his pleasure. Would she moan or cry out when he trailed his tongue down her stomach? Would she buck or shiver when he lapped at her sweet cream?

"You are a puzzle, sir," she said at length, drawing his attention from the dangerous paths his imagination had taken. "A man magical enough to attract the attention of a young gryphon, and not a citizen of this land. You do not travel as a mage, so I must believe you are here under false pretenses. Yet the child trusts you and I have yet to meet a gryphon who cannot see to the heart of another. They do not trust just anyone. Her opinion of your character counts a great deal and must be considered."

"I mean no one of this land any harm," Hugh unbent enough to explain.

"But you do mean harm to people of other lands?" One slim eyebrow rose as she picked apart his wording. Hugh had to chuckle.

"Only the people who would threaten Draconia."

She sat back in her chair, a slight smile gracing her lovely face. "Now we come to it. You are a soldier of Draconia. It is no use denying it. You carry yourself like a warrior."

"A warrior I am. I make no effort to hide it." He had given up trying to hide his stature when he'd taken Miss to the inn. He hadn't been very good at subterfuge anyway. Nico would be disappointed, but he'd also be the first to acknowledge that being a spy just wasn't in Hugh's nature.

"No, someone of your size and stature would have trouble pretending to be anything else. Unless maybe you wanted to pose as a blacksmith. You have the muscles for it." Hugh noted with interest the way her gaze roved over his body.

He had little doubt she liked what she saw. Most females liked his shape and appreciated a well-built man. He took that as his due. But the flare of something more volcanic in her gaze heated his blood.

Was he imagining that little frisson of heat that went from her to him and back again? It almost felt like a caress...the way her energy reached out to him.

Her magic.

Damn. She was probing him magically and he hadn't done anything to stop it. Well, that would end. Now.

As before, Hugh absorbed her magic, not allowing the energy to return to her with whatever information she had sought. He didn't slap her down, merely allowed her energy to seep into him where it would not return. Her eyes widened and he grinned. She knew she'd been caught, so she backed down for now. He got the distinct impression she was only forfeiting this minor battle, not the war.

"Not fair, lady. I have made no effort to use my magic on you, yet you persist on trying your luck with me and those I protect." He wagged a teasing finger in her direction.

She shrugged and sipped her tea. "You can't blame a girl for trying. You pose a unique puzzle to me, sir. One I would solve before I leave a child such as this in your care."

"And what right do you have to decide her fate?" Hugh really wanted to know. It was clear this woman held some kind of authority other than her high birth. The fact that she'd come here to investigate Miss's circumstances and the way the Hobsons deferred to her said as much.

"I work for the government. Specifically, it is part of my duty to right wrongs where the magical creatures of this land are concerned." She looked with compassion on Miss, who was dozing on Hugh's lap. "We have heard rumors of this little one for more than a week now. We've been searching high and low for her. Finally, today, Mr. Hobson was able to send word she was here and safe. I was greatly relieved."

"Then you are one of the caretakers of the gryphons in this land."

She looked uneasy, but nodded. "Yes, that's one of my responsibilities as Keeper of the Flame. I oversee those whose calling it is to help our feathered friends."

"And find those they reject," he said softly, saddened by Miss's situation. "You've come to take her away?"

"No! Sstay wif Hoo!" Miss hadn't been sleeping after all. Hugh grimaced at the fear and tension in her furry body. She was trembling again as her paws dug into his thigh. Her claws wouldn't damage him too much, given his own magical nature, but it did sting a bit.

"It's okay, little one. I won't let anyone take you anywhere against your will." He was quick to reassure her, stroking her neck and drawing her close against his chest. Even her wings bristled, the feathers sticking up at a low angle as he tried to soothe her.

The lady watched them closely, a small glint of kindness in her expression. It gave Hugh hope that Miss's fate would be good, not bad. Of course, he would take the child away before he'd let anything bad happen to her.

"There are others like you, little one. Not many. Just a few. They serve the Doge directly and live in the palace. You could live there, with them."

"Want Hoo." Her front paw kneaded his forearm.

"And what does Hugh want?" The lady's attention focused on him once more.

"I want her safe, no matter what. If it means taking her with me on my travels, then so be it."

"You would adopt her?" The lady seemed truly shocked by the idea.

"If that's what it takes, yes." Hugh was firm in his decision though it had only just crystallized in his mind.

Sure, he'd decided almost from the first to take her in and bring her to Draconia, if that's what had to be done. But adoption? How could a dragon shifter adopt a gryphlet? Then again, who better? At least he could teach her to fly and there was none better to guard her in the sky or on land.

"She will have special needs as she grows," the lady sputtered.

"I know all about it. Remember, I hail from Draconia. Baby dragons are common enough in Castleton and around the other Lairs. I know what mischief little things that can fly can get into." He smiled to soften his words, petting Miss indulgently.

"I have never seen a dragon—fully grown or otherwise. Aren't they quite different from gryphons?" She seemed embarrassed by her lack of knowledge.

Hugh could have taught her a thing or two about dragons. Heaven knew his body wanted to show her *everything* it could do to hers in bed...or on this table...or anywhere he could get her naked beneath him. Maybe on top of him. He wasn't choosey. He'd take her standing up if he thought she'd go for it.

"The flight characteristics are almost identical," he said, trying to get his mind back on business. "Large, long body mass with central wings. The only real difference is the feathers." Hugh ran his hand along Miss's folded wings. "Dragons have scales. Gryphons have feathers and fur. And Miss is not the first gryphon I've met. There are some nesting above Castleton now. They are frequent visitors to the city, curious as any tourist in a new place. Much of Castleton was built with dragons in mind—wide streets and oversized doors so they can join their knights in an evening's entertainment. The gryphons have found this to their advantage as well."

Hugh spoke no less than the truth any visitor to the growing city would note. The new gryphons were celebrities and flew often with the dragons who called the land home.

Keeper of the Flame

"You seem to know much of dragons. Are you a knight?"

Hugh laughed out loud at her suspicion. "No, milady. If I were, there would be a great hulking dragon lurking outside somewhere and I doubt any such thing could happen with your feathered friends all around. Someone would have noticed."

"Knights do not travel without their dragons?" She seemed truly interested.

"Once the bond between dragon and knight is formed, it cannot be broken except by death. They are closer than friends. They are family. They do not separate for long periods of time for any reason. It would be too great a handicap to both dragon and knight."

"I didn't know that." She seemed both intrigued and surprised. "There are many rumors about Draconia but little actual proof."

"Rumors go both ways, milady. To be honest, I wasn't certain of my welcome in Alagarithia. Until this little one ambushed me, my intention was to keep a low profile about my origins." That much was true at least. He wasn't going to divulge his real identity, but perhaps he could learn a few things from this highborn lady that would help his brothers.

"Helios has long been a friend of Draconia politically." Her tone was firm as if she truly believed what she was saying. That was good, as far as it went. If she'd shown the slightest hesitation, that would have been worth hearing.

"Then what has you worried about my origins? I assure you, dragons are honorable creatures. As are the folk they choose to associate with. They would not suffer evil magic to inhabit the land they have sworn to protect. This I know for fact."

"Strong words." She sipped her tea. "And you sound as if you truly believe them. Perhaps you should come back with me to the palace. There are people there who would like to learn more about your land, if you're willing to speak of it, and you could meet the others like your friend here and see that they

49

are not ill-treated."

Hugh was surprised by the offer. Surprised...and suspicious. This was way too easy. Did this woman—highborn or not—have the authority to invite guests to the palace? Or was this some sort of trap to get him and Miss out of the comfortable inn and into a place where she could spring some sort of ambush? Miss was just a baby. Though she had formidable claws, she couldn't fly yet and didn't know how to defend herself. She was small. A big enough man could subdue her. She wouldn't stand a chance.

Hugh could defend her, of course, but not if he were badly outnumbered. Dragon he may be, but if the lady had a platoon of guards out there ready to fight, he'd have a hard time getting Miss and himself free. If it were he alone, he would have jumped at the chance to get into the palace. But Miss was depending on him.

At that moment, as Hugh debated internally, he noticed the door bang open and a harried-looking woman run over to Hobson. A quick conversation ensued before the woman ran back out, shutting the door behind her. Hobson practically ran himself, approaching their table at a brisk trot.

"Milady, there are Eyes on the street. Mathilde from across the way saw a man in her alley and he had the tattoos." Hobson's tone was low and urgent. He sounded truly frightened.

"Did she see what kind?"

"Snake Eyes, milady," Hob answered in the gravest tone. "Where are your guards?"

"I did not bring them." She paled in shock.

"Snake Eyes? What does that mean?" Hugh asked. Something was going on. Something dangerous if he was any judge.

"Assassin. Stars!" She seemed near ready to faint. "I am dead."

Chapter Three

"Not yet," Hugh said calmly, lowering Miss to the ground as he stood, ready for action. "Are you certain they're coming for her?" Hugh asked Hobson as the lady sat frozen.

"Of course. There have been too many mishaps of late. We all assumed someone was trying to kill her, but to hire Eyes!" Hobson seemed as shocked as the lady was, but at least he was able to move. He grabbed Hugh's sleeve. "We must save her. What can we do?"

Hugh looked around the common room, noting the defensive spots again, as he had when he'd chosen to stay at this inn. It was better than most, but still a civilian building. It hadn't been built with true defense in mind.

"Close and bar the shutters for a start." There were a few windows that had been opened to let in light now that the freezing rain had stopped. "Tom," Hugh called to the boy. "Go to my room. Under the mattress, you will find a sword. Bring it here with all haste. And bring the pack at the foot of the bed as well." The boy ran off to do his bidding.

"Is there a door to the roof?" Hugh knew there was, but he wanted Hobson to feel as if he was helping and didn't want him to know Hugh had been prowling all over the building. Just in case he wanted to come back here someday.

Hobson nodded vigorously. "This way." He bustled toward the hall that led to the guest rooms. Hobson escorted the lady as if she were made of glass and Hugh made sure Miss kept up, playing rear guard to their little parade.

He sent his senses out to the limit of his abilities. The building was quiet for now, no intruders. Or at least, none that he could sense. Perhaps the woman across the street had given them the head start they'd need.

Tom met them in the hall and handed the heavy sword and pack to Hugh. He took them as he walked and Tom joined the little group, helping Miss up the stairs that would lead eventually to the roof.

The inn was a two-story structure. The innkeeper and his wife kept their family rooms upstairs. They passed through a modest living room to a locked closet that held another set of narrow stairs that led to the roof. This time, Hugh went first. Hobson handed over the key to the door at the top of the stairs without comment.

Hugh ascended soundlessly and paused by the door to listen before opening it. The rest of the group had stayed at the foot of the staircase, just in case. Pausing only a moment, Hugh opened the rusty lock and peered out over the roof. The inn was taller by several feet than the buildings around it. Its height was one of its main advantages as far as Hugh was concerned and a large part of why he had picked this particular place to stay.

Night had fallen, the days being shorter at this time of year. The darkness would work to their advantage. If worse came to absolute worst, Hugh could always shift shape and fly them out. He could carry the woman and Miss with no problem. He'd have to get them to agree, of course, but faced with certain death versus a fire-breathing dragon protector, he thought both females would choose wisely.

Hugh crept out onto the flat roof and looked over the edge. He checked all four sides, though two bordered on shorter structures on either side of the inn. One had a steeply pitched roof that would not be easy for an assassin to climb. The other was clear for the moment. He checked the back of the inn, where the open courtyard led to the stables. It was clear. That left only the front.

Sure enough, Hugh sensed danger before he spotted the cleverly hidden man in the shadows of the alley between two buildings across the street. The man looked up once but did not appear to have seen Hugh. His attention was mostly focused on the doorway and the barred windows of the inn two stories below.

If not for his better-than-human night vision, Hugh would likely not have seen the man, so well camouflaged was he. Hugh spun when he sensed someone behind him, only to find Miss padding up to him. He motioned for her to stop where she was as he crept back from the edge of the roof so they would not be seen by the watcher below.

Hobson had reached the roof as Hugh returned to the entrance with Miss at his side.

"She would not stay, Hugh. I'm sorry," the innkeeper said in a whisper.

Hugh shrugged. "It's all right. There is a man watching your front door from the alleyway across the street."

"Only one?"

Hugh nodded. "If he is an assassin, one is all it takes. It will be hard to get past him. The roof on the left is too pitched and the right is too exposed. Going out the back would take us to the stables, but they back onto the mountain. I don't suppose there's any way up the cliff from there?"

"No." Hob shook his head, muttering. "The only way out is by the street and he would have a perfect view. She is doomed. Dear Mother of All, why did she come here alone?"

Hobson was wringing his hands when Hugh stopped him. "She is that important to you?"

"To us all," the man said at once. "She must survive. Without her, the land is lost."

Hugh was taken aback by Hob's words. He hadn't thought the man was of a dramatic bent, but what could one highborn lady mean to Helios as a whole? She wasn't the ruler here. Her job was no doubt important, but the gryphons would find another champion should she fall. Still, Hobson's urgency cut through Hugh's conjecture.

Add to that the fact that the beauty had done nothing wrong as far as Hugh could tell. She seemed the innocent target of these Eyes—whatever they were. Based on Hobson's reaction and words, Hugh didn't think she was evil. Merely troublesome in that she wanted to take Miss away.

He could deal with that. What he couldn't deal with was if his inaction caused the lady's death. He was well and truly stuck. He could easily fly her out of danger, but that would expose his true nature. He didn't see a way around that at this point. With a sigh of resignation, he spoke.

"There is a way, but I cannot tell you what it is. I will tell the lady, and she will decide whether to take it or not."

Hope and fear entered Hobson's gaze. "Magic?"

"Something like that," Hugh answered. Let the man think he was a mage. The truth was even more surprising, and twice as effective.

The lady stepped out of the shadows near the door. It seemed nobody stayed where he left them tonight.

"Thank you, Mr. Hobson, for your service." Her tone was warm, but her words were a clear dismissal. Hobson turned to the door and seemed to hesitate.

"I will leave Tom at the foot of the stair should you decide to come back inside. Otherwise, I wish you all the blessings of the Lady on your journey. We will do our best to keep the Eyes off your path."

"Thank you." She passed a few coins to him and in the dark night. Hugh saw the gleam of gold. She'd paid the man well for his work this night.

Hugh stopped the man when he would have left, slipping a jeweled dagger bearing his mark and its silver-laced sheath into his hand. "Give this to Tom. He has been a good friend to me and the gryphlet. I will not forget him. Or you, Hob. You have my thanks."

He'd also have the purse of silver Hugh had left on the mantle in his room. Hugh was glad to give it to the kind innkeeper. Hobson had been a helpful contact and perhaps would be again.

When the door shut behind Hob, Hugh turned to the two females and sighed again. This wasn't how he wanted things to go, but he saw little alternative.

"So you *are* a mage?" The lady preempted his planned explanation.

"No, milady. I am a shapeshifter. One of very few in my land." He let that sink in.

"What kind of creature shares your soul?" His interest was piqued by her wording, but he didn't have time to delve into her beliefs just now.

"I am a dragon."

"Hoo?" Miss was clearly confused.

Hugh crouched down to meet her eyes. "I can become a dragon, sweetheart. I can fly, like you will be able to, once you are bigger. I can teach you to fly, if you like."

She seemed to like that, nodding so hard her whole body shook.

"Want fly!" She moved closer to him and butted his chest with her chin, ruffling her wings in excitement.

"All right, little one." He caressed her ears and met her gaze. "How about I take you flying tonight? You can ride on my back and I will show you what it feels like. Would you like that?"

She bounced on her forepaws, clearly excited by the idea.

"Now, milady, it's up to you." Hugh looked up at her from his crouched position.

She stood in front of him, closer to the back of the building. The gryphlet was at his side and he was turned so that his right side faced the street. A flicker of movement caught his eye and he knew in that split second that all choice had been lost.

The assassin had come.

Somehow the man had climbed to the roof without Hugh

having heard a thing. Hugh turned, as if in slow motion, already knowing what he would see.

The man from the alleyway, a weapon already in his hand. His gaze was fastened on the lady, but Hugh knew he would not hesitate to kill him and the gryphlet as well, if either stood in the assassin's way.

Standing to his full height, Hugh shifted shape as he moved, thankful for the drills that he and his brothers had practiced over and over again. He could take his other form with hardly any delay. Fractions of a second and a magical black fog surrounded him. Only scant fractions more and he was reborn as the black dragon that was his other half.

The look on the assassin's face would have been comical had the circumstances not been so dire. Hugh reared up, fanning his wings, keeping the baby gryphon and the woman behind his armored hide. It was up to the assassin now. If he backed down, Hugh would leave him be. If he advanced, he was toast.

Although, looking around, Hugh decided it would be inadvisable for him to use his flame up here. For one thing, it would alert every gryphon on the cliff to his presence. For another, it could very well start a raging inferno that might burn down half the city. No, this was a job that called for finesse.

Hugh showed his claws to the assassin. They gleamed ebony in the dark night. Each one a foot long, razor-sharp instrument of pain and death.

"Leave now and I'll let you live." The lady's voice rang out from beneath Hugh's right wing. Would the woman never stay where he left her?

The assassin shook his head. "You know it does not work that way." His voice was heavily accented in a way Hugh had never heard.

"So be it." Finally showing some sense, she ducked behind Hugh's wing once again, allowing him to shield her as best he could.

To his credit, the assassin held his position even as Hugh advanced. Closer now, Hugh saw the tattoos on the man's hands. Eyes. Slitted snake eyes. He'd never seen anything like it before. He had the impression the marks were indications of both his profession and level of skill. Too bad Hugh didn't know how to read the code. He'd make a point of learning more about it later, after he took care of this threat and got the lady to safety.

The assassin made a move. A feint to the right though his weapon spun to the left. It was a dart of some kind. Poison, most likely. Hugh wasn't concerned for his own safety. Unless the little darts had diamond-bladed tips, they would not penetrate dragon scale.

First one and then two and then a flurry of the little darts flew at him, but they bounced off his hide like so many gnats. The assassin hadn't counted on that. Hugh could read the anger on his face. Excellent. Anger made a warrior lose focus. An angry warrior was one who made mistakes.

Sure enough, the assassin's rage rose until he came at Hugh directly, a dully gleaming sword lashing through the dark sky toward Hugh's snout. It would bounce off, of course, though if he got lucky and hit his eye he might do some damage.

Hugh wouldn't allow the man to get lucky. He was about to step forward and use his claws on the assassin when a dagger sprouted out of the man's chest.

Shock replaced the anger on his face as his sword clattered to the rooftop and his hands clutched at the knife in his chest. It had struck his heart, Hugh realized when the man pulled it out and blood gushed. He fell to the floor. Dead.

Hugh looked around for the source of the dagger. He was a little amazed to see the lady standing at his side, a grim expression on her face as she watched the assassin. A matching dagger was in her hand. Hugh had no doubt she'd been the source of the amazingly accurate shot. At night. In the dark.

With only human eyesight to aid her. Or so Hugh thought.

Maybe she'd used magic to magnify her skill or make the dagger fly true. Hugh had never seen such a thing, but he'd heard stories about mages that could do just that. The question remained—was this woman capable of that kind of magic?

Or was it possible she was more than human? He didn't think so. Hugh felt certain he would have noticed if she'd had some other influence in her background. Maybe he was wrong. He'd been wrong before and probably would be again.

"Nice throw." He spoke directly into her mind, wondering if she would prove to be one of the rare females who could hear his thoughts when directed at her.

She jumped a bit and looked at him. "Was that...? Did you...?" She looked uncertain of her own senses.

"Did I talk in your mind? Yes." He felt the connection now, a brief meeting of her mind to his. *"Unlike your feathered friends, dragon vocal chords are not suited to verbal speech. We speak in this manner with our knights and the few others who can hear us. I'm glad you can. It will make our time together easier."*

He was impressed. She'd just killed a man and she barely shook. Most women he knew would not have handled this kind of thing with as much aplomb. Well, maybe his new sister-in-laws, and a few of the heartier Lair wives, but not the vast majority of court ladies he'd known. This one was a cut above. She had surprised him and that wasn't easy to do.

"I think we'd better go." Her tone was still calm. "There could be more of them. Eyes are never predictable."

Hugh moved away from the poisoned darts, sweeping them into a small pile with his tail. If anyone came up here before it rained and washed away the poison, at least the darts would all be in one place.

Once clear of them, he crouched, extending one forearm. *"Step on my elbow, then up the shoulder. The best place for you to sit is with your legs hooked in front of my wings."*

"Like a gryphon," she commented absently. "Speaking of

which..." She turned to Miss, helping her up.

"Hoo?" The little mewl was plaintive and questioning. Miss needed reassurance.

"I'm here, little one. Can you hear me?"

"Hoo!" Little paws bounced on his crest as the kitten settled into place. The lady took a seat behind her with more skill than Hugh had expected. She'd ridden before. No doubt on one of her gryphon charges. Interesting.

"Yes, sweetheart. I want you to hold on tight and let the lady help you stay in place. When I jump into the air, it may be bumpy at first. All right?"

"Yess, Hoo." Her little voice sounded so eager Hugh would have smiled if he could.

"Are you ready, milady?" He liked the feel of her riding him. It made him think of having her do it while in his man form and he couldn't help the little growl that came out of his throat accompanied by a trickle of smoke.

He felt her settle in and reach forward to grab one of the spikes on his neck. Miss was tucked between her arms and her body, as safe as they could get for now.

"Ready," she confirmed with a surety in her voice that made him curious about her flying experience.

One thing he thought he knew for certain...she'd never ridden a dragon before. She seemed to know so little about his land and its inhabitants—if she weren't misleading him for some reason. He thought with some amount of confidence that he was the first dragon she had ever seen.

Small by Draconian standards, the black dragons of the royal family were the rarest of all dragons. They alone could take human form at will. They were faster than most dragons and usually more agile because of their smaller size.

They were also the only dragons who were completely black. All other dragons in Draconia were colorful. Blue, bronze, silver, gold, red, green... Every color of the rainbow, in fact, though some were more common than others. There was even a young ice dragon living at the castle whose scales shimmered like frozen mirrored glass.

Tonight, though, it was good to be black. With no moon to gleam against his hide, he would remain hidden against the dark sky, even to the keen-eyed gryphons. He'd noticed that few of the birds flew at night. While there were a few darker-coated gryphons, most were lighter colors that weren't good for camouflage at night.

The stealthier gryphons were dark brown mostly and they worked the skies at night from what Hugh had observed. Still, they usually didn't come back to their cliffside dwellings until after dawn. At this time of night, nothing flying should be around to spot the strange black dragon flitting through their territory.

Hugh launched himself into the sky as smoothly as possible, mindful of the precious burdens on his back. He didn't want to drop either Miss or the lady. He winged out away from the cliffs and climbed to an altitude where he'd be unlikely to come across anything else in the air. From below, he'd be just another dark shadow against the inky black sky.

"All right back there?"

"We're good," the lady shouted to be heard over the rushing wind.

"*Where do you want to go?*" He probably should've discussed this on the ground, but they'd been in too much of a hurry to get away from a possible second attacker.

"The palace," she replied instantly. At least she knew where she wanted to go. The palace wouldn't have been Hugh's first choice, but she did work for the government and there would be guards there who might be able to help her.

Hugh veered off toward the largest structure in the surrounding area. It was lit by fires on the battlements and easy to see even at this distance. He'd come in cautiously, from high above.

While he could see the fires, there were no gryphons at the

posts where a gryphon guard usually stood watch twenty-four hours a day. He felt the tension in his passenger as her legs tightened around his shoulders. She knew the palace better than he did. As they circled far above, even she could see the missing sentries.

"Something's wrong," she shouted to be heard over the wind. "The guards should be manning the battlements even in this weather. And the gryphons aren't at their posts."

"I doubt the palace is safe for you, then. Is there somewhere else we can go?"

"Go east. My cousin lives on the sixth hill. She will help."

Hugh veered eastward, counting the hills in the distance and heading for the sixth in line from the coast. The lady's grip on his shoulders didn't lessen. She was filled with tension and it communicated itself to him in the stiff lines of her body.

She was a good rider, though. He had no doubt she'd been aloft many times before. No doubt the gryphons took her flying whenever she wished in return for her advocacy on their behalf. He wasn't sure of her exact position where the creatures were concerned, but the more he was around her, the more he began to form a good opinion of her. Good, but still wary.

He'd already made up his mind that he wouldn't leave Miss in the lady's care unless he knew for certain where and how Miss would be cared for. Hugh would go with the lady wherever she went until that need was satisfied. Either that, or they would part company and he would take Miss with him back to Draconia, cutting his mission here short. Roland and Nico could send somebody else. The child was more important to Hugh at this moment.

It took only a few minutes to fly over the dark city and enter the foothills where luxurious estates caressed the hillsides and vineyards rolled down the slopes in graceful lines. The sixth hill contained only one large estate and it was somewhat revolting in its opulence.

"*Your cousin lives there?*" Hugh tried to keep the horror out of his tone. The place was ghastly in its sheer gaudiness.

"Her taste is not mine." The words were muttered, but Hugh heard them and silently agreed with the sentiment. "Approach from the orchard," she went on in a louder voice. "Considering what we saw at the palace, we need to be cautious."

"I'll set down in the dark beyond that fence. I think I can fit between those rows of vines. We'll walk up to the house together."

"You're coming with me?" She sounded surprised.

"*I will not leave you until I'm sure you're as safe as you can be with assassins on your trail.*" Her safety had suddenly become important to him. Certainly, she could take care of herself to some extent. She had killed the assassin, after all. But he wouldn't have wanted her to come up against those poisoned darts on her own.

He also wanted to learn more about those mysterious Eyes. He'd never heard of such creatures before. Oh, Draconia had its share of secret groups—even some assassins—but nobody who used eyes as their symbol as far as he knew. At the very least, Nico would want to know as much about the mysterious assassins as Hugh could discover.

He backwinged gently, executing a perfect covert landing between two rows of grapevines. Once again, he thanked his brothers for the training they'd all done together to perfect their abilities. The weather had changed for the better over the past day. No pelting, freezing rain and more moderate temperatures. Still, it was cold and no leaves graced the spindly vines. In the dark, they looked like massive spider webs staked out between the poles.

The vineyard was well kept, even in its dormant winter state. No dead leaves stirred with the gusts created by his wings, or crunched underfoot as he came to rest on the ground. Hugh crouched low, allowing his passengers to climb down off his back. As soon as they were clear, he shifted back to his human form.

He emerged from the black mist clad in his own worn, black leather armor, his sword strapped to his side. It was a gift of his special kind of magic that allowed him and his brothers to take their clothing into the shift with them. Hugh had a bit more magic than his other brothers. So much so that he could influence the color and texture of what came back with him when he regained his human form.

He didn't know where the clothing went when he became a dragon, but he was able to leave certain items in the misty space between his two forms, secure there until he needed them. That's where his armor had been and that's where the clothes he'd been wearing before he shifted stayed for the moment. Wherever that was. Perhaps one day, if he ever met the wizard Gryffid in person, he could find out. If anyone would know, the last of the mighty wizards would.

But that was a question for another time. Miss looked up at him with wide eyes as he picked up the pack the lady had carried for him. The gryphlet seemed exhilarated by her first flight and Hugh would have loved to spend a few moments talking to her about it. But not now. Not when the lady could still be in grave danger.

"Sweetheart, I want you to stay here, among the vines. Find a place to hide and wait. I will go ahead to see if it's safe for you and the lady." Hugh looked at the woman who stood quietly at his side, scanning their surroundings intently.

"I must go with you. My cousin doesn't know you, nor do her guards. You would be arrested for trespass as soon as they saw you," she argued in a soft voice.

"I didn't plan on being seen," he quipped, but he understood her point. "Do you know this house well? Would you be able to tell from afar if something was wrong here, as you did at the palace?"

She nodded once. "I visit here often."

"All right, then. Come with me, but stay in my shadow as

best you can and if I give you direction, take it without question. Your life could depend on it."

"I understand." She nodded once more as they moved out.

He glanced back at Miss. "Stay hidden, little one. We'll be back shortly and I expect to find you here, safe and sound. Understand?"

The gryphlet nodded gravely and sank down into a crouch, scooting backward until she was partially hidden between the thick base of one of the vines and a fencepost. That would do for now. Her feathers and coloring were mottled enough that they acted like natural camouflage in the dark night.

"Good girl. See you in a little while." He patted her head before setting off with the lady walking quietly a step or two behind him.

She wasn't the stealthiest person he'd ever worked with, but she was better than he'd expected. She stumbled a few times over the uneven ground, reinforcing the fact that she had to rely on plain old human eyesight, which wasn't the greatest in the dark. Hugh tried to help her when he could but he had to keep his hands free in case of attack.

There were beacon lamps lit periodically along the wall of the vast estate. They were more decorative than functional, thankfully for Hugh's purposes. Guards patrolled at regular intervals, though they weren't the crisp military professionals of the palace guard. These men showed a bit of laxness when it came to the rigor with which they went about their duties. Hugh supposed they didn't often see action way out here in the vinelands, even if the family they were protecting was highborn.

Hugh paused in the shadows, watching them. The lady tugged on his sleeve, wordlessly communicating her impatience, but he would not move too hastily.

"Let me just watch them for a moment. Something seems..." he thought in her direction.

A more adamant tug on his sleeve made him turn his attention to her. Wide eyes looked up at him in the darkness as she tugged him downward so she could speak as quietly as possible near his ear.

"You can still talk in my mind?" She seemed fascinated by the idea.

He smiled slightly, relieved. *"Of course. Now that I know you can hear me, I have this ability no matter my form. In time, you might even learn to do the same."* He returned to his study of the house. *"There should be a guard right over there."* He gestured with the subtle movement of one hand. *"I don't see why—"* he broke off, sinking to a crouch in a smooth gesture and taking her with him.

"What's wrong?" she asked in a low, urgent voice.

"Good question." The words, spoken in an unfamiliar voice, made them both whip around to the left.

A black-clad man stood there, in the dark shadows of the vines. How had he approached without Hugh sensing him in some way? The lady shrank back in terror, crowding Hugh. Then he saw it. The snake eye tattooed on the stranger's forehead and the deadly gleam of blackened steel in his hands.

"Eyes." Hugh didn't need to hear the lady's frightened gasp to know what they faced. Another assassin. "Why didn't you just stick her with your blade while you had the advantage?" Hugh stood in the darkened field between the rows of vines to face the man and put some space between himself and the lady. He needed room to maneuver.

"Terms of the contract," the man replied offhandedly. "My employer wanted her to see it coming. There's a bonus for terror. Plus, I find it personally more entertaining to make the target suffer." He looked around at the dark vineyard. "And on her own land too. She'll like that, she will."

"In my land, assassins take pride in their silence." Hugh tucked away the news that the lady's cousin had put out the contract on her life, though he could tell by the way her face drained of all color that it came as a shock to her.

"It must be a very boring place, then." The tattooed man

moved, closing in as Hugh drew a short blade that had been sheathed in the leather strap over his chest.

"I would call it civilized," Hugh replied with a small amount of disdain.

"I see you plan to act the hero." The assassin sounded almost bored, but his eyes—the real ones, not the tattoos—missed nothing, actively watching Hugh's slightest move. "I'm only being paid for her, but I suppose watching you die first will garner me that bonus."

Without warning, the man engaged, closing with Hugh in a lightning fast move. Had Hugh been any less alert, he would've been dead within seconds. But he was a dragon and had supernatural reflexes even while in his human form. He could see better in the dark than a regular person and had the advantage of dragon magic that allowed him to harden his skin against the sharp metal blade.

While not exactly as strong as his dragon hide, Hugh's unique magic allowed him to take blows that would leave normal people slashed to ribbons. The assassin moved like lightning, but few of his strikes landed and those few that did didn't draw blood.

Eventually the man changed tactics, maneuvering Hugh around the darkened vineyard, almost herding him. Hugh tried to keep himself between the assassin and the lady at all times, but he hadn't counted on there being more than one attacker.

A gasp from behind made Hugh spin. The lady was in the grip of a second assassin, this one with a matching snake's eye tattooed on his forehead, directly between his real eyes. The blackened blade gleamed to Hugh's sight as the assassin pressed it against her throat.

"That's right, boyo," said the first man, closing on Hugh's unprotected back. Hugh could take him, but his partner would kill the lady without a second thought before Hugh could get to her. "Now, do we get one eye from this or two? Your choice."

"You get an eye for each person you kill?" Hugh was

sickened by the macabre practice.

The man nodded with seeming pride. "Twenty-seven I have today. My master there has double that number." From the corner of his eye, Hugh saw something move in the darkness to the left. Something that blended with the night in gray and black stripes. "My master can make it quick for her or make her suffer. Which would you prefer?"

"Neither, actually," Hugh said conversationally to the man. *"We need your help, sweetheart."* He directed his thoughts toward the baby gryphon. *"Remember how I told you about your claws? Unsheathe them and sink them into the man holding the lady. I will take care of the rest."*

A split second later, as if he'd timed it perfectly, though luck had more to do with it than planning, the gryphlet erupted from beneath the vines as Hugh sprang into action. Miss went for the man holding his knife at the lady's throat, claws bared, sharp teeth flashing in the night as she hit the man from the side, raking his arm. She jumped upward, using her wings to bat him with air and feathers, claws and teeth, blinding him and making him let go.

But not before the sharp blade cut into the lady's neck.

Hugh saw it in the split second as he shifted shape and slashed out with his much bigger claws, killing both assassins at the same time—one with his right hand, one with his left.

The lady was bleeding, but still standing when he dropped the lifeless men to the ground and beckoned to her.

"Get on my back quick as you can. We dare not tarry. There may be more of them."

The lady climbed aboard and Miss bounded up right behind her. Hugh lurched into the air with less grace and even more speed than before, heading out, over the hills, toward the sand flats beyond. He needed a place to take them where they'd see an enemy coming. Someplace safer than the city or its environs. Someplace close.

The sandy wasteland beyond the foothills was the only

place he could fly to fast that provided some of those tactical advantages. And it had to be quick. The lady was bleeding. He had to see how bad it was.

"How are you holding up back there?"

"All right," she said in a weak voice. Was the weakness from shock or blood loss? Hugh needed to land in order to find out.

He looked around for a likely spot and found something usable not far. He landed more rapidly than before, with less finesse, but more speed, absorbing the shock of meeting the ground with his elbows and knees. The lady tumbled from his back, followed by the gryphlet who glided downward using her fluffy, baby wings. She would be fledging before long, Hugh thought absently as he shifted form and knelt at the lady's side.

She was pale, blood flowing down the front of her dress. Hugh cursed and examined the wound, glad to see it was not as deep as he'd feared. He could heal this and in time, she would regain her strength.

All dragons had magic. Most had healing abilities. Hugh had trained his healing powers so that he could help humans and dragons alike should there be need. He blessed his teachers now for their preparation as he laid his hands over the lady's neck, summoning his power.

A fog surrounded them as the Dragon's Breath came at his call, enveloping her and healing her wound. Miss was sitting at her side and batted at the magical fog in curiosity but didn't back away. She seemed to bask in the magic that Hugh called and he was glad for it. He hadn't had a chance to see if any of the blood on the kitten's fur was her own. He thought not, but he didn't want to take any chances.

If she was injured, the Dragon's Breath would work to heal her as well. If not, it would still be good for her to bask in the magic he'd been feeding her in much smaller doses since they first met. As a growing creature of magic, she should have gotten such influxes of magical energy from her parents. Hugh had been acting as a surrogate of sorts until finally the baby gryphon's energy level was just about where it should have been for her age.

At length he drew back, recalling his healing power. The lady's eyes blinked open and she stared up at him with confusion.

"Are you feeling better, milady?" Hugh asked with a small grin, hoping to calm her and ease the shock of the startling news she had learned in the vineyard.

"A little dizzy, but better. What was that?"

"The Dragon's Breath. It is a healing mist most dragons can call. Some stronger than others." He tried to shrug off his very potent ability.

He was very close to her. So close, he had only to lean in a little farther in order to touch his lips to hers.

Following the impulse he'd had since almost the first moment he'd seen her, Hugh did just that.

Chapter Four

Warm, firm lips covered hers and she was powerless to resist. This man—this dragon—had quite literally swept her off her feet. Twice.

And he'd saved her life just as many times. In less time than it took to sit through a state dinner, he'd dispatched assassins with almost careless ease. And now he was kissing her. As if his life depended on it.

She would deal with her cousin's betrayal later. Though it shocked her to have confirmation of her worst fear, she could not think of anything beyond Hugh's strong arms that made her feel truly safe for the first time in a long time.

One thing was certain, he was definitely the best kisser she had ever known. Much better than the man she'd briefly considered making her life partner. Even better than the rebound fling with a flattering bard that had come after.

She'd never kissed a warrior before. Or a man so imbued with magic that he could transform himself into a dragon and back with seeming impunity.

What manner of man was he, really?

And why did he make her insides melt with the slightest touch? The slightest look?

Oh, yes, he felt so good against her as he deepened the kiss.

But this was all wrong. He was an outlander. A mage of some kind. Something her land had never seen before. He could be dangerous.

But he felt so good...

When the kiss ended it was because he drew back, not

Keeper of the Flame

through any willpower of her own. In fact, she wanted him to stay, for the kiss to go on and go farther. She wanted to be naked beneath him and learn what he felt like in true passion.

Instead, he drew back, separating their mouths and their disappointingly fully clothed bodies.

He sat on the ground at her side, holding her gaze for a moment that felt significant, silence stretching between them before he turned his attention to the baby gryphon.

Blessed Lady. How could she have forgotten the baby?

"Are you all right, sweetheart?" He held one hand out to the gryphlet. She moved a step forward to snuggle her cheek in his palm and lick his wrist.

"Good, Hoo." She sat on her haunches, her wings tucked behind her. "Yummy magic misst."

Hugh smiled, petting the kitten. "You liked that?"

"Felt good," she agreed, nodding her little furry head.

"I'm glad." Hugh looked around as if he really could see in the utter blackness that surrounded them. "I'm going to make things more comfortable for you both," he said, rising to his feet. "I'll be within hearing distance if you need me, but you should be safe enough here."

"Where are we?" She struggled to sit up, but her head was swimming.

"Out beyond the hills, on the sand flats," Hugh answered shortly. "Behind a boulder and small rise that should hide a fire, if I can find enough wood or something else to burn." He looked around, peering into the dark night. "Rest easy. I'll be back shortly."

She didn't like him leaving her alone in the inky darkness, but she had the gryphlet nearby and she discovered that she trusted him. He'd already proven himself her protector twice over this night. Surely he wouldn't leave her out here to die alone. He wasn't that cruel. If he'd planned to let her die, he would've just let the Eyes take care of it.

No, Hugh would be back.

She must've dozed, for the next thing she knew, a small fire leapt at her side, throwing off enough light that she could see a bit of her surroundings. Hugh was there, kneeling by the fire. If she believed the evidence of her eyes, he'd started the flame with nothing more than a touch of his hand.

She supposed it was possible. His magic was potent and he was half dragon, after all. In his other form he was probably able to breathe fire. If anyone could call flame, it would be him. The thought intrigued her.

"Handy," she commented, nodding toward the cheery fire.

Hugh's small smile made her tummy clench when he turned the full force of it on her.

The gryphlet stirred, fanning her wings out once before settling them snuggly against her back in neat rows of feathers. Which reminded her...

"I am in your debt, brave Miss." She reached out to the gryphlet, gratified when the baby gryphon walked over and sniffed her hand, then rubbed her cheek along her fingers. "Thank you for saving me."

"Hoo helped," Miss said, settling on her haunches.

That response made the lady smile, even through the pounding in her head. She was weak from blood loss and knew she wasn't thinking entirely clearly, but she knew the gryphlet had done an incredibly brave thing and deserved praise.

"Hugh is as brave as you are, little one." She sent him a smile across the short distance of the fire. "We really need to find you a better name. Do you have a preference?"

The baby gryphon tilted her head. She didn't understand the word.

"Are there any names you especially like? Something you'd like to be called?" she tried again.

"Don't know namess," Miss answered in a sleepy, slightly puzzled voice. "Like Misss."

The lady gave up. "I guess that'll do for now." She stroked the kitten's ears as the baby settled down, resting her head on her front paws, her wings folded along her back.

"Speaking of names," Hugh said as he sat down near enough to touch. "If I'm to keep you safe, I can't keep calling you milady."

"Will you keep me safe, Hugh?" She hadn't meant for that to come out so seriously, but it was the thought that weighed most heavily on her mind at that moment.

Hugh drew closer, reaching out to cup her cheek. His impossibly green eyes flickered in the firelight, seeming to delve into her soul.

"I'll do my best."

She already knew his best was better than at least three master assassins.

"That's good enough for me." She gave him a fleeting smile, even as her head spun. "You can call me Lera."

"Lera," he repeated, making her nickname sound exotic and mysterious. She liked the way it rolled off his tongue.

Hugh moved closer, his big body leaning over her, warming her with his inner heat. His lips touched hers as he breathed her name once more against them and she'd never heard a sweeter sound or felt a more delicious touch.

As he deepened the kiss, he lay her down on the ground and she realized that he'd been busy while she'd dozed. A soft wool blanket was beneath her and as he rolled them both fully onto it, she recognized the size and shape of it as the compact bedroll that had been tied to his pack. The same pack she'd held on to while he flew her off into the night from the inn's roof. The same pack she had a vague memory of Miss dragging with her teeth as she'd clambered onto the dragon's back the second time that night in the vineyard outside her cousin's palatial estate.

If they were to camp, she was glad they hadn't managed to lose the pack. If only for the small cushion of the blanket between her back and the sand. Hugh made a warm cover on top of her. Getting warmer by the second as he kissed the breath out of her.

Her life was so confusing right now. Her cousin had hired the most dangerous assassins in the world to kill her. They would try again. Hugh had promised to protect her, but what if he failed? What if they struck when he wasn't nearby?

She could easily die tomorrow, but if this was to be her last night of life, she knew one thing. She wanted to spend it with him. The dragon who had saved her life not once, but twice. Damn the possible consequences. This wasn't about her position or her land. This was about need. Her need as a woman to be with a man that stirred her senses as no other had before.

She pushed at the cloth and leather covering his shoulders. He was wearing too many clothes. Too much leather that didn't allow her to feel the true contours of his massive body.

"Hugh," she breathed against his lips as he let up slightly.

"What is it, sweet Lera?" He drew back fractionally, as if he couldn't bear to let her go fully. She liked that.

"Take off your clothes," she whispered.

He twitched, and she guessed she had surprised him. Well, good. She was through being taken by surprise for the night. It was time she doled out a surprise or two of her own.

Hugh's head swiveled to the left and he looked into the darkness. Lera realized he was checking on the baby gryphon. Good thing one of them was paying attention. How could she have forgotten the child's presence yet again?

Simple. Hugh crowded out every other thought from her mind. Every duty she owed to her land and people. Everything else but the sheer magnitude of his presence and strength of his body.

She couldn't focus on anything else when her body yearned for his warmth. She was glad he had thought to check, but very little would stop her from, at the very least, sleeping in his arms and taking what comfort she could from his nearness. At best, she wanted to share her body with him and learn his in return. She would leave it up to him, what would happen that night, but she'd do everything in her power to help things along.

"Is she asleep?" she asked hopefully.

Hugh refocused his lovely green eyes on her. She could just see him in the flickering firelight, though he seemed to have keener vision than she did.

"Fast asleep. The Dragon's Breath topped up her magical reserves, but physically it's still been a very long day for one so young. She will no doubt sleep deeply for many hours."

"Good." Later, Lera would have time to praise the misborn gryphlet as she deserved, but for now, all Lera wanted was Hugh. His lips on hers. His warmth heating her. His body joining with hers. She leaned upward and nibbled on his stubbly jaw. "Then what are you waiting for?"

"Are you sure about this?" His tone was breathless, which meant she was doing something right. Her hands roamed over his body, seeking the closures of his tunic and the leather pieces he wore over it.

"I want you," she whispered, enjoying the little growl that rumbled through his chest at her bold words.

He struggled with the lacings on his leather vestment even as she tried to help. Their hands tangled but managed to get the job done, though it took longer than she wanted. He paused when the lacings were undone, slowing his movements and capturing her attention. She read hesitation in his green gaze, along with regret.

"Lera, I know you've had a shock today. Two shocks, in fact. I don't want you to regret what comes next."

"The only thing I'll regret is if you stop now, Hugh. I'm not a maiden, if that's what has you worried." She felt her cheeks heat with the frank words, but hoped it was too dark for even Hugh's half dragon vision to discern.

"That's a relief," he admitted boldly, inserting his legs

between hers as they lay on his bedroll. "It means I can worship your body as you deserve."

Lera's blood heated at the promise in his gaze and the fire in his touch. She wasn't altogether certain if she should be insulted or gratified by his response, but either way, she was going to have him. Really, nothing else mattered. Just him. His body, on hers, in hers, as soon as they could manage it.

Hugh shrugged out of his shirt while his lips traced patterns down her neck. He paused only briefly to help her with the bodice of her fine lawn gown. The dress laced up the front so she could put it on without assistance. She used the plainer fabrics for times when she wanted to go out without an entourage. When she wanted to be as incognito as possible.

It didn't always work. The innkeeper had recognized her, for one. And the assassins had found her. But she'd been able to dress herself and get out of the palace alone. That, in itself, was a feat.

And the outfit was just as easy to take off as it was to put on. Hugh made short work of her lacings and she almost purred when her breasts fell free, into his waiting, warm hands. She liked the way he paused to examine her as if she were made of the finest porcelain.

He rubbed her nipples, making her squirm with arousal. As she'd expected, Hugh showed all the signs of knowing his way around a woman's body and she was glad he was here to share this night with her. For all she knew, the assassins would find her soon enough and Hugh might not be there—or he might be a split second slower—and she'd be dead. Just like that. She would enjoy this time with him while she could.

There was nothing like a brush with death to make a woman value the important things in life. A warm bed and an even hotter man to make her go up in flames.

Hugh's mouth covered first one nipple, then the other, sucking and licking, making her temperature rise. All the while his hands lowered to the tapes at her waist, releasing the skirt and pushing it downward. She helped, kicking her feet until the fabric was clear. Clever man, he'd undone all her bows and she was able to get free of skirts and undergarments in one move. Now there was a man after her own heart.

Hugh's hands traced the curves of her body as his mouth suckled and kissed its way over her skin. One hand delved gently between her legs and found the little button that sent her senses spinning. She stifled a moan, not wanting to wake the baby gryphon. She had to be quiet considering they were outside where anything—or anyone—might hear them.

Just the thought of it sent a forbidden thrill through her as Hugh's fingers moved on, seeking entrance to her wet passage. She was primed and ready. It wouldn't take much to set her off.

"Come into me now, Hugh." Her softly spoken words brought his gaze up to meet hers.

Surprise turned to deviltry in his expression. "Impatient, are you?"

"Needy," she corrected with a soft smile. "It's been a long time for me and I don't want to wait."

"But anticipation increases pleasure. Haven't your previous lovers taught you that valuable lesson, Lera?"

He was definitely fishing for information, but she saw no reason to keep her sexual experience—or lack thereof—from him. If anything, such knowledge might help him satisfy her.

"There were only two and neither for very long. It was several years ago. Since then, I've lived a quieter life. Less dangerous."

"Dangerous?" Hugh grinned. "Playing fast and loose with your favors is something you would consider dangerous to your position, then? I can understand that. Many a court lady has lost her standing and the respect of her peers due to loose morals. But I never expected that of you, Lera." His gaze turned serious and he removed his hands from her body. "That's not what I was implying. Forgive me if it sounded as if I was insulting you. That was not my intent."

He was drawing away and that was something she did not want. She grabbed one of his hands and tucked it against her skin, close to her heart.

"I never thought that, Hugh. Don't leave me like this. I want you."

"So you say, but you've had a rough night. Much as I want to be with you, I do not want this to happen for the wrong reasons."

"I want this for all the right reasons, as far as I'm concerned." She stroked his hand. "You've saved me twice this night, Hugh."

"Do you think giving yourself to me is some sort of repayment?"

Damn. That hadn't come out right and she was losing him.

"Never," she replied. "I meant that I know I can trust you. Above all those in Helios at this hour, I am certain only of you, Hugh. My savior. My protector. And I hope...my lover?"

The fire rekindled in his eyes and hope blossomed in her heart. Had she said the right thing? His actions would tell.

"I am honored by your trust and will not abuse it, Lera." He moved closer once more.

"I never thought you would."

Hugh smiled and lay back down at her side, his hand turning over in hers so that they were palm to palm. He lifted her hand and brought it to his lips, kissing her knuckles with lingering, licking little kisses.

The warmth of him amazed her. On one side the fire did its best to warm her bare skin. On the other side was Hugh. Warm, huge, smoldering Hugh. With him around, she would never be cold in any way.

"Now can we get back to where we were?" she asked breathlessly as her temperature resumed its climb upward.

"And where was that?" The wicked glint in his eye brought a smile of anticipation to her mouth as he climbed gently over her, insinuating his legs between hers.

She parted her thighs eagerly, wanting him with increasing desperation. Never before had she been so quick to excite, so eager to accept a man into her body, but she knew this was right. She felt it in the very marrow of her bones. This man. This time. This night.

There might never be another as perfect as this moment.

"Just about there," she agreed as he moved into position and then halted. She frowned. "A little farther?" she asked hopefully, looking up at him in the dim firelight.

His grin was sultry and the intent in his gaze made her tummy clench.

"You don't think we're moving a little fast?"

"I know we are, but I don't care. Don't you feel this?"

"I thought I was the only one," he admitted, making her gasp. She'd put herself out there not really expecting anything in return. He hadn't come out and said it. Not really. But he'd definitely implied that he was feeling some of the same magic she was at the moment.

"You're not in this alone, Lera."

She thought she read something deeper in his gaze, but she couldn't be sure. The feel of his skin against her body made her crave more and he still had his pants on.

"Too many clothes, Hugh," she complained breathlessly. "Please don't make me wait."

Hugh laughed and rolled a bit, taking the time only to release the vital part of his body and return. She felt the blunt head of him against her leg as he moved back into position.

"I'll make you a bargain. This first time will be quick, the way you want it. After that, it's my turn."

His smile widened as she began to pant. She was in a bad way and he'd barely even touched her. What was this power he held over her? If he was using his magic to inflame her responses, she couldn't sense it. And she'd been trained from birth to be able to deal with various forms of magic. Of course, she'd never come up against dragon magic before.

Still, did it really matter? She had been attracted to him since almost the moment she'd seen him in that inn. His appeal had only increased in the hours since when he'd saved her life. Twice.

He was heroic in a way she'd never really seen before firsthand. For the past twenty years or so, her land had been a mostly peaceful one. Her father had ruled during the last big conflict, when he'd moved the seat of power to Alagarithia after the assassination of the entire House of Alagar—the hereditary rulers of this city.

Since her father had come here and dispatched those who had killed off the House of Alagar, nothing else had caused such a military response. She'd known soldiers and guardsmen. She'd rewarded those who'd demonstrated bravery in the course of their duties, but there hadn't been a war in Helios since before she was born. The opportunities for real heroes to prove their worth were few and far between. Thankfully.

But Hugh had been where she needed him to be twice that night.

If he'd move a little closer, he'd make that three times, she thought with a wicked grin.

"What's so funny?" He moved, dragging the aroused head of his cock along her most tender skin. She hadn't seen him or even touched him, but she could feel the substantial size of him against her inner thigh.

"Not funny," she clarified. "More like desperate."

One of his hands slid downward, insinuating itself between them. His agile fingers zeroed in on her clit, rubbing lightly at first, then in harder, circular motions. Lera could feel the wetness seeping from her body, making ready for his entry. An entry she craved with every last fiber of her being.

She squirmed under him, trying to coax him closer to no avail. Hugh was too large for her to maneuver easily, but she liked the weight and heft of him over her. He was careful not to crush her, considerate of her smaller frame under his and she was grateful for his care. Everything about his actions proved how good he was as a man.

He'd impressed her by taking in the vulnerable misborn baby gryphon. He'd earned her thanks and respect for killing the Eyes and whisking her away from danger. And now he was in the process of proving how considerate a lover he was. Everything about this man made her like him more.

If only he would move his arse and get inside her.

Hugh's fingers delved deeper, pulsing within her as he watched her intently. She felt vulnerable under his scrutiny but could do nothing about it. Not at the moment.

"Are you ready for me, Lera?" She met his gaze, aware of how in control he was and how out of it she felt. He definitely had her at a disadvantage.

"I was ready ten minutes ago, but some fool of a dragon has been keeping me waiting," she whispered against his lips as he bent over her.

He chuckled and moved closer, sealing his mouth to hers as he used the hand that was still between them to line himself up with her opening. She felt the first gentle probe, followed by the steady slide inward as his tongue danced with hers.

He went slow, for which she was grateful. It had been years since her last foray into the world of physical pleasure. When this first bout was over, she wanted to examine that rigid shaft in depth, but the moment was too urgent just now to take the time.

"Oh, Hugh…" She gasped when he was seated fully within her. Stars, that felt good.

"All right?" he paused to ask, concern in his green gaze.

"Better," she replied breathlessly. "Keep going."

"I'm in all the way," he laughed.

She shook her head, wanting more. "I know. Just keep

going. Move!" Increasing desperation forced her to use simple, urgent words.

"As milady commands." Hugh dipped his head, placing sucking kisses under her ear and down along her neck as he began to move in shallow thrusts that nearly made her scream. It was so good. So perfect.

He picked up the pace, moving faster now as her body opened to accept him fully. She was wet and willing, ready for the pleasure she sensed only he could show her.

She'd had climaxes before, but she'd never heated up so fast for a man and had definitely never been so desperate. She wasn't sure she would survive the ecstasy that loomed just out of reach. She yearned for it. She wanted it so bad, it almost hurt. Would Hugh be able to take her there—to the place beyond mere pleasure? She thought she might have finally found the man who could show her the true power that waited just over there, on the other side of the massive orgasm that was even now building within her.

Hugh's speed increased again as his breathing began to match pace. His thrusts were harder, deeper, more compelling, and she welcomed every stroke, every contact.

"Hugh!" She fought hard to keep her voice down even as her senses began to explode.

It didn't take much. Hugh accelerated, grinding into her in short digs that put pressure on just the right places inside and out. Three strokes and she shot to the stars, stifling the scream she would have voiced if they hadn't been so out in the open. The real stars above her swirled as her vision faded and sparks flew behind her eyes. Her body trembled and shook under him as Hugh clenched, his cock spewing warm jets into her body, heating her from within as his blanketing bulk heated her skin.

"Lera... Sweet Lera..." His words came to her through the fog of pleasure.

Finally. Finally she knew what it was like to feel the highest of highs, the pinnacle of pleasure. Finally, she touched the stars with a man. Finally, she understood what it was really all about for her as a keeper of magic.

She had touched the place that had been out of reach with her other lovers. She had seen behind the curtain and learned there was ever more to see, ever more to experience. But at least she was on the path now.

Hugh rolled off her, never losing touch with her bare skin. He lay behind her, spooning her back with her front to the fire so she was warm on all sides. He'd proven himself a considerate lover in all ways, including now, in the afterglow.

Lera must have dozed, for when she woke next, Hugh's warmth at her back was gone. In fact, she was lying flat on her back on the bedroll, her legs splayed wide apart and Hugh was between them, his head very near the juncture of her thighs. He looked up when she tensed.

"Glad you're awake." He winked at her, an audacious smile on his handsome face.

"Why's that?" She felt strange, exposed like this, under the stars.

A quick glance across the fire reassured her that the baby gryphon was still fast asleep. She'd seen youngsters of that race before and knew they required more sleep than most infants and when they slept, very little short of an earthquake would wake them until they were fully rested.

"Because I was taught it's not gentlemanly to take advantage of a woman while she is sleeping."

"And now that I'm awake, it's all right?"

"Definitely." Hugh lowered his head, keeping his gaze locked with hers as he did something unexpected. His mouth opened over her clit, taking it inside the warm, wet cavern where his tongue waited to torture and play.

No one had ever done this to her before. Lera didn't know where to look, but that problem was solved by the fact that Hugh would not release her gaze, holding it with his own. The moment was far more intimate than when he'd been inside her.

They'd been in that together. This time, it felt like only she was being driven to distraction, and he was doing it to her. He was in control here and she'd given over her free will with no fight at all. Whatever he wanted to do to her, she was open and ready. That was the message her body was giving him and he was taking full advantage.

At the moment, she didn't give a damn. Let him take charge if this was the result. She'd give total control to him, and gladly.

A dangerous thought for a woman in her position. Danger, of course, had been following her for years. Only yesterday, two separate attempts had been made on her life. Now was not the time to deny herself any sort of pleasure Hugh had in store. She might not live much longer, in which case, she wanted to enjoy these stolen moments to their fullest extent.

Hugh delved lower, his tongue stroking out to tease and tempt until finally, it made its way into her body. Stroking, licking and thrusting, Lera had never known a tongue could work such magic. She shattered against his mouth, suppressing her cries lest someone hear.

Hugh rode her through the climax, taking his time before prowling his way back up her body, kissing and trailing that talented tongue against her skin as he went. He didn't stop until he was face to face, his mouth on hers. She thought she tasted a bit of herself on his lips, and the mere thought rekindled the fire in her belly. Never before had she been so easily aroused.

"One day we will make love somewhere you don't have to stifle your sounds of delight, Lera. You will scream my name when you come, for all to hear." His words were spoken between kisses as his hands stroked her nipples, pinching and squeezing in the most delightful way.

"But the baby..." she tried to explain.

"I know. And regardless of how barren this place looks, we do not fully know who or what might be around. No sense advertising our presence any more than we already have." He swooped in for a masterful kiss, then rolled to her side, propping himself up on one elbow as their eyes met.

He had added wood to the fire, for the flames danced once more, licking his skin with their subtle light. They reflected in the cool green crystal of his eyes. He really was the most breathtaking man, now that she could see all of him. Those dusty traveling clothes had not done him full justice.

The thought occurred that perhaps that had been deliberate. Perhaps he'd been in disguise. In a land full of very observant gryphons, it seemed odd to have a dragon shapeshifter walking without notice among her people. Was he the only one? Were there more such as him, roaming the streets of the capitol city? If so, what were their real intentions?

"I never knew there were people like you in the world, Hugh." She reached out to stroke his stubbly cheek with one hand.

She wanted to know more about him. Not just because his kind could pose a threat to the people and creatures of her land, but because he'd been as kind and gallant as a man could be, and he'd made love to her with a caring and skill she'd never experienced.

"There are a few of us. Not many, of course, and none that I know of, other than myself, in this realm."

The clarity of his gaze became clouded with unease. He wasn't comfortable with her implied question. That much was plain to see. But she had to ask. It was her duty to protect this land from all possible threats.

"Why are you here? Surely not just to rescue mistreated children and women on the run for their lives?" She tried to make a joke of her very real inquiry.

He smiled and stroked the hair back from her face. His touch was warm and gentle, soothing. She wondered again if he was using his magic on her, but had no way of knowing for certain. His was a kind of magic she'd never been trained to deal with. She wasn't sure her usual tricks for detecting magical energy would work on him.

"I came to discover more about this land. I can't tell you much more than that, but my intent was never hostile. I came here only to learn."

And report back. He didn't have to say it. She was savvy enough to know how these things worked. He'd been sent to gather first-hand intelligence on her land—whether for good or evil, only those he reported back to would decide. He was but the messenger. Or so he implied.

"And somehow you find yourself rescuing not only one female in peril, but two." She tried to make light of the situation, hoping to distract him so their night together would not end abruptly. She hadn't finished with his devastating body yet.

"I didn't plan any of this," he agreed ruefully. "But part of being...what I am..." he seemed to hesitate over the words, "...is protecting those who are innocent. Miss is clearly that." He glanced over at the sleeping gryphlet and his compassion was clear in his expression.

"And me? You really have no way of knowing if I deserve to die." She held her breath, waiting for his answer.

"Nobody deserves an assassin's blade." His words were unequivocal. "If you'd done something worthy of a death sentence—which frankly, I cannot believe—then it would properly be carried out by legal representatives in a formal proceeding. I know at least that much about Helios. It is not a lawless place run by assassins and thugs. Not from what I've seen."

She wondered what he'd been doing in Helios before their paths had crossed. How long had he been observing her city before he came to her attention by rescuing the gryphlet? What had he seen and done?

And why was she so fascinated by him?

Usually a woman of thought rather than action, Lera decided not to let this night pass in introspection. He was what he was. And right now, he was naked and if the hardness of that giant cock was any indication, he was more than ready to bring her pleasure again.

There would be time for thinking later. Or not. It was really up to the goddess how much time Lera had left and for right this moment, she planned to enjoy every last moment she had with Hugh.

She rose and moved so that he was under her, her legs straddling his middle. He seemed surprised, but helped her reposition them so that they were both comfortable.

Lera had never taken charge in bedsport before and was uncertain of exactly what to do. Hugh helped, cupping her breasts as they hung above him, bringing her hardened nipples to his mouth in turn as she squirmed over him.

"Do you like that?" Hugh whispered against her breasts.

She could only utter a soft moan of agreement as her hips moved restlessly against him. The friction of his hard body against her clit was good, but it wasn't enough.

"Do you need some help, sweetheart?" His tone held a humor she was far from feeling at the moment.

"I need you inside me," she said, desperation coloring her softly voiced words.

"So greedy," he chastised, playfully nipping at her breast. "I like that about you." He slid one hand between them, cupping her, letting his fingers roam through her curls until he found her clit and rubbed.

Oh, that felt good. But she needed more.

One long finger slid inside, as if testing her readiness. She wanted to scream. She was ready! Oh, so ready!

But he made her wait. The devil.

His finger pulsed inward, then out, and when it returned, there were two. Then three. Stretching, filling, pleasuring her.

"Hugh..." she whispered, a desperate plea.

"We're going to have to do something about this impatience

of yours, Lera," he teased, moving his fingers in delicious ways. "But not now."

"Praise the goddess," she breathed in relief as he withdrew his fingers, replacing them with the very hard, very large cock she'd glimpsed in the firelight.

He certainly knew how to fill her. And then some. In this position, she was able to influence the speed and depth and it occurred to her that he hadn't really given her all of himself that first time. He'd definitely been holding something in reserve.

Bright stars, had he! She sank onto him, annoyed by the hand he insisted on keeping between them. His care of her body would have been touching at any other time, but not now. Definitely not now.

She wanted all of him. No. She *needed* all of him, and he was holding back. The sneak.

"Move your hand." Her tone held a trace of the command she was used to wielding and she knew it surprised him when his gaze shot to hers, full of question. Never mind, she thought. This joining was too important. "Give it all to me," she tried again, hoping her voice sounded more coaxing than ordering.

"I don't want to hurt you."

"Let me be the judge of what I can handle." She surprised herself with the ability to speak a whole sentence. The way her mind fragmented at this moment, she hadn't expected more than a few disassembled words.

"Are you sure?" His hand flattened between them, decreasing the space, allowing her to take him glorious fractions deeper. But she needed it all. She was desperate.

"Positive. Please, Hugh." Her words came between pants of breath now, low and pleading.

He seemed to think about it for a moment more, then slid that big hand out of the way, bringing it to rest on her hip. A fiery brand of possession that felt so right.

She took him all the way, grinding against him when he was fully seated. She gasped at the sensations and met the fire in his eyes with abandon. She didn't care what he might read in her expression. She was open to him completely. Bared to the soul. And it was the right thing to do. She felt it in her bones.

This man was different from all others. With him, she could release the beast she kept carefully hidden within. She could be what she was born to be. With him. Only with him.

Hugh alone could handle her fire. She knew it instinctively.

She began to move, holding his gaze, wondering what he might see in her eyes if she let loose completely. She'd been told about the magic inside her all her life, but had never been in a position where it might come out whether she wanted it to or not.

Not until Hugh.

"Can you handle my fire?" she whispered, dipping to kiss his strong chin as she increased her pace.

"I'm half dragon. Fire is my element," he replied, his own breathing satisfyingly abrupt.

She felt the leap inside her at his words. A leap of magic. A leap of excitement. A leap of fire. A leap of faith.

She closed her eyes, knowing the flame was reflected there. She bent low to kiss him for all she was worth, needing to seal their bodies together in every way possible while the magic was riding her, glad he was who and what he was. Glad she needn't fear burning him with the power she'd been born with.

She pounded her hips into his, matching his upward thrusts from beneath her as they met in the center of the storm, a timeless place apart from the rest of the world. There, in the heart of the maelstrom, their souls met and fused, heated by the magic of two separate traditions, now joined.

Lera hoped it was the first of many such joinings, but only the goddess she served knew for sure.

There, at that blinding center, passion exploded, whooshing outward and then back in to take them both on the ride of a lifetime, upward into the heavens and back, toward the rushing sea of sensation. Lera clung to him, physically and mentally, knowing he was with her in this climax of climaxes, even as their souls and magic parted and drew back into their separate bodies.

The pleasure was like none she had ever experienced. It was on a deeper, more magical level than she had ever even imagined. Something she had not known existed. Something sacred.

The power rose up, engulfed her and drained her, all at the same time. A sweeping sensation beyond any she had heard of from all her teachers, supposedly so wise in the ways of magic. They had done their best to try to explain what she might find waiting for her if she ever found that once-in-a-lifetime partner who could match her both physically and magically. None of their many words had been even near adequate to describe such a thing.

The ecstasy rode her long and hard. She felt the strain in every muscle—and in the strong body that lay rigidly convulsed in matching pleasure beneath her. Long, long moments of utter bliss, followed by a long slide down into the satisfied oblivion of one who had given her all and had it returned twice over.

Sleep claimed her while the pleasure washed down into wavelets, lapping at her senses, lulling her into a heavy state of relaxation. Hugh was still joined with her body even as she felt the deep, even breathing that indicated he was following her into the abyss.

Chapter Five

When Lera woke, hours later, she knew something had changed on a fundamental level. Memory returned with the twinges of strain in her muscles as she came more fully awake.

She'd fallen asleep all over Hugh. She had to laugh at her own discourteous actions. She'd been his living blanket for most of the night, while he'd warmed her from beneath. At some point, he'd found the strength to cover them both with the thin blanket from his bedroll, and it had been enough to keep her bum from getting cold, but he hadn't moved her off him.

Maybe he liked the feel of her draped all over him. And by that, she meant *all* over. His impressive cock, even while soft, had stayed within her while they slept. As if it had found a home. Again, she smiled at her own thoughts.

Disengaging from him with some difficulty, she rolled to the side, watching him as he slept. The fire had died down to embers, but the faintest hint of dawn over the rolling dunes of the sand flats allowed her to study the chiseled angles of his face.

He was such a handsome man. Even in sleep, he was hard-edged and stunning. A warrior's warrior. He also had proven he had a kind and gentle heart. He'd taken in Miss and then rescued Lera and took it as his task to protect them both. He wasn't a glory hound. He did it all with no expectation of glory. It was just who he was.

And she was very attracted to this strange man who had come out of seemingly nowhere to seduce her senses and boggle her mind. He didn't mean to. It was just that when he touched her in just the right way, all coherent thought seemed to fly right out of her head.

It was time to turn the tables and see if she could do a little mind boggling of her own.

Sliding down his body, Lera spared a glance across the campfire to be certain the gryphlet was still asleep. Miss hadn't moved all night, her eyes still tightly closed, her wings folded neatly along her sleeping body. She'd be asleep for a while still.

All that much better for what Lera had planned.

Reaching out, she trailed her fingers along Hugh's muscular abdomen, playing in the thin arrow of hair that led downward to the rod that had brought her so much pleasure in the night. He'd given her more satisfaction than any man—not that she'd had that many lovers. But even the two who had professed to love her had taken their pleasure without giving her anything in return.

Growing bolder, Lera trailed her fingertips lightly over Hugh's cock, pleased when it stirred. She looked upward to gauge his level of slumber. Sleepy, sexy, half-slitted green eyes met her gaze.

"I'm glad you're up," she whispered, her touch growing bolder.

"Not yet, but I'm getting there." His deep voice rumbled through her mind in a mental caress that made her shiver with an added dimension of excitement. "Keep doing that, baby, and I'll be up in no time and ready to please you."

"Mmm." Lera licked her lips, moving closer. "I had something a little different in mind. I've never done this before, so let me know if I do anything wrong." Her voice dropped to an even lower pitch as she opened her mouth near his straining cock, reaching out with her tongue to lick a delicate line along his expanding flesh.

"Nothing you do with your mouth on my cock could be wrong."

She heard the excitement in his mental communication and smiled. There was no doubt he liked what she was doing. Emboldened by his reaction, she stroked her tongue over him again, this time more fully.

His legs moved restlessly as she lowered her mouth over the tip of his cock. He was rigid now, straining against the insides of her cheeks as she rolled her tongue around him. He had a faintly cinnamon taste. She'd noticed that about him in dragon form as well. He smelled of cinnamon, not brimstone. So different than she had expected.

Everything about this magical man enchanted her.

And she'd always loved cinnamon.

She sucked inward and he muffled a groan. No doubt he was as conscious of the child sleeping nearby as she was. She knew the gryphon baby would sleep for some time still, but they did need to keep the noise to a minimum. In a way, that made the encounter the tiniest bit more exciting.

Still, the faster they moved, the safer they'd be. That in mind, she redoubled her efforts, taking him as deep as she could down her throat. She was just getting into a rhythm when Hugh lifted her by the shoulders and rolled her under him.

Pushing her clothing out of the way, he slid into her body with little preamble, thwarting her plans to give him an early morning gift. Instead, he was giving them both pleasure—taking his from her body and giving her the same in return.

His cock was wet from her mouth, and her pussy, though tender from the night before, was wet with excitement. He slid in easily, rousing the sensitive tissues that had gotten to know him well already. Her body knew him now and knew he would bring her pleasure like she'd never known, except with him.

It was easy to join him at the fever pitch of excitement. The way he handled her body inflamed her senses. There was something about being with such a giant of a man. His immense strength made her feel small and feminine. At the same time, they way he tempered his power when he was with her made her feel cherished in a way she'd never experienced with any man.

Hugh was an original. A once-in-a-lifetime lover.

He began to ride her, his thickness making her want to cry out his name on every thrust. But she dare not.

Instead, she grabbed onto his shoulders, digging in her fingers, hanging on for dear life.

It didn't take long. The power of his thrusts increased as the magic between them rose to engulf them both. The fire came to her—his, hers—she wasn't sure which. It didn't matter. The flame in them was everything. It was nothing. It was heaven on Earth for the few life-altering moments while bliss rolled over them, holding them together in its grip.

She wanted to scream as she came but settled for muffling her moans against his shoulder as he did the same. They were wrapped around each other tighter than tight, his body possessing hers as she held on, claiming him with arms, legs and magic wrapped around him.

He didn't resist. In fact, it felt like he did the same, though she couldn't be certain. After such an explosion of feeling, she couldn't be sure of anything. She could only feel the incredible bliss, the unending and magical fire that he brought her.

She dozed in the predawn, blanketed by him, though he made a small effort to take most of his weight off her by rolling to one side. But he didn't let go of her. And she didn't mind at all.

A stirring on the other side of what was left of the campfire drew her attention as she woke again from her light doze. The baby gryphon was coming awake by slow degrees. Dawn was just breaking over the dunes and Lera was able to see better with each moment.

"I guess we'll have to postpone the rest of this interlude to another time." Hugh's voice promised even more naughtiness of the most delicious kind.

"I'll look forward to it."

She kissed him one last time, then slipped away under the

blanket he'd thrown over them, searching around for the clothes she'd discarded so carelessly the night before. The bodice was close enough for her to grab and wriggle into under the covers.

When she poked her head out, Hugh was already up. She saw him standing above her with a devilish grin on his face a moment before he flung a pile of fabric at her. It landed with a soft whoosh, making her laugh. It was her skirt and undergarments. She fought her way out of the yards of soft fabric to look at him.

"There's a bit of water and privacy over that dune." He nodded toward the east, a few yards distant.

Lera used her skirts as cover, making her way toward the dip in the sands that held the trickle of a clear-running stream. There was also a bit of vegetation they were using as an outhouse. She was able to take care of necessities, bathe somewhat, drink her fill and dress more fully before she returned to the campsite. Nothing could be done, however, about the nest her hair had become. It would take her hairdresser a week to comb out all the tangles, she was sure.

When she walked back over the dune toward the rekindled fire, the gryphon's sharp gaze was the first to spot her. Hugh turned his head and winked as he leaned over the fire, tending it.

In the golden light of dawn, he took her breath away.

The gryphlet flapped her wings, breaking the silence and drawing attention.

"Good morning, little Miss." Hugh addressed the gryphlet. "Are you hungry?"

The little kitten head nodded as she pranced over. She was careful of the fire, Lera noticed. Smart girl. Or maybe she'd already learned the hard way that fire, fur and oiled feathers didn't really mix well.

"Hungry," she agreed in her simple way as she butted her soft head against Hugh's arm.

"So am I," he agreed. "If you can wait just a bit, I'll go find us something to eat, all right?" He caressed the kitten's head with genuine affection just as Lera's stomach growled. He laughed and looked at her. "Sounds like Lady Lera is hungry too."

"Iss dat why sshe growlss?" Miss asked, her head tilting in question.

Lera had to laugh. "Sorry about that." She moved closer to the fire, enjoying the heat it gave off in the chilly morning air.

Hugh stood from tending the fire and walked over to Lera, stealing an all too brief kiss before striding even farther from the campsite. A blur of black fog and suddenly the dragon stood where the man had been only an eye blink before.

"I'll be back in a few minutes with something to eat."

The feel of his thoughts in her mind was comfortably familiar after the harrowing night before. She'd never even heard of anyone who could speak mind to mind before, much less experienced it, but with Hugh, it just seemed right. As did many things. He was comfortable to be with, which was something she had rarely experienced in her life of privilege.

People were usually uncomfortable with her elevated status. Either that, or worse, they courted her favor purely for their own gain. While not evil in itself, such self-interest tainted all her dealings with people to the point where she seldom had a simple, friendly conversation with anyone.

There was a saying that it was lonely at the top and Lera knew it to be true from firsthand experience. She gathered her skirts around her legs and sat at the fire on the folded bedroll. The gryphon looked at her suspiciously.

It was about time she set the little one straight and did her best to make friends. While Hugh had protected the child thus far, she would probably be better off among her own kind. It was up to Lera to give the little one the opportunity.

"My name is Valeria, but my friends call me Lera. I hope you will be my friend." The gryphlet took a tentative step toward her, skirting the rebuilt fire by a wide margin. "I'm sorry if I frightened you yesterday when we first met, but I was concerned that Hugh might not be a good man and I wanted to protect you."

"Hoo iss good," the baby insisted with a stubborn set to her pointy jaw.

"I know that now," Lera agreed. "He saved my life. As did you. I owe you a great debt, Miss. Thank you for helping when those bad men were trying to kill me."

"Trying to hurt Hoo too," Miss mumbled. "Don't like."

"You were right not to like those bad men. The men with the eyes painted on their bodies are dangerous. You were very brave to attack that man. Very brave indeed. You have the heart of a lioness, little Miss. Helios is proud of you. And I am proud of you and thankful. To show my thanks, I give you a boon."

"What'ss a boom?"

"Boon, dear one. It means that I owe you one special treat. When we get back to the city, you can ask me for anything that it is within my power to grant you and I will give it to you. It is a very rare honor given to only the bravest gryphons. It has been years since I have given one." The kitten moved closer, her folded wings gleaming with health in the crisp dawn light. She looked much better than she had only the day before. Perhaps the benefit of Hugh's magic? Lera wasn't sure, but it would make sense. "You must think long and hard about what you want. Do not waste such a gift on something simple. You should ask for something really important. Something that is your heart's desire. If it is within my power, I will give it to you."

"You have power?" The baby looked up at her with tilted chin and Lera had to laugh.

"A very good question," she congratulated the gryphlet. "As a matter of fact, I do. That's why my cousin sent those bad men to kill me. If I died, she would take my place and that's something Helios cannot afford."

Lera's attention was caught by the return of the black

dragon. He landed some yards distant. Far enough away that the wild game he held in one clawed hand wasn't recognizable. Hugh used those sharp ebony claws to slice whatever it was and tossed the remains farther away from the campsite.

He walked toward her and her attention was snagged by how gracefully he moved even in dragon form. She wouldn't have expected something that was so clearly born to be in the air could be as good on the ground. The gryphons were different. They were half cat and therefore able to prowl as well on the ground as their raptor could conquer the air.

Dragons? They were something altogether different. Purely their own species, not made by a wizard from two separate creatures like the gryphons had been.

"How do you like your mutton? Well done or pink in the middle?"

His voice in her mind made her feel warm in a good way. He was close enough now that he would hear her if she spoke aloud.

"Can you do medium well?"

"Most certainly, milady."

"But what can we cook it on?" She looked around, even though she knew there hadn't been any cooking gear in his pack.

"Watch and learn."

He stood a few yards from the campsite and raised one clawed hand that held two cut portions of the meat. Opening his jaw, he blew a small stream of fire at his own hand.

The sight of it made her jump and for a split second horror struck her that he might be burned. Then she remembered. He was a *dragon*. He was impervious to flame. She knew that. She could see it with her own eyes. But flame was so dangerous to her gryphons. She was used to being wary of any kind of fire when they were around.

Hugh closed his mouth, extinguishing the flame, and moved closer. He had another piece of meat in his other hand.

It was raw. He handed it to the gryphlet with due care for her soft skin, keeping her safe from his talons. Miss took it with eager paws and sat down again, nibbling on it with her sharp baby teeth.

A moment of black fog, and then Hugh stood there in his human form, holding two pieces of sizzling meat in his hands.

"I'm sorry we don't have any plates to eat this from. It's probably still too hot for you to handle safely." Hugh looked a bit sheepish, which Lera thought was adorable considering he'd just hunted a meal and provided for all three of them. There was nothing for him to feel the least bit embarrassed about.

"Hang on to it for a bit." She laughed when he brought his portion to his mouth and tore a chunk out of it. He grinned at her even as he chewed.

"Sorry, couldn't wait." The intimacy of the shared thought touched her once again.

"Just as long as you save me some. What is that anyway?"

"Nothing I really recognized. Some kind of sheep, though it wasn't domesticated. It was running wild with a small flock up on that hill over there." He gestured with his portion of the meat toward a distant hilltop.

"That's all right then. We allow the gryphons to hunt wild herds as long as they leave enough to keep each group viable." She sat on the bedroll and Hugh followed suit, sinking gracefully to the ground even though his hands were full.

"You seem to know all about gryphons and the rules governing them. Part of your job, I expect." The statement sounded more like a question and Lera realized the time had come for plain speaking.

"It is. Hugh, there is much I need to tell you." She turned toward him, wanting to clear the air.

"Let's eat first, talk later. I think this is cool enough for you to handle now." He offered her the piece of meat.

"I don't think I can handle all of that," she said dubiously, noting the size of the hunk he'd cut for her.

"Don't worry. Whatever you don't eat, either Miss or I will. Come on." He offered the meat once more, a coaxing note in his voice. "You haven't eaten anything in hours. You must be hungry and with all that's been going on, you need to keep up your strength."

She couldn't argue with that, even if mutton wasn't her first choice for a hearty breakfast. Beggars couldn't be choosers. She had to take what he offered and be grateful that she'd been rescued by someone who could not only defend her but provide for her as well. Truly, the goddess had been watching over her when she'd crossed paths with Hugh.

Lera bit into the juicy fillet, surprised by how good the salty meat tasted on her tongue. She'd been too upset to notice how hungry she really was, but things were safe for the moment and her hunger could no longer be ignored.

Silence reigned while they ate and Lera watched the baby gryphon a few feet away. Miss ate daintily for a gryphlet. Lera was impressed by her manners and the methodical way she concentrated on her task, not allowing the raw meat to come in contact with the sandy ground for even a second. Most children—even gryphon children—had more trouble with their coordination than this little misborn.

Within a few more bites, Lera began to feel full. The heavy meal wasn't something she was used to first thing in the morning, but her starving body had needed the nourishment. As her eating slowed, she became more aware of Hugh sitting next to her. Watching her. She looked over at him. He was smiling in a way that heated her insides.

"I can't finish this. Sorry." She handed what was left of the meal back to him.

"Don't be sorry." He ripped the meat in half and tossed the larger portion to the youngster. Miss caught it with her outstretched claws and immediately dug into the tasty meal. Hugh ate the other piece more slowly. "So now, what did you want to tell me?"

Keeper of the Flame

Now that the moment was upon her, Lera didn't know where to begin. She supposed it was always best to start with gratitude.

"First, thank you again for saving my life. Twice. Without you and Miss, I'd be dead now and my land would be in even more of an uproar than it already is."

"Your land?" Hugh's eyes narrowed.

"I told you it was my job to look after the gryphons of Helios," she began. She wasn't sure how he was going to take this and she wanted to break it gently. He nodded, his expression receptive. "Actually, there's a bit more to it than that." Maybe plain out was better than beating around the bush. She took a deep breath for courage. "I am the Doge."

"The Doge," Hugh repeated. She wasn't sure what she heard in his voice. Was it anger or disbelief? Or something else altogether? The moment dragged on.

Then Hugh began to laugh. Now that, she hadn't expected.

"I'm not kidding, Hugh. I am the Doge of Helios."

"I believe you," he said between chuckles. "I just find it funny that I came here to learn if the Doge was true friend or hidden foe to my land. I never expected an audience with the Doge herself."

"Or wanted one, I suppose. You're a spy, after all." She saw the humor and had to chuckle herself.

"Ouch." He winced comically, then relented. "You know, I'm not really a spy. Not the way you mean, at least. I'm just a...fact finder, you could call me. I certainly never intended to take in an orphan or rescue a damsel in distress. I don't think a real spy would've so badly compromised his mission."

"I guess you're right. Whoever sent you here might be disappointed."

"My brother sent me, and to be frank, I don't think he expected much in the first place. I think he came up with the idea strictly to placate a certain woman."

101

"His wife?" Lera asked. She wasn't altogether surprised to learn that Hugh's family was high-ranking in Draconian politics. With such abilities, it only made sense that they would be placed in the government of a land that favored dragons so heavily.

"No. Shanya is a... Well, I guess you could call her a friend of the royal family. She's a seer of some renown. She was the one who said I had to come here and big brother went along with it. Even though I'm not known for my spy work. Most of the time, I deal with soldiers. Training. Fighting those who attack us. I spend a lot of my time in the Lairs."

"Lairs? That's where the dragons live, right?"

"Dragons, knights and their families," he confirmed.

"Sounds nice." And it did. That the dragons had human counterparts as part of their family structure—or vice versa—was something she'd never anticipated.

"So you're the Doge." Hugh's tone was speculative. "I guess that's why someone is trying to kill you."

"My cousin, Sendra. That was her estate we landed at last night. You heard what the Eyes said. She hired them. If I die, she will most likely seize power."

"That doesn't sound good."

"It's not. She and I have not agreed on anything in recent memory. She would turn our peaceful land into a warring nation. She has been urging conquest for years now and has thankfully been outvoted at every turn. But those are my counselors. If she took control, she would no doubt remove most of my people and replace them with her own sycophants. She could get away with almost anything and it would all be legal."

"I don't really understand how your government works. In my land, we have a king who makes all final decisions, though he is often influenced by the wishes of both his own counselors and the Dragon Council."

"A Doge is sort of like your king, only the Doge can be

either gender. He or she comes into power when the previous Doge either dies or abdicates. My father was the Doge before me and ruled Helios for almost ninety years. The magic extended his life beyond that of regular people, as it will mine. Father always said that when I was born, the goddess gave them a sign that I would be the next Keeper as well as the next Doge. Their belief was proven true when I was tested by the Fire and chosen as Keeper of the Flame. From that day, I have been responsible for the welfare of all gryphons in Helios."

"So the Keeper looks after the gryphons," Hugh repeated. "I don't suppose there is anyone like me in your land. Someone who is both gryphon and human?"

"No. Gryphons were created from two creatures already part of this world. I believe dragons are an entirely magical creation. Though both were made by wizards, gryphons came from the land. Dragons, I now believe, probably sprang from the eternal fire itself. This is something I've thought through over the past day since seeing you transform. Though before meeting you, I never would have imagined there were people who were also dragons."

"The eternal fire," Hugh mused. "I like that."

"It is part of our beliefs and part of my knowledge as Keeper. Fire is the one thing gryphons must fear above all. Oiled feathers and fur do not have any defense against the eternal flame. And just as people have free will, so too do the gryphons. If one transgresses to the point of capital punishment, they are given to the flame. That is my heaviest responsibility as Keeper."

Hugh frowned. "The Keeper is also executioner of bad gryphons?"

Lera could see the little one watching them with wide eyes.

"No. Not really. I only keep watch over the eternal flame. It would be up to the gryphon court to carry out any sentence on one of their own. It happens so rarely, I've never been called on to unleash the flame. Goddess willing, I never will."

Hugh seemed to take that in before asking his next question. Both his expression and tone was serious and thoughtful.

"Was your mother Keeper before you?"

"Actually, no. Until me, Keepers usually came from the House of Alagar, the original rulers of this city, which carries their name. About twenty years ago, my father moved his court here after the assassination of the entire line of Alagar. It was a dark time and my family came here to restore order and catch those responsible for killing off the noble House of Alagar. It was a tragedy."

Hugh looked like he wanted to comment, but something made him hold his tongue. Lera filed that away for later consideration, continuing her explanation.

"From what I've been taught, the role of Keeper used to pass from mother to daughter in the House of Alagar, though it didn't always work that way. Sometimes it would go to a niece or female cousin. Since I have no daughter, my cousin Sendra is the nearest in line for both of my roles. She could be made Doge, though I expect another would be found to act as Keeper until such time as the goddess grants that responsibility to another family line. Unfortunately, that would leave my cousin in charge of the government and military for far too long. The Keeper holds a quasi-religious, magical power. She is not required to be a politician or ruler. Her responsibility is to the Lady's sacred flame first and foremost. And to the gryphons."

"Sounds like Sendra could cause some serious trouble for this land and others if she seized power," Hugh observed.

"I have no doubt of it. But I never thought she'd stoop to murder. Setting Eyes on me is something I never thought of. Never dreamed of. I knew we had disagreements of late about how the country should be run, but I couldn't bring myself to believe that she wanted me dead. She's my cousin. My blood. I didn't believe it until last night, when I heard that assassin say he'd get a bonus if he made me suffer before he killed me." The horror of those moments in the vineyard came back to her. "I didn't know she hated me so much."

"You can't let her win," Hugh said softly, drawing her attention. She was heartened by the compassion and strength in his expression. "There is really only one thing you can do. You must return to the city and reclaim your throne."

"But the Eyes..." She hated the fear that crept into her tone and made her hands tremble.

Hugh took both of her hands in his, warming them, stilling the fear.

"If you allow it, I will stay by your side. I will keep you safe, Lera. I promise you, I am a much better bodyguard than I am a spy."

His rueful smile invited her to chuckle at his words. He was such a good man. And he had formidable abilities in both his human and his dragon form. If anyone could keep her safe, it would be Hugh. More than that, she trusted him. After the night they'd had, between the assassins, the mad flights from danger and the sweet pleasure they'd shared, she felt she knew him better than most of the people who'd been in her life for years.

He certainly had seen her at her worst. And she'd seen him act with courage and chivalry. He was both a fighter and a gentleman. He had treated her so well throughout their adventure. He'd cared for her wellbeing both physically and mentally. He was a man she could easily come to depend on—or love.

"Would you really come with me? We'll be walking into certain danger. Eyes don't quit just because a job has become more difficult. They will send ever more skilled members of their brotherhood until the job is completed. As long as the holder of the contract keeps paying. I can't imagine Sendra will stop now that she is committed to this course. They'll keep coming until I'm dead."

"Or until I kill them all." Hugh's gaze went steely and she

could well imagine a pile of dead assassins at his feet. Hugh was a warrior who would not balk at killing those who confronted her with death on their minds.

Silence reigned for a moment while his words echoed through her mind. It would be dangerous, but she really did have to return to the city. Her people depended on her. If Sendra seized power, the land would suffer greatly. She could not let that happen, no matter the danger to her personally. The land and its inhabitants had to come before her own happiness and wellbeing, if necessary.

"I must go back," she said bleakly, knowing there was no alternative.

Hugh's arm came around her shoulders. "I'll go with you."

"I go too." Miss's simple words were punctuated by the gryphlet's small bow. Where had she learned such courtly manners? Perhaps it was instinctual, Lera thought, but it would bear investigation, if and when she was free to look into such things.

"Thank you, Miss. When we get to the palace, there are some others like you that I want you to meet. I believe you would be welcome among their number and they would treat you well."

"Want sstay wif Hoo."

"We'll talk about it when we get there, sweetheart." Hugh tabled the subject efficiently. She could see the concern in his expression. She felt the same worry. She couldn't knowingly put the child in danger and just being around Lera at the moment was a very dangerous place to be, indeed.

They'd have to sort it out when they got back to the city. For now, that was the best Lera could come up with.

Chapter Six

Things were moving quickly. Hugh was almost shocked when he realized how neatly events had unfolded. He'd spent the night under the stars with a woman who set his world on fire. True, she was running from assassins, but that was only a minor complication. He hoped.

Hugh would do everything in his power to keep her safe. He'd stay with her night and day if he had to. If she let him. This was her land and he'd play by her rules...as far as he could. If her life was in danger though, all bets were off.

"How do you want to do this?" he asked as they sat before the waning fire, making plans. "The last time I approached the palace with you on my back, something was definitely off. You said the guards weren't at their posts and the gryphons were out of place."

A worried look crossed her lovely face. "I've been thinking about that. We have to move in cautiously. Maybe work our way through the city a bit."

"Very dangerous," Hugh commented, not liking the options. "It might be better to do a little reconnaissance first. Is there anyone in the city that you can be certain of? Someone you trust with your life?"

"I thought I could trust my cousin Sendra." Her words were tinged with both sadness and betrayal. Hugh felt for her, but now was not the time to dwell on the disappointments of the past days. Now was the time for decisive action and carefully measured boldness.

"Is there anyone else?"

"Hyadror." She nodded to herself, confirming her own

thoughts. "He has saved my life before. He would not side with Sendra against me."

"How do we find this Hyadror?" Hugh could work with this. If only they had at least one ally within the city, it might make all the difference.

"If we get close enough, I think he will find us. If he's the friend I think he is, he will have noticed I am nowhere to be found and will be looking for me."

"What good can one man do in searching an entire city? The chances seem slim to me." Hugh had to be realistic. Lera's chuckle took him by surprise.

"Hyadror isn't a man. I mean...he's male, but he's a gryphon."

That sounded a lot better to Hugh. "A fully grown gryphon, right?"

"Of course. He was one of my teachers when I was in training." The fondness in her voice was clear.

"All right." He could definitely work with an adult gryphon on their side. "Let's fly closer to the city tonight, under cover of darkness. I'll do some scouting ahead and we'll see what's been going on during your absence. How does that sound?"

"Sounds about right," Lera agreed. "Do you want to stay here for the day or can we move a bit closer while there's light?"

"A black dragon is very visible against a light blue sky," Hugh mused. "But we can do some trekking on foot if you're game."

"It's better than sitting here, waiting all day."

"There are other things we could do, but not with the little one about." His wink made her blush and he found that he enjoyed teasing her.

"Behave, Hugh." The smile on her face was his reward.

"I'll start packing if you want to wash up. There's an empty water skin in my pack. Maybe you could fill it in the stream while I take care of the embers?"

"Certainly, my liege." She made a funny little bow as she stood, reaching for his pack.

Hugh wondered how she'd react when she found out that he really was of royal blood. He wasn't sure why he'd kept that fact to himself, other than some vague idea he had about being wanted for himself rather than his social rank. He didn't think Lera was like that, but all too many highborn ladies were. He'd felt hunted in his brother's kingdom by more than one court lady intent on marrying into the royal household.

Third in line for the throne wasn't a bad place to be. Or so many of those shallow women thought. One had even whispered to him that with the dangerous life Roland led and Nico's commitment to the Jinn Brotherhood, it was likely Hugh would wear the crown sooner rather than later.

Hugh had thrown the conniving wench out of his bed for even thinking such a thing. He'd had her banned from court as well, though he'd gone about that more subtly than the middle-of-the-night ouster from the royal apartments accompanied by armed guards. He'd alerted his brothers to the possibility of trouble from her, and Hugh had only been satisfied when Nico had sent one of his operatives to check on her noble family from the inside. Nico wasn't the Prince of Spies for nothing.

Miss pranced down to the stream with Lera and he watched his two females with a softness in his heart. They both had beautiful souls. Miss was so eager, so trusting, as only a child could be. Lera, on the other hand, was all woman, mature and strong, and more than a match for him on so many levels.

He'd been blown away by their night together and hoped it was only the first of many spent in her company. First, however, he had to take care of the threat against her. Those Eyes had been deadly and more skilled than he liked. Three times now, one of them had snuck up on them without his knowledge. It was unheard of. Such things did not happen to a man with the senses of a dragon. He should have smelled them coming even if he didn't hear their whisper-soft footfalls.

Or perhaps the woman had been too distracting. Now there was a thought. He was off balance, worrying about Lera when he should have had all his senses focused on the danger they faced. Hugh had to get over that. He had to be ready for the next time they faced Eyes. He had no doubt the assassins wouldn't quit. He'd have more blood on his talons before this was over. In a way, he almost looked forward to it.

Proving his strength and skill against highly trained opponents was thrilling in a primitive way. Even more primitive was his desire to protect his woman. Proving himself the victor when her very life was at stake was a dangerous game, but one he planned to win. He would die before he'd let harm come to Lera. Or the baby gryphon.

Miss was every bit as precious to him. He couldn't feel more protective of her if he'd fathered the little girl himself. Odd, that. But there it was. He loved the poor, brave creature and would do all he could to keep her safe from harm.

Lera and Miss came back in short order and Hugh had his bedroll and the few items he'd used from his pack back together. Lera gave him the filled waterskin when he reached for it. Slinging it over one shoulder, with the small pack on his back, he was ready to go.

They walked for a half hour or so, steadily uphill, though the grade was easy. The small sand dunes were hard packed and rolling across the landscape toward the much higher hills. The city of Alagarithia sat on the other side of the hilltops, in the triangular valley nestled between them and the cave-filled cliffs where so many gryphons nested. The sea was the third and final border to the city, which allowed some protection as well as easy trade via the many ships that docked there from other lands.

Their pace was easy, no hurry to their steps. Hugh wanted to time their arrival to take advantage of his natural, dark camouflage. They had hours to go before the sun would set. There was no reason to hurry. All rushing over the dunes would do is tire out the ladies and he didn't want to put either one of them through any more strain.

He coached the gryphlet as they walked, giving her little exercises she could do to strengthen her wings as she walk-hopped alongside them. A few times she actually caught air and the delight in her prancing steps was clear to see.

"Try cupping your wings when you hit the top of the next rise, sweetheart," he told her. "Gather a little speed and leap. You might be able to coast down to the bottom of the dip."

"I try," she promised very seriously, then ran ahead to test her wings.

Hugh lost sight of her for a moment, then had to laugh when he saw her practically galloping back up the dune from the bottom, triumph in every step.

"I fly, Hoo! I fly!"

She ran right up to him and rubbed up against his legs, her wings folded sloppily along her back. She was so excited, she hadn't even taken time to tuck her feathers in. He patted them into place as she pranced around his feet.

"Want to show me?"

"Yess!" Miss ran back toward the top of the dune.

Hugh glanced at Lera before following the gryphlet so he could witness her first little triumph in flight. As he expected, she instinctively caught the air and coasted beautifully down the small hill created by the sand dune. She was a natural flyer.

"Hoo! Did you ssee?" she asked from a few yards away at the bottom of the dune. She bounced on her front paws, excitement making her fur stand on end in places. She looked adorable.

"I saw, sweetheart. You did great." He crouched down to her level when she ran back toward him, nearly bowling him over with her enthusiasm as she jumped into his arms.

He praised her a bit more before she got impatient to try it again over the next dune. He let her go, enjoying the moment.

"You're very good with her," Lera observed, coming even

with him as they watched the boisterous gryphlet.

"She is a joy. It's good to see her like this. Especially after the way I found her. Or rather, she found me."

"I can imagine." Lera's focus was on the child as they walked along, side by side. "It was during the last round of storms, wasn't it?"

"She was shivering and half frozen. Her fur was wet through and through. It took hours to get all the mud out of her feathers and fur. She was so afraid of the fire at first. Her front paw was badly burned."

Lera turned toward him. "She was burned? Did she say how it happened?"

"No. She didn't want to talk about it. I assume, like most children, she didn't know that fire could hurt her until she tried it."

"You healed her, didn't you? I can't see any evidence of a burn on her anywhere."

Hugh nodded. "She might've been crippled otherwise. I couldn't let that happen."

"She's lucky she found you." Lera turned her attention back to the scampering child.

"I don't think luck really had anything to do with it. The more I think about it..." He trailed off, not sure whether he should share his suspicions.

"What?" Lera turned back to him again, her expression very serious.

"I told you that a seer's vision sent me here. I think Miss is part of the reason I was the one who had to come."

Lera regarded him intently for a long moment, then turned her attention very deliberately toward the gryphlet again.

"I think you might be right."

That was all she said before forging on ahead, in the gryphlet's tracks.

The rest of the morning passed much the same way, in a

Keeper of the Flame

leisurely walk over the sand dunes, enjoying Miss's antics and what little scenery there was to see. A few hearty souls were attempting to graze domesticated animals here and there along the sand flats. They crossed a few fence lines, but didn't see many animals. There wasn't much natural vegetation. Hugh doubted such vast and mostly barren land could support large herds. It was more likely the animals naturally gravitated toward the more verdant land near the coastline. Certainly, the few farmhouses he saw in the distance were all toward the coast, where trees sprang up to shelter them from wind and storms.

There were a couple of dilapidated barns along their path. No more than crude shelters for whatever animals might graze this far afield. Perhaps they saw seasonal use. Hugh didn't know enough about this part of the world to say for sure. He only knew that an empty barn could be useful on their journey.

In fact, he called a halt at one of the mostly empty structures at midday. They'd been following the stream all morning. He knew it came down out of the hills and it was as good a path as any to take, since the distant hilltop was their destination. They were close enough to take a break. One last push and they'd be climbing the hill in no time at all. Best to wait until near dark for that.

"Hungry?" Hugh asked as he shrugged out of the straps of his travel pack.

"I could eat something," Lera confirmed. "Are you going hunting again?"

"I have a ration bar or two in here. You can have them."

Her eyes lit up and he was glad he'd remembered the fruit and nut bars he had thrown into his pack in case of emergency. The consistency of boiled leather, they were rolled in waxed fabric because the boiled and concentrated fruit had a tendency to make everything sticky. That made it a natural for adhering any number of shelled tree nuts, seeds and dried berries into a compact bar. The result didn't look very good but tasted

113

delicious. Especially when you were hungry from the road.

Hugh rummaged around until he felt the familiar waxed fabric. There were two of them, each about half a foot long and half that size across. He took them both out and placed them on an upturned crate in the shadowed interior of the barn. Other than a few empty wooden crates, there were only a few bales of hay stored in the structure.

"You make a start on these. I'll just have a little word with Miss." Hugh met the gryphlet who stood poised on the threshold of the shadowy barn. He knelt down so he could talk to her at eye level. "Are you up to hunting, sweetheart? I hear some rustling in the corner over there."

It might not be appealing to the lady, but Miss needed every chance she could get to learn her natural skills. Both raptors and cats were natural born hunters. Miss was a little of both. She needed to learn how to hunt both on the ground and from the air, and if Hugh was serious about taking her in, he had to use every opportunity to teach her. The younger she was when she started to learn, the more readily such things would come to her.

Hugh knew he'd guessed right when he saw the way her eyes lit up and her whiskers twitched. Furry little ears swiveled to catch the sounds of scurrying rodents near the back of the barn.

"Where do you think they are, sweetheart?" He spoke in a low tone, near one mobile ear.

"There." She gestured with her right forepaw exactly where Hugh thought the critters might be hiding. "Good. Now how will you stalk them? What is your approach?"

The little head turned to him in question, tilting in puzzlement. "Sstalk?"

"When you crouch low and wait quietly so they don't see you coming."

"Oh. Like diss..." Miss moved silently on her paws, advancing carefully until she was only a few feet from the

Keeper of the Flame

corner where the rustling noises had been coming from.

She crouched, maneuvering her approach so that the rodents would be boxed in between the two walls in the corner of the barn and her. There would be little chance of escape unless they were much faster than a pouncing gryphlet.

Hugh watched as she waited, willing to let her demonstrate before he tried any further instruction. She seemed to know what she was doing. He'd watch this time and critique if necessary to teach her how to sharpen her skills.

He saw the moment when she moved to strike, as the first of two black round things with bald tails came running out from under a loose bunch of weed stalks that had blown into the back of the building. Her claws came out a split second before she pounced. Two slashes with her front paws and she went still. Neither of the rodents had escaped her incredibly accurate stabs.

Miss turned to Hugh, calm as could be, holding one of her catches up to him. "Want one?"

Hugh couldn't help the grin that split his face. "Thank you, sweetheart, but you earned them both. You did such a great job." He reached out to pat her head, bestowing the love and approval the little one needed so much. "Where'd you learn to hunt so well, sweetheart?"

"Hungry," she said simply, though she moved into his caress.

Hugh's heart broke again for the baby who had been roaming the streets on her own for who knew how long.

"I guess that would do it. Get hungry enough, you learn how to catch dinner, eh, Miss?"

The gryphlet didn't reply. She sat down on the ground to enjoy her catch, tearing into the dead rodent as neatly as she ate everything else.

Hugh headed back toward the doorway and the lady who watched with no discernable expression on her face. Lera was making good progress on the first of the fruit and nut bars.

"Sorry if that wasn't exactly the entertainment you're used to at table," Hugh apologized as he walked closer.

"Some of my best friends are gryphons." Lera surprised him by waving his words off nonchalantly. "I've seen worse table manners. She is really an incredibly neat eater for a child."

"I noticed that too. Most young dragons don't have her level of coordination or her natural grace. I haven't been around enough gryphlets to know if that's normal for the species."

"It's not. Most gryphlets are little fuzzballs of mischief. Of course, most are spoiled rotten from the time they're in the egg to the time they fledge." Lera smiled and handed Hugh a slice from the ration bar.

He noticed she was using the throwing knife he'd seen in her hand on the roof of the inn. The blade had to have been secreted somewhere in the fabric of her gown, though he hadn't seen it or felt it when he'd taken her dress off last night. There must be some kind of secret compartment in there somewhere.

"There's a sheath in the stays of my bodice." She must've noticed the direction of his curious gaze. The grin she gave him was both sassy and shy. An intriguing combination.

"You'll have to show that to me sometime."

Her smile deepened. "Maybe I will."

He took the slice of ration cake from her hand with a lingering caress. "I certainly hope so."

Hugh looked at the corner where Miss had been sitting quietly, devouring her catch, and found the baby gryphon fast asleep. He wasn't altogether surprised.

"What do you say we stop here for a few hours?"

"I don't think we have a choice," Lera replied with a soft smile toward the gryphlet. "She's already had a big day dancing up and down the dunes, testing her wings."

"Yeah, she'll probably sleep for a couple of hours, at least."

"Whatever will we do in the meantime?" Lera's question sounded innocent, but her expression was chock full of mischief.

"I don't know, but why don't you come over here and sit on my lap. I'll try to think of something."

The curve of her mouth promised a delicious kind of trouble as she walked slowly toward him. Far from the innocent miss, she prowled right up to him, hiking her skirts as she moved in a way that made his mouth water. She held his gaze as she straddled his thighs, perching on his knees, her arms looped around his neck.

"I can think of a lot of things I want to do to you," she whispered against his lips before joining them in an intimate kiss.

The kiss deepened as she slid forward on his lap so that her warm heat rubbed up against his straining erection. Their bodies moved and swayed against each other, bringing little tingles of excitement, while the kiss went on and on. Lera was in charge and Hugh didn't mind at all. She twined her tongue with his, commanding his response in a way that sent shivers of pleasure down his spine, through his insides and straight to his cock.

Quick as that, he wanted to be inside her. She enticed him like no woman before and though he let her call the pace, he was ready to go whenever she wanted him. Thank the stars, she seemed as quick to catch fire as he was.

Lera bounced off his thighs and his hands went to her waist in reflex. He didn't want her to go. But then he saw what she was about. Her clever hands were at the ties that held her drawers and she was working at the dainty little bows, loosening them. He wanted to help but knew his big fingers would just get in the way.

He watched, impatient as she seemed, while she conquered the knots and let the fine fabric slide down her luscious thighs. She still wore her skirts, but she was naked beneath. If he had his way, he'd keep her like that at all times—naked and ready to take him.

He just about died when she sank to her knees in front of him and coaxed him to move his knees farther apart. Her fingers went straight for the buttons on his fly and he forgot to breathe.

When her small hand wrapped around his cock and squeezed, he had to fight for control. Then she moved closer, her long hair sliding over one shoulder, and her mouth closed over him. Hugh gave in to the pleasure as she explored him, letting her do what she wanted with his willing body.

He only pushed her away when he was too close to the edge. He didn't want to come in her mouth. No, he wanted to feel her tight pussy around him before he gave up his seed.

Which reminded him of something.

"Lera, honey." He stroked her hair back from her face as she lifted away from his rigid cock. "I'm sorry. I never thought about the fact that you could get pregnant."

"Oh, don't worry." She smiled at him and he felt like the sun had come out on a stormy day. "I am not a virgin and though I have not been with many men, I do know how to take care. I eat a particular herb that helps regulate my system and prevents me from conceiving. I'd have to stop eating the herb for a few weeks in order for the effect to wear off."

She stood as she spoke, hiking her skirts up as she moved into position. She straddled his legs again and her intent was clear. Oh boy, was it ever clear.

Hugh's hands went to her hips and stopped her forward progress as she stood over him, her skirts around her waist and her thighs spread over his. It was probably an awkward position for her, but he wouldn't let her fall. He wanted a moment to savor her and be certain she was as ready for this as he was.

One hand stayed around her hips, steadying her, while his other hand moved to the juncture of her pretty thighs. His fingers searched for and found the little nub that made her squirm. He watched as her thighs trembled and her mouth opened in enjoyment. He played with her clit a few moments before delving deeper.

She was so wet. He liked how responsive she was to him. He liked it a lot.

Hugh slid one finger inside her narrow sheath and enjoyed the way her breathing hitched. He added a second finger to be absolutely certain she was ready to take him, pumping his fingers into her for a few moments, heightening her pleasure. Once he was inside her, he wouldn't last long. He needed to make sure she felt the same.

Hugh's fingers inside her felt wonderful to Lera, but she wanted more. She wanted his cock. And she wanted it now.

"Please, Hugh, don't make me wait," she whispered. She was so close to losing all control and she wanted his cock inside her when she did.

His fingers left her and his hand guided her downward as he finally gave her what she wanted so desperately. She sank onto his hardness by slow degrees, holding his molten gaze as they became one. The fire in his eyes singed her senses as she felt her magic rising to twine with his.

Their union was of more than just bodies. It was a joining of souls and the magic contained therein. It was a thing of beauty she had never before experienced and feared she never would again without Hugh. He was fast becoming the center of her existence. It was a frightening thought. It was also an exciting thought.

When she held him fully within her body she sat for a moment, enjoying the connection. He seemed to want to take a minute to savor the feeling as well.

"I love the way you feel around me, Lera. Like your body was made to fit mine."

"Like you're the key to my lock," she joked, squeezing her inner muscles a tiny bit around him. He really was the most perfect fit.

"You're skilled at torture, milady," Hugh gasped with a

smile as he pulsed lightly up into her.

"Not torture. Pleasure," she whispered in his ear as she began to move in subtle, slow pulses.

Wanting more, she sat up and used her legs as leverage to help her ride him, taking him deep then shallow, deep then shallow. His hands at her hips helped her move, his impressive strength lifting and releasing her as they worked together to climb higher.

Within moments it was all too much. He powered up into her as she did her best to keep control over her movements, but it was a losing battle. A battle she didn't want to win. For on the other side lay ecstasy and she wanted that more than control.

Hugh pumped in short, fast digs into her willing body, driving her higher with each movement. She whimpered when her body seized in the most amazing contractions of rapture. She came around him and a moment later she felt the warm jets of his come inside her body.

Things became even more slippery after that, both of them riding through the bliss together, joined as one.

"I love what you do to me, Lera," Hugh whispered near her ear as things began to calm down.

They were both breathing hard and the cool air wafted across her neck, making her aware of the perspiration that formed a light sheen on her skin. How she longed for a bath, but she was on the run from assassins. Such luxuries would have to wait until she was back home and safe from the threat—if they managed to accomplish that feat. Right now, she wasn't feeling very positive about their chances.

With Sendra against her, there was no telling who remained loyal and who had turned traitor. Sendra might not have the throne, but she had wealth. Vast quantities of wealth amassed over the decades, first by her family, and then by her varied business interests. She was a shrewd woman who was known to be both cutthroat in business and generous to those who helped her achieve her goals.

Lera knew that enough money could tempt many to put aside their principles. Lera would have to tread carefully if and when they returned to the city. She had no real notion of who she could trust outside of a very few.

"I didn't hurt you, did I?" Hugh asked in a worried tone, drawing back to look at her face.

She smiled lazily at him. "No, you didn't hurt me. How could you even ask that?" Her voice was pitched low and sounded a little raspy to her own ears.

"Then what puts that look on your lovely face?"

"Just worrying about things," she said, rising off him, separating their bodies while her skirts slid down to hide the evidence of their joining. He tucked himself back into his worn leather pants and buttoned the fly.

"Things?" Hugh prompted, moving to his pack and taking out a cloth, which he handed to her without comment. "Like going back to the city?"

Lera accepted the soft cloth and ran it up her leg, under her skirts, capturing the trickle of come that had begun to leak out of her. Hugh handed her his water flask and she used the contents to wash up as best she could.

"Sendra has a lot of money. She could use it to turn people against me," she confided.

"I don't doubt she has tried that tack already. A few have probably taken her up on it, but there are good people in every land. And you have me. My loyalty is to you, Lera. And my brother, of course, but in this situation, it's definitely with you. Roland wouldn't want to be allies with someone who sent assassins after their own cousin."

"Politics sometimes makes strange bedfellows," she reminded him.

"Not in Draconia. And especially not with Roland. We've had enough of treachery to last ten lifetimes. Rol won't deal with someone he knows is a snake in the grass. It's not worth his time to weigh every word and action. Truth is truth and honor is honor. There is no way to deal with someone who doesn't understand these simple concepts."

"I think I'm going to like your brother Roland."

"Not as much as you like me, though," he warned playfully, grabbing her around the waist and pulling her close for a kiss. "I saw you first."

Chapter Seven

Just before dark, Miss woke, stretching her sleepy wings and body. She'd used her fuzzy wings a lot more than she was used to that day and they were no doubt sore. Hugh went over to her and rubbed her muscles.

"Are you all right, sweetheart?"

"Yess, Hoo. Wingss hurt."

"I bet. You gave them a good workout before, flying down those dunes. But wasn't it fun?"

"Fun!" she agreed readily. "Want fly more."

"I'm sure you do. And you will. Later. For now, you need to build up your wing muscles every day and soon you'll be soaring over the land. I promise."

The gryphlet trotted beside him as he walked toward the doorway to the barn, where Lera waited.

"I want you to wait here with Lera while I scout ahead."

"Are you sure that's wise?" Lera asked, concern in her voice.

"I want to know what we're flying into."

"Good point." She didn't look happy about it, but he read the acceptance in her expression.

"I won't be long and I've already checked around here. There's nobody in this wasteland. We'd see them approaching from long distances in this flat place. And I can be back here in a heartbeat if you need me." He took her hand. "All you have to do is call out. Use your magic if you have to—that same probe you tried to use when we first met—I'll feel it and I'll fly back to you. But I honestly don't think you'll have any problem here for the short time I'll be gone."

"I trust your judgment." She leaned up and kissed his cheek.

Hugh felt like he'd won a great prize. Her trust and her open affection meant the world to him. It didn't seem possible after only knowing her such a short time. Still, he had recognized a connection between them almost from the first moment they met. Adversarial as that initial meeting had been, he couldn't deny he'd been attracted to her from the instant he saw her.

"I'll be back before you know it. Just stay here and keep to the barn, out of sight. Miss will protect you." They shared a smile at the idea of the baby being Lera's guard.

They both knew Miss was brave enough, and she had already played a key role in allowing them to escape that second set of assassins, but she was so small and…fuzzy. Sitting at their feet, licking her paws, she didn't seem nearly as ferocious as she had already proven herself to be.

Hugh leaned in and gave Lera a proper kiss. He'd be back quickly, but even the short parting tugged at his heart. Again he marveled at how close their bond had become in so short a time.

"Sit tight. I'll be back before you know it."

Hugh let her go and walked into the waning sun toward the top of the nearby hill. He felt the pull of Lera on his heart. The connection was so strong, it felt like a string tied between them, stretching as he left her, but not breaking. It felt a lot more comfortable than he would have expected.

Hugh hadn't ever expected to find the woman meant for him, regardless of the success of his brothers' relationships with their new wives. He'd been happy for Roland and Nico. Even the twins, Darius and Connor, had found a beautiful, otherworldly woman to share their lives with. He'd seen their joy in their wives and been glad they'd found such happiness, but somehow he'd doubted there could be a woman out there for him.

And now, he'd found her. In this foreign land. In a desperate run for her life. In danger.

Hugh renewed his vow to protect her with his very life. He wouldn't let anything happen to her. If she were hurt, Hugh knew his own heart would break.

He moved quickly up the hill, using some of his dragon strength and speed to move much more rapidly than they had earlier in the day. He wanted to get this mission over as fast as possible and get back to Lera and the baby.

He paused as he approached the crest of the hill. He had to be cautious because he wasn't sure what he'd find when he popped his head over the top of that hill. He crouched low to the ground, ready for anything.

What he found was something he hadn't expected.

Gryphons filled the skies. Everywhere he looked, gryphons flew in formations easily recognizable as search patterns to Hugh. Others circled higher above, operating independent of the more organized wings.

Hugh ducked down behind the hilltop. Something major was going on in, and over, the city. He wouldn't be able to sneak in quietly by air. At least not easily. He'd have to fly at heights that would be a challenge both to him and his passengers, but it might still be possible. He'd have to think this through and consult with Lera on possible landing sites. And there was always an approach from over the water. That might be the best way...to come in after full dark.

Hugh hightailed it down the slope, heading back toward the barn at top speed. Gryphons had the eyesight of their raptor precursors. It was possible, even at such a distance, that he might've been spotted.

Damn. He hadn't expected this complication, but he guessed he should have. Lera was the Doge, after all. Somebody had noticed she was missing and had called for a search of the city. Whether those running the search parties were good or bad, he had no way of knowing. If she were found by the searchers, it was all too possible she would be delivered into the hands of the same faction that had contracted for her death at the hands of assassins.

The only way Hugh could be certain she would remain safe and alive, was if he was the one guarding her. She had to go back to the city, but if Hugh had anything to say about it, she wouldn't be leaving his sight until the threat was nullified.

Hugh stretched his senses, on full alert as he approached the barn. He was almost to the entrance and could see Lera waiting there with the child when he heard the sound he'd been fearing.

Wing beats. Feathered wings at that. Very large feathered wings.

He spun on the sand to find a lone gryphon bearing down on them. Too late to do anything else, Hugh shifted shape to his dragon form, blocking the entrance to the barn as best he could.

"Wait!" Lera's voice called out from behind him, but Hugh couldn't let her interfere.

The gryphon wasn't slowing. In fact, he'd started a dive and was gaining speed. Hugh guessed those razor sharp talons would flash at him as the gryphon pulled up just short of the ground.

Nice maneuver.

Only Hugh wouldn't let the gryphon's fancy flying succeed. Hugh had a natural defense that gryphons feared.

He let out a breath of flame, aiming it up toward the sky. A warning shot across the gryphon's projected flight path. Hugh was gratified to see the beast swerve away from the flame, altering his path away from the barn.

The adult gryphon was clearly a warrior. He landed with a grace and speed that Hugh had to admire. He came to rest a few yards distant, out of what the gryphon was probably guessing was the reach of Hugh's flame. The feathers around his neck and head ruffled in what Hugh thought looked like either a show of bravado or annoyance. Either way, the bird looked like he meant business.

"Releasse her," the gryphon ordered in a booming voice.

Hugh wasn't going to shift shape in order to speak aloud to the gryphon. Protecting Lera and the child was his first priority and he could do that best in dragon form.

"It's all right!" Lera shouted from behind Hugh. "Hyadror! Stand down! This dragon is protecting me, not holding me prisoner."

"Then he will not mind sstepping asside." The gryphon's beak cocked in a superior way that demanded compliance. His words were only slightly hindered by the beak, causing his S's to slur in a slightly different way than Miss's, but he was perfectly understandable.

Too bad he'd apparently never met a dragon before. Hugh would not back down. Not when Lera's life was at stake.

"Hugh, please, step aside so I can explain to him."

"It could mean your life if he is not trustworthy," Hugh reminded her in the privacy of their minds.

"It's Hyadror, the one I told you about. I *do* trust him. With my life."

Hugh recalled the name from their earlier conversation. He wasn't thrilled with the idea of trusting someone he didn't personally know, but he'd have to take Lera's word for it. They needed an ally in this mess. Perhaps this gryphon would be the one.

"Are you sure?" Hugh heard the desperation in his own words. He couldn't help it. She was precious to him.

"Positive."

"All right then. Proceed slowly and stay near me. Do not go to him. I cannot protect you adequately if you are too far out of my reach." Hugh steeled himself and retracted his left wing, allowing the gryphon to see Lera, standing just behind him.

"Hyadror, this dragon saved my life twice yesterday. Sendra

sent Eyes to kill me. Tell me what's been happening in the city."

"We found the Eyess, though Ssendra did a neat job of disstancing hersself from the two found in her vineyard. Ssloppy work, that." Hyadror still looked suspicious to Hugh's trained eye. "I organized a ssearch. All wingss are ssweeping the city, even now. And the guard iss out looking too. Now where have you been, milady? With thiss dragon, I ssuppose."

"He is much more than just a dragon."

Hugh liked the tone of her voice when she said that. It felt like she was staking a claim and for the first time in his life, he didn't mind. He wanted her claiming him. Just as he wanted to claim her for all to hear.

Hugh felt the unexpected tickle of feathers against his wing as Miss slid out from under his protection to look at the adult gryphon. Hugh knew the exact moment that eagle-eyed gaze noticed the misborn baby.

"And who iss thiss?" Hyadror asked and Hugh was relieved to note the mild tone of his voice when he saw the child.

"Miss," she answered as if the adult gryphon had asked her directly. "Sseen you before," she went on. "Nicer than papa."

Hugh was stunned. In the days they'd been together Miss had never volunteered any information about her origins. She'd refused to answer when gently questioned about her parents and Hugh thought it wiser to leave the subject alone rather than upset her while she was recovering from being on the streets by herself.

"Who iss your papa, little one?" Hyadror asked gently.

"Mean," was all she said in reply to that very pointed question. Miss backed up, huddling under Hugh's wing, only her small head peeping out from under. "Want Hoo."

"Who?" Hyadror looked around, clearly puzzled, and Hugh let out a smoky chuckle.

He couldn't help it. His name and the gryphlet's pronunciation issues with it had become something of a comedy over the past few days.

"Hugh," Lera clarified, smiling too. "My dragon's name is Hugh."

Oh, he liked that. He was *her* dragon. He could live with that. Easily. For the rest of his life.

"Hugh?" The gryphon's gaze returned to him. "Can your kind not speak?"

"We can speak." Hugh sent the thought toward the gryphon experimentally. *"But not with our snouts."*

Hyadror's beak clicked shut, then open again. "I can hear you, dragon Hugh."

"Forgive my overabundance of caution, but my lady is in danger. She trusts you. I am more wary, but I trust her judgment—to a point."

"I have sserved Valeria and her family for three generationss. I would not ssully my honor now." Hyadror seemed both insulted and proud of his service.

Hugh noted the fading color in the dark gryphon's feathers and the streaks of white in his fur. He was definitely an older soul, and judging by his scars, a battle-tested one. They could do much worse than to have a creature such as him on their side in this mess.

Making his decision, Hugh shifted shape in the blink of an eye, standing before the gryphon in his human form.

To his credit, the gryphon didn't jump, though his eyes widened, giving away his surprise.

"You are a sshapsshifter?" he asked, unable to hide at least that much of his shock. His tone held a hint of alarm, if Hugh judged correctly.

Hugh bowed his head, but didn't break eye contact. "I am half human, half dragon."

"Wizard kisssed, no doubt," Hyadror concluded with a clack of his beak. He seemed to be taking the revelation well.

"My kind is descended from Draneth the Wise," Hugh agreed.

129

"He who made the dragonss." Hyadror obviously knew his history.

"As the wizard Gryffid made your kind."

"Praisse the maker'ss name."

Hugh wondered what this old, battle-scarred gryphon would make of the news that Gryffid was still alive. Now wasn't the time, though. The most important things right now were Lera and the child.

"You sseem to know gryphonss," Hyadror continued, nodding toward Miss, who cuddled against Hugh's leg.

"There are a few nesting above Castleton. I've flown with them a few times."

"Sstrange gryphonss. Iss it true they are from a new flock? One we have not heard from before?"

"I believe so," Hugh answered cautiously. It was up to his brother Roland whether or not to allow more gryphons into Draconian skies. Hugh had to tread carefully. "There is a young pair who have been granted leave to immigrate to Draconia. They mated before their parents were ready to let them go. Hard feelings caused them to seek a new land in which to nest." All three were listening intently, so he decided it was worth telling them more. "They arrived with both sets of parents and sought the permission of our king to make their nest above the capitol city."

"Your king agreed, I sssuppossse."

"He did. The parents were glad to see their youngsters forging new bonds in a new land. And it's been interesting flying with them. Feathers catch wind differently than scales."

"Fassscinating. I would like to hear more of these sstrange gryphonss ssometime." The older gryphon paused for a moment, then turned his attention back to Lera. "Milady, you sshould return to the city."

"We'd already decided to do so," Lera answered him. "Only we hadn't decided exactly how. I thought Sendra's home was safe until we met the Eyes waiting there for me."

"Sshe iss no friend to you, milady. I have told you thiss before."

"I'm sorry I didn't believe you. I feel like such a fool." Lera's voice cracked, and Hugh put one arm around her shoulders, offering comfort. The gryphon stared markedly, but did not comment.

"We can easily fly back to the city tonight. I was waiting for full dark to fall." Hugh gestured toward the darkening sky. It was sunset and the sky was a glorious golden orange.

"I am happy to give you a ride, milady," Hyadror offered.

"Thanks, but..."

Hugh cut in before Lera could answer. "She rides with me. That's the only way I can be certain she's safe."

Hyadror looked suspiciously from Lera to him and back again. "What iss going on here?"

"We are bonded," Hugh said simply, hoping Lera would not deny what he knew to be true.

"Iss thiss true?" Hyadror demanded of Lera.

"It is. Hugh of Draconia is my mate."

Damn. Hugh was proud of the fact that there was no hesitation in her voice. He let out a breath, unaware until that moment that he'd been holding it, anticipating her reply.

"A dragon?" Hyadror backed up a pace as if in denial. This news, finally, had pierced his steely demeanor.

The gryphon and all his feathery friends were going to have a lot to get used to now that Hugh had finally found his mate. He would not leave her and he knew in his heart, though they'd yet to discuss details, that Lera would not leave her people for any length of time. He was merely third in line for a throne he was happy enough to let his brother keep. Lera was the Doge. She held power and needed—for the sake of her land and people—to hold on to it.

It would be Hugh's duty, honor and privilege to help her do just that. First on his agenda was getting rid of the Eyes who were most likely still hunting her. After that, he'd see what needed doing and get to it. On that list somewhere was getting the gryphons of Helios used to seeing a black dragon in their sky.

He might also be the conduit through which they reconnected with their maker, Gryffid. Hugh had a feeling the renewed contact with the last of the wizards and his creatures was one of the reasons Roland had sent him here in the first place. Sooner or later, the gryphons of Helios would find out that Gryffid was still alive and they'd have to fly over Draconia to get to his secluded, magical Isle. Better they do it as friends than as potential enemies.

Hence Roland's interest in renewing ties with this distant land. And it was probably also why he'd agreed to Shanya's belief that it had to be Hugh that was sent here, not one of the other dragon princes or even one of Nico's many spies.

Then there was the whole House of Alagar issue. The last surviving member of the hereditary rulers of the city was a woman named Lucia who had recently married two dragon knights. From what Lera had said, it was believed the House of Alagar was extinct. Hugh didn't know Lucy all that well, but she did have a legitimate claim to leadership of this city if she wanted to return to the land of her birth someday.

The ties between Draconia and Helios were becoming more and more complex. One thing was certain—Hugh would be in the thick of it now that he had found his perfect mate in the Doge of Helios.

"You'd better get used to me, Hyadror. I'm not leaving." Hugh spoke no more than the simple truth.

Hyadror's ruffled feathers started to relax as he stood there, watching them, his beak agape. Miss picked that moment to flap her little wings, catching a tiny bit of air. The whooshing sound seemed to break the spell and Hyadror walked slowly forward, pausing about three yards in front of Hugh and Lera.

The gryphon bowed on one foreleg, showing his acceptance.

Miss, oddly enough, mirrored the elder gryphon's gesture gracefully.

Lera stepped forward and Hugh let her go, despite his desire to keep her close, within his hold. He knew there would be times when she would have to act as Doge. This felt like one of them.

Lera touched Hyadror's bowed head as if in benediction and spoke softly, though Hugh easily heard what she said.

"Hugh can withstand my flame, my friend. I have never met any man who could do that before. It's not just because he's half dragon. He is the mate to my soul. His fire twines with my own...as one."

Hugh felt a little arrow of joy pierce his heart at her words. He could not have put it better himself. He had felt the same thing when they joined, but he hadn't known how to describe it. Not in words. No wonder she was the statesman of their pairing. She could be very eloquent when she wished to be.

He was the warrior in their bond. He would protect her with his life, if necessary. They were a perfect match of skills and abilities that would deepen and grow with time. He just had to make sure they had the lifetime together that fate tempted them with. If they could just get through this crisis and nullify the threat of the Eyes, Hugh knew they could make this work despite his being a dragon in a land chock full of gryphons.

Starting with this one. He had to win Hyadror over. He'd be the first of many. Hugh thought he had a good chance of impressing the aged warrior. Hugh had dealt with old dragons and old soldiers before. He thought he knew how to approach the gryphon. Proving his worth by deed and not word was most likely the way to go.

"I accept your wissdom." Hugh thought he heard an unspoken *for now* on the end of that statement, but he wasn't worried. Hyadror was giving him a chance to prove himself. That's all he needed.

Lera stepped back and the older gryphon rose from his

bow. As did Miss.

"I don't ssupposse you fly yet, little one," Hyadror addressed Miss with a kindly tone.

"I fly," she said proudly, then withdrew her bravado. "A little," she admitted, shyly ducking her head.

"I can carry her," Hugh said gently. "Miss will be a natural flyer when she's grown," Hugh added, hoping to build up the child's self-esteem. He'd have to work on that with her. She'd been so ill-treated until he'd found her.

"There will be an uproar when the otherss ssee milady with you," Hyadror warned Hugh.

"I figured as much. But if you fly with us, hopefully they'll question first before trying to shoot me down."

Hyadror nodded once. "I will do my besst. It will be eassier, I think, if we make a ssteep approach, but I do not want to rissk your passsengerss."

"I know what I can handle—and what they can. Will you follow my lead in the dive?"

"I sshall. I take it we aim for the palace?"

"Is it safe? We tried to go there yesterday and even I could tell there was something wrong." Lera spoke the question for both of them.

Hyadror's eyelids dropped lower and his feathers ruffled, very easily conveying his annoyance. Hugh was learning how to read feathered faces the more he was around gryphons.

"I have taken thosse ressponssible to tassk. Ssomeone lured the duty gryphonss away from their posstss and Eyess murdered the guardss. North Wing disscovered thiss and killed the Eyess. My wing took over all duty at the palace and the guilty gryphonss are being held pending your return."

That sounded promising. If it was true. Lera trusted this gryphon and Hugh was willing to give him a chance. They were taking a chance going back to the palace, but it was good that Hyadror admitted to a problem yesterday. If he'd denied it all,

Hugh would have been much more concerned. As it was, Hyadror was still being given the benefit of the doubt.

It was getting dark, night creeping in like an ink stain on the sky.

"It is almost time to fly," Hugh observed. "We'll try for the palace, but if anything looks wrong, we'll divert to the roof of the large temple I noticed while flying over the first time. It looked like a defensible position and I assume Lera could find help there." He'd given some thought to this but hadn't gotten a chance to discuss it with Lera before now.

"The temple is actually a much better choice," she confirmed. "I doubt anyone there would be in league with Sendra. As Keeper, I hold rank among the priests who live there."

"Only priests? No women?" Hugh asked.

"Warrior priesstss," Hyadror added.

"The high temple is the training center for the Order of Light. They protect and serve the eternal flame."

"And you are the Keeper of the eternal flame," Hugh observed. This was sounding better and better. "Are they bound to protect you as well?"

"Yes."

"And you suspect no treachery in their ranks?"

"It would be impossible for several reasons but mostly because they are tested by the flame. No one of evil intent can withstand it."

Hugh would have to take that on faith for now, but if things went sour again he could at least fly her out—dodging gryphons all the way—but he had fire in his belly that singed them badly. He had confidence in his ability to fight his way free with her on his back.

It was dark enough now. They could fly at any time, his dark dragon hide would conceal them against the inky black sky.

"All right. We'll make for the temple. Hyadror, can you run interference for us?"

"My wing will come at my call. We will ssurround you in flight. Do not be alarmed when you ssee them closse in."

"Hyadror is one of the four senior wing leaders," she explained. "Actually, he's the eldest and most skilled. All the other gryphons will follow his orders."

"They sshould, milady," Hyadror added. "Of late, though, thingss have not been asss they sshould have been. Now I undersstand ssome of it."

"And we'll learn the rest when we get to the temple," she agreed.

Hugh liked the conviction in her tone. She was fearless, this woman fate had chosen for him.

Hyadror stood watching while Hugh shifted shape. Those keen eagle eyes missed nothing as Lera and the gryphlet mounted. By unspoken agreement, they launched into the air at the same time.

In only a few wing beats they were over the hill and Hugh puffed smoke when he saw the hoard of gryphons turn almost as one and head toward them. Hyadror went ahead to meet them, calling out to his brethren.

All slowed to listen except one group led by a large, dark gray gryphon. They came far too close for Hugh's comfort, angling in from a side vector, going around Hyadror and the others.

"Hang on, Lera. I'm going to climb higher," he warned, putting on some speed as he propelled them into the clouds.

As he went, Hugh released a shot of flame across the pursuing gryphons' flight path, close enough to let them know that Hugh would not be taken down easily.

Hyadror seemed to notice the flame and winged back to intercept the gray gryphon. Hugh was done messing around. He stayed in the clouds as much as possible, noting the rest of the gryphons were not pursuing, merely guarding. They'd followed

Hyadror's instructions. Belatedly, so had the wing of gryphons led by the gray one.

Hyadror led the way, flying just below Hugh and his precious burden, all the way to the temple. It was a harrowing ride over the city, but Hugh saw the temple, built close to the palace, but without the wide battlements. There was a small flat roof near the central dome. Hugh would land there. It was the only place that made any sense. All the other roofs in the complex were too steeply pitched or domed in a way that made landing on them much too slippery a prospect. From a tactical point of view, Hugh found that interesting.

Could it be that the Order of Light didn't welcome the gryphons of this land within their walls? It sure looked like they'd built their complex to defend against them. Except for that one small landing area. If gryphons intended to visit the temple complex, they'd have only one real choice for landing, and the priests controlled it.

Hugh could easily see a group of humans keeping watch up there, but no gryphons. In fact, there wouldn't be much room for more than a few winged creatures to land there at once, which suited him just fine. He would accept Hyadror's presence, but few others. Particularly not that dark gray beast who kept giving Hugh the evil eye.

Hyadror landed first to warn the humans guarding the temple roof, Hugh following close behind. Swords were brandished and the moment was tense until the guards got a look at Lera, hopping down off Hugh's back.

Miss bounded off and ran to hide under an awning that had been set up on one side of the flat roof. It looked like a windbreak where guards could rest away from the rains that had hit the city in the past week. Miss was shaking in what looked to Hugh like sheer terror.

"Go after her. Something's very wrong," Lera said as the warrior priests formed a protective circle around them at Hyadror's direction.

"Are you sure it's safe?"

"Hyadror is here and you will only be a few steps away. I need to talk to them anyway. To prepare the way. Take care of Miss. Please. She's terrified."

Hugh didn't like splitting his attention between the two females, but he had no choice. He could see Lera was right. He took quick stock of the warrior priests and all looked ready to defend Lera with their lives. Hyadror was also staying near to her and Hugh doubted the old bird would let anyone through who meant her harm. Quickly, Hugh followed Miss, moving into the shadows of the awning. He had to shift shape to fit down under the tables where she'd hidden.

A few of the warrior monks might possibly have seen him shift, but he couldn't be too choosy about it at the moment. There might be no way to hide his dual nature in this land after such a grand entrance. He hoped his brothers wouldn't be too upset with him for betraying the family secret to such a large number of beings—gryphon and human alike.

But Miss's behavior had him worried. She refused to come out and was shaking so hard, the table she hid under vibrated. A quick look outside told him Lera was still surrounded by warrior priests and well guarded by Hyadror. They were asking questions and listening to her explanations and orders.

He'd heard her order the priests to give Hugh a wide berth and they followed her instructions, leaving him and the baby gryphon alone inside the tent-like structure.

"Sweetheart, what's wrong?" he crooned to the baby, holding out his hand to her, hoping to coax her toward him. She was huddled as far back into a corner under a wooden table as she could squeeze her little body.

Miss refused to answer, shaking like a leaf and cowering in a way Hugh had never seen. She'd been frightened before, but this was much more alarming. She wouldn't even talk to him. It was like she'd withdrawn to the smallest corner she could find and was trying to hide from everything, Hugh included.

Keeper of the Flame

"Dear little Miss, did the big gryphons scare you? You have to know I would never let anyone hurt you. I'd flame anyone who even thought about laying a finger on you. You know I can. You saw it," he coaxed, glad to see her little head lift slightly and her slitted eyes open to gaze at him. "I would burn any creature that tried to hurt you. You're under my protection now. Do you understand what that means?" Her little head jerked to the side and she was still shivering, but at least she was listening to him. "It means I will keep you safe. Always. I put your life and safety before my own."

Her eyes widened. "Really?" she whispered.

"Truly. It's a matter of honor. You are very important to me, sweetheart." He held out his arms to her. "Won't you come over here? I will keep you safe, as I have before."

"Don't want to be sseen," she whispered, still shivering.

"By the men?"

She shook her head. "From above." Her voice pitched even lower as she crouched under the table.

"You don't want the big gryphons to see you?" Hugh thought that was significant, but he wouldn't push her any further at the moment. It was important to get his females together in the same place so he could keep an eye on both of them.

She nodded shyly but said nothing.

"I will keep you under cover. I'll shift back to dragon form and you can stay under my wing. Nothing will see you from above. Is that all right?"

"You hide me?"

"Yes, sweetheart. I'll hide you. None of those big gryphons will see you. Only Hyadror, and he already knows about you. I'll tell him not to mention you to anyone else, all right? You can stay hidden as long as you like."

"Nobody ssee me? Promisse?" She edged one paw out from under her, toward him.

"I promise. Nobody will see you from above. All they will see is me and none of them can hurt my scaled hide. If they come too near, I'll toast their feathers."

She crept out, moving a bit closer to him. He wanted to reach out and hug her, but she had to come to him. He would not use his strength and size against her. He had to build and keep her trust.

"Iss it really ssafe?" She looked hesitant, but hopeful.

"I will make it so, sweetheart. I will keep my wings slightly unfurled at my sides. All you have to do is stay underneath until we get inside. Lera is talking to them now and she will get us inside quickly. All you have to do is stay under my wing until we get there. I will shield you. I promise."

She crept a bit closer. She was still trembling, but less so. Hugh was glad. He really wanted to get back to Lera. She trusted these priests, but he hadn't had much chance to take their measure for himself. He had sworn to protect both females. The easiest way to do that would be to keep them together. If only Miss could be convinced.

"I go wif you, if you're ssure."

"I'm sure. Do you trust me, sweetheart?"

She thought about it for a moment, her furry head tilting to one side.

"Trusst Hoo," she answered finally, stepping closer to him, placing her head under his outstretched hand. He stroked her fondly, glad when her shivering dissipated under his touch as he fed a little tendril of magical energy and reassurance to her.

He turned around so he could see Lera and formulated a plan.

"I'm going to the edge of the awning where I will shift shape. I'll extend my wing and I want you to walk under it. We'll walk out from under the awning together, understand sweetheart?"

"Yess, Hoo." She trotted behind him, using his legs as a shield as he neared the edge of the awning.

As soon as he had enough room to shift, he did so, not allowing the gryphons above to see it. Only a few of the priests were paying attention to the shadows under the awning. Mostly because it looked like they were guarding Lera *from* him.

Good for them. They couldn't know what sort of threat a dragon in their midst might represent. It boded well that they had surrounded Lera and looked to be protecting her from all comers.

"We're coming out, Lera," he sent to her privately. "Miss is scared of being seen by the gryphons above. She will be hiding under my wing. Can you get us inside, away from the circling hoard above? Warn the priests to make way. I'm coming through."

He shifted shape under cover of the awning, making sure Miss was securely under his left wing as he moved back into view from above. The gryphons were still circling. A few had landed on nearby roofs, but Hugh knew their vantage point was poor. They would not be able to see Miss, even with those sharp eagle and hawk eyes. The secret of her presence was safe for now.

"Hoo?" He could just hear her uncertain mewl beneath his wing.

"It's all right. I'm here. Nobody can see you. Just stay with me and it will be all right. I promise. We're almost to Lera's side. She will make them take us inside where you cannot be seen from above. Trust me, sweetheart. You're doing fine."

The warrior priests made room for him to pass between their ranks with the gryphlet hidden beneath his wing. He arrived at Lera's side in time to hear her request entrance into the temple for herself and her party, which consisted of Hyadror, Hugh and the baby gryphon nobody could see from above.

There was a doorway large enough for Hugh to pass through in dragon form. Hyadror went first, followed by Lera and then Hugh, shielding Miss as she scampered through. He

141

watched the youngster cling to Lera's side, glad his two female charges were together. They could help each other should they run into trouble inside the warrior priests' temple.

Hugh looked around as the door shut behind him. Most of the priests had stayed behind on the roof and the door had been shut at Lera's order. There was an honor guard of priests flanking them on a wide stone ramp that spiraled downward. It was made of pure white marble and was ornamented in gold here and there, with lamps lit along the walls at intervals.

At the very bottom, down the center of the spiraling ramp, Hugh saw a bright point. A fire burned at the base of the tower, but oddly, no smoke or soot soiled the pure white walls. And the place reeked of magic. Its flavor was at once familiar and foreign, but it didn't feel threatening, so Hugh let it go for the moment. Still, something was definitely odd about that fire down at the center of the tower.

"Thiss iss the gryphonss entrance to the temple," Hyadror told him, noting the direction of his gaze. "It iss big enough for you, Ssir Hugh."

"The ramp leads down into the courtyard. It's the only way a gryphon can enter the temple grounds by air. There's also the main gate," Lera added. "That's big enough for a gryphon to walk through, but most prefer to fly, if and when they have business with the temple."

"Few of my kind come here," Hyadror said as he began the walk downward on the spiraling ramp. "Mosst fear the flame."

Hugh followed, keeping to his dragon form for now. He could shift in an instant should it become necessary. Lera and the child would come to no harm while he was around.

Chapter Eight

Lera was glad to be inside the temple grounds. Nothing could hurt her here. It was her place of power, even more than the palace. The loyalty of the priests could not be questioned. Each had been tested by the flame and found to be pure of heart. Only if the flame had forsaken her would they ever turn against her.

And the flame was still strong in her heart. Being with Hugh had only strengthened it, in fact.

"When we reach the floor of the tower, the flame will test you, Hugh. Do not be alarmed."

"When has a dragon ever been afraid of a little fire?" he replied with a humorous edge to his thoughts.

Hugh didn't really understand what he was in for, but Lera knew he could handle it. As could Miss. She would be frightened, of course, but Lera kept her hand on the baby's soft fur as she trotted between herself and the wall. Lera wouldn't expose her to the flame until the last possible moment. Miss was scared enough as it was. But she had to walk the gauntlet of the flame, like any other gryphon who sought entrance to the temple grounds.

"Hyadror, when we reach the bottom, will you guide the little one?"

"Of coursse, milady. Sshe will have no problem. Sshe iss pure of heart."

"I think so too. But something has her frightened. She will need all our reassurance."

"Asss you wissh." The gryphon bowed his head slightly in respect as he led the way downward.

When they reached the bottom of the ramp, their honor guard of priests went ahead, spreading out to ring the circular chamber. There were no windows and only one door large enough for a single gryphon to pass through at a time.

The flame greeted her as it always had, leaping and bounding with iridescent tendrils of magical power. When Miss saw it, she cowered back, afraid. Lera stayed with her, allowing Hyadror to go first.

As Lera expected, the old gryphon passed around the half circle of the chamber, heading for the door, allowing the central flame to examine him. It sent out tendrils that never quite touched his feathers or fur, retracting before they could cause any harm, but taking stock of the purity of his great heart. For such was the consciousness of the eternal flame. It could see into a being's true nature and it judged harshly should it see any sort of contagion within, burning from the inside outward.

It could singe or it could decimate. The flame alone knew what was required in each case brought before it. No being was allowed on the temple grounds without undergoing this test. The flame that burned here was only a small part of the eternal fire the priests kept alive in many parts of the temple complex.

Miss shivered against Lera's legs as she watched Hyadror face the flame. He turned when he was more than halfway to the door and looked at the little one.

"You ssee, child? There iss nothing to fear if your heart iss pure." Hyadror dared the flame, spreading his wings in silent salute as he continued around the room to wait by the closed door.

"Iss my heart pure?" Miss asked, looking from Lera to Hugh and back again in clear distress. Her eyes were wide and her whole body trembled.

Hugh bent his head to her level, blowing warm air over her in comfort. *"Yours is the purest heart I have met in many a year, my dear. You have nothing to fear from the Lady's fire."* Lera could hear the words Hugh sent to Miss. *"Is that not right,* milady?"

"Hugh is right. As Hyadror said, you have nothing to fear from the eternal flame." Lera tried to inject confidence and faith into her tone.

"I'll go with you, sweetheart," Hugh offered, stepping forward. Lera was touched by the tender tone of his voice in her mind. He was so loving with the child. If she'd had any doubt about the goodness of his heart, she had only to watch him with Miss to know he was as straight as an arrow and would fly as true.

He led the way, allowing Miss to go as fast or slowly as she wanted. He kept himself between her and the flame. Lera knew how little protection even a dragon would be for anyone of ill intent, but Miss didn't realize it.

The flame licked out with its pink, gold and orange iridescent tendrils, touching Hugh's scales. It hadn't touched Hyadror, but when the dragon paused before it, the fire embraced him. For a moment, his entire body was engulfed in a magical phosphorescence that all within the chamber viewed with awe, Lera included.

And then it was over. The tendrils stopped short of Miss's feathers and fur, though they gave her a close examination as well. Wafting around her and over her, under her belly and through her legs. Delicate wisps of flame that never burned, only touched the very surface without causing one bit of harm.

She made a mewling sound. The whimpers of distress turned to sounds of joy as Hugh turned to watch the child bat at the little wisps that seemed to play with her for a short moment. Her paws struck out, claws hidden, trying to touch the elusive tendrils.

"Tickless," she said, enchanting a smile from even the most hardened of the priests in the chamber.

"It likes you," Lera proclaimed, somewhat surprised by the playfulness of the eternal flame in the child's presence.

"See? That wasn't so bad, was it?" Hugh's voice was warm

in Lera's mind as he spoke to Miss.

"Fire hurt before," Miss said, her head tilted to one side, clearly perplexed.

Lera looked at Hugh. Little puffs of smoke came from his nostrils as he chuckled.

"That was ordinary fire. The eternal flame is very special, Miss," Lera explained. "Very magical and sacred to the Lady we all serve."

Lera walked toward the fire, glad to be in its presence as Miss scampered back to Hugh's side. She raised her arms, greeting the flame and taking it within herself. All was well. The eternal fire welcomed her as it had always done. She was still its chosen. Being with Hugh hadn't changed her so much that the flame no longer wanted her.

She felt empowered by the flame. Fleeing for her life had put Lera in a position she'd seldom been in during her privileged life. Hugh had saved her and taught her about real passion, but the feelings of vulnerability persisted. Her cousin wanted her dead. The most expensive—and successful—assassins that money could buy were following her, lying in wait, anticipating her every move.

Hugh had foiled them and taken her away from danger for a precious few hours. But sooner or later, the threat had to be faced. She was back in the city to do just that. Like it or not, things would be coming to a head soon. On her terms, hopefully, this time.

Leaving the tower and walking into the courtyard, which was covered by a leafy trellis, hiding them from above, Lera and her party found the High Priest and his Council of Elders waiting for them. They greeted Hyadror first, with a respectful bow for his age and station. Lera walked with Miss. Hugh guarded them from the rear. Lera noted the widening of the High Priest's eyes when he saw the dragon, even though she knew he had to have known by now that the black dragon had brought her to his temple tower. The priests had efficient ways of passing information among their number. Even Lera didn't know the extent of their magics.

"Greetings, milady. We are relieved to see you well." High Priest Gregor greeted her with concern in his eyes.

"Father Gregor, may I introduce Hugh of Draconia and his ward, Miss." Lera kept to the formalities while they were standing in the middle of the courtyard, in full view of anyone who could possibly see or hear them. She trusted the priesthood in general and had even more respect for the elders and High Priest, but there were always a few brothers-in-training around who had not yet been fully embraced by the flame.

She'd never questioned their presence before. Then again, she'd never had the most fearsome assassins in the land set on her trail before. Bitter experience of the past few days made her leery of anyone and everyone.

"The flame has welcomed you, Hugh of Draconia and young Miss. Be welcome in our temple and among our brethren."

Miss bowed on her forelegs, her manners impeccable, as usual. Lera had to wonder again where she'd learned such dainty ways, but the child had so far refused to discuss much about her origins.

Hugh bowed his head, holding eye contact like most warriors she'd seen. He did not initiate telepathic communication and she wasn't sure he'd show his human form to these warriors, which left her unsure how to proceed.

"I invite you to the main audience hall. It should be big enough for our flying friends," Gregor said, neatly taking the problem out of her hands.

"I would request only that you limit the meeting to you and your Council, Father Gregor. I trust you, but I have reason to doubt all others until proven otherwise." She tried to phrase her request politely. She may be the Doge and the Keeper of the Flame, but the warrior priests of the Order of Light operated under their own aegis for the most part. They were autonomous

147

and dealt with transgressions within their own order separately, away from the justice system she administered either as Doge or as Keeper.

Gregor frowned but nodded. "I heard about the bodies in your cousin's orchard."

"Eyes, Father. She set Eyes on me." Lera's voice broke with emotion. She'd had some time to let the fact of her cousin Sendra's betrayal sink in, but it still hurt. Badly.

Gregor sighed as some of the elders in the Council shook their heads in disapproval of Sendra's actions.

"Your cousin is missing, milady. Our brethren have been assisting the Guard, looking for her trail with no luck."

"Thank you for trying, Father. Much as it pains me, she must be brought to justice."

"We agree," Father Gregor said, including the elders that surrounded him in his statement as they nodded in agreement. "Let us go indoors where we may sit and make plans."

"Thank you." Lera almost collapsed in relief. She had feared somehow the priesthood might have turned against her. Or they could have denied her assistance. They often kept to themselves and did not choose to interfere in secular matters. She had been hoping they would help her but couldn't fully count on it until she saw Father Gregor in person.

Judging from his responses and tone, he would give as much help as she could wish for. Lera's heart lightened as they stepped toward the main audience hall. Once again, Hyadror led the way. Miss scampered under Hugh's wing when they came out from under the arbor and were exposed to the sky and the gryphons who still circled above in agitated spirals.

The giant arched doorway to the main hall was open and large enough to fit both gryphon and dragon. They proceeded through in the same order—Hyadror taking point, Lera in the middle and then Hugh acting as rear guard. She had never felt safer. The priests fanned out and the elders and High Priest took seats around a long table that had been set to one side in the large chamber.

Place settings and platters of food were already on the table and an area behind held pillows enough for both gryphons and the dragon. Lera wondered if Hugh would stay in his dragon form. She would have liked to have him seated at her side, but it was his secret to share.

"If you can get the younger priests out of here, I will shift form. I believe these elders and Gregor can be trusted after what I learned from your flame."

Hugh's thoughts came to her, as if in answer. She wondered what his first experience of the eternal flame had told him. She was curious to know what he'd learned from it. Sometimes—in very special circumstances—the flame communicated with those it touched. She assumed, from his words, that Hugh had experienced something like that. It meant a great deal that the flame had chosen to converse with him. A great deal, indeed.

"Father, can we be private? Just the elders and yourself? There are many things I wish to discuss with you, but I am hesitant to do so in front of others." Lera looked at the priests stationed all around the large hall. They didn't shift their stance but Lera could tell they were probably surprised and a little suspicious of her request. "The flame has already tested my companions. They mean no harm within your walls. Isn't that so?" She turned to the non-human shapes gathering behind her as she took her seat at the table.

"I have no quarrel with the priessthood," Hyadror confirmed. He turned to Miss, prodding her gently with the tip of one long feather.

"I won't hurt anybody," she said softly, as if afraid of the large audience in front of her. She was adorably shy, which went a long way toward putting the rest of the room at ease about her.

It was the dragon the younger priests eyed with distrust. Hugh stretched his long neck as if allowing them to study his form—especially the spikes along his neck and the scales that shone a gleaming black all along his body.

"Do you agree to withhold your fire, Hugh?" Lera asked him directly.

"For you, I'd do just about anything, my dear," he answered in her mind. His teasing tone made her warm inside. He then made a great show of nodding his scaled head for benefit of the priests.

"I am satisfied," Gregor said, nodding as well. "Brothers? What say you?" He looked to the elders for their agreement.

The elders agreed readily and the lower ranking priests were ordered to leave. When the last one had cleared the area, one of the elders sealed the doors, going from portal to portal, erecting a barrier of magical flame around the edges. Lera had seen it only once before and was satisfied they would not be disturbed or overheard.

When he was finished, he returned to his place at the table. Lera turned, sensing Hugh was gathering his magic.

Sure enough, he'd gone from dragon to human as the priests watched in amazement.

"What is this?" Father Gregor asked, standing in shock from his chair.

"Father, as you just witnessed, Hugh is a shapeshifter. He is half dragon and half man, as you have just seen for yourself."

"And I would appreciate it if that fact remained a secret among ourselves. There are those who would hunt my kind if our existence was widely known. There are very few of us as it is."

Gregor resumed his seat. "I had wondered how a dragon could enter unseen into our city."

Hugh dipped his head in acknowledgment. "I did not reveal my dragon form until the threat to Lera was imminent."

"You saved her from the Eyes." Gregor seemed to put everything together.

"More than once," Lera said, touching Hugh's arm as he took a seat at her side.

"You had best start at the beginning of your tale," one of the elders put in. "We will not be overheard or spied upon in any way with the flame guarding us." The man who spoke was the same one who had erected the magical wards around the doors.

"I'm impressed, elder," Hugh addressed the man. "I've never seen such casual use of magic."

"Says one who can change from dragon to man and back again," the elder replied dryly. The smile on his crinkled face was friendly enough and Hugh responded in kind, Lera was glad to see.

"Point taken, sir. Perhaps I should say, I have never seen *your* kind of magic before. As I said, it is very impressive."

"As is yours," Gregor added. "How do you come by it?"

"I was born this way. My line is descended of Draneth the Wise. It was he who made a pact with the dragons and humans of Draconia long ago to allow him, and his descendants, to rule over both races by being part of each." Lera wondered about that verb he used—to rule. Was he more than just a soldier?

"A clever and interesting solution." Gregor seemed to think about the ramifications of the wizard's bold move so long ago. "It is no wonder they called him wise."

"Why were you in Helios? Had you come to spy on us?" the elder asked pointedly.

Hugh shook his head. "Sadly, I must admit, I came here to learn the true feelings of your people and government toward Draconia."

"We have long been allied with that distant land. Nothing has changed as far as we have heard," Gregor answered.

"That is what I have observed, to my gratification. We'd heard rumors in my land that made us doubt the old alliance, but that's something we can address further after the threat to Lera is neutralized." Hugh brought the focus neatly back to her problem, Lera was glad to see.

The political stuff was something to be handled later between herself, her council and the kingdom of Draconia. The priests need not be involved. Where she did need their help was in stopping the Eyes her cousin had hired. They might also extend themselves to help apprehend her cousin. In fact, they were working on that already, since Gregor told her they'd been assisting the Guard looking for Sendra.

"How did you come to be in the company of our Doge?" the elder asked of Hugh.

"I guess the sequence of events started when Miss came to me." Hugh motioned to the child, patting the wide seat of the cushioned chair next to him. It was just large enough for her to perch on and she hopped up and settled her wings while Hugh scratched behind her ears. "I took her back to the inn where I'd been staying to weather that last big storm. I believe the innkeeper sent his son to report Miss's circumstances to the Doge and Lera arrived shortly thereafter to check on her."

Lera nodded. "That's exactly how it happened. I went to the inn to take custody of the child, but Hugh wanted to be sure she would be safe with me. I stayed there longer than I expected to and alert neighbors sent word to the innkeeper that Eyes were seen on the street. The innkeeper delivered the warning and Hugh agreed to protect me. We went up to the roof and that's when I discovered Hugh's secret. He shifted shape to protect me and flew me away from there."

She remembered those moments as she described them. She'd been so shocked by the dragon, yet so grateful for the fierce protector. Hugh had been the next best thing to a stranger, but he'd proven to be a man of honor and a warrior to be reckoned with. Looking back, she thought maybe that was when she'd started falling in love with him.

Hugh took up the story. "I tried to fly her to the palace, but we both saw right away that something was wrong there. Lera wanted to go to her cousin's home next, so I landed in the orchard, preferring to take an oblique approach. There were Eyes waiting in the orchard, as you know."

"Hugh dispatched them, with Miss's help. I was slightly injured, but Hugh healed me." Lera helped by pointing to the bloodstain she'd tried unsuccessfully to wash out of her bodice.

"After that, I was taking no more chances. I took Lera and Miss into the wasteland over the hills to regroup."

"We had just decided to head back when Hyadror intercepted us," Lera added, glossing over the time they'd spent alone together. Her personal life wasn't really any of their business. As long as the flame accepted her—and Hugh—the priesthood couldn't say anything about it.

"The resst you know," Hyadror added from his seat in the cushions behind the table.

"We came straight here," Lera added. "I wasn't sure if the palace was safe."

"Until Sendra is caught and the Eyes are called off, you're better off here," Gregor stated.

"Thank you, Father Gregor. I'd hoped you would say that."

"We convened our Council last week," Gregor admitted. "Portents led some of our number to believe a nexus approached. I believe this is it. Especially since meeting your new friends." He nodded toward Hugh and Miss. "Things have been changing in the surrounding lands—not necessarily for the better. It was only a matter of time before Helios could no longer avoid becoming involved." Gregor turned his sharp gaze to Hugh. "What can you tell us of the Citadel?"

Lera was shocked. There appeared to be a much deeper game being played here than simply—though there was nothing *simple* about it—the threat to her life. She looked at Hugh, noting the momentary surprise cross his features before he suppressed it.

"That is something we have been learning about in my land. Apparently the last of the wizards were imprisoned in the far north, in a place called the Citadel. Certain forces have been working toward releasing them. King Lucan of Skithdron was working with both the barbarian horde in the north and the witch, Loralie, who has been aiding them. We've discovered Lucan was behind multiple murders and kidnappings in our land over many years."

A moment of silence greeted his revelations. Lera was the first to speak.

"Is this firsthand knowledge or merely rumor?" she asked.

"Knowledge from myself and my family." Hugh's expression seemed resigned and she didn't quite understand why.

"Who is your family?" Gregor asked, though she kept her focus on Hugh. Something was up. His tension level had risen more than a little.

"I am third in line for the throne," he admitted. "My eldest brother Roland sent me on this mission, with advice from Nico."

"The Prince of Spies," Lera whispered. Hugh's sharp look made her shake off her surprise. "Even in Helios, Prince Nico's reputation is known."

Hugh smiled. "As you can probably tell, I am nothing like Nico."

Lera chuckled with him and touched his cheek. "Lucky for me, you're more honorable warrior than spy."

The moment was almost intimate as she gazed into his eyes. Only when one of the elders coughed did she realize they weren't quite alone. She removed her hand, but Hugh caught it on the way down, interlacing his fingers with hers as he held her hand under the table.

"Prince Hugh." Gregor addressed him and nodded in respect. "Thank you for saving our Doge's life."

"It was my honor and pleasure, Father Gregor."

Lera would talk to him later about hiding the fact that he was not only noble, but also royal. It didn't matter to her if he'd been the commoner she'd thought, but he had to know from personal experience that his being royal would be both helpful and create difficulties in their relationship being accepted by her people and her court. Of course, that was if they *had* a relationship. She wasn't sure what the future would hold at this point.

"It becomes clearer why you don't want your ability to change shape widely known," the elder put in shrewdly, bringing her back to the matter at hand. "I assume your brothers are the same as you."

"It is a gift of the royal family alone. Only those of us descended from Draneth the Wise have the possibility of shifting," Hugh confirmed.

"It is not guaranteed?" the elder pressed.

"Forgive me, but there are some things I cannot divulge. Suffice to say, the ability does not always pass down to every member of the family." Hugh was firm but respectful, striking just the right tone with the nosy elder, Lera thought.

"What is being done to find Sendra? Tell me what happened on this end while I've been away," Lera asked.

"As I mentioned, we have been asked to assist in locating her. When you went missing, the entire Guard, all the gryphon wings and most of the novitiate were alerted. The palace tracked your movements to the inn and heard the tale of Eyes on the street, the child and the stranger who had promised to protect you." Gregor's gaze went from Miss to Hugh and back to Lera. "No one could understand how you'd made it off the roof, though of course, now that is clear." He nodded in Hugh's direction.

"They thought it was something supernatural? Is that how the temple became involved?" Lera guessed.

"Exactly so. The Guard asked us to allow our novitiates to join some of their search parties to look out for signs of magic. Sendra's was one of the first places they searched. She was already gone." Gregor's raised eyebrow spoke volumes. "They went over her estate and found the bodies in the orchard. One of our young brothers was with the group that found them. Two master assassins—we discovered later by counting their tattoos." Gregor looked at Hugh with respect. "We feared the worst, but I knew that if those two were dead, you had to have help. Good, able help. I went to the scene myself and noticed small paw prints in the soil, so I knew at least part of the story the innkeeper told was true. I didn't know what to make of the giant claw marks. Not all of them looked like gryphon tracks."

"Did you actually see gryphon tracks near the site?" Hugh asked, leaning forward slightly.

"I did. And oddly enough, some of them were over what I know now were the dragon's footprints."

"Well, you said the gryphon wings had been out searching for me," Lera said, searching for some kind of explanation.

"True, but none had been in Sendra's orchard before the Guard got there and any who came after were directed specifically not to land in the orchard."

"One of uss wass there after the attack, but before the official ssearch," Hyadror concluded, sitting up on his front paws. He looked angry to Lera's knowing eye.

"It couldn't have been soon after, or they would have followed us over the hill," Hugh said quickly.

"But why would any gryphon not report the bodiess?" Hyadror asked.

"Good question. They were in plain sight. Judging by the paw prints I saw, the gryphon got very close to them. Close enough to examine. Yet the bodies remained where they'd fallen until the Guard found them," Gregor supplied.

Silence fell as everyone considered what that meant.

"At least one of the gryphons is working with Sendra," Lera said with a sinking heart.

Hugh's arm came around her and she leaned on him. She didn't care that Father Gregor and the elders saw her moment of weakness. The idea that one of the gryphons had betrayed her—that one of them wanted her dead—was almost more than she could bear. As Keeper of the Flame, she was responsible for them in so many different ways. She thought they liked her. That they respected her. That they were loyal to her. It was hard to conceive even one of their number being willing to help those who were trying to kill her.

Hyadror was conspicuously silent. Lera hoped his tongue was stilled by shock. She dared not look to see his expression. Gryphonic faces were hard to read, but she had come to understand the subtle shifts of their feathers and angles of their heads over time. She couldn't bear to see if he had been expecting something like this.

Suddenly there was a pounding on the main door to the great hall. Bounded by magical flame, the sound was muffled, but distinct in the silence. Father Gregor grumbled and signaled to the elder who had posted the magical barriers.

Lera belatedly remembered the old man's name. Seldom seen in public, she'd met him when she had first been blessed by the flame. He'd overseen her initiation, but always from afar. His name, she recalled, was Edon. He was something of a hermit who lived a secluded life here in the temple. She hadn't realized until now just how conversant with the flame's magic he was.

He took down the ward with a wave of his hand and opened the door. Gregor had followed him and his voice carried easily across the hall as he chastised the young priest who had disturbed them.

"But Father, you have to come," the man protested and Lera could easily see he'd been through some kind of shock. His face was pale and his hands shook.

She straightened away from Hugh's warm shoulder and stood. She noted Hugh stood as she did, as did many of the elders. Something was clearly wrong.

"What is it?" Gregor demanded.

"Something stirs in the cauldron. You must come."

Lera started in surprise. The cauldron was the source of the eternal flame in the main part of the temple. She knew it well. It was where she'd first encountered the flame that had changed her life so greatly, but she hadn't been to the cauldron chamber since the last high holiday. Seven times a year she performed ceremonies in that sacred space.

Gregor turned to look directly at Lera. "We all must go." His words fell like blows on the hard polished stone of the hall floor. Lera felt the seriousness of his pronouncement and knew in her heart, he was right. If the flame had chosen this moment to become active in some heretofore unknown way, it had to be significant.

Lera moved first, Hugh at her side. Predictably, Miss followed her guardian and Hyadror took up the rear guard position as they walked with the elders, moving quickly out of the great hall. The cauldron chamber was nearby, at the heart of the temple building. The great hall had been built onto the central structure, which meant they only had to traverse a long corridor to get to the sacred cauldron.

They made an odd-looking parade as they headed for the chamber. Priests lined the hall, scooting out of the way as they passed, then closing in behind the gryphon to follow the group. Everyone seemed to want to know what was happening in the cauldron chamber—one of the most sacred places in the temple.

The elders arrived first and arrayed themselves around the chamber to allow room for Lera and her party. Hugh escorted her, standing side by side with her as they faced the deep stone pit from which the flame shone in pink, purple, orange and gold glory. It shimmered against the polished stone that picked up its coloration, bathing the room in a golden shimmer.

Lera stepped forward, to within a few feet of the gold-rimmed bowl. There was no discernable source for the flame's combustion and indeed, the priests never fed the fire. It burned magically by the grace of the goddess the priests served. It was Her light. Her power. Her flame.

As Lera was Her servant. Just like Gregor and all his

priests.

Lera sank to her knees, awed as always by the presence of the flame in this chamber. It was here that it burned brightest and largest. She stared into the heart of the flame and there definitely was something in there she had never seen before. Something...moving. Growing larger.

No wonder the brothers who always stood guard in this chamber had sent for the High Priest. Gregor knelt next to her on the curved, cushioned rail that circled the fire pit a few feet back from the actual golden rim that contained the cauldron.

"What iss it?" The big gryphon was terrible at whispering. Hyadror's question echoed in the chamber.

"A miracle," Edon stated.

The flame suddenly spiked, reaching upward to lick the high, arched ceiling of the chamber. The thing within it grew in proportion, as if it had waited until everyone had gathered before continuing its evolution.

Wings began to take shape within the tendrils of fire reaching toward the domed ceiling. Wings of flame fanned upward from the white-hot center of the sacred fire. Lera watched in fascination as it grew to unheard of proportions, the thing in its center becoming larger.

Hugh was behind her, guarding her back. She could feel his tension and knew he thought to protect her. He did not realize the flame—or anything it contained—would never hurt her. If the one she served had turned against her, Lera would have known it when they'd arrived and walked near the testing fire. She'd been welcomed by it then. She knew whatever was happening now, it would not hurt her.

The form took shape quickly, the wingtips flaring with licks of flame toward the roof as the body moved forward out of the cauldron. Paws touched the golden rim, followed by a furry face bathed in glistening flame that did not burn. The front paws moved out of the fire pit and were followed by a cat's face, then body. The wings emerged from the flame after that, followed by the hindquarters and two more cat-shaped paws.

It was a gryphon, but not a normal one.

"Sshe'ss like me," Miss whispered, more successfully than Hyadror.

The cat-faced gryphon looked at the child and a purr erupted from its chest that sounded like the roar of a conflagration. Her fur was white, bathed in orange, pink and golden flame at the moment. The feathers of her wings might be white as well, though they shone more orange than her body. Perhaps they would prove more colorful when they were free of the flame's influence. Lera was eager to know more about the goddess's servant.

For there was no doubt in her mind that this strange gryphon had been sent by the goddess Herself. Why the Lady had chosen to act in this way at this time, Lera didn't know, but she assumed she was about to find out.

"Welcome, Lady." Lera spoke to the gryphon and the spirit that shone in her eyes.

"Valeria." The white gryphon spoke Lera's full name as her sparkling gaze settled on her. "We are glad you have not perished."

Lera knew then that the gryphon was inhabited—at least for the moment—by the spirit of the Lady she served. Whether it would continue to be so had yet to be learned. For the time being, Lera and all in the chamber were being granted an audience with the goddess Herself. A rare and momentous event.

"Dearest Lady, ask what You will of us. We are Yours to command." Gregor, it seemed, could see the Lady's presence in the cat's eyes as well.

"Gregor of Helios, you have been a good and faithful servant. You have done well in aiding Valeria and her mate." Unlike the gryphons and even Miss, this winged cat had no problem speaking clearly. Everything about her was different than Lera had grown to expect.

One thing she was coming to understand more fully. It looked like she was destined to rule over interesting times for her land, upheavals for her many subjects and seemingly, all kinds of unexpected goings on in the land of Helios.

Chapter Nine

Hugh felt many eyes in the room shift to focus on him. Both the priests and the goddess-possessed feline turned their attention to him. Hugh fought the urge to shift form to meet the creature at a more comparable size, but he couldn't leave Lera or the child unprotected, even for a moment. He needed to stay close to them, to protect them with the last breath in his body if necessary.

He didn't have a lot of experience with deities in physical form. This was a once in a lifetime sort of event and he wasn't sure how it would work out.

That She'd called him Lera's mate was a step in the right direction. They hadn't talked about their union much, but Hugh was there to stay. There would be no return to Draconia for him. Not without Lera. And he already knew she was as dedicated to her land as Roland was to Draconia. In order to be with Lera, Hugh would have to give up his homeland and stay in Helios. If they'd let him. He wouldn't give Lera up without a fight.

"Hugh of Draconia." The white gryphon addressed him directly, which he wasn't expecting. "Be welcome in Helios. Your family has served Me for many generations. I come to make it known in no uncertain terms that this land should remain allied in unity with yours. Evil has long been working against My desires. Draconia, Helios, and others must continue to oppose it. I will give you tools, but you must act and exercise your free will. For it is My desire that all beings be given choice. The evil you must oppose would take all choice from you."

"We will continue to fight against such evil, Dearest Lady," Hugh vowed. "My brothers and I are united in service to You, as we have been since Draneth the Wise."

"Draneth was one of the few wizards to gain My favor," the Lady replied. "Gryffid was another. You must send word to him. He may not like the alterations to his creations, but I will not interfere with evolution. I have given life to this one to help those who are evolving." The white gryphon seemed to indicate its own body, though the words undoubtedly came from the goddess temporarily inhabiting it. She turned her fiery gaze away from Hugh to look at the assembly, addressing them all. "She will protect and serve, as you all do. She will also aid with the gryphons. At least one among them, as you have already surmised, is a traitor."

Edon stepped forward. "Blessed Lady, we have kept faith with you as best we were able. No gryphon lives within these temple grounds, but we would be honored to have this one stay."

"Stay she shall," the goddess affirmed. "And she will bring others. Not all, but a few chosen others who will train with your brethren to fight the way the dragons in Hugh's land partner with knights. He will show you the way of it. The white gryphon will choose those of her kind worthy of such an honor. Hugh will choose the priests who have the right temperament for aerial battle. This task I give directly to you, Hugh of Draconia, mate to Valeria. Your brothers will see to Draconia. You are for Helios now. But I think you already knew that."

"It is my honor to serve You, Dearest Lady." Hugh bowed his head but did not lower his eyes. It was the proper way to show respect to this aspect of the goddess, come to Visit them in a warrior's body. "And yes, nothing will part me from Lera now. I will stay with her in Helios, if she will have me."

Lera gasped and turned to look at him. His heart leapt at the joy in her eyes.

"Of course I will. I love you, Hugh."

"As I love you." He declared his love boldly, not caring who heard him. They'd have to get used to the idea of Lera and him as a couple because he wasn't going away. Not ever.

"You have My blessing," the Lady said, through her surrogate. "You may wonder why I have taken such extraordinary measures." She addressed the group at large again. "The answer is simple. These are extraordinary times. Your world is at a crossroads. I have an interest in seeing things turn in the direction I wish. Yet I do not choose for you. As is My way."

"You are wise and just, Dearest Lady," Gregor intoned.

"And now I will leave you. I will not return in this form again, but I will leave this creature of My creation that you will have a reminder of Me."

"Thank you, Lady. We love and serve You, all the days of our lives." Hugh was impressed by Gregor's reverent tone. It almost looked as if the old man had the sparkle of tears in his eyes. And he wasn't the only one. Several of the elders were weeping openly at this unprecedented visitation.

The cat's face seemed to smile, turning her glowing eyes on each person in the room in turn.

"Your love and service are well appreciated. You are loved in return and your service is never taken for granted. Blessed be you all your days and be welcome in my hall when you move on to the next realm."

Everyone dropped to their knees to receive the Lady's blessing. The two gryphons bowed before Her and the fire increased, whirling around the circular chamber in a glistening golden whirlwind. The conflagration touched all but did not burn. It brought joy and strength to each person it touched, a blessing from the Lady they all served.

The light grew so bright everyone had to close their eyes against it until in a flash, it was gone. The Lady had left and only the white gryphon remained. She blinked her glistening purple eyes and dropped to her haunches, sitting in front of the cauldron and the fire that had returned to its usual size and intensity.

"I am the emissary." The cat spoke without the Lady's influence for the first time. Her voice was different—less robust, but still just as articulate. "Like you, I am simply another child of the goddess we all serve."

"Be welcome, emissary." Gregor spoke. He, of all the priests, looked the most recovered after their divine visit.

"Thank you. My name is Jalinar. The Lady gave me knowledge of your names and positions. Greetings, Father Gregor, Doge Valeria, Prince Hugh." She nodded to each person as she named them, then went on to name each of the elders and priests in the room. The list was long but she didn't hesitate. It was clear to Hugh that the goddess had given her creation a vast store of knowledge along with life.

The white gryphon turned last to the others of her kind. She addressed Hyadror as an equal, giving him the respect due his age and station and having it returned in kind. When it came time to greet Miss, the larger cat bent down to meet the little one's eyes.

"Hello, Miss." Her tone was non-threatening and almost...motherly, Hugh thought.

"Hi," Miss replied shyly. "You're pretty. Missborn, like me."

"You are not misborn, little one. The goddess does not make mistakes and She made me like this. Exactly how She wanted me to look. As you are exactly how you should look. Do not let anyone ever tell you there is something wrong with your appearance. You are a creature of the Lady and She loves you well. Or do you forget so soon Her words and blessings?"

"I don't forget," Miss said, ducking her head a bit, almost looking embarrassed.

"Fear not, little one. I am here now and no one will question the new breed of gryphon that has a mouth instead of a beak. No disrespect to you, Hyadror. There is room in the heavens for both kinds of gryphon and I have no doubt those with beaks will continue to be the majority of gryphon-kind. But there must be acceptance of those with differences. I am here to demonstrate the Lady's will in this matter."

"And a better repressentative I cannot imagine," Hyadror acknowledged formally.

"Thank you." The white gryphon preened. "Now, I must converse with the elders for a short while." Jalinar prowled forward on silent paws toward Gregor. "Father, if you would send word for all your order to convene in the great hall, it would make it easier to explain my presence once and let them get their gawking over with. There is much work to do."

Gregor laughed at her words and tone. "It shall be as you wish, milady." He motioned to a few of the younger priests and sent them to gather the others. The elders filed out of the chamber to oversee the gathering and bring order to the ranks.

"I will be with your shortly, Father." Jalinar's words were a clear dismissal, but Gregor took it well, leaving the chamber with only the gryphons, Hugh and Lera inside. Jalinar turned to address them once more. "Milady, I would like to meet with the others of my kind as soon as possible. For now, I would like your permission to take this little one under my wing. I know she is your charge, milady, and you, milord, have become her guardian. I would like to be a mentor of sorts until she finds her way."

"I have no objection," Lera said softly. "I imagine she could learn a great deal from you." Lera turned to Hugh and he valued the fact that she didn't try to speak for both of them. She was a woman used to being in charge. Hugh was a prince used to having his own say in all matters. It boded well for their future that she asked his opinion, as he valued hers.

"I have no objection, as long as it is what Miss wants." Hugh turned to the child, reaching out to scratch behind her ears affectionately. "Do you want to learn from Lady Jalinar, sweetheart? Since she is blessed of the goddess, there is no doubt she can be trusted."

Miss looked from the cat-faced gryphon to Hugh and Lera and back again. "I'd like to." She spoke in a timid voice. "But want be wif you too, Hoo."

He had to chuckle at the unintended rhyme. Miss was just so incredibly adorable sometimes. He bent his head to hers, going forehead to forehead, nose to nose with her.

"I want you to be with me too, little Miss. Did I ever tell you that in my land, in dragon families, all the adults parent all the children? That means the human knights and their ladies act as fathers and mothers to their dragon partner's offspring and vice versa. It is no stretch to my imagination to consider you my daughter, sweetheart. You are the daughter of my heart and nothing will ever change that. You are part of my family now. If you want to be, that is."

"I do! I do, Hoo!" Little paws walked up his chest until they rested on his shoulders. He embraced her furry little body as she hugged him, cementing the deal.

"Then I will formally adopt you according to the laws of this land, if such a thing is possible. If not, we'll do it under Draconian law, since I am still—and always will be—a prince of Draconia, no matter that I make my home in Helios now." He looked up at Lera, gratified to see her indulgent smile and the joy in her eyes. "We'll figure this all out later, when there's time. For now, know that you are loved and wanted, Miss. If you go with Lady Jalinar, that will not change. Lera and I will be here for you no matter what."

He hugged her for a moment more before letting her go.

"Well spoken, my prince," Jalinar complimented him. Hugh thought it interesting that she used his Draconian title. "The child must gain her rightful place in the world. The Lady has made this my task, but I would have taken it on regardless." Jalinar turned her attention to Miss, who had turned to face her. "You are well loved, little one. The Lady Herself saw you and decided on my form because of you. That is a high honor, one you will grow to be worthy of in time. Already, you have proven to have the heart of a lion and the courage of an eagle. An admirable combination. I will teach you how to best utilize your talents. It will be my honor."

The white gryphon stretched out her paw to the youngster, touching her small head gently and stroking downward over the striped fur. Miss not only allowed it, but moved into the almost human gesture of affection. Hugh knew how starved the child was for loving attention of any kind. It was good to see her bask in the approval of a gryphon. Especially one as special as the emissary.

"I must attend to the priesthood now," Jalinar said. "I fear this will take a while. I would like for Hyadror and Miss to be part of this presentation, since the priests are not accustomed to having our kind in their midst. Best get them used to it."

"The honor iss mine, milady," Hyadror intoned. He seemed to be a bit in awe of the newly made, magical gryphon.

Hugh got the idea that he and Lera weren't necessarily wanted at this gathering and they'd already had a long, eventful day. For the moment, Lera was safe within the walls of the temple.

"We will find a place to rest," Hugh decided.

"There's a small, private room just down the hall, where I usually prepare before ceremonies and rest afterwards," Lera put in. "We can go there. It's reserved for the Keeper's use and no one will disturb us." She took Hugh's hand and he marveled again at the warmth of her touch.

"Good." Jalinar's voice held the hint of a purr. "We will be busy for a few hours at least. I will watch over the little one for the night so you can rest easy. We will not leave the temple and I promise to keep her safe."

What better guardian could the child have than a creature created by the Lady Herself, Hugh thought. He need not worry about Miss tonight. She would be safe and well cared for.

"Thank you," Hugh said simply, meaning so much more than he could express. The creature seemed to understand.

They had left their hiding place on the sand flats just after dark. With all that had happened, it was well after dinnertime. Lera put her arm through Hugh's and accompanied him out into the hallway. The gryphons preceded them and kept walking down the longer hall toward where the priests were gathering.

The door Lera was aiming for was nearby. The Keeper's Quarters was a ceremonial place now, though when a Keeper not of the ruling house had occupied the position, they had actually lived in the temple. She only used the quarters on ceremonial days. It was actually a suite of rooms that had a bedchamber, private bathroom and sitting area. It also had a walk-in closet that held almost all of her ritual robes. She had another like it back in the palace that held her robes of state.

Luckily, she also kept some regular clothes—plain dresses and lounge wear—in the Keeper's Quarters for when she was too tired to go back to the palace after particularly long or strenuous events.

If they had to, she could stay here in these quarters, safe in the temple, until it was clear to go back to the palace. In a way, she liked the idea of staying here, in this sanctuary with Hugh for a while. When they got back to the palace, real life would start up again, meaning court functions, council meetings, petitions and a million other things she had to deal with as head of state.

She'd enjoyed the time away from those duties with Hugh—even with Eyes on her trail. She knew he would keep her safe, and being with him made her want to chuck all her responsibilities and just be a woman in love for a little while. Was that too much to ask?

"What makes you frown so?" Hugh whispered in her ear.

"I wish we didn't have to go back to the palace," she admitted in a small voice.

"We don't. Not yet at least. There's still the matter of the assassins to deal with. For now, you're safer here."

"I know," she admitted as they walked. "Is it wicked of me to be glad to be away from my responsibilities for a while?"

"No, my love." Hugh patted her hand. "Remember, I am a prince. I have never envied the burden that lies so heavily on my eldest brother's shoulders, but I do understand it. You don't have to bear it alone anymore. I'm here to lean on when you need to."

The thought made her pause in her steps. She turned toward him, realizing just how well he did understand what she faced for the first time. So much had been happening, it hadn't really registered fully before.

"Oh, Hugh. The Lady certainly knew what She was doing when She brought us together."

He dipped his head to kiss her. It was a tender salute of his lips that could have turned into something much hotter in an instant, but a throat cleared down the echoing hall and she remembered they were in a public thoroughfare—in the temple, no less. She had to at least try to be a little more circumspect.

Lera pressed her hands to his chest, enjoying the feel of his strong muscles under her fingers as she pushed back slightly. She broke the kiss, but spent a moment looking up into his eyes. They were such a lovely green. She could get lost in his gaze.

The throat cleared again and a chuckle followed. Lera thought she recognized the sound. Sure enough, when she looked down the short hallway to the Keeper's Quarters, she was pleased to see the old monk who kept the rooms in readiness for her standing outside the doorway. A smile lit her face as she turned to him, stepping out of Hugh's embrace.

"Hugh, come meet an old friend." She tugged his hand, leading the way with joy in her heart toward the small doorway.

Just seeing Brother Hubert's familiar face brought her immediate comfort in these troubled days. She let go of Hugh's arm to give the oldster a hug.

"Child, it is good to see you unharmed." His hug was that of a surrogate father. Indeed, it was Brother Hubert who had taught her to read and write when she was a child. He'd been her tutor for many years and had become a trusted friend.

"Brother Hubert, this is Prince Hugh of Draconia." She pulled back to make the introductions with an exuberant heart.

Hugh was the first to offer his hand in a greeting of equals. Lera liked that. She'd never held with formality among her inner circle of friends. Brother Hubert was one of the closest to her and she was glad Hugh treated him as such.

"It is an honor to meet you, Brother."

"The honor is mine, sire. The tales have spread quickly through the temple of how you saved my little Lera's life and brought her to safety. I am forever in your debt, as are all the people of Helios. Lera is the bright star that leads our land."

"I see that readily, Brother." Hugh's smile lit her insides as he gazed down at her.

Brother Hubert's smile widened. "Then it's true what they're saying? You have found your match?"

"Yes, Brother," Lera said, almost overcome with shyness. Brother Hubert's opinion of her chosen mate meant a great deal to her. "Hugh is very special to me. He is my heart's desire."

She looked up at Hugh again, almost getting lost in his gaze.

"Momentous events are taking place," Brother Hubert said with a good-natured chuckle. "The Lady sends an emissary and my little Lera brings a dragon to our temple. A dragon who disappears when Prince Hugh shows up." Brother Hubert winked. "Fear not, no one else has thought to question it yet, but be prepared, others will make the connection."

Hugh grimaced and shook his head, but she was glad to see he was taking the news well. The Lady had caused a lot more fanfare with Her visitation than anyone had expected and as a result, keeping Hugh's presence here low key was not going to happen.

"The Lady works in mysterious ways," Brother Hubert intoned. "Perhaps it was Her plan all along."

Her plan that Hugh not be able to hide his dual nature, Lera reasoned. Yes, that could very well be it. Perhaps it was time for all of the dragon princes to come out from the secrecy that had shrouded their existence to this point. Starting here and now with Hugh—and the remarkable, once-in-a-lifetime visitation by the Lady Herself.

Hugh seemed to agree. His expression was thoughtful.

"I think you have a point, Brother. The Lady has plans far deeper than we mere mortals can fathom. Or so I have always been told."

"When you get to be my age, you may see the truth of that statement is greater than we know." Brother Hubert opened the door to the Keeper's Chambers and entered first. "I have prepared your rooms and laid out clothing for you and your companion. I apologize in advance for the fit and quality of the spare clothing I procured for you, Prince Hugh. We are simple monks who do not wear finery."

"It's quite all right, Brother. I have always been more warrior than courtier. I prefer to live simply when I can. I will just be glad to have something clean to wear. We have been living rough the past day or so."

The words seemed to please Brother Hubert and his smile widened as he swept through the chamber. He opened the door to the bedchamber, the bathing room and the closet for Hugh's inspection.

Hugh motioned for her to stand in the middle of the sitting room while he searched every nook and cranny of the suite, looking for any possible danger. When he'd seen everything to his satisfaction, he returned to her. Of course, he'd never really taken his eyes off her, even while he searched the place. He took her safety very seriously, which made her feel cherished rather than insecure.

"I know you brought a small gryphon with you. I've ordered some nesting material brought in for her. It will be here shortly, though as you can imagine, everyone is in a tizzy after the

Lady's visit." A tear came to Brother Hubert's eye as he paused for a moment. "If I never live another day, I can die easy having heard our Dearest Lady's words with my own ears. I was one of the many who crowded in through the open doors to hear Her."

Lera touched Brother Hubert's arm. "It was an amazing experience, Brother. I'm glad you were there to see it."

"As am I." He patted her hand. "I go directly to order all those who witnessed anything this night to write it down for posterity as soon as possible. The last visitation from the Lady was over a century ago and as you know, Her words were recorded in many different ways depending on who was writing the account. I want to collect everyone's memories of Her words as soon as possible to create the most accurate record for those who come after. Who knows when She will visit us again?"

"Brother Hubert is the temple historian and a learned scholar," Lera explained to Hugh.

"If you have time, I would encourage you both to record your observations of the past days as soon as you can," Brother Hubert suggested.

"We will," Lera promised. "As soon as we have time."

"There is the matter of the assassins to deal with first, I'm afraid," Hugh reminded them.

"Of course." Brother Hubert's tone turned serious as he released Lera's hand. "You must have had a hard time of it these past days. I will leave you to rest, for I'm certain you will be in demand again all too soon." He moved toward the door to the outer hallway. "Once this door is barred, it is one of the most secure in the temple. I will also post a full priest outside in the hall. Ask him if you need anything. He will send someone to fetch whatever you want."

"You have thought of everything," Lera complimented the man as he turned to leave. "Thank you, Brother Hubert. You are a treasure."

"Anything for you, my dear." He smiled once more and left. Hugh bolted the door behind him.

And they were alone.

Hugh leaned back against the barred door, gazing at her, his broad shoulders relaxed for the first time in hours. He had to be exhausted after all he'd done for her that day.

"It's been one hell of a day."

"I know. Can you believe it?" Lera sank down onto the couch, glad to finally be at ease. It seemed like forever since she'd been able to relax, when it had only been a day or two. So much had happened in that small amount of time.

Hugh walked over to her and sat at her side, putting his arm around her shoulders and moving her close to his side. She snuggled happily, liking his warmth.

"My brothers will not be pleased that so many know our secret," he said finally, sighing heavily. It seemed she wasn't the only one nearly overwhelmed by all that had happened that day. "But if it is the Lady's will that our true nature is known, then who are we to argue?"

"It did seem like She had many purposes in what She's done here tonight. Sending an emissary has only been done once before and then it was a human—the first High Priest of this temple was said to have walked out of the flame, speaking for the Lady. But that was hundreds of years ago. Since then, She has spoken through the Keeper twice, but not for a very long time. And that she chose such a form..."

"Miss seems to inspire many of us to do extraordinary things. It will be interesting to hear what Gryffid makes of this."

"That is the second time you've said something that made it sound like the wizard was still alive." She turned in his arms to look at him. "As did the Lady, now that I recall. What's that all about?"

"Simple." Hugh shrugged. "Gryffid is indeed alive and well. Living on Gryphon Isle with an enclave of fair folk and many, many gryphons. My youngest brother spent a few years with him, learning. When he returned, he was no longer the youngest brother."

"How so?" She was puzzled by his words.

"Time passes differently on his island. Or, it did until recently. It is some kind of complex magic he worked to hide his existence for these many years. He slowed time on the island. Then, when he learned what was transpiring in the outside world from some of his folk who had left the island and returned with news, he reversed the spell. He had his people kidnap my brother Wil—which I am still not pleased about, though we got him back mostly unharmed, just older. While Wil was on the island, time had sped up so that he lived there for years while only weeks passed in our land. Wil disappeared as a youngster and returned a young warrior with excellent knowledge and skills taught him by both the wizard and his warriors."

"Amazing." She settled back in his arms. "The gryphons will be shocked at the news. They all revere Gryffid's memory. He is their maker and they praise his name often. To learn that he's still alive..." She trailed off as she thought through what that might mean to her charges. "There will be an uproar. Some of them will want to make pilgrimages to meet him, I'm sure. This is going to be big."

"I don't know what he's going to make of the emissary," Hugh said dryly. Up until I met Miss, I'd never seen a gryphon with a cat face. Are there many like her?"

"A few. They live in the palace. I keep a tower set aside especially for their needs. They are not well accepted by most of the other gryphons, so they've been living separate and not flying out with the warrior wings, though they have sharp skills. I've been working toward getting them better accepted for a while now, but there's been resistance in some quarters."

"There won't be after those birds get a load of the emissary."

"How can you tell for sure if the dragons in your land are loyal?" The idea that at least one of the gryphons was plotting her downfall made Lera wonder how the dragons of Draconia proved their loyalty.

"Well, fighting dragons partner with knights who have to be of pure heart, or else they don't get picked. The knight and dragon are joined mind to mind, heart to heart. If they're lucky, the two knights partnered with two dragons who are mates, find a woman to share their lives. Once the knights have claimed their wife, the dragons are free to be together and everyone settles down to the business of family life. It would be hard to hide evil intent unless every member of the family was in on it and that's too horrible to even think about." He pulled her legs across his lap, snuggling closer. "You're thinking about the gryphon who is working with Sendra, aren't you?"

"I can't believe one of them is working against me. I thought I could trust them all. The fact that this must have been going on for a while now, right under my nose, has me worried."

"Me as well," Hugh replied, stroking her arm in a soothing way. "Maybe that's another part of the reason the Lady came to us. That part about the priests partnering with gryphons sounded very ambitious to me. Particularly when I see this temple and how little contact the priests have with gryphons now. It would take an edict by the Lady to get them to work together. It probably won't be exactly the same as we have in Draconia, but if the priests are all tested by your flame, then they would act as a check on the gryphons they partner, and vice versa, I suppose."

"You're right. I wonder how the gryphons will take the news."

"A thought for another time." Hugh stood, lifting her with him in his arms. The man was impressively strong. "I think there's time for a bath and then bed. We will, no doubt, need our rest for what is to come on the morrow."

"I like the way you think." She looped her arms around his neck and tucked her head into the hollow of his shoulder as he moved them both into the large bathing chamber.

The sunken tub was already half full of water, much to her

surprise.

"I took the liberty of turning on the tap when I checked the room earlier." Hugh deposited her on the bench seat in front of the vanity mirror off to one side of the marble-tiled tub. She watched him kneel and dip his hand into the water. A moment later, steam rose from the pool. "Lukewarm, hot or very hot?" he asked, looking back over his shoulder at her. He was the most handsome, magical, magnificent man she had ever known.

And he was all hers. The Lady had said so, miraculous as that seemed now.

Lera smiled at him. "Hot sounds good."

He stood and disrobed slowly, holding her gaze. The way he moved made her mouth water and the intent in his eyes made her want to rub herself all over him. Now.

But he was moving slowly.

His magnificent chest was revealed as his shirt fell to the floor, then his hands went to his waist and the buckle of the belt that held up those black leather pants he wore so well. She wanted to help, but it was clear from the hot look in his eyes that he wanted her to stay put. From the way her knees felt, she wasn't sure she could stand even if she wanted to. He made her weak, and oh so strong. A paradox she would spend the rest of her life exploring, however long that proved to be.

He dropped his pants a few feet away from the steaming tub and walked toward her. The evidence of his arousal bobbed invitingly and she couldn't help but stare. He was a well-built man, in every possible way.

When he reached her, he knelt before her on one knee, taking her by surprise. His hands rose to her shoulders, pushing the sleeves of her gown downward. His fingers moved to work on the lacings that held her bodice and lingered to touch and caress her skin as he bared her from the waist up. He paused then, cupping her breasts as he looked into her eyes.

"I have looked all my life for you, never thinking I would be blessed enough to find you."

177

His words touched her deeply, bringing tears of joy to her eyes.

"I feel the same, Hugh. I never thought..."

"I know." One of his hands moved to cup her cheek, stroking gently as he moved closer. He touched his lips to hers and time seemed to stand still and drift away.

While his mouth conquered hers, his hands were busy releasing the ties that held her skirt. She kicked off her shoes and lifted when he coaxed her, so that her skirt and stockings flowed down her legs to bunch near the floor. His hands stroked after the fabric, flaring warmth wherever he touched.

She lifted her feet out of the pile of fabric, completely bare now as Hugh pushed her thighs apart and settled between them. She was completely open to him.

"Touch me, Hugh," she whispered as his lips released hers.

"Your wish is my command." He grinned as his hands swept over her tummy and downward to rub over the insides of her thighs.

They reversed course and moved upward until the palms of his warm hands rested just inside the apex of her thighs and his thumbs teased her folds, spreading and dipping within, sliding in the wet heat he found there. She couldn't help the sounds that came from her throat as his touch inflamed her senses.

"You like that, don't you?" The dark rumble of his voice fanned the flames. The whisper of his breath over the sensitive skin of her inner thighs made her squirm on the bench as his thumbs parted her outer lips and delved within. "Yes, I can see you do. What about this?" His words trailed off as his tongue reached out to lick over the tiny nub that yearned for his touch.

She moaned and he swirled his talented tongue around her clit, making her cry out until she climaxed hard and fast against his mouth. He rode her through the storm and she couldn't get enough of the scandalous sight of his head between her thighs.

When he lifted his head, he was smiling. His green eyes sparkled with humor and deviltry.

"I love the way you respond to me, Lera." He straightened, patting her curls as if in praise before he stood, picking her up easily in his arms once more.

He walked over to the sunken tub and stepped in, then lowered her gently into the heated water. The temperature was perfect against her skin and her body still thrummed with desire for more of his attention.

His cock was hard against her thigh as he sat with her in the tub. She had never appreciated before how large the tiled wonder was—big enough for two and then some. Of course, she'd never had anyone to share her bath with before Hugh.

She felt boneless after the quick orgasm he'd given her. Relaxed but still up for anything. Judging by the hard rod against her thigh, he was too.

Lera squeaked with delighted surprise when he lifted her up and spread her thighs, seating her on his erection with little further ado. She was ready and the heat of the warm water made it easier to take him. Her back was to him and his hands were slick with the water and a small amount of fragrant bath oil he must've added to it before he'd brought her into the room. It made her skin slippery as his hands roamed up her torso, cupping her breasts and playing with her nipples.

She pulsed gently on his hard cock as he teased her delicate buds, the warm oil causing a pleasant tingling sensation on her skin. The fragrance of the oil was wild and exotic.

"I love how you feel around me, Lera. How your tight walls caress me inside and squeeze me when you come." His words were harsh against her ear as his teeth bit down on her earlobe gently, but with enough force to make her squirm in pleasure.

She couldn't think straight with him inside her and his hands and the oil making her body seek an even higher peak than she'd already achieved. She began to move on him more forcefully, needing the friction, the feel of his hardness slamming home inside her as she neared the precipice.

"I love the little sounds you make and the way your skin feels against me," he growled as she increased her pace again. She was close now. Close to something earth shattering. Mind numbing. Life changing.

She grabbed onto his arms, needing to anchor herself to him in any way possible. She held his palms to her breasts and he squeezed, obliging her need for more stimulation. His teeth continued to tease her neck, biting more harshly as deep sounds erupted from his throat. She took that to mean he was as close as she was to coming apart at the seams.

One of her hands reached downward to balance on his thigh and her nails dug in, causing him to growl. The sound was like that of the dragon, only sexier, and it drove her over the edge. She screamed his name as she came, writhing on him and rising out of the water as his hips lifted under her. He came with a shout, uniting them in pleasure.

When it was all over, he slid them down in the water until only their heads rested on the tile rim of the tub. His fingers trailed lightly over her skin under the water.

"I love you, Lera. Most of all, I love *you*."

She realized then, the list of things he'd given her while they were making love had led up to this most important declaration of all.

"I love you too, Hugh. With all my heart."

Lera dozed against him as they lounged in the water. With his dragon nature, he could keep the water hot indefinitely, but he couldn't prevent her skin from wrinkling up from the excess moisture. He thought it was kind of cute. But then, he loved everything about her. Including, apparently, the way her fingers pruned up from too long in the bath.

Speaking of which, Hugh decided it was time to get dry and make use of that comfy-looking bed he'd seen in the other room. He didn't want to rouse her unless he had to. She'd been through a lot the past day or so, and it didn't seem like things would get easier until the assassins were stopped for good. Lera needed her sleep while she could get it. There was a lot on her agenda for tomorrow.

He lifted her in his arms and allowed the water to drip off as much as possible before stepping out of the tub. Large towels were laid out on a shelf and he snagged one for Lera, propping her on the bench while he dried her sultry skin.

As a testament to how tired she was, she didn't wake even while he rubbed the towel over her body. Giving his own skin a quick swipe, he used his dragon magic to warm the air around them a bit to accelerate the drying process and keep Lera comfortably warm.

After they were both dry, he lifted her in his arms again, walked into the bedroom and deposited her gently onto the fluffy mattress. Scooting in next to her and snuggling her into his arms, nothing had ever felt so perfect.

He fell asleep with that thought in his head and didn't know anything more until a bell chimed hours later.

Chapter Ten

Hugh blinked awake, wondering where the sound was coming from. It was then that he noticed the bronze bell hung near the high ceiling. A ribbon led from it through a small hole in the wall, into the other room. Hugh assumed it ended in the hallway outside the door. A tug on the bell pull that hung decoratively alongside the door, and visitors could announce their presence in a discrete way.

Lera woke the second time the bell rang. One of her dainty hands rubbed at her eyes. She was adorable when she woke from a sound sleep, bleary-eyed and confused for a moment before she remembered where they were and why she was sharing her bed with him. He saw the moment she remembered and loved the sudden shyness that was quickly overcome by a leap of fire in her gaze as she looked at him.

"Someone is at the door," she said unnecessarily.

"I gathered that." He couldn't help but be amused by her slow approach to waking up. "Shall I go see who it is?"

"Would you?" She looked relieved. "I'm not much of a morning person." She covered her mouth with her hand as she yawned, then stretched one arm above her head.

He could have stayed there, watching her, but the bell rang a third time. Whoever was at the door must *really* want to talk to them.

He dropped a kiss on her forehead as he left the bed, shrugging into the clean shirt and simple, cloth trousers Brother Hubert had left for him as he headed into the outer room. He sent out a tendril of his magic before opening the door, as a precaution, even within these temple walls. He

Keeper of the Flame

sensed a familiar presence on the other side. Brother Hubert had returned and Hugh's sensitive nose caught a whiff of bacon and eggs. The priest had brought breakfast with him.

Even armed with the knowledge of who waited, Hugh unbarred and opened the door cautiously. He could never be too careful with Lera's safety.

"Good morning, Brother Hubert," Hugh greeted the old man with a sincere smile. He sobered instantly when he saw the grave expression on the old priest's face. "What's amiss?"

"I bring breakfast and news. There is a party of dragons sighted approaching in the western sky. They should be over the city within the hour."

"Dragons? How many?" Hugh took the heavy tray laden with breakfast from the old man.

"At least two. And a strange gryphon as well. All have riders."

"Will they be allowed to land on the tower, where we came in last night?"

"Is it wise? Do you believe they can withstand inspection by the eternal flame?" Brother Hubert's eyes narrowed as if in worry.

"Yes, Brother. I have no doubts about any fighting dragon or their knight. As for the gryphons in the party, it will be up to them if they want to chance an encounter with the sacred fire."

"As you wish, sire. I will relay the message to guide them here. Hyadror is going out to meet them, but only awaited your instructions."

With that, Brother Hubert bowed slightly and left Hugh at the door, holding the tray.

Hugh would've liked to ask a few more questions, but no doubt time was of the essence. He kicked the door closed and used his elbow to lower the bar to lock it. Placing the tray on the low table in front of the couch, he went back into the bedroom to wake his lady.

By the time the dragon party was within sight of the temple tower, Hugh and Lera had eaten, dressed and were ready to greet them. They'd encountered Miss and the emissary in the hallway before leaving the temple to make their way to the tower. Miss bounded up to Hugh happily, full of energy and life. He was glad to see her so happy, but catching up with her about her activities since they'd parted the night before had to wait.

The emissary had taken the little one into another part of the temple that was being prepared for gryphons under her guidance while Hugh and Lera made a dash for the tower. They climbed the spiral ramp upward, reaching the roof in time to see the party approach in the distance.

Two dragons were flanked by at least two complete wings of gryphons acting as honor guard. Or maybe just *guards*. Hugh had no doubt the gryphons of Alagarithia were very suspicious of anything but their own ranks in the skies above their cities. Especially dragons.

"Do you know them?" Lera asked at his side.

Hugh smiled wide. "Oh, yes, I know them. And I believe you may know at least one of the knights now approaching. See that beautiful orange dragon? She is the Lady Jenet. That handsome bronze fellow flying at her side is Sir Nellin, partner to Sir Mace, one of the most steadfast and capable young knights I have ever known. We should be able to see the riders shortly...oh, now...that is interesting."

"What?" Lera sounded eager. Hugh supposed her eyesight probably wasn't as good as his. Being half dragon had many advantages, even while in human form.

"They're riding double." He couldn't quite recognize the people on the dragons' backs, but he began to suspect who the extras might be. "The lady is probably Krysta, wife to Jenet and Nellin's partners. And the other is male. I think..."

"*Hugh, is that you?*" The thought struck his mind from one

very familiar.

"Collin? Is your evil twin lurking around here somewhere?" Hugh broadcast his words to both minds he suspected would be nearby. The twins never went anywhere without each other.

"Nice to see you too, brother," answered a similar, but separate voice in his mind. It was his brother, Trey, Collin's twin. "Roland sent us to check up on you, and Nico figured you'd probably already blown the spy job anyway. Seems he was right. Good thing I didn't place a bet on it."

Hugh almost laughed out loud, but caught himself in time. "Nice of you to have such faith in me," Hugh answered dryly, enjoying the joke even though it was at his expense. It was obvious that out of all his brothers, he was the one least suited to spy work. "But where are you? I only see one of you riding on Nellin's back."

"I'm the one being choked by feathers," Trey answered.

Hugh looked sharply at the gryphon bringing up the rear of the party. Sure enough, there were two riders on its back as well. One was his brother. The other...

"Did you bring one of the fair folk with you?" Hugh could hardly believe it.

"You're quick," Trey teased. "He and this bird bring a message from Gryffid."

"So you didn't come just to check up on me." Hugh didn't bother asking it as a question. He knew the truth of the matter just from the make-up of the party. Things were about to get even more interesting than they'd been already.

The group was within landing distance of the tower, so Hugh made no further comment. He wondered what the priests and his new mate would make of the changes coming in on the wind. One thing Hugh knew for a certainty—he was glad to have trusted help to keep Lera safe. His brothers and the dragons and knights were all above suspicion and would aid him greatly in his quest to end the threat of the Eyes against his lady love.

Hugh watched them land, one by one, crowding into the small space on the tower's top. The two dragons and lone gryphon took up most of the space, forcing most of the priests to squeeze into positions along the crenellated wall. Hugh, Lera and the High Priest stood near the doorway into the tower, the greeting party.

Hugh waited only for his brothers to dismount before orchestrating this little tableau. He sent his thoughts out to the dragons, knights and his brothers all at once.

"Collin, Trey, I want you both to hold back. Drake, you should be first, since you've been to Helios before. Introduce the fair one and the gryphon, but leave the rest for later, if possible. I want to downplay the rest of you for a bit. Things are happening here that you need to be aware of. Let's just get you all into the tower and away from the circling hoard."

Once again, the gryphons of Alagarithia circled in agitation high above the tower. Hugh thanked the Mother of All that there was no room on the tower for more to land—and that gryphons had to run the gauntlet of the eternal flame if they wanted to enter the temple complex. At least one of those circling could have deadly intent where Lera was concerned. Hugh would take every advantage to keep that particular gryphon from getting close to her.

They arranged themselves as Hugh instructed, and within a minute, Drake led the party of two-legged beings forward, the fair one at his side. He made a great show of bowing and Hugh saw the little start of surprise, quickly concealed when Drake saw Lera. But true to his bard training, Drake of the Five Lands didn't miss a beat.

"Your Highness, it is so good to see your lovely face once again. It has been much too long since I visited your beautiful land," Drake said as he bowed somewhat flamboyantly.

"Drake?" Lera seemed truly shocked. "Drake of the Five Lands? Riding a dragon?" She looked from Drake to the fire-colored dragon and back again.

Drake made a show of his embarrassment, though Hugh knew for a fact the newly made knight would never be embarrassed of his dragon. Rather, he was probably still operating under some misapprehension that he wasn't good enough to partner the dragon. Such foolish thinking had already caused Drake to stay away from his homeland—and his dragon partner—for fifteen years. Now that they were truly united, he would never leave the dragon he'd been raised alongside ever again.

"Some remarkable things have happened to me in the recent past, milady. One of them is my partnership with Lady Jenet. She chose me as her knight and has forced a change in profession on me." Drake smiled as he said the words, his expression rueful and inviting others to grin with him as he reached up to stroke the dragon's cheek. Jenet had stretched her elegant neck upward so that her head hovered just above Drake's.

"A true loss for the musical world, but a gain for Draconia, I'm sure," Lera commented, seeming to regain her balance and better hide her surprise. Hugh marveled at her political skill. This woman he'd found was more adept at statecraft than he'd ever been.

"Please allow me to introduce my partner, the Lady Jenet," Drake added politely. The dragon nodded respectfully at Lera.

"I am charmed to meet you, Lady Jenet. Your scales glisten with the colors of flame, which is something you will learn is quite significant in this land. You are most welcome."

Again the dragon nodded, then pulled her head back, retreating from the immediate party. Drake turned to the fair folk male at his side.

"And may I present Liam Eliadnae of the fair folk from Gryphon Isle and Reliendor, First Wing Leader of the Gryphon Isle flock."

"I know our gryphons will have many questions for you both. I have heard only legends of your island," Lera surprised

Hugh by saying. "And I have never met one of the fair folk before. I will enjoy speaking with you both and learning of your land and people. Be welcome in Alagarithia."

"Thank you, milady." The man's voice was almost musical, in the way of his people. He had pale blond hair cut short in a warrior's style, but his clothing was that of a diplomat. Rich embroidery and fine fabrics marked his status.

"It iss my honor to meet you, milady," the gryphon answered. Though initial meetings with gryphons could be tricky, this one was more diplomatic than others Hugh had observed.

"The honor is mine, sir," she replied politely, returning his small nod of acknowledgment. "While I am the Doge of Helios, we are currently within the temple grounds of the Order of Light," Lera said tactfully, gesturing to the High Priest at her side. "This is Father Gregor, High Priest of the Order. Father, this is Drake of the Five Lands, the famous Jinn bard. He has entertained in my court, and I know him to be a good and talented man with a kind heart and a glib tongue."

Drake laughed at her teasing introduction and smiled when she did, reaching forward to shake Father Gregor's hand when he offered it. When he turned to Hugh, they exchanged a more hearty greeting. After all, they'd grown up together. Drake had been friend to all the princes when he lived in the Castle Lair with his parents.

Father Gregor made the official greetings and invited them into the tower. Hugh was glad the older man had apparently picked up on his desire to get them under cover. The two-legged folk entered first, allowing the dragons and gryphon to bring up the rear.

They paused on the wide ramp as soon as everyone was within. Father Gregor turned to address the newcomers.

"It is our tradition that none may enter the temple grounds without first being tested by the eternal flame. The flame rests at the bottom of this tower and you must all pass through it before you may proceed farther. Perhaps your colleague, Prince Hugh, can answer any concerns?" Gregor turned to Hugh and politely allowed him to take point on the issue with his landsmen and their guests.

"I have tasted this flame," Hugh assured the dragons and knights. "It welcomed me as I have no doubt it will welcome you."

"It is a magical flame?" Liam asked, his pale face showing only interest.

"It is the flame of the goddess we serve," the High Priest added helpfully.

"Then we need never fear it," Reliendor said confidently. "We alsso sserve the goddessss."

"Thank you for allowing us to conduct the rest of the introductions inside, Father," Hugh said to the High Priest. "As you know, not all of those circling gryphons may be trusted."

Father Gregor frowned in agreement and turned to the rest of the party for further introductions. Lera also looked expectantly at the newcomers.

"The pair of bookends you see are two of my many brothers. Collin and Treymayne are just after me in age, fourth and fifth in line for the throne."

"Our brother, King Roland sends greetings to the Doge, and our compliments as well, to you, milady. And to you, Father Gregor," Collin started.

"Thank you for making us welcome," Trey finished. They often finished each other's sentences. Hugh had gotten used to it over the years.

Hugh went on with the introductions. "Let's see, the quiet knight back there is Sir Mace and his dragon partner, Sir Nellin. Both Drake and Mace grew up with us in the Castle Lair, so I've known them both most of my life, as I know their dragon partners. They are all close friends and newly mated to Lady Krysta."

As he mentioned her, she stepped forward. "My father,

Rulu, former leader of the Wayfarer Clan of the Jinn sends his greetings, milady."

"Krysta Vonris?" Lera surprised Hugh by asking.

"Yes, milady," Krysta answered with a smile. "My father will be pleased that you remember our family. He always speaks of his many years in Helios fondly."

"Where is he now?" Lera wanted to know.

"He has settled in the new part of Castleton. My sister, Malin, leads the Clan now and continues to gather them for the move to Draconia."

"We'd heard a little about the Jinn disappearing from our land, but nobody seems to know where they're all going," Lera said.

Krysta smiled. "All the Clans are gathering in Draconia. Our Queen has been found and a time foretold in prophecy is upon us."

"Queen?" Lera seemed really surprised.

"My new sister-in-law, Riki," Hugh put in. "They made Nico King-Consort of the Jinn and his wife is their Queen."

"So the Prince of Spies is now King of the Jinn?" Lera addressed her question to Hugh.

"A ceremonial title only, so he assures us," Hugh said, rolling his eyes.

"And soon you'll be sharing my throne," she said as their gazes locked. For a moment it felt like they were the only two people in the world.

"Wait a minute," Trey said.

"What's this?" Collin asked, finishing the thought.

Hugh was brought back to reality. "Uh...Lera and I..."

"You don't say." Trey grinned, as did the rest of the group.

"Another royal sister-in-law?" Collin teased. "You're putting a lot of pressure on us."

"Where are we going to find a couple of princesses?" Trey laughed at his own joke.

"None are likely to have you, that's for certain," Hugh teased back good-naturedly.

His brothers stepped forward to pound him on the back in congratulations.

"We look forward to getting to know our new sister," Collin said, grinning from ear to ear.

Lera took their enthusiastic congratulations well, though Hugh noticed neither of the twins were comfortable enough with her to give her a hug or kiss. They'd only just met, of course. And she was the ruler of a country. This older set of twins had always been a lot more aware of what was polite and what wasn't than some of their other brothers. All in all, they were a good choice for this mission. They wouldn't inadvertently insult anyone if they could help it, as some of his younger brothers might.

But they'd soon learn that Lera was the perfect mate for their brother. They'd learn to love her and welcome her warmly into the family. Hugh was certain of it. They just had to be around her a bit more to learn more about her.

Providing, of course, they could nullify the threat of the Eyes. Which reminded him...

"Actually, you could be of help. Lera's life is in danger."

That got everyone's attention in short order.

"What sort of danger?" Drake asked, moving closer, Mace and Krysta flanking him.

"Eyes," Lera answered. Drake and Krysta both frowned. Hugh found their reaction interesting. Both of them seemed to know more about these Eyes than Hugh did.

"What are Eyes?" Collin asked.

"Assassins of the highest caliber," Drake answered. "They originate in the Kingdom of Talinor, across the sea. They get a new tattoo for each person they kill. The masters of their cult have eyes tattooed on their faces and all over their bodies."

"We have killed three with those markings already," Hugh

was proud to state.

"Impressive," Krysta said with what appeared to be genuine admiration. "Do you know who hired them?"

"My cousin, Sendra," Lera admitted. "But let's get you into the hall, where we can sit and discuss this more comfortably. I'm sure you're fatigued from your long trip here. You must all pass before the flame, but I don't think any of you will have a problem. At least, Hugh doesn't think you will. The eternal fire welcomed him readily. I believe it will do the same for you."

Lera turned and started slowly down the wide ramp, indicating that everyone else should follow. Hugh stayed at her side, knowing she was disturbed by talk of the assassins still on her trail. He didn't want to upset her, but he knew the situation had to be forced to a head so as to eradicate it.

"Did you have a quiet flight?" Hugh asked his brothers, who loped along beside him.

"Quiet enough," Collin answered with a shrug.

"To think, Rol and Nico were worried about you, and here you've been wooing a beautiful maiden all this time," Trey teased. He could always be counted upon to lighten a situation.

"If you call fighting assassins and fleeing for your life wooing," Lera answered with a rueful shake of her head.

"Hey, whatever works," Trey quipped. Hugh punched him on the shoulder, but not too hard.

They made quick progress down the spiraling ramp. Hugh could see the surreptitious looks everyone was giving the flame down below. He understood how they felt. Only the day before he'd never seen anything like the Lady's eternal fire. Now, it almost felt like an old friend.

"Is it dangerous?" Collin asked, nodding toward the flame they could now see at the bottom of the chamber.

"It can be, if one has evil intent. The Order of Light serves the goddess. The magic of the eternal flame is Hers alone, though it has been entrusted to the priests of this order. If Her flame sees evil in a being's heart, it can burn. It can injure or even kill, but that happens only rarely. Those of evil intent seldom come voluntarily to the temple. They know the flame will see into their hearts and they avoid its judgment."

"Good thing we're on the same side then," Collin observed.

"It kind of tickles at first," Hugh told his brothers. He was so glad to have them here. Even if there was danger—no, especially if there was danger—he couldn't ask for better men to fight at his side than his brothers and the knights and dragons they partnered. "Don't worry. You'll all do fine."

They arrived at the foot of the ramp in short order, and the High Priest demonstrated the path the visitors should take.

"Let the dragons go first," Hugh counseled.

Nellin was the first to move, walking bravely toward the unknown fire. Jenet followed, with Mace, Drake and Krysta not far behind. As expected, the flame licked out and Hugh watched it embrace Nellin for a moment, seeming to welcome him like a long-lost friend. It did the same with Jenet and she rustled her wings happily before moving along to make room for the others. She and her mate waited by the large, arched doorway for the rest of the party. Hugh felt reassured to have them here. The more dragons to protect his lady, the better.

When Mace and then Krysta walked before the eternal flame, it engulfed them slightly more than Hugh had seen it take any human, but when Drake entered the area, it completely enveloped him. Hugh started forward, but Drake's voice came to him in his mind.

"Fear not, my prince. The magic meets and feeds my own. All is well."

For a moment, Hugh had almost forgotten that Drake was a Firedrake, who had the ability to call fire and control it. It was Drake's heritage, shared among his family. Their visit to the Wizard Gryffid had awakened Drake's dormant magic—a residue from his ancestry. Gryffid had revealed that Drake was a descendant of the Wizard Draco, who had the same abilities. Draco had been the very first Firedrake.

Apparently the Lady's eternal flame recognized his fiery quality and reveled in it.

"It likes him and his partners," Lera observed. "I've never seen a man so fully engulfed."

"Drake is special," was all Hugh would say in public. It was Drake's secret to reveal, if he so chose.

"Fire is something gryphons are always wary of. Are you certain this will be safe for my colleague?" Liam asked politely, coming up beside them.

At that point, Hyadror, who had landed behind the rest of the party, moved forward.

"Allow me to demonstrate," the gryphon said, moving swiftly toward the fire. It sent out a gentle iridescent tendril of greeting to him, which he bravely faced before moving forward to join the dragons by the door.

Not to be outdone, the foreign gryphon followed him. The flame embraced him a little longer than the previous gryphon, with smoky, iridescent wisps of gentle magical glow that did not burn. Reliendor handled it well, shaking his feathers as he emerged unharmed on the other side of the gauntlet. There was no doubt he was a brave creature, willing to take risks, who kept his cool under uncertain circumstances. The eternal fire had showed them that much at least.

Liam went next. He paused before the fire, seeming to examine it as it examined him. Cheeky of him, Hugh thought privately. But the eternal flame kept glowing cheerfully, whirling happily around the fey diplomat before retreating once more. The twins went next, greeted much as Hugh had been by the tendrils of sacred fire. Hugh and Lera went after them, followed by the remainder of the priests who'd been up on the tower as honor guard.

It was a large group that headed across the courtyard into the main temple, but they were soon settled in the great hall. It was the only room big enough to hold all of them—two-legged and four-legged alike.

Before the princes and knights were seated, they shared a more informal greeting with Hugh. A lot of back pounding and manly hugs were distributed among them, and it was clear to Lera that the two knights and her new mate were old friends.

She found herself observing them as Krysta came up beside her. Without realizing it, she had drawn slightly away from the rest of the group, so the two women were essentially alone, off to one side. The priests were busy organizing seating for the newcomers, Father Gregor directing them while speaking privately with the fey diplomat.

"You'll have to pardon the boys, milady," said the Jinn woman. "They like to trade war stories when they haven't seen each other in a while. They won't say it, but I know my mates have been worried about Prince Hugh. He is not the first of the royal princes to find himself in distant lands, but of them all, Hugh has never been very good at blending in—or so my men tell me."

Lera had to chuckle at that. "No, he'll never be very good at espionage, but that's only part of what I love about him. Far too many people in my life have ulterior motives. It's refreshing to know that he would never be able to pull something like that off."

"Then in the interest of full disclosure, I would make it known to you that I am the Spymaster of the Wayfarer Clan."

Lera turned to her companion in utter surprise.

"Please, milady, this is something I disclose to you alone, since I can be of help in your current situation. Plus, I've married into the world of dragons and knights." She looked fondly at her family—the men and dragons standing a short distance away. "I find my world utterly changed by finding my mates. My cause is their cause. Our purposes run together and if at some point they diverged, my loyalties would be first with my new family, not my old one. But I can't see that happening. The Jinn are now more strongly allied with Draconia and its

195

inhabitants than they have ever been before."

"You've been tested by the flame," Lera said cautiously. "I have no reason to doubt your words, except for the fact that you just admitted to being a spy. A master spy at that." Lera didn't know what to make of the woman and her candid speech.

Krysta smiled understandingly. "A lot has happened to you in a short matter of time. There are many things we must all adjust to. I just wanted it clear from the beginning, who and what I am, so that you know you may call upon my skills and knowledge. Drake will say the same. He's an even better spy than I am." Krysta winked as she moved away from Lera's side, a mischievous smile lighting her features.

Lera wasn't truly surprised at the idea that the master bard was also a master spy. It was taken as a given that most court musicians listened in on any conversation one was foolish enough to hold while in their range of hearing. Lera had been taught discretion from an early age.

Hugh rejoined her when the extra seating was arranged, though he'd kept an eye on her all along. He placed one arm around her waist and drew her near. She liked the possessive gesture and accepted the pointed smiles of his friends with good humor. It felt nice to be part of a couple. Strange, but definitely good.

The High Priest began speaking, welcoming the newcomers once again, less formally, and asking questions. Unexpectedly, he turned first to the gryphon and the fey man who sat near him.

"I can't imagine you traveled so far on a whim. Have either of you a message for us?" Gregor asked rather bluntly.

Liam stood with a flourish and bowed. "I do. The Wizard Gryffid sends his regards and has tasked me with delivering these two letters—one for the Doge and one for you, sir, the High Priest of the Order of Light." Liam reached into a small, richly embroidered satchel that was slung across his body.

It was so ornate, Lera had taken the strap to be a banner of office rather than the more functional satchel strap it really was. Only now did she notice the flat square of fabric resting near his hip had a flap and closure hidden among the heavy embroidery. From within Liam produced two flat folded pieces of parchment, each sealed with an elaborate seal and ribbon that glowed with a hint of magic that was tangible when Lera touched the paper.

Wary of the magic but sensing nothing evil from it, Lera decided to break the seal, releasing a little glimmer of sparks that floated like twinkling dust motes on the breeze, shining with golden light before dissipating harmlessly into the air.

"So the Wizard Gryffid is truly alive?" Gregor asked. "Gryffid himself, from ancient times, not his son or grandson?"

Liam nodded, smiling politely. "The one and original Gryffid, who created the gryphons with the Mother of All's blessing. Is that not so, my friend?" Liam turned to the gryphon at his side.

Reliendor nodded his powerful beak. "The maker livess."

Hyadror's beak opened in an expression of shock. "Truly?" he asked in an astounded tone.

"Truly," Reliendor said gently to the other gryphon. "He ssendss hiss greetingss to all the gryphonss of Helioss. If you permit, I will fly out with you to bring hiss wordss to our brethren."

"That would be mosst welcome. Praisse the maker'ss name," Hyadror replied, more humble than Lera had ever seen the proud creature.

Lera unfolded the parchment and scanned the formal words of greeting and goodwill. It was a straightforward communication seeking to open diplomatic relations between the folk of Gryphon Isle and Helios. It introduced Liam and Reliendor as ambassadors and representatives of the two major races found on Gryphon Isle—fair folk and gryphons.

"For my part," Lera said, passing the parchment to Hugh, "as Doge, I welcome the opening of diplomatic relations between our lands. As Keeper of the Flame, I suppose I could speak preliminarily for the gryphons and say that they will most like be very interested in learning more about the Wizard Gryffid, if at all possible. Isn't that so, Hyadror?"

"Indeed it iss," the native gryphon agreed readily.

The High Priest didn't say much about his message and Lera didn't push him. She'd learned over time that Father Gregor spoke only after he'd had time to think, and only when he had something of import to say.

She watched as he refolded the Wizard's missive and pursed his lips. He gathered the attention of all just by the expression on his face. At length, he spoke.

"There are a few things you should know." Father Gregor addressed the ambassadors directly. "First, and most important, we had a remarkable event happen yesterday, from which this temple is still reeling. A Visitation by the Lady, Her words spoken to us through an emissary created out of Her eternal flame." The ambassadors both looked suitably impressed. "Our Blessed Lady has charged this temple and our Order to work with the gryphons of Helios—those selected by the emissary—in the way I believe the gryphons of Gryphon Isle work with your folk, Ambassador Liam."

Liam nodded. "We work with the feathered folk and fight alongside them. Several highly trained wings allow us to ride into battle on their backs."

"As I suspected. The Lady has charged some of our priests to do the same and I believe your folk could help us greatly in learning these new skills."

"We would be pleassed to help," Reliendor replied with all due gravity.

"Thank you. The second thing you need to know is the nature of the emissary." Lera remembered only then that Hugh had wondered what the other gryphons would make of the new breed of gryphon.

The doors at the far end of the hall opened as if on cue, to frame the magnificent white gryphon in the carved stone archway. She paused for a moment, allowing everyone to get a good look at her before padding forward on four, silent paws. No clicks of claws on stone heralded her presence as they did for other gryphons who had the front end of the bird, including the front claws.

Lera watched the shock on the ambassadors' faces. It was clear neither one of them had ever seen anything like the Lady's emissary.

It was Miss who broke the tension, bolting in the doorway at a run before she'd had a good look inside. When she saw all the people at the table, watching her, she skidded to a stop, dismay in her eyes as her wings swept out to help her stop, displayed to their full extent.

"It's all right, little one," Hugh said to her in a coaxing voice. "Come meet everyone."

Hugh stood and held out his hand. Miss started walking again, clearly bashful with so many eyes upon her. She walked in a hesitant pattern of fast and slow, then made a mad dash to Hugh's side. He crouched down to her eye level and greeted her quietly, stroking his hands over her fur and speaking reassuring words to the frightened child.

While Miss held everyone's attention, Jalinar had drawn near. She walked right up to the foreign gryphon, showing strength in every line of her proud body.

"Greetings, Master Reliendor. I am Jalinar, emissary of the Lady. Long has She waited for your flock to rejoin the timestream. As you can see, things have changed among gryphon kind over the many years your maker kept himself away from these lands and the normal flow of time."

"I can ssee that. Iss thiss the normal appearance for gryphonss in this land?" Reliendor looked from Jalinar to Hyadror and back again.

"No," Hyadror replied. "Only a few have been born thiss way. And it hass only happened in recent yearss."

"What caussess it?" Reliendor asked, probably not realizing how rude the question sounded to Lera's ears.

"Evolution," Jalinar answered shortly.

At that point, Reliendor backtracked, tucking his feathers close to his body and withdrawing slightly. It was the gryphonic version of tucking his tail between his legs.

"I meant no dissresspect."

Jalinar eyed him dispassionately for several moments. "The Lady gave me this form after observing what happened to the young one. She is called Miss because her sire called her misborn rather than give her a proper name and threw her out of the nest to die."

This time, Reliendor's reaction was satisfyingly shocked. "Ssuch thingss sshame uss all. It iss not right for a parent to behave sso."

"No, it's not. Which is part of the reason the Lady chose to make me in this form," Jalinar agreed. "To teach tolerance of those who are different."

Reliendor looked from the emissary to the child and took a small step toward Miss. "It iss good to meet you, little one. I am Wing Masster Reliendor of Gryphon Isle. You may call me Masster Rel, if you wissh."

"Say hello, sweetheart," Hugh coaxed. "It's all right."

Her head down, her paws hesitant, Miss moved slightly forward, toward the much larger gryphon. "Hi," she whispered. "I'm Misss."

Reliendor clacked his beak gently in what Lera recognized as gryphon laughter. It was a kind sound coming from the much older and very highly ranked creature, meant to put the youngster at ease. Lera was glad to see the sound did the trick. Miss looked up to meet Reliendor's gaze and he lowered his head to her level before speaking again.

"You have very pretty coloration, child. Sstripess like yourss are rare in my flock."

Miss ducked her head slightly, this time in pleasure at the compliment.

At that point, Jalinar reclaimed everyone's attention, sitting on her haunches, very close to the table, her head at the same height as most of the seated humans.

"Before we can get to the very important business of diplomacy and defeating our common enemies, we have two even more urgent local issues to deal with," Jalinar said, her words well modulated and perfectly enunciated.

"Assassins known as Eyes set to kill my lady," Hugh put in as he sat next to Lera, Miss in his lap. He addressed his words to the newcomers.

"And a traitorouss gryphon who plotss againsst her asss well," Hyadror added.

"Exactly." Jalinar nodded. "The Eyes will not stop hunting Valeria until their employer is stopped."

"They were sent by my cousin Sendra," Lera admitted with a pang in her heart. She'd thought Sendra was at least loyal, even if they'd grown apart over the years.

"Stop Sendra, and we stop the assassins," Hugh summed up. "That must be our first priority. Until Lera is safe, statecraft must be put on hold. My apologies to our new friends."

"Not at all," Reliendor said with a respectful bow of his head. "We will aid you in whatever way we can. I can perhapss be of asssisstance in tracking down your traitorouss gryphon, since I am new to the flock."

"And I can help the priests search for the woman by magical means, if they will allow it," Liam added, looking from Lera to Hugh to Father Gregor.

The High Priest nodded his acknowledgment. "If we can give the soldiers a direction in which to look, it would help considerably. We have tried all our usual methods, but Sendra grew up in Alagarithia and was trained in the temple. She has probably covered her tracks in ways we cannot follow because she knows our methods. Perhaps a new perspective will be more effective."

"I would be honored to help," Liam reaffirmed.

"What do you need?" Lera asked, wanting to get the fey mage started as soon as possible.

"A quiet room in which to work. An object the woman may have touched. A bowl of water and perhaps a tankard of ale. After all, scrying is thirsty work." Liam grinned and broke the mounting tension in the room.

"You shall have all of those things," Father Gregor replied. He signaled to one of the young priests near the door and he went scurrying off to prepare everything Liam had listed. "But refreshments first. You must be hungry after your trip."

The High Priest's words heralded the arrival of platters of food and flagons of ale and wine from the temple's stores. A simple but sumptuous meal was served in short order. Meat was brought for the dragons and gryphons and a selection of cooked and seasoned foods for the two-legged group. Everybody settled down to a companionable meal, the first of many they would share in the coming days, Lera hoped.

Chapter Eleven

While everyone had been talking, the twins had been uncharacteristically silent—out loud. All the while, they'd been keeping up a more or less steady dialog with their elder brother.

Hugh had told them in no uncertain terms that they were not to go out on search parties with the priests. He needed them close, to help keep Lera safe. Once they realized the threat to his lady, they had agreed readily enough. Already, they were making plans for watch schedules, splitting the duty between themselves and the knights and dragons.

None of them would be available for other duty until the assassins had been stopped.

"So who's your little friend, brother?" Trey asked, humor clear in his tone, though it was communicated mind to mind while the spoken conversation went on around them.

"We call her Miss." Hugh included the dragons, their knights and his brothers in the conversation, as Trey had. *"She found me in an alleyway, following me by the scent of my magic. The poor creature was abandoned in an ice storm to fend for herself."*

"So you took her in." Connor didn't even bother phrasing it as a question. Unspoken was the thought that Hugh could have done nothing else.

"One of her front paws was badly burned and even so, she'd managed to teach herself how to hunt. She wasn't starving for food—though she was pathetically thin. It was the magic she needed most. I could not leave her like that."

"She seems to trust you," Trey commented.

"She is just a baby and already she has helped save my

lady's life by attacking one of the assassins who held a knife to Lera's throat. Miss has the heart of a lion." Hugh felt he was justified in the pride he felt for her accomplishments.

"She has the face of one too. Or at least some relative of a lion. Is that why her parents abandoned her? They did not like her cat features?" Jenet asked in her rumbly, warm voice in his mind.

"Yes. Apparently there are a few others like her. The innkeeper where I was staying said he'd seen a kitten like her abandoned once before. It's one of Lera's duties to find such creatures and take them in. That's how we met. The innkeeper sent word of Miss to the palace and Lera came to take her."

"Obviously that didn't happen. Did you not want to give her up?" Collin asked.

"Lera came in disguise. I didn't know she was the Doge. She wanted to take the child and I wanted to know more about her before I let a stranger take Miss anywhere. If you could have seen her in that alley… She had a very rough start in life."

"I can imagine," Collin replied. The silent conversation ceased for a while when the food came and everyone settled in to eating.

Hugh fed Miss from a bowl of tidbits the servers put in front of him. He selected a small piece and handed it to her. She took it between her little paws and nibbled at it with impeccable manners.

"She's very dainty," Collin observed. He looked from the gryphlet to the larger gryphons seated with the dragons. Miss was a neater eater than all of them, except perhaps the emissary.

"I don't know if that's because of her differences from other gryphons or if it was something her parents taught her before she was thrown out," Hugh confided.

"It would be interesting to discover the truth of it," Collin went on. "If her parents are such sticklers for manners, it could help us identify them. She has not spoken of them, you said?"

Keeper of the Flame

"No. She refuses to say much of her origins. Only that her papa was mean and that she'd seen Hyadror before and thought he was nicer than her papa. Hyadror had never seen her before, so that means she was watching him from concealment. She was also very afraid of being seen by the gryphons circling above us when we landed on the tower yesterday. I had to hide her under my wing whenever we were outside."

"We'll keep our eyes open while we're here and see what we can learn," Trey promised. "No youngster should be treated this way. Justice must be served and her parents taught a lesson."

"I agree." Hugh was greatly pleased by his brothers' support.

If there was any way to discover who Miss's parents were, he'd take it. He needed to have a few stern words with them at the first opportunity. Lera probably would have something to say to them as well. Regardless, he had to discover who they were first.

"I still have many contacts in this land." Drake spoke after a short break in the silent conversation. "I will put out feelers first thing and see what we can learn about these problems we face."

"I am grateful you came here. All of you. I've been handling things, but it will be so much easier knowing I have a team I can trust beyond the shadow of a doubt."

"I am flying out with Hyadror to meet the various Wing leaders after we finish here." The emissary spoke aloud, making a sort of general announcement, garnering everyone's attention. Hugh knew that meant Miss would be staying with him for the day. He looked forward to having her around. "I was sent, among other reasons, to choose those gryphons best suited to forming fighting partnerships with the warrior priests. This may be a good opportunity to begin looking for the traitor among them."

"I would go with you, if you don't mind the company," Reliendor put in, a slight smear of blood on his beak from the hunk of raw meat he'd just consumed.

"We would welcome your pressence, Masster Rel," Hyadror replied politely. "I ssent word lasst night to convene an open meeting of the Gryphon Council today, at which all the Wing Leaderss will be pressent. Many otherss will be in attendance, as well. I thought only to introduce the emisssary, but now that you are here, you may deliver your messsage from the maker. I think it iss clear from thesse passt dayss that masssive change has come upon our land. We besst gear up for it."

"Well said, Wing Leader." High Priest Gregor spoke into the heavy silence that descended after Hyadror's grave words. "Emissary, many of my brothers have already volunteered to train with the chosen gryphons. I will arrange to have all the candidates ready for your assessment at your convenience. Simply tell us how you wish to proceed and we will accommodate you in every way."

"Very kind, Father Gregor." The great cat bowed her head slightly in acknowledgment. "I will fly out shortly and return when the meeting with the Gryphon Council concludes. If all goes as planned, I will bring four gryphons with me. We will start there. Your brothers have already begun the expansion of the temple garrison that we will require once the fighting pairs are made."

"Excellent. That just leaves the problem of the Eyes." Father Gregor turned his attention to Lera once more.

"We can protect Lera," Hugh put in quickly. "Between myself, my brothers and the knights and dragons, she will never be unguarded."

"And a formidable guard contingent it is," Gregor agreed. "But we must get to the root of the problem if we are to stop the Eyes."

At that point, their conversation rolled back around to the main problem they had been discussing before the meal was served. They ironed out a few more details as they finished eating and soon all were leaving in different directions, purpose in their steps.

All except the Draconians. That core group of knights, dragons and royal princes stayed behind with Hugh and Lera at his direction.

Mace spoke first, uncharacteristically stepping forward. "We've been thinking about how best to work this." Hugh was glad to see the new confidence in his actions, wrought by his mating with two such dynamic people, no doubt. "Drake and Krysta have the skills and connections needed to elicit the most information in the shortest amount of time. We propose they go out into the city and see what they can learn. The dragons and I will stay here. Nellin and I will take first watch."

"A sound plan." Hugh nodded. "What about you two?" He addressed his question to the twins.

"We go where you go," Collin stated.

"Until this is all sorted out," Trey put in.

"Then I think we should go back to the palace and put things to rights," Lera said, unexpectedly. Hugh turned to her and noted the firmness in her expression. "Hyadror said he'd already sorted out the gryphon guards. I trust him to have done a good job. Now we have to see what's happening with the human part of my palace guard."

"We can help with that," Trey said eagerly.

Hugh knew his brothers and the dragons were more than up to the task, but outside the temple grounds Lera's danger would increase a hundred fold. There was no all-seeing flame to test all the people she came into contact with before they were even allowed into the palace. They could get much closer to her without ever being examined, or even seen.

"It will be dangerous," was all he said. She knew the risks as well as he did.

Lera nodded, swallowing her fear visibly. He was so proud of her. This was a woman of true courage, meant to share his life. Hugh knew he was the luckiest man alive.

"It's something we have to do. We can't continue living here in hiding, sharing three small rooms with all the help we have at our disposal now." Her smile brightened as she gestured toward the group. "Plus, there are others like Miss at the palace. They have all been with me since they were born and are loyal to me."

"Are you certain?" Hugh wasn't so sure. Until recently, Lera had thought all the gryphons were loyal.

"As certain as I can be." Her expression clouded.

Hugh wasn't pleased by that answer, but he understood her need to be doing something rather than just hiding in safety while everyone else put themselves in danger on her behalf.

"Can you test them with that eternal flame in some way?" Collin asked.

Lera's eyes widened as she turned to look at the twins. "An excellent idea. I can't be as efficient as the flame here at the temple, but I do have certain powers as Keeper of the Flame that can be extended with some effort. At least enough to test the beings in my immediate vicinity."

"I bet our brother's magic could augment your power," Trey said with a calculating grin.

Lera looked back at Hugh, and he had to smile. "An excellent notion. I bet you'll find you have more magic than you thought now that we are a couple," Hugh said.

"I hadn't even considered—" She broke off, her expression full of wonder.

"I know. But he makes a valid point. Together, we are stronger than either of us was alone. We need to use that to our advantage. To keep you safe."

He drew closer and deposited a soft kiss on her forehead. He didn't give a damn that his people saw the tender moment. He would kiss his mate if he wanted. He'd waited a long time to find a woman he could call his own.

Miss squirmed in his lap from where she'd been dozing after the meal and he moved back so she could jump down. She looked at all the faces watching her and shied away, rubbing against Hugh's legs for support. Hugh patted her fur in reassurance.

"Sweetheart," he addressed the child. "I want you to meet my brothers, Collin and Treymayne. They are both dragons like me."

Her head perked up to really look at the two identical, black-clad warriors when she heard that and the two princes crouched to be closer to her level.

"I'm Collin," the one on the left said.

"And I'm Trey," said the one on the right.

"Hi," Miss replied shyly, but with more confidence than Hugh had ever seen her display with anyone other than the boy from the inn, Tomlin. Hugh made a mental note to reward the boy when this was all over.

"They will be guarding Lera over the next few days. Until she is out of danger," Hugh added. "As will my human friends, Drake, Mace and Krysta, and the dragons, Jenet and Nellin." Miss looked at all of them, huddling against Hugh's shins but looking carefully at the humans and much larger dragons.

"They are all from my homeland and I trust them all with my life," Hugh said very seriously. "They will never harm you, Miss, because you are under my protection. That means, you are under their protection as well. If you ever have a problem of any kind, you can go to any of them as you would come to me. All right?" He looked deep into her eyes, hoping she understood the importance of his words. She was so young, after all, he wasn't always certain of her grasp of certain concepts.

Hoping she'd understood, Hugh went back to the strategy session. After a few more minutes, Drake and Krysta took their leave. The dragons stayed behind while the rest of the group discussed the logistics of removing to the palace.

After a while, Miss seemed to become more comfortable and began to stretch her legs and move around the room a bit more. She was a curious little creature, like the cat she partly resembled.

Hugh stopped talking when she walked up to Jenet and

placed one paw on the dragon's foreleg.

"You change?" Miss asked, looking up to meet the dragon's jeweled eyes. "Change like Hoo?"

"*Sire?*" Jenet looked from the curious kitten to Hugh for guidance.

"*I think she's asking if you can shift shape to a two-legged form,*" Hugh replied to Jenet.

"*Oh.*" Jenet lowered her head to the gryphlet's level. "*No dear, I am only a dragon. I cannot shapeshift like Prince Hugh or his brothers. Like you, I am what I am. I take no other form.*"

"Talk in head like Hoo," Miss insisted.

"*That is because I cannot talk with my mouth like you do. Being in this form has its limitations and not all beings can hear me when I speak. You are luckier than I am in that respect. You can speak out loud.*" Jenet had always been good with young creatures. She would be an excellent mother one day, Hugh thought.

"Pretty color," Miss said, moving on. She patted Jenet's foreleg with her little paw, watching the sparkle of magic that passed between them. Jenet was indeed one of the prettiest dragons of her generation. She was a cross between a red dragon and a golden one. She was the exact mix of their coloration—a lovely peachy, shimmering rose-gold. She was absolutely stunning.

"*Thank you, Miss,*" Jenet said politely. "*I like your stripes,*" she added. The kitten seemed pleased by the compliment. If Hugh wasn't much mistaken, a friendship had just been struck.

They spent a few more minutes making plans but the time for action had come. Like it or not, Lera was set on going back to her palace. He could understand her desire to do so, but he would have preferred keeping her in the safe environs of the temple.

"I don't really like this," he said to her privately as they stood from the table.

"I know. I don't either. But it must be done. A monarch

cannot hide behind temple walls, and with your people here, I doubt the Eyes will get another real chance at me. Plus, appearing to be out in the open might tempt Sendra into revealing herself. You don't know my cousin. One thing about her—she always likes to gloat. I think she'd want to be present if and when her assassins strike."

"She wasn't present before," he countered.

"As far as we know. Now that I've had time to think about it, I'd bet she was somewhere in the vicinity of the inn, and when that failed, she probably went back to her estate, where we were accosted next. Either there or the palace, which was also in disarray. She would have wanted to be nearby."

Hugh definitely didn't like the sound of that, but he had to trust Lera's judgment regarding her cousin. She knew her. Hugh did not.

"If we do this." Hugh spoke louder so they could all hear their words, "I want your agreement, Lera, that you will not leave my sight—or that of my people. They are the only ones I trust in this land to defend you as I would."

Put on the spot, Lera paused, looking at the newcomers. Sir Mace and the twin princes stood with their expressions solemn, their heads bowed slightly though they held her gaze with purpose. The dragons also bowed their heads downward to be on a level with hers.

She faced Hugh, taking both of his hands in hers. This was a serious moment and she had to treat it as such. From this moment forward, Hugh would be her partner in all things. She had to give him the respect he was due as she knew he would give her.

"I will stay by your side, Hugh. And I will accept the protection of your people with grateful thanks. You also have my thanks for joining me in going on the offensive. I will not hide any longer. I want to go on the attack—even if my attack is a subtle one." She released one of his hands and turned so that they were both facing the group. "You will be my defense, but also my offense. I thank you for your willingness to help me and my land. Helios and I will not forget your valor."

The time had come. She was not going to stay in the temple any longer. She had allies now. Allies and a mate who was fiercer than any man she had ever known. With such things in her favor, there was no way Sendra could succeed.

Or so she hoped.

The flight to the palace was accomplished quietly. The only hiccup was Miss's refusal to go anywhere outdoors unless she was hidden. She would only agree to fly on Hugh's back if Lera kept her under her cloak. It was a little awkward, but Lera didn't really mind humoring the child. She just didn't understand the fear that drove the gryphlet.

When asked, Miss refused to explain exactly why she didn't want to be seen. She clammed up and declined to say anything more, her little body quaking in fear. At that point, Lera calmed her and held open the cloak under cover of the wall so Miss could scurry up onto Hugh's back and hide her shivering body between the dark cloak and Lera's body.

It had to look a little odd, but Lera hoped nobody would note the extra bulk under her cloak. It was only a short flight to the palace, after all, and once there, the halls were designed to allow easy passage of gryphons within. The dragons would fit nicely and Miss could climb down once they were inside.

The princes didn't shift shape, preserving their secret. Instead, they rode on Jenet's back, while Mace rode with his fighting partner, Nellin. Lera liked the way they worked together. It was clear they had trained to work that way in both the air and on land. She wondered if her gryphons would find it as seemingly easy to do the same with the priests.

No doubt, the experience of the dragons and knights would come in handy when fulfilling the Lady's wishes to create the new, integrated wing of fighters. Once again, Lera had to marvel at the Lady's plans and the way she had drawn them all together in perfect timing for Her plans.

This time when they approached the palace and the landing platform nearest the throne room, to which she guided Hugh, the guards were exactly where they were supposed to be. In fact, they looked more vigilant than they had in a long time. Had she grown so complacent over the years that she'd let a lax attitude in her guards develop? Perhaps. Though her Guard captain should not have let his men grow sloppy.

She would have to look into it. Or better yet, ask Hugh to take the matter in hand once things had settled down. She almost smiled to think how he would deal with any warrior who had grown negligent of his duties. Yes, that was a job Hugh would enjoy.

The temple had sent a runner with the message that dragons would be arriving at the palace in order to clear the way for them. A set of gryphons waited on the platform—a pair Lera had known most of her life. She didn't think they would be in on the plot to dethrone her, but she'd agreed to let Hugh's people see to her safety and she would defer to her mate's judgment.

She had been wrong in the recent past, to her own detriment. Now was the time to allow Hugh to exercise his area of expertise. He was a warrior born and bred. He knew how to keep her safe. All she had to do was let him and not interfere.

They landed without incident, Jenet going first with the twin princes, followed by Hugh and Lera, with Mace and Nellin acting as rear guard. The gryphon pair, Taldor and Rulith, eyed the dragons with suspicion. The mated pair had been members of Hyadror's elite wing for the past ten years or more and were both accomplished aerial fighters.

Hampered by Miss's terror of being seen, Lera kept her seat, allowing Hugh to walk her under cover of the roof. He'd landed neatly in the center of the platform instead of near the edge where it might've been more dangerous to her, and it was only a few of his large steps to the pointed arch that led inside.

The gryphons watched in bemusement as she rode on the black dragon's back until they were inside. Once there, Lera hopped down, holding out her arms to help Miss untangle herself from the voluminous cloak Lera had unbuttoned and left behind on the dragon's back.

"Ssafe?" she asked.

"It is safe, sweetheart," Lera promised. "Only Taldor and Rulith will be able to see you. Is that all right?"

She stared toward the archway, wide-eyed as the two gryphons followed the dragons indoors. Relief was evident in the relaxation of her small body when the gryphons were fully visible.

"Is it all right?" Lera repeated, keeping low to talk to the gryphlet.

"Don't know dem," Miss whispered. "Iss all right."

Lera looked at Hugh. He had shifted shape as soon as Miss had jumped down off his back. He was clearly as puzzled by the child's words as she was.

But there was no time to discuss it further. The gryphons tried to get close and Sir Nellin stepped into their path. A confrontation was in the making and Lera had to make a few things clear to her gryphon friends.

"Taldor and Rulith have been members of my court and Hyadror's fighting wing for a long time." She spoke to Hugh as he stood beside her. "I cannot believe they would be involved in a plot against me, but I understand your caution. Please let me explain to them."

"Do it from here, milady. Once again I would remind you that I cannot protect you if you are too far from my side."

"Please, Sir Nellin, stand aside so that I make speak to my friends," she said in a louder voice.

With a more graceful move than Lera would have expected

from a creature so large, Nellin swept aside, allowing the puzzled gryphons to see her.

"Milady, are you all right?" Taldor asked, stepping forward. His motion was intercepted by Nellin's tail. It whipped around, sitting across the gryphon's path. The feathers around Taldor's neck rose in agitation as he shot a glare in the dragon's direction.

"I am well, my friend. Please do not take offense. Prince Hugh of Draconia has saved my life several times in the past two days. I have put my safety and my life into his hands until this crisis is over." *And beyond*, she added mentally. When this was all settled, there would be a party for the two-legged and four-footed alike to celebrate their marriage in the more traditional way.

"Milady, I know we were in dissarray, but iss it wisse to trusst thesse foreignerss?" Rulith stood forward, beside her mate, concern clear in her raptor's gaze.

She made the formal introductions. "Lady Rulith, Sir Taldor, please meet Prince Hugh of Draconia. It is not widely known yet, but he is my mate. I trust him with my life." She could see that her news startled the gryphons, but there wasn't time to let them adjust. They had to know the decisions she had made that would affect them all. "These two identical gentlemen are his brothers, the Princes Collin and Treymayne," Lera went on with the introductions. "Sir Mace is a knight and his fighting partner is the dragon, Sir Nellin. His mate is the Lady Jenet." Lera motioned toward the gorgeous peach-gold dragon and saved the best bit of information for last. "Lady Jenet's knight partner is someone known to you, I believe." She smiled, wondering how they would react. These two, more than any other gryphons in Helios, had a soft spot in their hearts for the golden-haired bard.

"Who iss your knight, Lady Jenet?" Rulith asked, her head cocked in puzzlement.

"*Drake,*" Jenet said simply, broadcasting to everyone

present.

"Drake?" Taldor's crest feathers ruffled again in surprise as he looked from the dragon back to Lera.

Lera grinned. "Indeed, Drake of the Five Lands is now a knight of Draconia. I saw him myself not two hours past. He's out in the city right now, but I believe he will be back at court in time for dinner. Perhaps we can persuade him to sing."

Taldor and Rulith settled down once they'd all moved into the throne room. Big enough to hold a few wings worth of gryphons, there was plenty of room for the gryphon pair and the dragons as well. Hugh and his brothers were in human form and Mace stood guard over all. He seemed such a serious man. Lera liked his dedication and his quiet capability. He made her feel more confident. If all of the knights of Draconia were like him, it was no wonder that land was such a strong one.

Lera looked at her simple throne, a large, straight-backed chair set on a slightly raised platform at one end of the big room. That would soon change. Instead of a single chair, there would soon be two.

"What brings that little smile to your luscious lips?" Hugh asked, his voice pitched low near her ear as he came up behind her and took her into his arms from behind. His warm hands wrapped around her waist and she felt enveloped in his warmth. It was a heady feeling.

"I was thinking about my throne and how I'll be sharing it with you from now on."

"And that makes you happy?" He turned her in his arms, his gaze serious, which she hadn't expected.

"Having you in my life, at my side, makes me very happy indeed." Her voice held the same seriousness she saw in his eyes.

"I feel the same way," he replied. He leaned down to place a chaste kiss on her lips, then drew back. "But I'm not marrying you for your throne, Lera. I would love you no less if you were a beggar in the street. I have no desire to steal your power or usurp your authority. I need not have a throne. As long as I have a place in your heart, that is enough for me."

His words nearly made her melt into a puddle on the spot. She felt the truth of them. She knew he meant every word.

"Which is exactly why you shall have a throne of your own, my gallant Hugh." She wondered how she got so blessed to have this magnificent man for her own. "I loved you when you were a simple warrior and I will love you as my co-ruler. Your wisdom and skill will help Helios—and me. I love you, Hugh. And so will Helios."

He kissed her then, the emotion welling up between them, firing their individual magic to glow and spark and twine around each other. Lera lost track of her surroundings in an instant, caught up in the perfection of being with the only man who was meant for her. The man who completed her and embraced and met her inner fire with his own.

"Your majesties," came a warm female voice in their minds. It had to be the dragoness, Jenet. *"The child is watching."*

Lera pulled back, looking around in surprise. Hugh had that effect on her. She'd forgotten they were in the middle of the throne room with a small crowd of beings all around, including one very inquisitive young gryphlet.

Sure enough, Miss was at their side, staring up at them. Hugh released Lera and bent to the child, rubbing behind her ears, trailing sparks of magic over her fur that danced and played with Miss's own replenished magic.

"Magic feels good," Miss observed. "Warm and cuddly."

"That's love, sweetheart," Hugh told her in a quiet voice that carried only to Lera as he looked up at her.

"Love's nice," she answered simply. Lera wasn't really sure how deeply the child understood the concept. She'd known so little love in her young life. Lera would see that changed, if it was within her power.

"One of the nicest things in the world," Hugh agreed, scratching Miss behind her ears as he smiled up at Lera.

She had to agree. Loving Hugh was amazing. Breathtaking. Incomparable.

A commotion near the interior entryway to the throne room caught their attention and broke the spell. There would be time to explore the love between them later, she hoped. Now that Hugh and his friends were here, she had powerful allies in the fight to stop Sendra and stay alive. For the first time since she'd first realized someone was trying to kill her, Lera had hope. Hugh would do everything in his power to keep her safe.

The twin princes and Mace moved to surround her, while Hugh took point, placing her slightly behind him. The guards at the door seemed uncertain with the Draconian contingent inside the room. She recognized one of them—a young warrior named Kendrik, who was the nephew of the leader of the Palace Guard, newly arrived from his home in the country. He'd been introduced to her the week before.

"Kendrik," she called to him from over Hugh's shoulder. "What's going on out there?"

"Milady." The young man stepped into the room and faced her while his companion held someone back, just out of sight. "Counselor Orin and a few others seek an audience. He does not have an appointment and he is being rather...difficult." The young man threw a disgusted look over his shoulder.

"I demand to see Milady Valeria!" A voice boomed from the hallway, just outside the door. She recognized both the voice and the tone.

"Sounds like word of your arrival has already spread. Do you want us to get rid of him?" Hugh asked at her side.

Lera sighed heavily, wishing she could lean on Hugh and not have to deal with this, but this, after all, was the reason they'd come back to the palace. She had to stand firm and root out the traitors in her court. Orin might not be one of them...but then again, he might also be plotting her death. It was time to find out which.

"Orin was one of my father's friends. He's also a distant

relation. I've kept him on as a counselor, but more often than not I don't agree with his hardline stances on things. We mostly don't see eye to eye, but I do value his opinion as a dissenting voice. Sometimes he has valid points that help me make better decisions."

Hugh seemed surprised by her frank appraisal of the man.

"I want you to know my opinions on who we're dealing with," Lera went on. "If we had more time, I wouldn't say a word so you could form your own opinion, then we could compare notes later, but with the current state of things..."

"This is a much wiser course of action, Lera." Hugh squeezed her hand. "I need to know the cast of characters to this play before the curtain goes up."

She was relieved he agreed with her strategy. "Good. Then you should know that Orin is married to Sendra's mother, Yasmin. It's a second marriage for both of them. Sendra's father was my father's brother. Her mother was a noblewoman from the kingdom of Talinor, across the sea. She's always been a social climber, and marrying Orin gave her access to his considerable wealth. Sendra inherited almost everything from her father upon his death. He'd been estranged from Yasmin for some time and cut her out of his will as much as possible before his death. I should also mention that he died under suspicious circumstances."

"This Orin seems closely tied to your enemy."

"He is, but he is also very much his own man. I don't think Yasmin has any control over his beliefs. She is very beautiful and the entire court watched the concerted play she made to ensnare him after her husband died. He was the richest single man at court at the time and it was widely believed that all she cared about was his fortune. Yasmin and Sendra do not speak. Sendra refused to continue supporting her mother out of her father's estate. She cut her off completely."

"Nice family," Hugh said dryly. Lera agreed. That branch of the family had turned into a nest of vipers the moment her uncle's riches had come into question.

"Orin is tough, but not as devious as his wife. At least, that's my read on him. I've known him my whole life and he's always been a tough man, but he does have a quick mind and principles he sticks to."

"We can work with someone like that. As long as he's on the right side of this mess."

"Shall we find out?" Lera gave Hugh a mischievous look, raising one eyebrow as she tilted her head toward the doorway, where Orin was still arguing with the guard.

"Let him in, but don't let him too close. Follow my lead." Hugh motioned with a jerk of his head toward his brothers. Both stepped forward on either side of him and Lera, a few feet in front of them to each side.

Lera called to Kendrik. "Allow Counselor Orin to enter."

The man that entered a moment later looked genuinely concerned. When he would have moved close to Lera, the twins blocked his path. He looked angry at first, then reconciled himself to keeping a certain distance, with the men watching him warily. Hugh had even positioned the dragons closer behind them, and the gryphons had followed. Lera saw Orin's eyes widen at their presence, but he didn't seem outwardly intimidated, only surprised.

"Milady, are you well? You had us all worried when you disappeared." To his credit, he did look truly worried about her welfare.

"As you can see, I am well. Thank you for your concern, Counselor Orin." She turned to Hugh, aware of Orin's interest in him from the looks the older man kept darting to her side. "Allow me to introduce Prince Hugh of Draconia and his brothers, Prince Collin and Prince Trey." She indicated each in turn. "They have been helping keep me safe."

"Tales of assassins have been spreading through the city," Orin said, with a deep frown furrowing his brow. "I am glad to see you have such fierce and noble protectors. Were you the man who saved milady at the tavern, Prince Hugh? If so, Helios is in your debt."

"You are well informed, Counselor." Hugh nodded.

A flutter of giant wings from the opposite end of the room caught everyone's attention. A gryphon had landed.

Miss took one look at the dark gray form stomping into the room and dove for cover behind Lera's throne. It wasn't very effective. Her tail and the tips of her wings stuck out from behind the chair and her paws were clearly visible under it. Her entire body shook with terror and Hugh wondered why the sight of this particular gryphon had caused such a marked reaction.

Hugh turned to face the newcomer, as did Lera. She noticed as she turned that the twins had moved close to Orin, securing him while everyone assessed this new possible threat.

Lera recognized the gryphon. It was Ylianthror. He was a distant relation to Hyadror through his sire's line, but there was very little similarity between the two gryphons except that they were both big brutes that fought well. Their fighting styles were very different and their coloration was on opposite ends of the somewhat limited raptor spectrum. Where Hyadror was brownish and tawny with a whitish underbelly, Ylianthror was dark gray with some lighter speckling on his underbelly. His wings were a dark, uniform gray and his talons were almost black.

His hooked beak swept from side to side as he took in the occupants of the throne room. His feathers ruffled at the sight of the dragons, but he showed no fear. When he laid eyes on Lera, she felt a cold sort of dread creep down her spine. His eyes were not friendly. In fact, he looked mad—both angry and somewhat unhinged.

Unconsciously, Lera reached for her magic. The magic of the eternal flame might protect her if the worst should happen. Hugh squeezed her hand and she looked at him, realizing that she wasn't alone in this. His magic tingled against and along with hers. He'd probably felt her call her power and had done the same in response. They were a team now and it would take more than one enraged gryphon to harm them. After all, she had a dragon prince and all his allies on her side.

Chapter Twelve

Hugh felt the tension in the air as Lera called her magic. First Miss had gone running for cover and then Lera had tensed. Hugh recognized the big brute of a gryphon who'd just crashed their party, uninvited. He was the same one who had dived at him while Lera was on his back on their way into the city. Hyadror had run him off that time.

This time, Hugh would have something to say to the ill-mannered bird.

"What is his name?" Hugh asked Lera silently. She hadn't mastered the skill of speaking back to him this way yet, but he could at least ask questions and give direction, if necessary.

"Wing Leader Ylianthror," she answered Hugh's question and addressed the gryphon. "What brings you here unannounced?"

"I wisshed to ssee if you were unharmed, milady." The gryphon's voice was smoother than most Hugh had heard. Hugh didn't like the bird's tone or the way he moved closer, looking around the room as if measuring the odds.

"She is fine, no thanks to you. Did you not see her on the dragon's back when you dove at him?" Hugh could not contain his anger.

"Who are you to quesstion me, human? I am a Wing Leader. You are a sstranger here and would not undersstand the wayss of gryphonss."

Oh, Hugh didn't like that answer at all. This beast was angling for a set down and Hugh was just the one to deliver it.

"I understand more than you think, gryphon." He wouldn't give the insulting bastard the dignity of his title. "I am Hugh of

Draconia and well acquainted with the etiquette of the skies. One does not dive on another unless you wish them harm. You dove on Lera and the dragon who flew her. Your actions suggest you are no friend to the Doge of Helios or her allies."

The gryphon's head reared back in a clear show of anger and surprise. His feathers ruffled all around his neck again and his expression—what Hugh could interpret of it—seemed altogether too hostile for Hugh's liking.

"You dare greatly, dragon lover. You would not speak so if your ill-conceived companions were not here to back you up."

Hugh refused to take the bait. The gryphon was goading him into an argument—probably to divert attention away from his actions. Hugh would have none of it.

"You do not deny diving on the Doge and her dragon from above?"

Ylianthror's beak clacked shut. He hadn't expected Hugh to meet his anger with fire of his own. At length, the gryphon found something to say.

"I do not answer to you, human."

"No," Lera said from behind Hugh's shoulder. "Since I am Keeper of the Flame, you answer to me, Wing Leader. Is what Prince Hugh said true? Did you intend to harm me when you dove out of the sky?"

"Harm was never my intent, milady." The gryphon made a courtier's bow that Hugh had seen before. Suddenly, things began to fall into place in his mind. Now all he had to do was trap the bird and cage him in his own words.

"No," Hugh agreed. "Your intent was to kill her. Only my flame, and Hyadror's intervention, prevented it, you traitorous bastard." Hugh advanced on the gryphon. Simple mental commands sent the dragons to Ylianthror's rear, to keep him penned. The twins had the Counselor under control and that only left Lera. *"Stay put this time, my love. I have a grievance with this bird and I intend to have it out with him."*

Hugh was glad when Lera remained behind him, even

backing off a few feet, moving toward Mace, who'd come closer to be ready should he be needed. Good man. Hugh knew Mace would protect her with his life if necessary. Right now, that was good enough for Hugh.

"You accusse *me*?" The gryphon's voice rose in outrage, then he seemed to gather his control. "Under our lawss, you cannot, ssince you were not there. You have no true knowledge of the eventss, sso you cannot sstand in protesst."

Hugh smiled evilly. "Oh, I was there, all right." So saying, he released his magic, bringing on the change from human to dragon. "*You tried to kill my mate, gryphon. And I believe you threw your own child out into the storm to die. For that alone, you should stand trial.*"

Hugh was sure to broadcast his words to all who could hear him. Everyone needed to know what was going on here.

"*Miss,*" he went on when the gryphon seemed about to burst with mounting anger. "*Come here, little one. I do not want you near that bad gryphon.*"

Hugh held out his wing and wasn't surprised when the child dashed out from behind the poor concealment of the throne. She ran to his side in a blur of gray and white stripes. He noted with satisfaction when Ylianthror laid eyes on her.

"You!" Ylianthror shouted, clearly out of control. Rage boiled over behind his raptor eyes as he lunged. Hugh blocked and the sound of talons scratching along impenetrable dragon scale resounded through the throne room.

The moment the gryphon attacked Hugh, the two dragons moved in unison to subdue him. They were all about the same size and the odds were not in the gryphon's favor. Jenet and Nellin pinned Ylianthror to the ground and held him immobile with their talons and tails. Between them, Ylianthror couldn't move.

Hugh changed back to his human form and crouched down to comfort the gryphlet who crowded close to his legs.

"He can't hurt you anymore, sweetheart. I promise. Will you

tell us who he is?" He tried to be as gentle as possible with the traumatized child, but he needed her to acknowledge his suspicions.

"Papa," she whispered, but all within the throne room could hear her. The room had been built with acoustics in mind and Hugh was glad the confrontation had taken place here for that reason. He wouldn't have to make her repeat her fearful testimony.

"This gryphon, Ylianthror, is your sire." Hugh spoke the words with finality and looked up at Lera. Tears streaked down her face as she stood with Mace guarding her, off to one side, away from Orin and the twins.

It was all out now. They'd found a least one gryphon who was a traitor to Lera. There could be more, but there had only been one set of gryphon footprints in the orchard, according to Father Gregor.

"What do you want to do with him now?" he asked Lera privately. *"We need to find out if he was the gryphon that inspected the scene in the orchard or if there's more than one gryphon traitor we need to look out for."*

"Kendrik?" Lera motioned to the guard by the door. "Send for the gryphon restraints."

"Already here, milady," the young man replied proudly.

Hugh was glad the guard was on top of his game. The longer this traitorous gryphon remained unfettered, the less Hugh liked it. He would not rest easy until Ylianthror had been put into a hole from which he could not escape.

"Ylianthror," Lera said in a clear voice as four men entered the room holding a giant collar and chain made of iron. "You will be questioned under the eternal flame and judged by your actions and the purity of your heart." The words sounded like part of a ritual to Hugh and he realized there must be some precedent for this kind of thing, since they had the restraints available.

As the men drew closer, Hugh felt the magic coming off the

metal collar. It was very old and imbued with a foreign-tasting magic of immense power.

Taldor and Rulith moved closer and took the collar from the men, each taking one side of the open metal ring.

"The maker left thiss asss a reminder that to whom great power iss given, great ressponssibility followss. Ylianthror, you have abussed your power and you will sstand trial by fire for it. Accept thiss yoke now and prove yoursself worthy of the name gryphon." Taldor's words only seemed to irritate the trapped bird. He tried to wrestle out of the dragons' hold, but he was no match for two adult dragons.

Jenet and Nellin eased back away from Ylianthror's head so the collar could be clasped around his neck. He struggled with them all the way, but Taldor and Rulith were able to snap the collar shut and Ylianthror's struggles ceased immediately. All within the throne room felt the blast of magic when the collar snapped closed.

Ylianthror was well and truly subdued.

The male gryphon was led from the throne room and put in a cell at the base of the palace. He would face trial by the eternal flame after they'd had time to question him. If he would not answer on his own, it would go against him when the flame tested him. Either way, they would eventually get the truth out of the defiant gryphon.

Lera was suddenly very weary of everything. They'd caught one traitor and it made her sick at heart to think that one of her Wing Leaders—those who were supposed to be among the most trustworthy of her gryphon warriors—had plotted against her.

She turned to Counselor Orin, who had said nothing throughout the ordeal. He was under close guard by the twin dragon princes and seemed content to be so. His actions counted in his favor. He seemed truly shocked at the turn of events and even a little bit appalled.

His face echoed the feelings in Lera's own heart. She turned to Hugh and knew he read her expression.

"I'll take care of the rest of this, my love. Why don't you and Miss sit down and rest while we clean up?"

Hugh's voice sounded in both minds as he prodded the gryphlet to walk the few feet to where Lera stood. Her throne was too far away, so instead, she took a seat on one of the comfortable benches that lined the room. She patted the cushion and Miss jumped up, snuggling against her side as she placed her head in Lera's lap.

"It's going to be all right, little one," she whispered to the gryphlet. "Hugh is here and he won't let anyone hurt either of us."

Lera noted the tears in the child's eyes and she reached out to hug the oversized kitten. They comforted each other as Hugh dealt with all the people and creatures left in the throne room. She watched him move, grateful the Lady had chosen such a capable and trustworthy man to be her mate. It was clear Hugh was well used to state craft. He dealt with Counselor Orin like a professional politician, giving the man reassurances while escorting him toward the door.

Taldor and Rulith had gone with the guards who'd brought the collar. Of the four-footed, only Miss and the two dragons remained, sitting steadfastly by the large balcony entrance. No other creature would land and enter without challenge. Sir Mace stood nearby, guarding her. The twins had stationed themselves on the inside of the door to the hallway until Hugh went over and had a few words with them and Kendrik. A moment later, the three of them had walked out into the hall, leaving Hugh to turn back to Lera.

His reassuring smile lifted her depressed heart. All would be well as long as Hugh was with her. He came over and crouched in front of the bench she sat on, placing one hand on the gryphlet's fur and the other on Lera's hand.

"I sent my brothers with Kendrik to scout out the path to your chambers. They'll make sure it's completely safe before we settle you there for the night. Drake has been in contact with me through Jenet and he'll bring dinner with him when he comes back to make his full report. I don't want to trust the palace kitchen just yet. So far, neither Drake nor Lady Krysta have been able to turn up anything useful. Most of the Jinn have pulled up stakes and gone. Only a few traders remain and it seems your cousin wasn't dealing with any of them."

"That makes sense." Lera hated the fatigue in her voice. So much had happened, though, she supposed she was entitled to be a little sick of it all. "There's room to eat in my chambers if we bring in a large enough table."

"Good. I was hoping we could do that. Drake, Mace, Krysta and the twins will eat with us. And Miss, of course. Jenet and Nellin probably won't fit inside, right?"

Lera smiled at the thought. "Not with all those people. Maybe one of them." She looked at them, considering. "They're bigger than you are when you shift."

"We black dragons are the smallest and most agile of all dragons. Jenet and Nellin are fully grown but young. They have only just reached adulthood and may get a little larger over the next twenty years or so. Of the black dragons, I'm the largest in this generation. It's proportional to our human size. I'm the tallest and widest of my brothers, so I make the bigger dragon." He smiled as he talked about something light rather than the serious deeds of the day.

"Is Miss all right?" He sent the thought to her mind alone. Lera nodded and shrugged her shoulders. *"Has she said anything to you?"* This time, she shook her head slightly.

Lera stroked the gryphlet's head and scratched behind her ears as Hugh shifted his attention to the child.

"Sweetheart, how are you feeling?" Hugh asked her.

Miss sat up a little, lifting her head off Lera's right thigh. "Ssad, Hoo."

"I know, sweetheart." His voice gentled as he moved closer, surrounding her and Lera both with his arms in a loose hug.

More importantly, he was warming them with his dragon heat, encompassing them within the circle of his heart.

"Can I have my boom?" Miss asked suddenly, looking up at Lera with wide, hopeful eyes.

"Boom?" Hugh repeated, unsure of what the gryphlet had said.

Lera smiled gently. "Your boon? Yes, little one, you can have anything you want that is within my power to give. All you have to do is ask. But make sure it's something you want with all your heart. Something important."

"Very 'portant," she said with all seriousness. "Want Hoo be my papa. Dat make you my mama too, right?"

Lera felt tears gather in her eyes. Her heart opened wide to this hurt child and tucked her inside.

"I'll be your mother." That was all she could manage. She looked at Hugh, knowing tears were running down her face unchecked.

"And I'll be your papa, little one. It would be my honor." He reached down to hug her, including Lera in the embrace and she felt something click into place in her heart and soul. They were a family. An odd sort of family, to be sure, but a family nonetheless.

The sparkle of magic surrounded them as Miss purred. Her sorrow at coming face to face with her sire was erased as she forged new bonds of love with Lera and Hugh. Lera felt it all through the connection that opened between them, never to be severed. A connection of the heart. Of love. Blessed by the flame that lived inside her.

They stayed like that for a long moment, enjoying the magic that swirled around them.

When they broke apart, the twin princes were back, standing a few feet away. Both wore puzzled grins.

"What was that about?" Collin asked.

"You were surrounded by some of that magic fire we saw

when we arrived," Trey added.

"Were we?" Hugh asked, moving back. He was smiling and Lera could tell he was touched deeply by the moment they'd just shared.

"It was a sort of purple, pink and orange flame. Just little tendrils of it," Collin confirmed.

"And it sparkled. Heavy magic in the air, Hugh. What for?" Trey cocked his head in question.

"The making of a family," Hugh replied, getting to his feet. He took Lera's hand as Miss jumped down from the bench and stood at his side. She seemed to want to stay very close to them both, but Lera understood. The poor child had just been through a traumatic and life changing event.

"Miss," Hugh addressed the child. "These two are my brothers. Do you know what that makes them to you?"

Her head tilted and she didn't answer right away. "What, Hoo?"

"Since you're going to be my daughter, they will be your uncles. Part of your new family, sweetheart." He reached down and stroked her head as her eyes widened. "Say hello to your Uncle Collin and Uncle Trey."

"Hi, uncas," she said shyly.

Everyone smiled at her cute phrasing. She was still so young. She didn't speak perfectly yet, but that would come with time and patience.

Collin and Trey welcomed her warmly, crouching down to her level and letting her decide if she wanted to be touched or not. Lera was impressed with how they handled the youngster. She also felt the little tendrils of magic they gave her in greeting. She soaked them up, preening under their warm welcome.

"When you're big enough we can all fly to visit the rest of the family," Collin promised the gryphlet.

"More uncas look like you?" she asked him, seemingly fascinated by the idea that the twins were identical.

"More uncles," Trey confirmed. "But they don't look exactly like us. Close, but not exact. And you have aunties too. Some of our brothers are married."

She seemed to consider that for a moment, then brushed it off without asking more.

"We've cleared the path from here to the royal chambers," Collin reported.

"What do you say?" Hugh turned to Lera. "Time to make a move?"

"Sounds good," Lera agreed.

The move to her chambers was accomplished with a minimum of fuss. The two dragons were left in the hallway, close by the door, standing guard while Mace and the twins performed a second search of the suite of rooms set aside for Lera's personal use. Hugh stayed by her side, as did Miss. Now that they'd declared themselves a family, it seemed like the gryphlet wanted the reassurance of being near her new mama and papa. Lera didn't mind. She needed the reassurance of Hugh and Miss as well.

Hugh settled the two females on a long, plush couch in the outer room while his brothers arranged the table and chairs they'd had moved into the large chamber. While Mace and the twins watched over her, Hugh took a little tour of the suite, sending a few pointed comments directly to her mind when he found the sunken bathtub in the marble bathing chamber and the four-poster bed in her bedroom.

Lera did her best not to blush.

When the door to the hallway opened, Lera was at first surprised. Then she saw who it was the dragons had admitted.

"Drake," she greeted the handsome blond bard-turned-knight. "And Lady Krysta. Welcome."

"Milady, it is good to see you looking so well," he replied gallantly.

"We come bearing gifts," Krysta announced, walking in beside him. She hefted a large wicker basket looped over one

Keeper of the Flame

arm. Her mate held an even bigger one, along with a cloth bag slung over his shoulder that clinked as he walked. Lera could see the outlines of wine bottles inside it as he moved farther into the room.

They laid their burdens on the table, exchanging greetings with the twins and Mace, who helped them unpack the feast they'd brought. Lera went over, Miss accompanying her, and helped. She found they'd even brought some raw chicken tidbits for the gryphlet. Lera placed the small dish next to hers and Hugh's, snagging a chair for Miss to perch on. This night—and for as long as she was small enough to fit—she would eat with them at the table. She was a member of the family now. She would be treated as any other daughter would. There would be a formal ceremony later, but in their hearts, they had already completed the bond. Miss was theirs and they were hers.

Hugh nodded his approval when he joined them. The others sat as soon as she and Hugh did, followed by the princes and then the others. For her part, Lera didn't care to stand on ceremony, especially not here, in her personal chambers, but it was kind of nice that the others showed their respect in this small way. After all, these people were loyal to Draconia first. To have their respect meant something to the ruler of another land.

The meal was one of the nicest she had ever shared. They kept the conversation light for the most part, for which she was grateful. Too much had happened that day. She needed time to take it all in. Just an hour to eat without having to deal with anything too weighty.

When the last crumb had been consumed and they were all enjoying a final glass of the excellent wine Drake had brought, the discussion turned to more serious matters once again. Lera didn't mind. She'd had her moment to recharge. She was ready to face the awful truth of traitors in her court once again.

"Our Jinn contacts turned up nothing, I'm sorry to say," Drake reported as the conversation evolved. "We stopped in at the temple to see what progress had been made. Father Gregor will be sending a Brother Hubert to you after dinner, milady, to give a full report, but when we were there about three hours ago, Liam was working with an elder named Edon. Although they hadn't come up with anything definitive yet, they said they were making good progress."

"Any word from the emissary or Hyadror?" she asked.

"They returned to the temple late in the day with four gryphon recruits. They are getting things started with the new gryphons and choosing four priest volunteers to work with them. When they are finished there, I was asked to tell you that the emissary and Hyadror will come here for the night. He will assist with guarding you and the emissary sent word she wanted to meet with a few special gryphons who live in the palace, if that is agreeable to you."

"That's right. You said there were a few like Miss who lived here," Hugh said, turning to her.

"I'm surprised they haven't shown up already, but they are a little shy."

Talk flowed around her for a bit while the men sorted out the guard schedule. One of the dragons would be outside her door at all times throughout the night. The suite was large enough that the knights and their lady could bed down in the outer chamber. The bedchamber had only one entrance, through the outer chamber where they were now, and no windows, having been designed for safety and placed on the interior of the palace structure.

A bell sounded inside the chamber a little while later and the warriors tensed immediately—meaning everyone in the room except her, and maybe Miss, though she seemed startled by the unfamiliar sound.

"It's just the door chime," Lera said, touching Hugh's forearm. "Like in the temple," she said in a lower voice, for his ears alone.

"It's probably Brother Hubert," Drake said, rising to go to the door. Mace rose at his side and joined him, just in case.

Keeper of the Flame

But it wasn't a human at the door at all. Instead, it was two small gryphons. Two small gryphons that looked a lot like Miss. One was a speckled brown and the other had a more reddish coloration. Lera smiled, rising from her seat. Hugh accompanied her and she knew he worried for her safety.

"Don't worry. I personally tested these children with the eternal flame when they came to me, and they are in and out of the temple all the time. Come, let me introduce you."

Lera moved confidently forward with Hugh at her side and Miss trailing cautiously behind.

"I was wondering where you two had gone. I'm sorry I was away so long." Lera crouched down to give the two juvenile gryphons hugs as they came up to her. Like Miss, they had cat faces. The only parts of the raptor that showed in their bodies were the wings. When she pulled back from the reassuring hugs, Lera turned to introduce them to Hugh.

"I want you to meet Prince Hugh of Draconia, who is my mate." She looked around, but Miss had gone into hiding for the moment, no doubt shy of meeting others like herself. She'd come out once she realized these two were friendly. Or so Lera hoped.

"My name iss Pruelle," said the spotted female. She was a few months older than the male but only a little larger. "Lera helped me pick it. It meanss *ssteadfasst* in the old tongue."

"And I'm Gerald," the reddish-brown male added. "The man who ssaved my life iss called Gerald, sso I honored him by taking hiss name. He visitss me every week."

Hugh crouched to be more on their level. "I'm Hugh. It's a pleasure to meet you both. And I know someone else who would like to meet you." He looked around theatrically. "Ah, there she is. She's just a little younger than both of you, I would imagine. This is Miss." He held out one arm and the shy striped kitten peeped around the couch, then ran to his side.

"Hi, Misss," Gerald said eagerly.

"Hi," she answered in a shy tone, ducking her head.

235

"I like your sstripess," said Pruelle.

"Pretty sspotss," Miss answered with a little more strength in her voice, daring to look at the other gryphon. "Bofe like me," she went on in an unguarded moment when she realized the two small gryphons were shaped like she was.

"Yess," Gerald answered very seriously.

Lera knew their cat faces had been the source of great difficulty in these young gryphons' lives. She decided to steer the conversation away from such things for the moment. There would be time later to examine the sad parts of their backgrounds with each other.

"Have you two met the emissary yet?" Lera asked the palace gryphons.

Both youngsters nodded. "Sshe ssent uss to you," Pruelle answered.

"Sshe iss on her way here now, but had to sstop to check a few thingss firsst, sshe ssaid," Gerald added.

"Sshe iss wonderful," Pruelle gushed.

"She was born of the sacred fire in front of my very eyes. She is very special," Lera agreed.

The bell rang again and this time the door opened to show the emissary, waiting in the hall. The arched doorway was big enough for her to fit through, but with so many people and so much furniture already in the room, there was little space for her inside.

The dragons blocked the hallway on either side while the emissary sat upright in the open doorway. The three small gryphons scampered over to her and rubbed their faces lovingly on her forelegs while she fussed over them for a moment.

Lera had known Pru and Gerald longer than she'd known Miss and she'd never seen either one so open and loving with an adult gryphon. Not even Hyadror, who was something of a grandfather to the two little ones and a part-time teacher to the older cat-faced gryphons who lived in the palace.

"It's good to see you again, emissary. I'm sorry there's not much room in here for you to maneuver."

"Do not fret, milady. Your safety must come first for the moment and you are safest here. I came to tell you of my progress today. Things are going well, I'm pleased to report."

"That is indeed good news, emissary."

"Please, call me Jalinar," the emissary invited, surprising Lera. Gryphons were usually much more formal until they'd known someone a long time. Then again, Jalinar was an altogether different kind of gryphon.

"It would be my honor, Jalinar. And I would be honored if you would call me Lera."

The giant cat bowed her head in acknowledgment. "Thank you, Lera." The little ones scampered around her feet and the big gryphon indulged them, but Lera got the impression there was more on her mind.

"Will you stay here in the palace tonight, Jalinar?" Lera asked. "I think the children would benefit from your presence in their nest, now that they have met you." She wanted so much for the children who had known such rejection from their kind to be around a fierce adult who looked like they did and could act as a very positive role model. It was clear Jalinar had a big heart that reached out to the babies in a motherly way these little ones had probably never experienced.

"I will nest with them tonight," Jalinar decided.

"Pru, Gerald, why don't you show Miss your nest and tidy up a bit for when Jalinar joins you?" The children looked at Lera and she could see their excitement in the twitching of their little tails.

Pru and Gerald shared the tower nest with the older cat-faced gryphons and there was plenty of room for Miss and Jalinar up there. With so many of them all in one place, Lera knew Miss would be safe. One of Lera's biggest fears was that the child would be harmed just by being around Lera while the threat remained so strong.

"We'll sshow Misss and make room," Gerald promised eagerly.

Miss ran over to Lera for a quick hug and then to Hugh.

"Rest well, sweetheart. We'll see you in the morning." Hugh cuddled the baby for a moment, then released her and stood. *"And if you want to talk to me in the night, do it this way."* Hugh shared the thought with Lera and the child. *"You can always reach out to me with your mind. Anytime. Anyplace. Do you understand?"*

"Yes, Hoo. Wuv you."

"We love you too, sweetheart," Hugh assured her as she walked back to the other gryphons near the door.

"Misss, you can sshare my favorite comforter. It'ss really ssoft," Pru promised the smaller girl as they walked out the door. Lera was glad to see that Miss was positioned protectively between the two slightly larger children.

Sir Mace discretely followed behind the three small gryphons.

"I'll just make sure they get where they're going safely," he explained with a small grin as he left the room a few paces behind the four-footed trio.

"When word reached the temple that you had arrested Ylianthror, Hyadror raced out with his fighting wing to take Ylianthror's mate, Xerata, into custody. She went quietly and is now being held in a cell beneath the palace, separate from her mate. I visited her before I came up here and she showed no remorse for having allowed her newborn to be kicked out into the rain. In fact, she disowned the baby with vile words I will not repeat." Jalinar's tone showed her heavy distaste. "I believe she is probably involved in the plotting of her mate. I also believe she should be subjected to questioning by the flame, along with her mate."

"I will need time to prepare for the ceremony," Lera said, feeling her heart drop. She'd held some small hope that Miss's mother would at least regret losing her child. No such luck.

"It will drain you, Lera," Jalinar reminded her. "Ambassador Liam and the elders may be able to locate your cousin. I believe you should give them a chance to do their work first before you take the chance of depleting yourself by questioning the gryphons. They will keep in the dungeon for now."

"How badly will questioning them deplete milady's energy?" Hugh wanted to know. "Is it something I can assist with? Can't my energy replace hers?"

"It could, but then you both would be at half-strength, my prince," Jalinar said respectfully. "With the current level of threat, I do not think it wise to let either of you take that kind of chance."

Hugh nodded, his expression grim. "You have a very good point, emissary."

"Jalinar, please," she said in a friendly tone.

"And I am Hugh. Thank you, Jalinar. We dragons don't tend to be as formal as most gryphons we've met." He flashed her one of his charming smiles and Lera found herself amused. Her Hugh could charm any female, it seemed. It didn't matter what her species.

"I suppose then we'll hope the ambassador and the priests can come up with something on Sendra. If they can't find her direction in a couple of days, we'll question the gryphons under flame." Suddenly, Lera was exhausted. It had been a long day and even though it wasn't that late, she wanted to sleep in her own bed and forget the craziness of her life for a little while.

With Hugh beside her, of course. That would be new, but oh-so-welcome. He made her feel safe. And loved. She reached for his hand as her shoulders began to slump the tiniest bit.

"I see you are fatigued." Jalinar spoke quietly. "Fear not for the little ones. I will watch over them for you tonight."

"You are a treasure, Jalinar," Hugh replied for them both. "We cannot thank you enough."

"I will leave you for now. If you need me, simply send out

your magic. I will know." She bowed her head and retreated through the open door. Jenet the dragon shut it behind her, using her very flexible tail.

When Lera turned back to the table, she noted that Krysta, Drake and the twins had begun clearing the dinner things.

"I'm sorry. I just feel so tired all of a sudden," Lera said as Hugh put his arm around her waist and guided her toward the double doors that led to her bedchamber.

"Don't worry," Krysta replied with a grin. "You've had a busy couple of days. We'll camp out here for tonight and keep watch. You rest easy. You're safe for tonight. Just pop your head out the door if you need anything. One of us will be awake and on watch all night."

"Thank you for your vigilance. And indulgence." Lera smiled at the small group as Hugh opened her bedroom doors. He went inside to check things before he'd allow her in, even though the room had already been checked and rechecked earlier.

When he came back to her, still standing in the doorway, he took her breath away by picking her up and carrying her across the threshold. It was a tradition in her land for newly married couples, but from what she had heard, Draconians had no such custom.

"Where did you hear about carrying a bride across the threshold?" she teased as he kicked the door shut behind them. He didn't let her go, only lifting her higher in his arms as he walked toward the four-poster bed.

"Am I doing it right?" he asked, instead of answering her question.

"Any righter and I'd swoon."

He laughed as she stroked the dark hair at the base of his neck. She had her arms looped around his shoulders as he walked her across the room to the bed.

"We don't want you swooning. Not yet, anyway." The devilish twinkle in his eye made his naughty meaning clear.

Keeper of the Flame

As far as she was concerned, it had been too long since she had been in his arms. He had become necessary to her continued existence. Having him at her side all day had brought comfort like she had never known before. Having him in her bed at night was even more important. They were a couple now, their union blessed by the Lady. Neither of them would be complete without the other from now on. And rather than frighten her, that thought brought such total joy to her mind and heart that she knew it was utterly right. He was her life mate. Her lover. Her husband.

He was hers. As she was his.

Hugh deposited her gently on the bed, then leaned over and kissed her, his hands working on the fastenings of her dress while hers went to his shirt. She wanted nothing between them. Not fabric. Not space. Nothing.

She got her wish as the cool air of the room flowed over her skin, followed swiftly by Hugh's warm hands. He knew just how to touch her to make her squirm in delight and it didn't take long for her to feel the driving need that only he inspired.

Hugh broke their kiss and stepped back, away from the bed, looking down at her while he stripped out of the rest of his clothing. She hadn't been nearly as efficient as him with undressing her partner. He still wore his pants and he had to bend down to remove his boots first before he could tantalize her with the removal of his well-worn, black, leather leggings.

He went slow when she was feeling desperate enough to tackle him where he stood. She knew he felt the same tension. It was easy to read by the massive bulge behind his buttoned fly. He wanted her as much as she wanted him. Yet he moved slowly, drawing out the moment, holding her gaze as his fingers went to the top button.

He smiled as her gaze dropped. She could see the satisfaction in his eyes the moment before her attention was snagged by the motion of his fingers as they undid the buttons on his fly, one by one.

241

Oh yes, it was clear how much he wanted her. She loved looking at the evidence before her eyes as Hugh stripped the black leather down his legs, muscles rippling as he moved. He was such a fine specimen of a man. She'd never seen better. She'd never dreamed she'd have such a man as her lover. Her life partner. Her husband.

How did she get so lucky? Lera still didn't know. All she could think of at the moment when he stepped fully out of his clothing and advanced toward her was that he was hers and she wanted him. Badly.

"Come here, Hugh," she whispered, hoping to urge him closer, but he was moving slow, giving her time to watch...to anticipate. "Stop teasing."

"Teasing? Who? Me?" He pretended innocence, but finally, he placed one knee on the bed and moved next to her.

She finally had him alone and she wanted to play. Lera got to her knees on the big bed and moved closer to him, placing her hands on his shoulders. With gentle pressure, she pushed him down until he was lying flat on his back across her bed. Right where she wanted him.

"I think it's my turn," she whispered as she moved over him, kneeling on either side of his hips.

She leaned down to place hot kisses on his neck, moving down over his chest. She paused briefly at his flat nipples until he shivered.

"What are you doing to me, woman?" Hugh asked.

"I'm playing. Learning your body the way you've learned mine. For example," she trailed her hands down his torso, scraping his skin lightly with the tips of her fingers, "I've been wondering if you're ticklish."

"I'm afraid not. We big, tough warriors have all ticklishness beaten out of us from birth."

She laughed out loud when her fingers reached a particular spot near his waist and he practically curled into a ball, laughing hard. He was ticklish and she found that adorable.

Not that she'd ever let him hear her use that word. Hugh had a really good sense of humor, which she loved, but she liked keeping just a few of her thoughts to herself, hugging the secret observations to her heart.

She wanted to play with him, but she also wanted him inside her in an increasingly desperate way. She was torn between delaying and taking what she wanted. She'd dreamed about riding him since almost the first moment she'd seen him.

Up to this point, he'd been mostly in control of their love play. This time, she wanted to take charge and she was gratified to know he was willing to let her. Some men, she knew, wouldn't be so easy to give up control of the situation to their partner.

"So you *are* ticklish." She trailed her lips down his torso, leaning in to nuzzle his erection. "Hmm. I wonder what else you're not telling me." She licked him, taking him deep a few times before his hands scooped under her shoulders to lift her mouth off him.

"Keep that up and you'll never find out." He winked and she had to laugh at his actions. He was apparently much closer to the edge than she'd thought.

Maybe it was time to give them both what they wanted. She stalked up his body on hands and knees, trailing her lips along the sensitive places her fingers had just explored. He wasn't squirming with laughter now. No, this time, if he squirmed, it was with ever expanding desire.

Lera was doing more than a little squirming of her own as his warm hands swept slowly down her body, cupping the cheeks of her ass and squeezing gently. Oh yeah, there was no doubt in her mind that she liked the way he touched her.

His hands dipped lower and she knew he could feel the wetness he inspired. She was more than ready to take him. She'd been ready since he'd swept her off her feet in the most romantic gesture she'd ever experienced.

So the question was, why wait? She needed him. And she

would have him. Just the way she wanted him.

Lera leaned up, reaching between them to align their bodies. She couldn't resist giving him a little squeeze as she took him in her hand and placed his cock at the mouth of her pussy.

She held his gaze as she sank slowly downward, enjoying every incredible inch of the slide, feeling him touch her insides in delicious ways. Oh, yeah. He felt amazing inside her.

She paused to savor the moment, enjoying the leap of fire in his eyes, the way his fingers tensed on her skin. His hands had moved to her hips, as if guiding her, but she was in charge of this joining. She reveled in her power.

"How do you like that?" she asked, feeling strong and full of joy that this special man would give her so much of himself in so many ways.

"If I liked it any more, the top of my head would blow off."

She laughed and enjoyed the feel of him inside her, making her whole. His head dropped back on the pillows, his eyes shutting in bliss.

"You have no idea how that feels. Laugh some more."

She couldn't help herself. Laughing with this man was easier than with anyone she'd ever known. He brought the fun back into her life. He made rainbows appear on a cloudy day. He was her everything. Her sun, her moon, her stars.

She began to move, rocking at first, testing the waters. More confident with each passing moment, she increased her pace, allowing his hands on her hips to guide her into a rhythm he seemed to enjoy.

Her breathing became more labored as excitement rose fast and hard inside her body. She reached out for him, at first cupping his strong hands with hers, then angling downward to rest her palms over his chest, near his shoulders.

The new angle made the feelings even more intense. Her breathing hitched as her pace increased. She had to move. She had to reach...something. That inevitable end of the road of passion. The glory that awaited them both.

Hugh's grip on her hips tightened and his muscles flexed as he helped her move on him. She needed the help, her body straining as it neared the awesome peak. Her thigh muscles were barely answering her demands, but still she strained onward, wanting what was just barely out of reach.

She pushed, he pulled, faster and faster until there was no her or him. There was only them. Together. Riding a burst of fire toward the sky, an explosion of sparks that tingled against every one of her senses.

Hugh shouted her name as he came with her and the sound of his ragged voice and rough breathing only heightened her pleasure. They were so in tune. She collapsed over him after the soul-shattering climax and he wrapped one arm around her back, dragging the coverlet over them both with the other.

"Now that was worth waiting for," he murmured near her ear, nibbling on her earlobe in a lazy caress.

She was too wrung out to reply, but she felt exactly the same way as she drifted off on a wave of bliss, held fast in his loving arms.

Hugh woke her an hour or so later when he repositioned them to his liking. This time, he used his considerable wiles to learn each and every sensitive spot on her skin, taking extra time with the ones that made her squeal in delight. By the time he'd finished his minute examination, she was fully awake and more than ready for anything he had in mind.

"Want to try something a little different?"

"I'm game," she replied instantly. With Hugh, every time was a new and exciting adventure and he'd never steered her wrong.

Hugh surprised her by rising from the bed. He held out his hand and she took it trustingly as he helped her off the wide expanse of the giant bed.

There was a cushioned chest at the foot of her bed and he led her around to it. She went along with him, bemused by his movements but willing to give anything a try where he was concerned.

He paused in front of the wood-framed chest and took her into his arms for a deep, hot, wet kiss that made her knees go weak and her senses swim. Releasing her, he spun her around so that her back was to his front and pushed gently on her shoulders until she was leaning down against the cushioned top of the chest.

She realized immediately that her ass was up in the air, presented to him. Lera looked back over her shoulder and had to smile at the rapt look on his handsome face. He was staring at her ass and as she watched, his hands reached out, cupping her soft cheeks, squeezing and separating, exploring and making her squirm in anticipation.

"I've been thinking about this since I first saw that piece of furniture, but it needs one more thing to make it perfect." His gaze swept the room and then he reached out to his right with one long leg, snagging the small footstool she sometimes used to reach the top shelf of the bookcase along that wall. It was a sturdy little device, wide enough to stand on with both feet spread apart and upholstered to match the rest of her furniture.

He positioned it for her and helped her step up onto it. She watched the smile that lit his face as he stepped up behind her.

"Perfect," he approved. "The height is just right."

She didn't have to ask for what because his next move stole her breath. Without preamble, he stuck his cock right up into her well-lubed pussy, all in one go.

"Oh!" She couldn't keep the little gasp of surprise from escaping.

Hugh immediately stilled, hilt deep within her.

"Are you all right? I didn't hurt you, did I?" He sounded concerned and she craned her neck around to look at him again.

"No, I'm fine. Sorry. You just took me by surprise."

She saw the devilish smile return to his face as he pulsed

once within her, holding her gaze.

"Good. Then I suggest you hold on for the ride. I have plans for your pretty little ass."

Could he mean...? No, she decided. They'd never discussed it and he had to know she wasn't experienced in that sort of thing.

Although...she had thought about it. She'd wondered what it would feel like to take a man that way. She wouldn't trust any other man, but she might just let Hugh try it if he wanted to.

He slid in and out, the position giving him control of the depth and speed of penetration and she was content to let him have his way. The feeling was indescribably good. She lowered herself fully onto the cushioned top of the chest and the fabric rubbed against her sensitive breasts with each long stroke.

She was starting to push back against him on each thrust when Hugh put one of his hands between them. His fingers rubbed against her clit and paused a moment where they joined, gathering moisture. He then moved back, pressing one slippery finger against the puckered opening of her anus.

Lera gasped as he slipped inside, past the tight ring of muscle. It didn't really hurt, but it felt really odd. And kind of exciting.

"All right, sweetheart?" he asked, beginning a slow in and out motion with his finger as he sped up his thrusts into her pussy.

She moaned her agreement.

A masculine chuckle greeted her incoherent response.

"I take it that means you like what I'm doing to you?"

"Yes." Lera tried to speak clearly this time, but the word stretched out, as did her pleasure.

Emboldened, Hugh pushed deeper and faster on both fronts. Lera began to sweat and strain against the building tension. The added sensations that were so strange, yet so exciting, pushed her right over the edge into oblivion as Hugh pounded into her in short digs.

Time froze as they came together, each groaning in utter completion. She shuddered and her knees buckled as wave after wave of pleasure broke over her spent body. Hugh caught her, his arms around her waist. Her shoulders and chest rested against the upholstered top of the chest. She was completely drained when the ecstasy finally released her from its addictive grip.

Boneless, she lolled in Hugh's arms when he lifted her and placed her gently on the bed. He disappeared into the bathing room for a moment, then returned and joined her, slipping the covers over them both and spooning his big body around hers as they both drifted to sleep.

Hugh woke in the middle of the night to an urgent knock on the door.

"Hugh? You awake?" His brother Collin's voice came to him in his mind.

"What's wrong?" The knock was designed to wake them. There had to be something amiss for his brother to disturb their sleep. He left the bed quickly and donned his pants, heading for the door.

"The gryphons have escaped. Helped by traitors in the palace guard. Someone paid the night watch handsomely to open the cells and remove the collars. The traitorous guards are dead, struck down by loyal guardsmen, but the gryphons were already free and able to fight their way out of the dungeon. They flew away before anything flying knew what was going on."

Hugh cursed inwardly, his anger rising swiftly. Then a thought occurred to him.

"Are the children secure? Is Miss safe?"

"The emissary is watching over her and the other children. She'll stay with them. And she said to tell you she has magical means of defending them. Nothing will get through her guard."

"Thank the Lady for that."

Hugh was at the door, shrugging into his shirt as he opened it. Lera was still asleep and for now he'd let her rest. He'd figure out exactly what had happened, then wake her when he had all the facts. She'd been through a lot in recent days and was fragile emotionally as well as physically. He wanted her to sleep as much as possible before having to face this new problem.

He closed the door softly behind him and faced the beehive. Everyone was awake and buzzing back and forth, gathering information to have ready to pass on to him. Hugh had a strange thought for a fleeting moment. This is what his older brother, Roland, must go through whenever there was an attack on Draconia. Hugh had never envied Roland his position of power. It was Roland who needed all the facts before he could make a wise decision.

Usually, Hugh was one of many who supplied those facts to his older brother. This time, Hugh was the one in search of information in order to decide their course of action. The decision wasn't his alone, of course, but he wanted to know everything before he burdened Lera. If what he suspected was true, their partnership would be a joint effort, but one that left military matters more in his bailiwick and political situations in hers.

It made sense. He was the warrior. She was the stateswoman. They each had their talents and it would be sensible to utilize each other's best abilities.

"Tell me what happened," Hugh asked as soon as the door was completely shut. He spoke in low, urgent tones, hoping they could make good progress on this thorny problem before he woke Lera.

What followed was a report from each of the people present—the two knights and their mate, the twins, Brother Hubert and the dragons. Hugh took it all in, learning the sequence of events that had led to the gryphons' escape. His thoughts were grim as he listened to the treachery that had taken place that night under their very noses.

The night watch had been caught in the act of releasing the gryphons. Unfortunately, the magical collars that kept the beasts under control had already been removed by the time the loyal guards had discovered their fellows doing the deed. A battle ensued where the loyal guards had just barely managed to win, but in the process the gryphons had been able to fight their way free.

In the present situation, it seemed obvious that whoever paid the night watch to turn traitor was deeply involved in the larger intrigue. If they knew who had done that, they would have a solid clue that might lead them to Sendra, the bad gryphons, and whoever else was plotting against Lera.

"Who paid off the guards?" Hugh asked after the last report was made.

"A nobleman named Portu," Brother Hubert supplied. Hugh had at first been surprised to see the old priest here, then remembered he'd been supposed to arrive earlier in the evening but hadn't shown up. "I was able to find out that much before the last of the night watch died of his wounds. He wanted to confess his sins. I do not doubt his word. Portu came himself to bribe the guards and deliver payment. Each of the traitors had a hefty purse on his person when he died."

"Portu was found trying to flee the city. He is under arrest but is not talking," Trey supplied. Both twins looked angry.

"We wanted to follow the gryphons, but we'd already lost the trail," Collin added.

Ah, so that was why they were mad. The twins were good trackers, but even they couldn't track a pair of dark-feathered gryphons at night, with no moon.

"All right. It's time to wake Lera," Hugh declared. "This is her land. She will know more about her noblemen and their holdings than we do. She must also be made aware of the situation, much as it pains me to bring her more grief."

"It's all right." Lera's voice came to him from the opening doorway to the bedroom. "I've been eavesdropping." She blushed as she stepped into the room.

He'd left her naked and she'd taken time to dress in a gown of soft blue. She was beautiful as she glided to his side, taking a seat at the table around which they were all gathered. Only a slight frown marred her lovely face and Hugh knew he would do all in his power to remove that expression from her for all time. If he had his say, she'd never worry again, foolish as that sounded. He knew he couldn't protect her from everything in life, but he certainly wanted to try.

"Portu has family lands on the sea, bordering the sand flats. It is sparsely populated except for his people and would be an excellent place to hide for both the gryphons and Sendra," she stated in a calm voice, when Hugh knew she was feeling anything but calm on the inside.

They had put a map of the city and its environs on the table and Lera pointed to a place just north of where he had flown her when they'd fled the second batch of assassins. They'd been close to her enemy and he hadn't even known it.

"Perhaps you two will get your wish," Hugh said to his brothers. "There's no moon tonight. Nobody could possibly see you unless you do something rash." He eyed Trey when he said the last bit. Of the two, Trey was the more likely to act first and think later.

"We'll fly out and scout the area. If the gryphons are there, we'll find them." The twins stood and were about to head for the door when Lera stopped them.

She went to the mantle on the opposite wall and retrieved a small frame, then walked back to where the twins stood. "This is a recent likeness of my cousin, Sendra. She will most likely be wherever the gryphons had fled."

The twins studied the portrait for a moment before handing it back to Lera.

"We'll find her, milady," Trey said.

"We'll find them all," Collin added with conviction in his tone.

They left and Hugh had only one further word of advice for his brothers as they walked down the hallway toward the balcony where they could shift and fly.

"Be careful."

Chapter Thirteen

"We have about two hours until dawn," Hugh said. "The twins should get where they're going in a less than a half hour, if I gauge the map accurately. I suggest we all prepare for action. We should be hearing back from them very soon. What forces do you have in the area?" he asked Lera.

"Not much. The responsibility for securing the area around a noble's lands is up to each noble. Portu isn't a high-ranking man and I doubt he has a large force, but whatever soldiers he does have won't be loyal to me if he's thrown his lot in with Sendra."

"She probably promised him an elevation in rank if he helped her," Drake suggested.

Lera nodded. "He's definitely the type of man to be swayed by the promise of power or wealth."

"Or both," Drake added. "I remember your cousin well, milady. I entertained at her home once, and once was more than enough for me."

"I saw it from the outside and it was pretty bad. Gaudy and overblown," Hugh commented. "Is it as bad on the inside?"

"Worse." Drake and Lera spoke in unison and both laughed, breaking a bit of the tension.

Mace was quietly lacing up his armor and even Krysta was checking her weapons. Drake was more leisurely about it, but he stood and went to his pack, which was resting against the wall, and began removing bits of leather armor from within.

It was clear the knights were bracing for battle. Hugh didn't have to, it seemed, because he would be flying and Lera had noticed that when he changed from dragon to man, he could be wearing armor, or not. He always seemed to have the same pants and boots, a shirt of soft black fabric and either a jerkin of black leather or boiled leather armor. There was definitely a lot of leather involved in his clothing choices and that probably had to do with the fact that he was a warrior and when he shifted form, he was a midnight-black dragon.

She'd ask him about it someday when they had less to deal with. For now, she was glad he'd be able to have the protection of both his nearly impervious scales and his armor should he need to shift shape from dragon to man.

"If you have no further need of me, I will return to the temple," Brother Hubert said, rising from the table. "It's just possible that we can be of some assistance. The gryphon volunteers were more eager to help than I had imagined they would be. If nothing else, they could ferry their chosen partners out to Portu's estate, even if Sendra is not there."

Lera was surprised by the offer. "Do you think Father Gregor will allow it?"

"With all that has happened in these few short days, everyone in our Order knows it is the Lady's will that you remain in your current position. The elders decided to support you in whatever way necessary until the threat against you has been eradicated."

Lera was shocked by the lengths to which the religious order was willing to go on her behalf. It was unprecedented. It was downright amazing.

"Thank you, Brother Hubert. And please pass on my thanks to Father Gregor and the elders. Their support is all that I could have hoped for and much more than a secular leader deserves."

"You are also the Keeper of the Flame, milady," Brother Hubert reminded her. "In that role, you will always have our support." He bowed his head and took his leave on that reassuring thought.

Hugh took her hand and tugged her toward her bedroom.

"Come on, let's see if there's something in your wardrobe that will offer the slightest bit of protection."

She was surprised he wasn't going to argue that she should stay here, safe in the castle while he went out and dealt with Sendra. Other men would have. But then, other men wouldn't have been the perfect man for her. Hugh was. And he probably understood how important it was for her to face her problems head on.

Oh, it would have been nice to let big, strong Hugh and his knights and dragons go out there and fight her battles for her. They'd return victorious with her enemy's head on a platter. But that wasn't her style. Not at all.

Lera believed in self-reliance for her people as well as for herself. She couldn't ask Hugh to fight all her battles. Certainly he'd take care of the physical side of the actual fighting—that wasn't something she was capable of doing herself. She wasn't stupid. She wouldn't go out there and fling a sword around to make herself feel better. That was a good way to get killed.

No, what she had to do was quite different. She had to be there. To pass judgment. To carry out sentencing, if necessary. To be the ruler—and Keeper—she was born to be.

She had to be there. Whether she wanted to or not.

In this case, she wasn't sure if she really wanted to face Sendra and her cronies, but she knew, deep down, she had to. If she didn't, Lera feared she'd always carry a secret terror of assassins in the night. No, she had to see Sendra and know once and for all that she'd faced her demons and they could no longer hurt her.

The Eyes would do what Sendra wished. If Sendra called them off, Lera might be lenient. If not, the only way to stop the Eyes would be with Sendra's death. There was nobody after Sendra to carry on the vendetta. She had no children, and her other relatives might be snakes, but they had never acted openly against Lera before. Now that Sendra's treachery was known, they would be even more careful to hold on to what power they still had.

Lera followed Hugh into her bedroom and watched him close the door. Before he could do more than that, she walked into his arms and gave him a full-body hug.

"Not that I mind, but what is this for?" Hugh asked as he snuggled her into his arms.

"For realizing that I need to be there. For being the perfect man for me. For being you, Hugh. Because I love you." She looked up at him with all the love she felt in her heart shining out through her eyes and in the magic that twined and swirled whenever they touched.

"I love you too, Lera. You are my heart." He dipped his head to kiss her, but it was all too short. Both of them knew they had a mission to carry out soon. They had to prepare.

"We'll finish this later, my love," Hugh promised as he let her go with something that felt like regret and moved toward the small room where her clothing was stored. "Now let's see what you've got in here that might work. First thing, we're going to order you some warm leathers and furs for when we go out flying together. And maybe a little light armor, for added safety." He opened the large wooden door.

"You'd turn me into a warrior queen?"

He smiled at her as he turned, surrounded by silks and satins in a myriad of colors. His black leather stood out against the rainbow, incongruously masculine against the frippery.

"Personally, I think you'd look stunning in leather." His humorous leer made her laugh.

"Then stand back, my prince. I think I've got something in the back that you might approve of."

Lera went into the large walk-in closet and selected a set of dark brown riding leathers. She enjoyed horses and had participated in hunting parties on country estates from time to time. She'd never worn them in the city and never in public—other than among the small groups at the estates. They were a bit daring. Very form-fitting, and the skirt was split right up the middle so she could ride astride.

The lacings were of leather through metal grommets along the sides of the over-dress and the matching leggings. They formed what she thought was a very attractive X pattern all the way up her thighs and could be adjusted at top to put them on and on bottom to accommodate various kinds of footwear. She chose matching dark brown leather boots with a low heel made for walking.

Hugh's eyes leapt with fire when he saw the outfit on the hanger. She couldn't wait to see what he thought of her in it. Feeling devilish, she placed her palm in the center of his chest and pushed him gently out of the closet, closing the door on his smiling face.

Quickly, she donned the garment. It was even more comfortable than she remembered and she wondered idly why she put up with the scratchy, stiff court garb. Maybe she should wear soft leather all the time, like Hugh did. It certainly looked good on him, and he was royalty. Why couldn't she be comfortable too?

She laced up the sides with little difficulty and put on the boots. As a last touch, she braided her hair simply, in one long tail down her back. She looked in the mirror at the back of the small room, next to a slit of a window that let in the light. She looked like a hunter.

Well, then. She would *be* a hunter. And her prey was Sendra and whoever else had tried to kill her. Lera was through running away and hiding. Now was the time to go on the offensive. Now was the time to become the hunter instead of the hunted.

With Hugh's loving help and support. With him at her side, she could do anything.

She opened the door and found him waiting for her. His gaze roamed up and down her body, like a warm caress.

"Will this do?" She stood before him, feeling fierce in her toughest bad-girl outfit. It wasn't much by comparison to the light leather armor Krysta sported, but it was certainly different than anything Hugh had seen her in before.

He had to clear his throat before he could speak, and that made her smile. She'd gotten to him. He couldn't seem to tear his gaze away from her body.

"It's perfect."

He walked closer and touched the thin, supple leather. It was warming as she moved, taking heat from her body and recirculating it back to her skin. The clothing would be more protective than simple cloth and would help keep her warm.

He frowned a little when he slid a layer of the soft leather between his fingers.

"It's thin. Not much protection. Makes me want to throw you down on the bed and have my wicked way with you, though."

"There is that." She answered his wicked smile with one of her own. That throwing her down on the bed thing sounded really good to her, but they both knew they didn't have time for fun and games. "There's also this..." She trailed off as she reached for the hidden weapons in her costume.

Quick as a flash, blades slid down her arms. He stepped back with a bloodthirsty grin when he saw the glint of steel throwing daggers in both of her hands.

"Now that is hot." His words purred with approval. "And I've seen your skill with a dagger. I'll worry less knowing you're armed. Are there more where those two came from?"

"A few more secreted in other parts of the outfit. Almost all my gear has daggers hidden somewhere in the seams or bodice. I haven't had to use them often, but I drill with them all the time to keep myself sharp."

"Very sharp." He lifted one of her hands in his, kissing her knuckles as he admired the sharp, flashing steel blade. "It comforts me to know you take your personal security seriously. We'll work on that more once this crisis is over."

"You're going to teach me self-defense?" The thought tickled her mind. "Are we going to wrestle?" she teased, liking the way he responded. The ability to laugh and flirt with a lover as an equal was something new and very tantalizing. And to think—she'd have this for always. The Lady had indeed blessed her with the perfect mate. The more she was with him, the more compatible she learned they were.

"Wrestle? Perhaps." He delivered a scorching kiss to her lips before stepping back and becoming more serious. "However, there are some techniques I think Krysta could teach you that would come in handy in court. Have you ever seen fighting fans?"

"Fans? Like ladies' fans?"

"Exactly like, but Krysta's fans have sharp steel blades. She is quite an expert with them, and it's the kind of weapon that can be easily concealed and carried everywhere by a lady. It's perfect for you, if you can learn the technique. Daggers are good for throwing, but you need something unexpected for close-in fighting. The fans could really work for you if you have a talent for it."

"Sounds intriguing. When this is over, maybe we can convince her and her mates to stick around for a bit so she can teach me." Lera tucked the blades back into their hiding places as she spoke.

Hugh surprised her by coming up from behind and wrapping his arms around her waist, tugging her back against his front. His embrace made her feel protected, wanted and loved. It was such a new feeling. She wanted to bask in it, but they didn't have much time. At any moment, the twins would reach Portu's estate and be reporting back.

"I think Drake has been chafing a bit, being stuck in Draconia," Hugh admitted. "He's used to the traveling life and likes it. Plus, he has to deal with his family when he's home and even though his blood father has mellowed in recent years, they still don't get along all that well. Krysta is Jinn and likes to travel too. Poor Mace and the dragons have never been far outside the borders of Draconia. I think they'd enjoy extending their visit. I can ask Roland to assign them here for a bit. I don't think he'll mind having one of Draconia's best spy teams in your court. As long as you don't mind that they'll be reporting back to Roland from time to time."

"I suppose Drake was doing that all along anyway, so I can't very well begin to object now. He was a favorite in my court for a very long time when he was still just a simple bard, and I did always suspect he was a spy. I sent him to your brother with a message when I heard about King Lucan's desire to kidnap one of your brothers, after all. I figured Drake was always a little more than he seemed, but what he's become...well, it's quite a change. A good change. He looks happier than I've ever seen him. I'd be glad if he and his new family could stay for a while."

"I'll arrange it. But for now..." Hugh tuned out for a moment, then came back. "My brothers are at Portu's. So is Sendra and the two gryphons."

There it was. The confrontation was imminent. Now that they were at the moment, Lera found she felt calmer than she would have expected. Having Hugh and his people there—people she could count on because she trusted Hugh beyond the shadow of a doubt—made her feel much more secure than if she'd been facing this alone.

"I guess we'd better get moving, then."

Hugh gave her a puzzled look as she moved toward the door.

"Are you all right?" He joined her near the door and put one arm around her shoulders.

"I'm fine." She smiled up at him, trying to find the words to explain what she was feeling. And what she wasn't feeling. "I'm not scared. I think I'm relieved more than anything. I know the coming hours won't be easy, but at least we have a chance at ending this thing."

Hugh squeezed her once before letting go. "All right. Let's

do this, and after all is settled, I'm locking this door for a week and not letting you out of bed."

"That's a promise I will hold you to, my prince."

The flight to Portu's was uneventful and thankfully short. Hyadror had shown up on the palace balcony when they were ready to leave, along with the four temple-tested gryphons newly partnered with warrior priests. Hugh had observed them in flight and knew they still had a lot of work to do to cement each partnership, but for now, it was good to have them along on this mission.

The emissary had come as well, leaving Miss with the other cat-faced gryphons and Brother Hubert. He was teaching the younger ones their letters, as he often did. She would be safe with the old priest.

Hugh and Lera flew in the midst of a large formation, a knight and dragon on either side. The emissary had agreed to carry Krysta, which had at first surprised Hugh, but then he realized the gryphon understood the dragons and knights would be more effective as two-being teams. Having Krysta ride with either of her mates might cause an imbalance that would hamper that dragon and knight's fighting abilities.

Hyadror was out front, the only gryphon with no rider. Hugh and Lera were behind him, with dragons on either side. Jalinar and Krysta were behind them, followed by the four gryphon-priest pairs.

They'd talked about how they were going to do this on the way. One major advantage the dragons and knights had over their newly paired gryphon and priest counterparts was that they could communicate silently, mind-to-mind. The twins kept up a steady stream of information as they observed and reported back on the movements within and around Portu's estate. Their black hides kept them well hidden in the darkness.

Hugh estimated they had another hour or so until dawn.

They would be able to use the darkness to make their approach and surround Portu's estate. He hoped this would all be over by first light.

But that all depended on the players who had yet to realize they were part of this drama, hiding out at Portu's. How the gryphons, Sendra and those loyal to them reacted would play a role in how this night's work unfolded.

Hugh and his party approached cautiously. The twins had laid the groundwork and were guiding the flyers in one by one to advantageous landing sites all around the property. This was where the constant training and drilling Hugh and his brothers had undergone with their knights came in handy. They worked as a cohesive unit and knew each other's strengths and weaknesses.

They didn't know as much about the gryphons, so Hugh conferred with his brothers and they decided together on the best supporting positions for the gryphons and priests. They would be helpful in securing the perimeter, to help ensure no guilty party escaped this night's business.

So the attack consisted of two rings—an outer ring of gryphons and priests who would contain anything that might escape the inner ring of dragons, knights, Hugh, his brothers, Krysta, the emissary and Lera herself. Hyadror would coordinate and lead the paired gryphons. The emissary and dragons would work to contain the two gryphons who were hiding at Portu's.

Everyone on two legs would work together to find, neutralize and arrest Sendra and her allies. Sendra herself was Hugh's top priority. Without their leader, Hugh believed the fight would be taken out of her followers. And Sendra, after all, was the biggest threat to Lera. If Sendra's bid for power was halted by her arrest, the assassination attempts would cease as well. Or so Hugh believed.

When all the others had landed and were in position, Hugh waited above for the right moment to pounce. His brothers would work in tandem to flush out their prey from the small manor house and stables, then the battle would be engaged.

Hugh watched as two frighteningly fast, matched black dragons swooped out of the sky. Flame leapt from their mouths, lighting the scene when they ignited small objects around the inner courtyard, away from the danger of setting the whole place on fire. They had chosen their targets well. Little dots of fire illuminated the targets that began running around inside the manor's walls.

Seconds later, screeches of outrage sounded as two gryphons rushed out of the stable. They tried to take to the air, but were brought down by four dragons, lashing with their tails and raking with their claws. The battle was fierce but Hugh had to trust his brothers to take care of the gryphons. Hugh had other quarry to hunt.

Patiently, he waited, looking for his opportunity. Lera clung to his back as he circled, a black shadow against an even blacker sky. Dawn approached, but for the moment, he was cloaked in his element—darkness.

"I see her." Lera's voice came to him from where she straddled his shoulders. "Sendra. She's coming out of the manor house wearing a red robe. Do you see her?"

Hugh zeroed in on his target. *"I see her. Hang on."*

He made a swooping dive as he passed on the information and his intentions to his brothers, the dragons and the knights. They would watch his back and help ensure the confrontation with Sendra was uninterrupted.

Hugh timed his dive, mindful of Lera on his back and the speed with which Sendra was moving. At the last moment, he backwinged, dropping into a fast, graceful landing that cut Sendra off, the backwash of his wing beats blowing debris into her face and whipping up the nearby flames.

Lera jumped off his back and Hugh changed swiftly from dragon to man. Lera, thankfully, stayed just behind him as he advanced on her cousin.

"Halt, Sendra, in the name of the Doge."

"Dragons and their filthy riders have no authority here," Sendra shouted, clearly angry. She was blinking rapidly and her eyes were tearing. Perhaps she hadn't seen him shift shape with all the dust he'd kicked up.

"Things have changed, cousin!" Lera shouted to be heard above the screeching of the gryphons, who still battled for freedom against the dragons holding them down, flat on the ground. "These dragons are my allies and I finally know that you are my enemy."

"You dare come after me, Valeria? I didn't think you had the guts," Sendra sneered.

"I came in person because, even after everything you've done, I'm still willing to hear you out and give you a chance at reconciliation. You are family, after all."

"Reconciliation?" Sendra laughed, and it wasn't a pretty sound. "The only way there can be peace between us, cousin, is if you are dead. Then we'll be reconciled."

"I'm sorry to hear you say that." Lera's voice held her sorrow and Hugh knew it to be real.

He signaled Mace, Drake and Krysta silently and, quick as a thought, Sendra was surrounded. No one from the manor seemed to want to come to her rescue or pit themselves against the warriors and chaos in the courtyard. The few that had fled were most likely in the custody of the perimeter guard gryphons and priests. The rest seemed to have taken one look at the dragons and decided to stay hidden inside the manor house.

Sendra was trapped outside, in the open, surrounded by armed and dangerous warriors. She looked around as if for some route of escape but seemed to understand that she was well and truly captured.

Hugh felt the gathering of Lera's power behind him and knew she was calling the eternal flame. It felt warm at his back and tickled his own inner dragon magic in a friendly way.

But the flame would not be so friendly to Sendra. That he

knew for a fact.

"As Keeper of the flame, I have several questions to ask you, Sendra, traitor to your Doge and your land." Lera's voice held the power of her magic.

"I should be Doge," Sendra raged. "Not you, Valeria. You were always too weak for it. You didn't deserve it."

"Perhaps not. Nevertheless, I *am* the Doge and you will obey me. If not, you will suffer the consequences," Lera snapped, her temper clearly gaining the upper hand for the moment. Hugh didn't blame her. This cousin of hers was truly a nasty piece of work.

"I'll hire more Eyes. You'll be dead!" Sendra shrieked, clearly irrational in her anger.

"How many, Sendra? How many Eyes did you send to kill me?"

Hugh felt an odd shift in the magic of the flame and was surprised to see little tendrils of that purple, pink and orange phosphorescence develop around Sendra's body, seeming to come out of nowhere to wrap and twine around her body in loose wisps.

This, then, was what it looked like to be questioned under the influence of the eternal flame. Hugh had heard about it but hadn't seen it done to a human being before. The way the magic wrapped around Sendra was fascinating. He could almost feel it compelling the truth from her lying lips as she struggled against it.

"Three!" she shouted suddenly, seemingly against her will. "I paid three. And you killed them all. Somehow." Sendra seemed both enraged and puzzled at how Lera had managed that amazing feat.

Hugh was gratified by the true number of assassins. They had indeed killed them all.

"Did you contact any others to do the job when those three failed?" Lera persisted asking her questions as the little licks of flame still enveloped her cousin.

"I tried, but with no success. I will hire more Eyes given the first opportunity." The words were coming easier now, less shrill as the eternal flame did its work and compelled the truth from Sendra's lips.

"How long have you wanted my position, Sendra?" Lera's voice was less powerful as she momentarily succumbed to her own emotions.

"From the moment I first understood what it meant. You were seven and I was twelve. Foreign ambassadors gave you gifts. The old man from Jirahal gave you a pony and I wanted it. Nobody ever gave me things like that."

"Sendra, your family was wealthy. You are one of the richest women in the land. You could have anything you want." Lera's voice cracked.

"I want the throne." Sendra's avarice sounded in her nasty words, for all to hear.

Lera paused and seemed to gather her strength. Hugh wanted to go to her, to put his arms around her and support her, but there were many reasons that would be the wrong move. For one, he was her main line of defense should someone find a way to attack her in this dangerous situation. He also had to let her stand on her own against her cousin.

He hoped she knew he would be there for her if she needed him, but he didn't want to rush in and appear to be doing her thinking for her. She was the Doge. She had to be strong. He would be the silent strength that supported her when she needed it. Just as she was his. It was for her to decide how publicly she wanted to acknowledge that fact, considering some might see it as a sign of weakness in a woman in her position. He would take his cue from her. So far, she was holding up remarkably well.

"You cannot have the throne, Sendra," Lera said at last, regret clear in her tone. Regret and fatigue. "You will stand trial for what you have done." Lera released the magic that held her cousin in place, calling it back.

Hugh nodded at Mace and Drake. They moved forward to take Sendra into custody, binding her hands and leading her away.

Hugh turned to Lera just as one of the gryphons managed to claw Jenet in the one vulnerable spot on a dragon—the softer skin where the wing joined the body. The scales were smaller and less dense there to allow freedom of movement for flight. Jenet roared as her blood spilled over the ground and moved just enough for the male gryphon, Ylianthror, to escape her hold.

"Col! Trey! Where in the hells are you?" Hugh shouted in their minds as he went to Lera, transforming his body into that of his dragon.

Hugh sheltered Lera under his wings while the male gryphon made a run at Lera, talons outstretched. He didn't make a sound when sharp claws tried to make a hit on his shoulder, much like they'd done to Jenet. Hugh's body shuddered, but he kept Lera out of reach of the feathered menace.

"We were checking the barn in case there were more gryphons," Collin answered.

"Shit!" Trey added as the twins reappeared and saw what had happened.

It was already too late. Ylianthror dove on the male dragon, Nellin, as he tried to hold the struggling female gryphon. The emissary interceded, putting herself between Ylianthror and Nellin, but Xerata managed to roll unexpectedly and claw her way free. Nellin wasn't as damaged in the escape as his mate had been and he launched into the sky after the two gryphons, flaming as he went.

The twins jumped skyward after them, as did the emissary, and between them, the three dragons and cat-faced gryphon managed to herd the two traitorous gryphons with flame and flashing claws as the sky began to lighten from the east.

"Bring them back if you can," Lera said, peeking out from

under Hugh's wing.

"We can fight them in the sky. They can't be faster than my brothers and they're susceptible to our flame."

"They need to be questioned and then judged by the eternal flame, Hugh. That's the only way to do this. If they fall in battle, we'll never know if they're the only two involved with Sendra. And they must answer for what they did to Miss. They are her parents."

"And they threw her away. As far as I'm concerned, they lost all right to call themselves her family when they threw her out into the storm to die."

Hugh was wary as he kept a careful eye on their surroundings. Krysta and Mace had charge of Sendra while Drake did his best to help his dragon partner, Jenet. Hugh couldn't see much, but Jenet's wound looked bad. It had to be. If it were a flyable injury, she would be in the sky with the others.

"I can help the dragon," Lera said. "She is badly injured."

Hugh kept vigilant, scanning the skies and the ground, keeping one eye on the chase and one eye on those around them. Sendra struggled, but Mace and Krysta had her under control. Mace was tying her hands and feet while Krysta held her still. Or as still as possible. Drake was trying to stop Jenet's bleeding. He had been raised with the dragon. They were siblings and Hugh knew Drake would not rest until he was sure Jenet would survive. If Jenet were to die of her wounds...Hugh didn't even want to think about it.

"All right. Stay as close as you can to me. We'll go over, but don't run out ahead of me. Got it?"

"Got it," Lera agreed. "Let's go."

Hugh took a quick glance at Lera's expression. Her face was filled with resolve and a calm sort of seriousness that boded well for how she was dealing with this chaotic situation. He was still concerned for her safety, but she was handling each new curve of this evolving situation better than he'd

Keeper of the Flame

expected.

They made their way to Jenet and Drake with deliberate, coordinated steps. Hugh didn't want Lera exposed to the air for even a moment, if he could help it. Those damned gryphons could dive like raptors and if they saw her as a target, they just might make a try for her. Hugh wouldn't let them succeed.

"Drake," Lera called out as they neared the struggling dragon and frantic knight. "Let me help her."

Hugh kept watch as he felt Lera draw upon her magic and send it into the grievous wound on Jenet's shoulder. He wasn't surprised when the magical flame manifested around them all, coming from he and Lera and going to the injured dragon. Hugh felt the intention of the outpouring of energy and knew if Lera had anything to say about it, Jenet would live to fly again, regardless of how much blood she'd lost or how grievous her wound.

Even before the magical flames had fully done their work on Jenet, a horrible screech sounded above them. Hugh looked up to see one of the gryphons falling from the sky, its tail feathers on fire. Nellin or one of his brothers had gotten close enough to singe that one badly and it was having a hard time staying in the air.

In fact, the air flowing over the embers only made things worse. The gryphon—the female, Hugh could see now—was spiraling downward at an alarming rate. She landed in the courtyard with a crash and the unmistakable crunch of bones. He could tell without even examining her that she wouldn't be flying again anytime soon. If ever.

As the magical flame around them faded, Jenet stretched her wing cautiously. She was weak from losing blood but whole once more, Hugh was glad to see. Drake looked relieved for a moment before his gaze turned to the fallen gryphon.

"We should not fly, but I think we can secure the female. What do you say, sweetheart?" he asked his newly healed dragon partner.

Jenet agreed and the duo walked slowly over to the unmoving gryphon. Hugh wanted to keep Lera away from the female gryphon in case she was still dangerous, but Lera followed and wouldn't be dissuaded.

Hugh kept an eye on the sky. The dragons were able to herd Ylianthror more effectively now that their attention wasn't divided, but the gryphon was proving a more difficult capture than he'd expected. He evaded the dragons' fire skillfully and to Hugh it looked like the emissary was holding back, observing. Perhaps she was judging her best angle of attack? He wasn't sure, but she was observing more than participating. Hugh found that interesting.

"Xerata," Lera called in a strong voice—the strongest Hugh had heard yet from her. This was the Keeper, calling one of the gryphons she was responsible for to task.

The female gryphon's head lolled to one side, responding. Incredibly, she was still conscious. Hugh kept Lera well away from the gryphon's claws and out of reach of her wings—though he strongly suspected both wings were broken in several places after that horrific fall.

"I accept your judgment, Keeper." The gryphon's pained whisper surprised Hugh. She was conceding victory?

"I haven't judged you yet, Xerata. There can be no judgment without a few answers first."

The gryphon whimpered as she tried to lift her head, then gave up the effort.

"I will anssfwer," she replied as her breath came in pained pants.

Hugh felt the magic build again. The flavor of it was different this time. More intense.

"Did you conspire with your mate, Ylianthror, against the Doge?" The question had the force of Lera's unique magic behind it.

"Yess. I could not sstop him." Xerata's pain was evident in every ragged breath.

Her answer made Hugh pause. Lera too. It was unexpected.

"Did you want to stop him?" Lera asked in a much softer voice.

"I..." Xerata gasped. "I don't ssuposse it matterss anymore. I did not want any of thiss."

"You didn't want to get caught? Or you didn't want to turn traitor against me?" Lera's questions became more impassioned.

"Neither."

Lera paused, taking a step back both figuratively and physically. She bumped into Hugh's shoulder, as if for support. He wished he dared change back to his human shape so he could hold her in his arms, but this form was safer for now. With so many large creatures about, being in human form was a distinct disadvantage.

"Then why?" Lera's voice was weaker now, showing her emotion more than before.

"Ssendra sstruck a deal with my mate. He wanted power. He wanted to lead all gryphonss." Xerata grew more fatigued with every word, her eyes showing the intense pain she was in. Hugh felt sorry for her, but he wouldn't let Lera near the potentially dangerous creature. "He would be king of our kind," Xerata added with disdain in her voice that Hugh felt could not be faked.

She was being questioned under Lera's magic. The flame didn't touch her volatile feathers, but its magic influenced the gryphon. She could not lie. Not under this kind of questioning.

"Did you not want to be his queen?" Lera persisted, stronger now.

"I could not dissobey my mate. I jusst wanted him to be happy. When the egg wass warming, he began to get ideass about a dynassty. Then, when it hatched and it wass...wrong, he ssaid...missborn..." The gryphon's voice trailed off painfully.

"Did you not feel the same way? What did you think of the child?" Lera asked the question, and Hugh waited for the

271

answer. They were talking about Miss. The gryphon child he'd found freezing in the rain.

"I loved her. Sshe wass sstrange, but sshe wass mine. He threw her out."

"Why didn't you stand up to him? Why didn't you stand up *for her?*" Lera seemed as angry and confounded by the female gryphon's actions as Hugh was.

"I could not. He iss my mate." That seemed to say it all for Xerata, and Hugh couldn't understand it. He would never understand that kind of blind acceptance of something so very wrong.

"If your mate had not set you on this path, would you have allied yourself with my cousin, Sendra?"

"No." The answer puffed out of the gryphon's beak.

"If your mate had not disapproved of your child, would you have thrown her out into the storm to die?"

"No." This time the word broke in half. In agony. A mother's agony.

"Would you have kept her, even with her differences?"

"I wanted to keep her, but I could not. He would not allow it with the way sshe hatched," Xerata admitted brokenly. "I tried my besst to keep her out of hiss way. To teach her how to be resspectful and quiet. But that lasst night, sshe did ssomething to anger him and he forced her out of the nesst. Sshe fell down the cliff to her death."

The gryphon mother made a sound the likes of which Hugh had never heard from one of her kind. It was of pain. Of soul-deep anguish. Of a mother's loss. Her desperate hopelessness.

"She's not dead," Lera whispered.

The gryphon stirred. Her head rose the few inches she was able to lift it. Her raptor's eyes blinked in surprise—and something that looked like hope.

"Sshe ssurvived the fall?"

"A prince of Draconia found her in the storm. She was

attracted by his magic and he took her in and protected her for days. He gave her the love and magic she needed to survive and he has offered to adopt her."

"My girl will be raissed by dragon folk? Will sshe be ssafe with them?" The mother's concern for her baby was genuine and truthful considering she was still under the watchful magic of the eternal flame.

"Safer than she has been with her own kind," Lera reminded the gryphon.

"I am glad sshe lives. If sshe ever asskss about me, pleasse tell her I tried but I wassn't sstrong enough to sstand up to her ssire." The gryphon's head lowered back to the ground. She was clearly losing what little strength remained. "Tell her I loved her and that I'm ssorry I failed her."

Chapter Fourteen

Lera had heard enough. This gryphon was weak, but neither Lera nor the flame judged her failures worthy of the ultimate penalty. The eternal flame dissipated. It did not want Xerata's life in payment for her sins. There would be punishment, but the sentence would not be death.

At least not by the flame's power. If the gryphon died, it would be of her wounds, though Lera didn't think Xerata's injuries were fatal. She was in bad shape. There was no doubt of that. She had broken bones and contusions from her fall. And her tail feathers were badly burnt.

She would heal, given time. For now, she was immobilized, which was the safest place for her to be with her mate still on the loose.

Lera looked to the sky, watching the action up there for a moment. The race in the sky looked like a stalemate. The dragons and the emissary were able to keep Ylianthror in the area, but they couldn't pin him down or run him to ground. Something had to tip the balance and end this standoff.

"Hugh, can you take me up?"

"I'd rather not. I can't guarantee your safety up there. And what about her?"

"The flame does not want her death this day. She will keep for now." Lera felt a mixture of anger and sorrow for the female gryphon she would examine in depth later. Now was still the time for action. "You need to be up there, Hugh, and I need to be with you."

The dragon that was Hugh craned his long neck upward to study the sky for a moment.

"Dammit, you're right. I don't like taking you up into that, but I dare not leave you here."

"You need to be up there, and so do I."

The dragon nodded. *"Yes. All right."* He seemed to come to a decision and bent downward so Lera could mount. She moved quickly and a moment later they were airborne.

As Lera looked backward, she could see Jenet and Drake standing guard over the fallen gryphon. Drake was doing some preliminary work on immobilizing Xerata's broken wings and dressing her wounds. Drake of the Five Lands had a big heart and Lera was glad he was there to help Xerata. Perhaps someday the female gryphon could redeem herself. Lera didn't know how or when, but perhaps in time, there might be some way for her to atone for what she'd done. At least the eternal flame seemed to think so...else it would not have left her alive.

Lera noted the coordinated way in which the dragons flew. No doubt, Hugh was orchestrating their movements with silent discussion. The way they flew as a unit was a thing of beauty.

"Are you all right back there?" Hugh took a moment to ask. His acrobatic flying continued as he worked his way around into the formation that would force Ylianthror down.

"Fine," Lera shouted above the wind. She'd flown on gryphons before. She'd even flown with Hugh before. She was an experienced rider, but this kind of flying was something vastly different than anything she'd experienced.

"Hold on tight, Lera. This is going to be tricky."

He didn't have to tell her twice. She could feel the way his wings sculpted the wind. He was flying fast and making incredibly tight turns as he joined the chase.

The sun was beginning its rise, but it was still dark enough for Hugh to take full advantage of his inky hide. He coordinated with his brothers and managed to tip the scales in one fell swoop, coming up in front of Ylianthror's flight path and hitting him with a warning burst of flame that brought the acrobatically talented gryphon up short.

He tried to backwing, but some of his feathers were on fire. He had to land or the feathers would continue to smolder and burn. The only way for him to stop the damage would be to land and brush his feathers through the dirt. Only when the fire was out would it be safe to take to the skies again.

It was a masterful bit of flying that forced the gryphon down. He screeched all the way and Hugh never let the pressure off. He followed Ylianthror down, spiraling and shooting bursts of fire all around him with the help of the other dragons, to make Ylianthror go where they wanted him to go.

Finally.

They had control of the situation. Or, at least *some* control. Which was a lot more than they had before.

The gryphon landed and dragged his wings in the dusty dirt of the courtyard, putting out the fire. He screeched at the dragons that landed around him, hemming him in. Unless he got another lucky shot in at the wing joint, his claws couldn't do much to dragon scale, which was one of the hardest substances in the world. Only diamond blades could pierce it. Gryphon talons were no match for it unless he knew just where to aim and the dragon was foolish or unlucky enough to let him close enough.

Jenet had been unlucky. Nobody else would suffer that kind of damage, Lera vowed as she jumped off Hugh's back the moment he set down. It was time to end this.

Lera called the eternal flame. It came to her hand, to her soul, stronger than it had in a long, long time. The flame was ready. And Lera was more than ready.

"Ylianthror! Stand and be judged by the eternal flame," she ordered as she strode forward. She had no fear. The flame surrounded her with its gossamer tendrils of power.

Lera knew that while it held her in its embrace, she could not be harmed by conventional means. It was the first time the flame had chosen to manifest in this way for her, though the skills to handle it were taught to every Keeper. The flame could not have picked a better time. Silently, she thanked the Lady for helping her stand strong against this threat.

Ylianthror screamed in feathery outrage but didn't speak. Lera reached for more of her magic, finding the link she shared with Hugh and drawing on their joined power. The eternal flame leapt inside her in answer to her summons.

Lera pointed her fingers, and tendrils of gossamer flame reached out to wrap around each of Ylianthror's front feet. His claws were tethered to the ground. He could not fly while the flame held him prisoner.

She didn't know how long this unprecedented ability would last. She hoped she'd at least get to question the gryphon and let the flame make a judgment. That was important. It was her duty as Keeper to dispense the flame's justice. But every creature of the goddess deserved to be heard before judgment was passed. This was Ylianthror's chance.

"I do not ansswer to you," the gryphon finally growled when he'd given up tugging at the bonds of flame around his ankles. As long as he didn't move his front feet, the fire did not burn. It encircled him, but would not harm him unless he fought it.

"All gryphons of Helios answer to the Lady," Lera argued.

"Only the weak do not forge their own desstiny," Ylianthror countered.

"Ssacrilege!" Hyadror's voice came from behind Lera. She noted that the gryphons with priests led by Hyadror had drawn closer, ringing the scene in the center of the large yard.

"You are weak, Hyadror!" Ylianthror screamed back, irate. "You alwayss were!"

"And am I weak as well, Ylianthror?" The emissary padded silently up to the imprisoned gryphon. "The Lady made me in the image of your daughter. The daughter you kicked out into the storm. For that transgression alone you should be judged. But for plotting against the Keeper..." Jalinar growled in outrage. "That is a killing offense. For only the truly evil would try to subvert the Lady's will."

"You are not a gryphon," Ylianthror screeched. "You are an abomination!"

"Was your daughter an abomination?" Lera asked carefully, trying to control her temper.

"That...*thing*...wass no daughter of mine."

"Then by my authority as Keeper, I take the child under my protection. From this moment on, you can have no claim on her. She is no longer yours."

"Good riddance." He fairly spat the words and it was all Lera could do to hold her anger at bay.

There was more she needed to do here and she had to do it quickly. She didn't know how much longer the flame would imprison him. She had to work faster.

"What was your deal with Sendra?" Lera changed tactics, invoking the eternal flame's truth seeking power. Tendrils wrapped around the gryphon, squeezing the truth from his traitorous soul.

"In exchange for my help, sshe would make me king of all gryphonss in Helioss when sshe took the throne."

"Why?" Lera wanted to know. "Why did you want so much power? What would you do with it?"

"I wanted my kind to be free of human rule. We are bigger, better, sstronger and fasster than you. Why sshould you order uss around? Why sshould the Keeper threaten uss with death by fire if we don't do what sshe ssayss? We are better than humanss. Ssuperior in every way. You need uss. We do not need you at all."

Lera begged to differ, but she wouldn't even try to reason with this creature. His heart was so filled with hate. She could feel the evil of it pulsing at her through the protective flame. The magic of the eternal flame connected them, but it also protected her from his malice. She'd never had it do that before. It had never had to.

Never before had she run up against a creature so intent on defying the rules the Lady had set forth to govern not only gryphons, but humans as well. This was a first. And Lera prayed with all her might it would be the last she ever saw of this kind of hatred directed at her or any other creature of the Lady.

The simple truth was gryphons and humans needed each other. In Helios, the balance had been struck long ago. Both races contributed to the health and welfare of all within the borders of her land. They had a symbiotic relationship. If Ylianthror didn't understand that very basic tenet, she held out little hope he would ever come around.

"Did you agree with Sendra hiring Eyes to kill me?"

"Agree? I ssuggessted it!" he roared. "It wass I who flew out to make contact with their brotherhood. You needed to die and if sshe would not do it hersself, ssomeone had to be found who would."

Lera's heart plummeted. There could be no reconciliation with someone who hated her this much.

"I'm sorry, Ylianthror," she whispered, unable to say more. The flame was making it hard for her to talk. It was fluctuating with her emotions and becoming more difficult to hold steady as a binding around the gryphon's front ankles.

Suddenly, he broke free, lunging for her with outstretched claws. She was too close!

Fire erupted from the dragon at her side. Hugh had come to her defense, using his fire to push the gryphon back.

But the gryphon didn't move back. In fact, he didn't move at all. And there was something strange about the stream of fire coming from Hugh's dragonish mouth. It wasn't the normal orange and yellow of dragon fire.

It resembled something much closer to the magical, eternal flame of the Lady. It was a phosphorescent orange, pink, yellow and purple, billowing out in waves that were almost translucent with the sparkling magic that flowed on every lick of flame.

The fire engulfed Ylianthror, freezing him in place. This time, rather than just holding him, it burned. Not like fire normally burns, but in a way that only the magical flame of the Lady burns. Everywhere it touched Ylianthror, he began to sparkle, then to shimmer, then to...dissipate.

Lera felt the pull of the Lady's magic out of her, into her mate. The way it twined and meshed with Hugh's dragon fire was familiar but at the same time altogether new. It was like the way their magics joined when they were intimate, but this was so much...more.

More powerful. More magical.

More dangerous.

Ylianthror disappeared particle by particle, caught up in the sparkling magical smoke that rose where the eternal flame met his body.

The unearthly screech he made as he disintegrated echoed into the dawn.

Ylianthror was gone.

Lera had never seen the like.

Hugh shimmered and turned into his human form. He looked surprised—as if his transformation wasn't voluntary.

"What just happened?" he asked, clearly stunned.

"I'm not sure."

He stood still a moment more, then wrapped his arms around her, hugging her close. His chin rested on the top of her head protectively. She felt his love, his fear for her safety, his wonder at the power that had just coursed through him.

"Are you all right?" Hugh asked her as he rocked her slightly in his embrace.

"I'm fine. But are you? Hugh, I've never seen the flame act through another person like that. When the priests use it, it's very different. It's only an echo. What you just did..." She trailed off, at a loss for words.

"Yeah, that was pretty amazing, but no harm done to me. Ylianthror, on the other hand... He didn't fare so well." He drew back and looked at the place the gryphon had been. Not even a singed spot on the ground marked the place he had...burned, for lack of a better word. "I'm sorry I acted without consulting you, but it was in defense and I had no idea that was going to happen. I only meant to keep him away from you."

"It's all right. The flame worked through my link to you. It had already judged Ylianthror and found him guilty of the most heinous betrayal. I delayed because I didn't want to be the instrument of his death. I've never had to do something like that before and I wasn't looking forward to it, even after what he'd done."

"Then perhaps this is the way it was meant to be." He held her hand, squeezing it gently as they looked at each other.

The emissary interrupted their moment, padding up to them and fanning her wings. "You are correct, my prince. Valeria is the Keeper of the Flame. You are now the first and only Guardian of its true power."

"What did it really do? Where did he go?" Lera asked, flummoxed by the way the flame had acted.

"There are many worlds and many dimensions unknown to us. But all is known to the Lady. Perhaps She sent him to another place and time where his desire for power in this realm could not harm anyone else. Or maybe She took him to abide with Her. It is not for us to know. It is for us to believe in Her wisdom and mercy. His blood is not on your hands—either of you. You were only the conduits through which the Lady's justice was dispensed. As it should be. Do not let it burden your heart."

"Thank you, emissary." Lera spoke softly, truly touched by the gryphon's words.

"If you would permit it, milady, I will assist in the clean-up here. I believe you and your mate should go back to the palace to recover from what has just transpired. Within an hour, you will both slumber and it will be some time before you wake. Neither of you are used to channeling that much magical energy. You're running on adrenaline right now, but you should get to the safety of the palace as soon as possible."

"We'll take that advice," Hugh answered for her, putting one arm around Lera's shoulders. "And we thank you for your willingness to take over here. The dragons, knights and their lady will stay also. Jenet shouldn't move much, but the others can help you. My brothers will come with us, just in case there are still enemies out there."

"It is only right the rulers of Helios travel with an honor guard," the emissary replied. "I only wish there were more of us to go with you."

"Thank you, emissary, but we will be fine with my brothers," Hugh replied politely.

Hugh didn't waste much time. He signaled the twins silently and within moments he had changed back into a dragon and she was on his back. They lifted off in the pearly orange of sunrise and headed back toward Alagarithia.

Lera's heart was both heavier and lighter. They'd found the traitors and dealt with them. While she was sad for the way the night had ended with injury, bloodshed and death, she was glad there was no longer any reason to believe assassins were on her trail. She was still in a position of power and there would always be danger, but professional assassins had ratcheted up her fear to the highest level.

Finally, she would be able to relax somewhat. Relax and enjoy time with her new mate.

After all, there was a state wedding to plan.

True to the emissary's predictions, Lera and Hugh slept for the entire day and night following their return to the palace. The twins did not let anyone in to see them except Father Gregor, who pronounced them healthy—just completely exhausted—after a quick examination.

The dragons and knights stayed at Portu's estate with the prisoners. Xerata could not be moved, but would survive. She was in worse shape than the dragoness, Jenet, and would require several weeks—perhaps months—of healing before she would fly again. By contrast, with her knight's help, the Lady Jenet would be able to fly within a few days.

The warrior priests who had paired with gryphons stayed at Portu's also to act as guards. The emissary had questioned each and every one of Portu's people and found a few sympathizers she judged to be dangerous to the harmony of Helios. The manor house had been partitioned so that a few windowless rooms were used to hold prisoners and the others housed the warrior priests and the knights and their lady.

Those servants who had no knowledge of Portu's treachery were allowed to stay on, if they wished, to serve those who used the house and stables. The temple gryphons had made nests for themselves in the disused barn and had helped Nellin make a place for himself and his mate, poor, injured Jenet. The dragons and gryphons were working together quite well, from all accounts, as Lera was pleased to learn when she finally woke up and was able to read the reports being sent back three times a day.

Much to her disappointment, when she and Hugh had finally woken a full day later, she was not allowed to laze in bed with her new mate. No, there had been a full schedule waiting for her of things that absolutely could not wait. Hugh too, had been occupied from almost the moment they woke until dinnertime.

Reliendor, the gryphon from Gryffid's court, had needed to see Lera to obtain a formal reply to his message. He'd flown off as soon as he got it, leaving the fair folk ambassador, Liam, as the beginning of a delegation from Gryffid to Helios. Lera had spoken briefly with Liam and thanked him for assisting in the search for Sendra. She'd been surprised to find that Liam and one of the temple elders had struck up a friendship and were teaching each other different ways to access and use magic.

Then there was the matter of the prisoners to deal with. There were a few here in Alagarithia proper and even more on the outskirts of the city, at Portu's estate. The manor house and farmland was forfeit to the crown for Portu's treason. He didn't have much family and those few who had been living with him were now imprisoned in their former home, having been found guilty of aiding in the treason by the emissary.

The temple petitioned and was granted the buildings and grounds as a training facility and possible housing for the newly formed partnerships between priests and gryphons. The emissary had suggested it and after some consideration, Lera saw the benefits of the scheme. The peasants who lived on the land would continue to farm it, only instead of coming under the jurisdiction of a minor nobleman, they would now turn to Father Gregor and the elders put in charge of the estate.

Lera also had to draft formal documents to send back to Draconia with the twins, whenever they decided to leave. She also wanted to include a more personal, informal letter of greeting between herself and her new extended family, explaining a bit about what had happened and how Hugh had helped. She also wanted to explain privately—outside the diplomatic documents—that Helios could be depended on as a steadfast ally now that the traitors had been dealt with.

Hugh had helped her all through the day. He'd had to write a few letters back home as well, so they did that together. But he'd been out around the palace as well, seeing to the Guard and making changes in her security. He'd trained with the Guard that morning and used the time to not only exercise, but also to evaluate those men he'd been able to observe and spar with.

Hugh was in his element and Lera was only too glad to let him do as he willed where the warriors were concerned. Over time, she hoped, they would find things he was suited to more than she, and they would divide up their tasks and areas of responsibility, sharing the burden of rule between them. Theirs would be a true partnership.

Lera had a million other items on her daily agenda that had piled up while she'd been away, fighting for her life with Hugh.

Keeper of the Flame

She tried to get through as much as possible with her private secretary's help. She was a conscientious leader and didn't like making her people wait on decisions that could be made quickly. She listened to as many of the petitions as she could, but eventually, she had to give up and leave the rest for later. There was much too much to do all in one day.

It was only later, after Lera and Hugh had fled the public areas of the palace and locked themselves into Lera's bedroom that they finally had some alone time where both of them were conscious and had the energy to play.

"Should I even ask how your day was, my love?" Hugh asked as they ate a private meal together in her chambers.

"You saw most of it. It was every bit as difficult as I supposed it would be. It's always hard for me to take time off, even when I prepare for it. This time, there was no preparation, no clearing of my schedule. As a result, everything just piled up and it will take some time to untangle the confusion and get back on track." She speared a green bean with her fork. "But you were a great help to me today, Hugh. Thank you for that."

"Anything I can do, I will."

"I know." She paused a moment to smile at him. "And I love you for it."

"Just for that?" he prompted, making her smile turn playful.

"For that and for a few other things."

"Maybe one thing in particular?" He waggled his eyebrows as he coaxed her over to sit on his lap. He fed her the last of her meal—a few final string beans, which were to be followed by a chocolate custard.

When she would have reached for the custard dish, he pushed it just out of her reach.

"Not fair. That's the best part of the meal." She pouted playfully.

"I know how to make it even better."

"Oh, really?" she challenged.

"Most definitely, milady. If you'll carry the dish, I propose we adjourn to the bedroom for desert."

He stood, holding her in his arms. He dipped her close enough to the table that she could grab the two dishes containing chocolate custard. Each had a generous dollop of freshly whipped cream on top. She was also able to snag a single spoon before he lifted her up again and whisked her into the bedchamber.

Once there, he lowered her to her feet next to the bed and took the two dishes and spoon from her hands, placing them on the night table next to the bed. Hugh moved close and lowered his mouth to hers, seducing her with his expert kisses while he undressed her.

Lera worked on the fastenings of his clothing as well, but she was much less proficient than he was. She managed to get him bare from the waist up in the same amount of time it took him to strip her naked. She figured he deserved some sort of reward for his ingenuity, and she had the perfect thing in mind.

Lera's fingers went to the fastening of his leather pants and unbuttoned the fly, pushing them down around his thighs, freeing his hard cock. She moved back to admire him for a moment, reaching out to snag some of the whipped cream off one of the custard dishes on her finger.

She brought it back, stroking the fluffy white concoction over his rigid length, smearing him liberally with the sticky cream. She held his gaze, gratified when she saw his eyes flare with excitement as she dropped to sit on the edge of the bed. It put her at the perfect height to lick him clean.

Lera leaned forward, taking her time, teasing him with light strokes of her tongue. She watched his face from under her lashes, knowing from prior experience how he liked to be touched. She had learned her lesson well over their relatively short time together and knew how to please him. She employed all her knowledge to bring him to the edge of pleasure, taking him deep into her mouth and making sure all of the whipped cream was cleaned off by her efficient tongue.

"Damn, sweetheart. Any more of that and the party will be over before it even started."

Hugh pushed her away gently, using a little more force to lay her back on the bed. He lifted her and positioned her in the center of the big four-poster bed. Only then did she notice the cords tied to each of the posts. He must have put them there sometime before dinner.

"Hugh?" she asked, uncertain, when he took one of her ankles and tied it to the corresponding bedpost.

"Ssh." He dropped a quick kiss on the arch of her foot. "Don't worry. You're going to love this. I promise." He moved to tie her other ankle to the opposite post.

She tested the hold and realized he'd tied her with something soft that wouldn't abrade her skin. He also hadn't tied her so tightly that she'd never be able to get out. She was secure, but with some concentrated effort and a little time, she could wiggle out if she had to. That reassured her.

When he moved to her hands, she went along with his plans willingly. He looped the soft cord around one wrist, then the other, tying them to opposite bedposts until she was spread-eagled, naked, before him.

Hugh stepped back to admire his handy work and smiled. It was the smile she had come to know and love from him. It was the smile that meant she was in for a really amazing few hours of pleasure. It was the smile he reserved for her alone and it meant the world to her. This was her man. Her life. They would be together now and for all time and she knew in her heart, he would never stray. His inner dragon wouldn't allow it. They were mated for now and for always.

She was finally free to give her heart, knowing it would never be rebuffed. Knowing he would never knowingly harm her in any way. He had her trust and her love, forevermore.

Hugh took one of the dishes of chocolate confection and sat

on the bed at her side. Holding her gaze with promises in his eyes, he scooped some of the chocolate custard onto his finger and placed it on one of her nipples.

The slightly chilly sensation of the wet custard made her jump and her nipple puckered into a tight pebble. He smiled at her reaction and repeated the action, placing a small dollop of the desert on her other nipple.

She lay there, waiting for him to do more, anticipation making her insides quiver.

"Have I ever told you how much I've always loved the flavor of chocolate?" Hugh asked conversationally as he licked the residue off his fingers and placed the dish back on the bedside table. "There is a place in Castleton called Pritchard's Inn on the High Road. They have the most amazing chocolate confections and sticky buns. As youngsters, my brothers and I used to go there whenever we could to buy treats from Mrs. Pritchard."

Why was he telling her all that when she was lying there dying of anticipation?

"I thought I'd tasted every kind of chocolate dessert there was to taste. Little did I realize they would all pale in comparison to this." He leaned over her and licked the custard off one nipple. She tensed.

"Mmm. Just as I thought. It tastes even better when licked from your skin. You were the missing ingredient," he whispered as he kissed his way across her chest to arrive at the other nipple.

He opened his mouth over her breast, sucking her in and tonguing her with concentrated effort. Oh, yeah. He knew just what she liked and how far to push her. Lera felt close to a peak from just this contact alone. Being tied up and unable to touch him was adding an extra little jolt to the experience that she hadn't expected.

The vulnerability. The trust. It all heightened her senses, which was something she didn't know would happen. She'd never allowed anyone to restrain her before. And no one had ever eaten dessert off her body before either.

Hugh's hands moved out of her sight while his mouth never left her skin. He sucked her nipples until they were sensitive to his slightest touch. He nipped the undersides of her breasts playfully, not hurting, but letting her know he was there. He swirled his tongue over her skin and then she felt the cool wetness of more custard being dropped onto her abdomen.

The difference between the heat of his mouth and the coldness of the custard made her shiver as he worked his way downward. He lapped at an increasing trail of custard all the way down her belly. One dollop at a time, he set her on fire. And she was unable to move. Unable to think beyond the pleasure that started to build inside her.

"Hugh," she pleaded as he moved between her legs, settling there, spreading her pussy so that he could place his mouth over her clit.

Her hips lifted involuntarily, reaching for more. Hugh didn't disappoint. His teeth nibbled gently on her most delicate and sensitive skin, holding her in place for his talented tongue. Lera almost came up off the bed as pleasure broke over her in a short, fast climax that was only the beginning. Hugh rode her through it and two more like it, all the while working his wiles on her with fingers, teeth and tongue.

After her third small peak had come and another was building within her straining body, Hugh finally moved, taking his mouth back up her body as he replaced his fingers with what she really wanted. His thick cock slid inside her and immediately went to work. He stroked deep and hard, increasing both the speed and pressure as he went until she was swept up in the passion they shared.

"Hugh, I can't take much more," she warned as the biggest climax yet started to peak.

"Don't hold back, Lera. Come for me now," he coaxed, driving harder and faster even as the words left his lips. With each pulse he treated her insides to a loving friction that rubbed her in all the right places.

She screamed his name as she came and only dimly heard his answering shout as his seed jetted into her. The feel of his come heightened her pleasure and it went on and on as she lay under him, needing him, loving him.

She must have passed out at that point because the next thing she was aware of was sitting naked in Hugh's lap in bed as he spooned what was left of the custard into his mouth. When he realized she was awake, he fed her as well, alternating with her as they shared the single spoon.

The bed was a bit of a mess, but she could honestly say she'd never had a better dessert in her life.

Epilogue

Weeks later, after everything had settled down and all the traitors had been dealt with, the twins had flown back to Draconia. Prince Nico and his wife, Riki, had arrived to perform a royal state visit. Nico was the Prince of Spies and also a talented diplomat. He'd managed to charm both Lera and her courtiers, and his wife, Riki, was just as popular, though she was by nature a quieter sort of person than the larger-than-life Nico.

Hugh and Lera were settling in, each day discovering some new facet of their relationship and learning how best to divide their public duties. Hugh had taken over the training and deployment of the palace guard. He'd also found many different areas in which Helios could benefit from his warrior skill.

Every night they spent together and every day they worked out how their new lives together would be spent. One important facet of their life was Miss. She continued to thrive under the emissary's watchful tutelage and Hugh and Lera's unrestrained love.

Lera worried about the gryphons of Helios. Something had to be done to renew the bonds she'd thought they had. Something also had to be done about Miss's insecurity. The baby often had worries about where she fit in, though she seldom discussed them unless coaxed into it.

Hugh and Lera had decided to formalize their adoption of Miss as a way to help the child with her fears and hopefully begin to repair what had been done to her. Miss's mother was still alive, but imprisoned. There might one day be a chance for reconciliation between them, but for now the baby needed a stable family. Hugh and Lera could provide that.

And that's why they were gathered in the throne room with all the dignitaries and courtiers present. Today Hugh and Lera would officially become Miss's parents, and they'd name her as well. Miss didn't know it, but Lera thought she had a solution to amend the child's name. She would try it out today.

"I, Valeria, Doge of Helios, Keeper of the Flame, adopt you, Miss, as my daughter for all time and through all obstacles. I love you and will protect and provide for you until you are of an age to take care of yourself." Lera couldn't deny, there were tears in her eyes as she spoke the words in front of the assembly, the gryphon standing before her, trembling with excitement.

"And I, Hugh, Prince of Draconia and mate of Valeria, adopt you, Miss, as my daughter for all time and through all obstacles. I love you and will protect and provide for you until you are of an age to take care of yourself," Hugh repeated, adding a wink for the nervous gryphon.

"Do you agree, Miss? And do you accept Hugh and Valeria as your adoptive parents from this day forward?" The emissary was officiating the ceremony and stood between the child and those who would adopt her.

"Yess!" Miss almost shouted her joy and bounced up and down on her front paws. Her little wings spread to balance her and she made a beautiful sight, all unconsciously. "Want Hoo and Lera to be mama and papa."

"Then so it shall be," the emissary said with finality. They could all feel the magic in the air at her pronouncement, sealing the ceremony with the blessings of the Lady. "Go to your parents, little one." Jalinar pushed Miss with one of her wingtips, but Miss needed no goading to run up the steps of the dais on which Lera's and Hugh's thrones stood.

Hugh bent and caught the child in his arms, hugging her as he stood. Miss ran her little tongue over Lera's cheek in kitty kisses as the three of them hugged each other with joy in their hearts. The court around them applauded the making of the family for some time.

When the noise settled down, Lera and Hugh sat. Miss sat between them, in a space deliberately left for her between their thrones. Hugh hadn't been officially crowned yet, but the state wedding was in the works and it would only be a matter of time before he became her official consort. Lera saw no reason why he couldn't sit with her on the dais now, since he was royalty already, albeit from an allied land.

One or two of her advisors had wanted to stand on formality, but Lera had dismissed their concerns. The court had gotten used to the arrangement after the first few days and had seemed to accept the new order. They would accept Miss too. She just knew it.

To that end, she had one more thing to take care of.

"Miss," Lera began in her public voice. The courtiers listened, knowing she was addressing them as well as the baby gryphon. "We have to do something about your name. I believe I have an idea, but it is up to you to decide if you like it or not."

Lera could see she had the child's full attention.

"My mother had a sister named Emisselde. She was very dear to my mother and to me. I have fond memories of my Aunt Emisselde and I think she would be proud if you would bear her name. And of course, my aunt's nickname was Missy, so we could keep calling you Miss or Missy. Or Emisselde. Whichever you prefer. But you'd have a proper name, from my family. As my adopted daughter, you deserve no less. Does that appeal to you? Would you like to be called Emisselde?"

Miss seemed to think about it for a few seconds. "Iss pretty."

"Yes, it is," Hugh agreed. "Do you want Emisselde to be your name from now on, sweetheart?"

The little cat head tilted in thought, then nodded once, very decisively.

"Yess. I like."

"Good then. You are now Princess Emisselde of Helios."

"Princesss?" Miss seemed confused by the idea.

"Of course, little one. Your parents are royalty. Now, so are you." Jalinar winked at the child, clearly amused.

It was fitting, Lera thought. The brave little girl had gone from half-frozen street dweller to heroic fighting feline to princess. She had the heart of a lion and the wings of an angel. To Lera, there was no more beautiful soul than Miss. She was proud to call her daughter and even happier to have the lovely little girl in her life.

Lera wondered once more how she got so lucky. In the space of a few weeks she'd gone from running for her life with assassins on her trail to finding the love of her life and a beautiful child to call her own.

Life didn't get much better than this. At least, it hadn't until now. Who knew what Hugh had in store for her? With him around, each day was a new adventure of the most incredibly joyful kind. As she looked at her new family, Lera knew she was well and truly blessed.

About the Author

Bianca D'Arc has run a laboratory, climbed the corporate ladder in the shark-infested streets of Manhattan, studied and taught martial arts, and earned the right to put a whole bunch of letters after her name, but she's always enjoyed writing more than any of her other pursuits. She grew up and still lives on Long Island, where she keeps busy with an extensive garden, several aquariums full of very demanding fish, and writing her favorite genres of paranormal, fantasy and sci-fi romance.

Bianca loves to hear from readers and can be reached through Facebook, her Yahoo group or through the various links on her website.

Website:
http://biancadarc.com

Yahoo Group:
http://groups.yahoo.com/group/BiancaDArc

SAMHAIN PUBLISHING

It's all about the story...

Romance

HORROR

Retro Romance

www.samhainpublishing.com